Praise for CONSIDER Y

'*Consider Yourself Kissed* is a love stor[...]
warm, heartfelt and funny but with a [...]
I absolutely loved every moment and didn't want it to end!'
Liane Moriarty, author of Here One Moment

'I'm annoyed I didn't write this book myself. Combines rom-com
breeziness with sharp political observation, plus one of the best
depictions of stepmother-hood I've ever read.'
Madeleine Gray, author of Green Dot

'*Consider Yourself Kissed* is a smart literary love story and an
absorbing family drama. Jessica Stanley follows her characters
over the years as they make their way in the private, intricate,
fragile world they create for themselves, and in the always-changing
larger world. This is a deeply appealing and winning novel.'
Meg Wolitzer, author of The Female Persuasion

'Jessica Stanley's principal subject is romance, which she renders—
in all its mess and glory—masterfully. But the real delight in
Consider Yourself Kissed is how the novel confidently thinks about
love more broadly: the feeling we can have for family, for work,
for art and books and our homes and our friends, for the very
world around us. It is an exhilarating read, a marvel of a book.'
Rumaan Alam, author of Leave the World Behind

'*Consider Yourself Kissed* is ringingly original and just
absurdly good. Jessica Stanley captures all the tenderness
and brutality of young motherhood without dulling either,
and the relationships and writing are so bracingly, deliciously
fresh that I wish there were a fresher word than fresh. And
that the book were 1000 pages longer.'
Catherine Newman, author of Sandwich

'Utterly brilliant—so astonishingly clever, but with a core of love. It's generous, it's hopeful, it's one of the very best grown-up love stories I have ever read. And wears its smartness so lightly, but it captures the strangeness of the past few years perfectly. I could not have adored it more.'
Daisy Buchanan, author of *How to Be a Grown-up*

'Fabulous…It's clever, joyful, familiar and awkward, and so funny.'
Nina Stibbe, author of *Reasons to be Cheerful*

'Sweet and tender.'
Pandora Sykes, author of *How Do We Know We're Doing It Right?*

'Warm, funny, clever and real, *Consider Yourself Kissed* is at once a charming romance, a social history and a profoundly authentic study of the complex work of love. A wonderful novel.'
Eleanor Elliott Thomas, author of *The Opposite of Success*

'Immersive, truly funny, brilliantly smart, and full of lovable characters, *Consider Yourself Kissed* is a joy. In her novel spanning ten years of one woman's life, Jessica Stanley balances domesticity and politics, contemporary British history and the pursuit of love—and she makes it all seem effortless. I cried when I read the last page, simply because I was bereft that it was over.'
Claire Dederer, author of *Monsters*

'Jessica Stanley captures all the quiet ecstasy and devastation of being a lover, a mother, a woman in the world, and wondering what is left over for yourself. In Coralie's endless labour to do everything right and try to write, I felt achingly seen. I want to hand this gorgeous book to every mum I know with a hug.'
Clare Fletcher, author of *Love Match*

'I loved it, I loved them, I loved the Cazaletty interior details,
I loved the social politics, I loved the actual politics, I loved
the time span, I loved how complicated everyone was. I already
know I will read it again…A beautiful romcom for grown-ups.'
Ella Risbridger, author of *The Year of Miracles*

'*Consider Yourself Kissed* is a tender, layered novel and one of the
sharpest portrayals of marriage and motherhood I've ever read.
It's also warm and clever and funny. I completely inhaled it.
As with all my favourite novels, I wished I could read it forever.'
Alice Robinson, author of *If You Go*

'Oh, how I loved and empathised with Coralie! *Consider Yourself
Kissed* is funny, tender, authentic and incredibly moving.'
Jennie Godfrey, author of *The List of Suspicious Things*

'Set over ten years, this wonderful, sweeping novel doesn't
just make the political personal, but the personal political.
It shows us how life is a series of negotiations and situations
over which you have little control, but that loving and
being loved is central. Beautiful and life-affirming.'
Araminta Hall, author of *One of the Good Guys*

'A beautiful, harrowing, wild ride through everyday life,
Consider Yourself Kissed is a love song to women everywhere.'
Annabel Monaghan, author of *Nora Goes Off Script*

'Beautifully written, wise, funny, moving. Deftly fuses the
personal and the political. A proper grown-up love story.'
Beth Morrey, author of *Lucky Day*

'The platonic ideal of reading experiences!…So funny,
so smart and deliciously well observed! A real treat.'
Lizzy Stewart, author of *Alison*

Jessica Stanley is an Australian novelist living in London. She grew up in Melbourne, studied in Canberra, and worked in journalism, on the set of the TV show *Neighbours*, for the trade union movement, and in advertising, before moving to the UK in 2011. Her first novel *A Great Hope* was published by Picador in 2022 and was widely praised.

jessicastanley.co.uk
@dailydoseofjess

Consider Yourself Kissed

Jessica Stanley

TEXT PUBLISHING MELBOURNE AUSTRALIA

The Text Publishing Company acknowledges the Traditional Owners of the country on which we work, the Wurundjeri people of the Kulin Nation, and pays respect to their Elders past and present.

textpublishing.com.au

The Text Publishing Company
Wurundjeri Country, Level 6, Royal Bank Chambers, 287 Collins Street, Melbourne Victoria 3000 Australia

Published by The Text Publishing Company, 2025

Cover design by Vi-An Nguyen, based on original design by Ceara Elliot
Cover images by iStock and Shutterstock
Page design by Imogen Stubbs
Typeset by J&M Typesetting

Printed and bound in Australia by Griffin Press, a member of the Opus Group. The Opus Group is ISO/NZS 14001:2004 Environmental Management System certified.

ISBN: 9781923058255 (paperback)
ISBN: 9781923059191 (ebook)

A catalogue record for this book is available from the National Library of Australia.

The paper this bound proof is printed on is certified against the Forest Stewardship Council® Standards. Griffin Press, a member of the Opus Group, holds chain of custody certification SCS-COC-001185. FSC® promotes environmentally responsible, socially beneficial and economically viable management of the world's forests.

For Kitten,
Boppy
and Nonny,
with love.

2022

Laundry she could do. Tidying wasn't a problem. She made up her daughter's bed with the summer duvet, and the handmade quilt that said FLORENCE. She arranged Catty with his long legs crossed, his plush black arms open in a hug. Maxi's special toy was a sheep; she laid him on his side in the cot. The colourful magnets went in one basket, the Duplo in another. Upstairs, she made Zora's bed with sheets she'd brought in from the clothesline. They were warm and smelled of the sun. Her tired mind surveyed her luck—a home, the children, Adam. In so many ways, her dream.

Something was wrong with Coralie, something that set her apart—she couldn't be *in* love, but she couldn't be out of it either. If she didn't love, she was half a person. But if she did love, she'd never be whole. Her hands shook as she packed her bag. Mother, writer, worker, sister, friend, citizen, daughter, (sort of) wife. If she could be one, perhaps she could manage. Trying to be all, she found that she was none. A high-summer night, still light outside—the seagulls soared and screamed. She loved him so much, more than anything. But when Adam came home, she'd be gone.

1

2013

It was a Sunday morning in March, one of the coldest London winters in modern memory, and—although she was totally alone—Coralie Bower, aged twenty-nine and a half, was certainly *not* unhappy!

Which superpower would you prefer: to be invisible or able to fly? Her first and only *Guardian* Soulmates date had asked her that question at Nando's. (An agronomist from Walthamstow, he identified as a 'contrarian', had worn a full Tour de France-style cycling kit, and had asked if Australia had 'any universities'. Never again.) The answer was invisibility, and she had that power right now. All it had taken was moving to the other side of the world.

She marched down the canal, dodging bikes and strolling couples. As she reached Victoria Park, she realised she hadn't spoken a word all morning. She cleared her throat a few times to loosen up. In her mind, she rehearsed her order: 'One latte, please…' She said it out loud: 'One latte.' Was that weird? It was weird! She'd spent the whole weekend writing, books and papers spread out across the flat, and she'd forgotten how to exist in public. It was so incredibly cold—whippets on their walks shivered in double jackets. Only the thought of coffee kept her going.

The night before, the pub on the corner had held a 'private event' in the function space next to her bedroom. 'Private events' were not subject, apparently, to the opening hours she'd carefully reviewed before signing her one-year lease. A few weeks after she moved in, she'd emailed the landlord about the noise. The pub was clearly visible to the naked eye, he'd replied. Besides, it had been 'factored in to the rent'. The rent was 43 per cent of her take-home pay. She still had six months to go.

It was far from ideal. (It was terrible.) But she'd learned her lesson during the Christmas-party season: better to stay up and keep busy than to lie in bed, failing to sleep, questioning every life choice. By midnight, she'd hung her hand-washing out near the radiator to dry. Her work emails were up-to-date, replies in Drafts for Monday. She'd dealt at last with her brother's scrupulously non-judgemental update from what she supposed she should call home. *Don't worry, it's fine, keep your distance*, his polite email seemed to imply. *You're totally not wanted or needed.* Coralie managed other people's emotions for a living! She didn't welcome having the tables turned on her by Daniel! She'd drafted and deleted several hurt responses before accessing a higher plane. *You're doing an amazing job with Mum*, she'd replied. *I bet she's so glad you're there. Please keep me*

4

updated on it all. The truth was, she could hardly bear to know.

Inside the Pavilion Café, every seat was taken, and the warm breath of laughing friends and families had fogged up the windows and even the high glass dome. ('One latte, please'—it had gone well, though she'd been forced to freestyle some small talk when the barista had been nice.) She took her coffee outside and stood by the lake to drink it. Soon the wind changed, and the fountain's spray changed direction too. The sun came out for a brief moment; the mist glowed with a streak of rainbow. She slipped her hand in her overcoat pocket for her phone. Images like that killed on her nascent Instagram, and performed an important function by reassuring friends in Australia she was alive.

'A rainbow,' a man said. 'Zora, look, a rainbow.'

The lake, at least the part next to the cafe, was bordered by a low fence of interlocking cast-iron semicircles. A small girl raced right up and bumped it with her scooter. 'A rainbow!'

She was so sweet, with bobbed hair, a little fringe, and serious dark eyes and brows—Coralie glanced up to take in the man, enviably warm-looking in his woollen jumper, scarf and coat. To her surprise, he was already studying her, turning on her the full force of his gaze. Did they know each other? But the whole point of Coralie Bower was that, apart from her colleagues at the office, she knew no one in London at all.

'Dada, see the baby ducks?'

'I can see them.' He sounded amused, and from the direction of his voice it seemed he was still looking at Coralie, even though she'd turned away and drifted off, staring down at, although not seeing, her phone.

5

'Can you get me one? A baby duck?'

'I could get you a croissant. Or a pain au raisin—would that do?'

'I don't want the duck-ning to *eat*,' the girl said.

The man laughed and picked up her scooter. 'Why do you want it then?'

'To love it and take care of it!'

They were walking off—the man carrying the scooter in one hand, the other hand holding the girl's.

When Coralie was five or six, her neighbour's cat had kittens. The cat received visitors like a queen in a pile of towels in the laundry, her babies fanned around her, their eyes closed. If Coralie could've got away with it, she would have stolen one—she'd wanted one of those kittens so badly. She knew exactly where the little girl with the fringe was coming from. Now she studied the ducks, very fluffy and newly hatched—hatched too soon, surely, in this cold. A sudden yearning filled her, too; although the ducks must have been swimming near her for five minutes without her even noticing.

She was back, suddenly—the girl, leaning on the fence by the lake. Coralie glanced through the windows into the cafe, and thought perhaps she saw the man, his head thrown back in a laugh. The wind changed again, and a wall of frigid spray advanced on them from the fountain. She raised her hand to shield her face. When she lowered it, the girl was in the water, face-down. Fuck!

Was it an emergency? It was an emergency. As in a nightmare, her throat ached with panic, but she couldn't scream for help. Seconds passed in a horrible flash. Why was the girl so still, her coat puffed around her like a life-jacket? Coralie climbed over the fence, steadied herself, and jumped in. The water was up to her waist. She scooped the girl up and lay her over the crook of her arm. She gave the top of her back, right between the shoulder blades, one tremendous thump with her fist. The girl coughed, spluttered, and gave a quick, outraged shout. 'Ahh!'

Coralie looked up towards the cafe. People had begun to spill out—silent, open-mouthed. She waded the few steps to the edge, reached up, and tipped the girl over the fence. Now she had no visible reason to be in waist-deep freezing water, and she could feel new people arriving at the scene and staring at her as if she was mad. She realised with horror that her phone was in her pocket, submerged. Oh well. She climbed up to the ledge, balanced herself, and stepped awkwardly onto dry land.

The girl's face was white with shock. Coralie crouched and rubbed her back. 'Did you want to see the ducks?'

The girl nodded. There was a graze under her fringe where she'd bumped her head on the way in. Tears filled her eyes. She began to cry.

People were surrounding them. A woman took off her coat and put it around the girl. There was an accusatory element to the crowd's murmured remarks, as if someone, probably Coralie, had been remiss and, now that the danger had passed, it was time to apportion blame.

'I'll just get her dad,' Coralie said to no one, but as she struggled towards the cafe in her sodden jeans and boots, the man emerged with a big cup in one hand and a small one in the other. When he saw the crowd at the water's edge, he dumped the cups on a bench and ran.

'Zora!' He crouched and heaved her up into his arms. In his embrace, water squeezed from her coat and dripped to the ground. He talked closely into her ear. Her cheek rested against his. For a moment, he locked eyes again with Coralie—the circle of onlookers drew closer, offering jumpers, scarves, lifts home. The man and his daughter were cut off from view. Walking as normally as possible, so no one would notice her leave, Coralie trudged home, shaking with cold and inwardly freaking about lake-borne parasites. But something had changed. She was no longer invisible. The man had really seen her, and she had definitely seen him.

'If you can't write, you can work.' That had been the advice of an author she'd heard on an otherwise-forgotten podcast. A week after the lake incident, she spent all weekend organising the notes she'd taken for her project, in emails to herself, on receipts and scrap paper, and in notebooks. What actually *was* she writing? (Her childhood friend Elspeth asked delicately in her email.) It wasn't that clear, even to herself. Something about the distance between Coralie and home, her past so far away, decisively 'the past'—her future here so blank and unknown— no one around to see her try, and probably fail, to get words on the page and keep them there. There weren't actual events from her life in her notes, or real people—it wasn't memoir. It was more like: feelings she'd had that she couldn't explain. Or: things she'd done that she couldn't understand. In the absence of fresh intel, she found herself starting to invent. That was something new—that felt like proper writing. By early afternoon on Sunday, it was so cold and so dark she couldn't face going far for coffee. She pulled the door of her flat shut and crossed the street to Climpsons, a small cafe with rough wooden bench seating and good coffee.

'Is that her?' she heard as she ordered. 'That's her!'

It was the man from the park. He stood up from his seat at the window. 'It's you!'

Coralie waved at the girl next to him. 'It's you!'

The girl waved back, her legs swinging.

The man came towards her. She wondered for a moment if he'd embrace her, shake her hand, or even, for a crazy second, kiss her—he seemed to be contemplating all three. He stood with his arms open wide. He was her height (not tall). They gazed at each other. 'I can't believe you ran away,' he finally said.

'I didn't *run*!' Coralie said. 'I sort of squelched.'

'Zora said it was you.' He called over to her. 'Didn't you?'

Zora, busy eating raw sugar from the bowl, didn't reply.

'Mmm,' the man said. 'Healthy!'

They both laughed, and then smiled, and then were silent for a second. 'She's okay then?'

'She's perfectly okay! I thought she'd be traumatised for life, have a fear of ducks and water, but she's living a normal life, taking baths willy-nilly, quacking—she's fine! Thanks to you,' he said, suddenly serious.

She waved her hand. 'God, no, not really. It was fine.'

'It must have been fucking freezing.'

It *had* been freezing, she'd had to buy a new phone, and her good overcoat was ruined, the wool all rough and misshapen.

9

'No, I really elegantly…*plunged* in, loving it, like Mr Darcy taking a dip in his lake.'

'People often say *I* look like a young Colin Firth.' He angled his face to help her see it—which she could, immediately, but what was she supposed to do? Agree?

'Colin Firth is a hundred and eighty-seven centimetres tall.' (Unlike you, she didn't add.)

He laughed, unoffended. 'Did you write his Wikipedia?'

'I might have.'

She waited for him to say she looked like Lizzy Bennett, a known fact at school, and something she'd—for a short time— loved about herself.

Instead, he was serious again. 'No, really. You were so brave, and acted so quickly. The knock on her head was really nasty— she could have drowned! About forty women with dogs lined up to tell me off.'

'I don't understand how it happened. She was on one side of the fence. Suddenly she was on the other.'

'She must have done a flip, against the fence, like—' He started to mime bending in half at the waist.

'Dada!' Zora shouted from her place by the window. 'Stop telling the story!'

The man winced an apology. He looked at Coralie, and seemed to gather himself, taking a breath to ask her—what? She had a sudden horror it would be to babysit. Hackney was full of Australian nannies pushing Bugaboos and ordering babyccinos.

'Latte!' the barista called.

'Oh, that's me.' Would she have sat with them? She thought

she probably would have. But the takeaway cup was in her hand. She was walking towards the door. It was too late. Anyway, her whole mind was spread out and waiting for her in the flat. It was time to get back up.

'Come and sit with us,' the man said.

'Oh, I can't. I have to...' She nodded towards the exit. 'Sorry, thank you, so nice to see you!'

'Snow!' someone exclaimed.

'Snow, Dada! Dada! Snow!'

Coralie turned. Everyone was looking out onto the street. Snow was falling steadily; each flake seemed suspended in mid-air. Snow! Coralie pushed open the door of the cafe. Halfway across Broadway Market, she wished she hadn't left. What was she doing? It was deranged, perverse, an act of self-harm—to leave a warm conversation in a warm cafe with a shorter, and younger, Colin Firth! But he was a man with a daughter, which implied the existence somewhere of a mother. Besides, she was out of practice with cosy chats.

She must look mad now, frozen in the middle of the road, in the snow. Was he watching? He was, giving a brief (perhaps regretful?) farewell wave. Coralie smiled. He was smiling too. When she opened the door leading up to her flat, she turned for one last look. The man had his arms around his daughter and his chin resting on her head. Now Coralie was waving, and they were both waving back.

The 'any plans for Easter?' workplace small talk was already in full swing. She considered a little trip somewhere just for something to say. But the weather had been so bad for so long—even English people agreed it was awful. It wasn't a tantalising prospect to be trapped in a bed-and-breakfast while outside it constantly sleeted. On the Thursday, their stern and impressive creative director, Antoinette, hadn't come into the office. By three-thirty, Coralie and Stefan were sinking house reds in the Coach and Horses.

When she'd transferred from the Sydney office the previous September, Coralie had been informally paired with Stefan to work as a creative team. They'd liked each other, and they'd got on, but did not become close until some weeks later, when Stefan woke one morning to discover his boyfriend had moved out silently in the night. Marcus went dark on phone and email. After a week, Stefan was so frantic he notified the police. At that point, Marcus texted, *Stefan, I am still alive.* 'But I'm not,' Stefan sobbed at his desk, while Coralie searched *Psychology Today* for links about avoidant personalities and toxic narcissism. His mother booked him flight after flight back to Nuremberg. He refused to leave the flat on weekends in case Marcus changed his mind. He became so thin someone offered him their seat on the tube to work. He was so weak with shock and grief that he took it.

Analysing 'the Marcus thing' from every angle was the foundation of Coralie and Stefan's friendship. Then, just as suddenly, and again without explanation, Marcus asked to move back in. Stefan was happier, and Coralie was glad for him, but she struggled a little with the speed of her friend's reversal, and—more selfishly—the sudden end of the crisis that had gripped them. Now, even as they talked about TV shows and laughed about their colleagues, she could feel his magnetic pull towards Marcus, who'd soon be finishing up work for the day at a rival brand agency in Soho.

Stefan leaned forward: gregarious, coy, heartbroken no longer, the dark circles gone from under his eyes, his blond hair bright once more. 'Anyway, is it true—about the Sydney boss? About Richard?'

She thought she'd escaped all that. 'There's so much about him.' Dread flooded her. 'Which bit do you mean?'

'His surname, Pickard—but nobody called him Dick Pic?'

'No!' She laughed with surprise and relief. 'At least, not to his face.'

'Seems like a missed opportunity.'

'It does,' Coralie said. 'Though actually...'

But Stefan's phone screen lit up and the moment to confide was gone.

She turned down his invitation to join him and Marcus for dinner and drinks. As she walked home from Clerkenwell, her body was in London, but her mind was back where she came from, revisiting her past, her failures, her exile, her disgrace, all scattered around her flat in the form of notes and drafts and questions. Her work was taking shape. She rushed to get back to the page.

But when she reached Broadway Market, she saw the pub next-door was having a late one. People spilled out onto the street, falling into each other's arms and shouting. Inside, the music pounded away, ignored by everybody, enjoyed by nobody, ruining Coralie's mental health, sleep and life! The mood she'd created, the head of steam she'd built up, her drive to make herself clear and known—it turned grey and drifted

13

away like a cloud of second-hand smoke. She liked the city, and her life in it, which she knew was only just beginning, and which she was sure would become deeper, more rich. But she could just as easily (and she felt it very strongly at that moment, standing there in her tiny flat, listening to other people's songs) disappear right then—simply evaporate! And no one would really care.

When she woke late the next day, the connection to her writing remained dead. She made a lentil soup to take in for work lunches. She sprinkled the kitchen sink with bicarb soda and scrubbed until it was spotless. She took down the fan grille in her windowless bathroom and vacuumed it. She straightened her papers into piles. By mid-afternoon she was exhausted, famished, and overwhelmed by a critical internal voice telling her, not incorrectly, she'd wasted her entire day. She slid her journal into a tote bag, walked down the length of the market, and ordered fish and chips at the Dove.

Wine in hand, she ducked away from the crowded main dining room to the smaller, more private tables at the side. At one of them, newspapers open and spread messily around him, sat the man.

Amid the hustle and crowding in the pub she felt safe, standing there, studying him for a bit. By the lake, she'd been startled by the directness of his gaze. At Climpsons, or—more accurately—afterwards, in the privacy of her flat, in the form of an email to Elspeth, she'd considered his brown eyes, his brown hair, his smile. As he looked down, studying the papers, she was able to study his profile. He had a big nose and a nice square chin. Wasn't that what had driven Sylvia Plath so wild she'd bit Ted Hughes's cheek? Her glass wobbled in her hand. She stepped back around the wall.

Down in the depths of the pub near the toilets it was too dark and pokey to take out her notebook and write. From the bench next to her, a small Italian greyhound stared mournfully at her plate. 'Can dogs eat fish and chips' she typed into her phone. 'By feeding your dog human food such as fish and chips, they could miss out on the forty-one essential nutrients required for optimal canine health.' Forty-one? She admired, from a professional standpoint, how using an unsourced fact added extra weight to this vague advisory from a pet-food manufacturer. 'I'm sorry, I can't. Don't hate me,' she told the Italian greyhound. He turned his back on her and placed his tiny head in his owner's lap.

'Breaking a dog's heart now,' a man said. It was *the* man. 'Is that really true about Colin Firth being two metres tall?'

'One point eight-seven,' she said. 'And I'm so sorry, but Elspeth—my best friend at school—was already very tall by the time we saw *Pride and Prejudice*. So we checked it very thoroughly.'

'To see if he was suitable for her?'

Coralie nodded.

'Actually, I'm half an inch taller than the average British male,' the man said. 'And I've got a really nice table upstairs.' Coralie laughed. 'If your friend from school would like to join me.' She laughed again. 'No, of course I mean—if you'd like to join me.'

She did.

*

15

It was almost comical, being plucked from her cramped bench near the toilets and set down at a coveted table near the fire. Adam was his name; she'd found that out already. With the Walthamstow agronomist, she'd felt like a robot programmed to conduct a polite conversation in a language she hardly knew. With Adam, it was *fun*.

'So why did you leave Australia to come here?'

'Oh!' She gave an enormous shrug.

'Are you mad?'

'Probably!'

'Okay, you don't have to say why, but when?'

'When did I move? Just after the Olympics.'

'I see, you waited until London was good again. Some of us were forced to be here the whole time. And what do you do? Is that…'

'Boring!'

'Boring! Sorry! You're right. It's too boring to ask.'

'It's fine to ask, but it's boring to say. Basically, I'm a copy-writer.'

He cupped his chin and said, mock-fascinated, 'Go on.' They laughed. 'But don't you miss home? Where did you grow up?'

'I mainly grew up in Canberra. Which is…' *the capital city*, she was going to helpfully add.

But Adam knew it, had been there, was enthusing about it. 'It was ages ago now—nine years? I was doing a profile of the Australian Labor leader at the time, Mark Latham. We thought he was a sort of heir to Blair, the Third Way, all that.'

'No way, wow…' Coralie did remember Mark Latham—

vaguely. 'I can't believe you've been there!'

Did she miss home? She would let that one go. She didn't know the answer.

It was her turn to ask questions. Adam was thirty-seven. He was a journalist. 'Just a sec,' she said. 'When you tell me who you write for—please don't be offended if I don't know it. I might! I just might not. I've only been here a few months.'

'You won't know it,' he said. 'You know the *New Statesman*?'

'Oh, I do!'

'Well, it's not it!' They laughed, they seemed to be non-stop laughing. That was what had been missing from her life: jokes! Hearing them, making them. 'No, I write for a modern pretender, *Young Country*. Never heard of it—okay! It was set up in 1996, when I left university, by a multi-multi-millionaire with a packaging fortune. Charlie Tuck? Charles, Lord Tuck? None of this means anything to you. It was right before the Blair landslide—Blair? Tony Blair? No?'

They laughed again, because of course she'd heard of Tony Blair, Cool Britannia or whatever, and Iraq.

'The title actually comes from a Blair speech.' Suddenly Adam dropped into character, his shining eyes fixed on a point behind her, his voice vibrating with passion. 'I want us to be a young country again, with a common purpose, ideals we cherish and live up to, not resting on past glories, fighting old battles and sitting back, hand on mouth, concealing a yawn of cynicism, but ready for the day's challenge. Ambitious! Idealistic! United! Not saying: This *was* a great country.' He held out two fists. 'But: Britain can and will be. A great country! Again!'

'Extremely intense, wow! Tony—is that you?'

He wasn't coasting on his floppy hair and knitwear. Adam was performing—for her.

'Probably my best impression,' he said. 'I can't do accents, which limits me. Yes, I'd missed out on all the good trainee-ships, like *The Times*, and I was rejected by the civil service fast-track scheme, and obviously I couldn't take the slow track.' He made an appalled face. 'So I was very lucky to be hired at *YC*. Not as a writer then, as a general dogsbody.'

'Like Bridget Jones,' Coralie said appreciatively. 'Fannying about with press releases.'

'In my little skirt. Bridget Jones came out that year! The book. Everyone was talking like her: V.G. Very good. Those were the days. Now I write for *Young Country*, and I host their award-winning podcast, also called *Young Country*, regularly in the top twelve, or fifteen, in the News bit of UK iTunes, and I freelance at other places, and I also do a bit of...' He coughed modestly. 'Broadcast.'

'Wow!' Coralie gave him the reply he clearly craved. 'V.G!'

It was nice he liked his job—she wouldn't be able to conjure a single anecdote from hers. Except maybe the time she'd asked how many people worked there. Stefan had said—so dry she hadn't at first realised it was funny—'About half.'

'Same again? Do you fancy a bowl of chips?'

WWAFD: what would a feminist do? Strictly, it was her round, but although she wouldn't dream of complaining, her crap new second-hand iPhone had cost £300. 'I'd love the same again,' she said. 'Thanks!'

When he sat down again, she asked about Zora. He leaned

18

forward: she was perfect, he said. Hilarious, maybe a poet—definitely a genius. They once had a powerline go out on the street, and Zora said something amazing about the torch Adam used: it 'moved the dark out of your way'. She was three at the time. Wasn't that amazing? Coralie agreed sincerely that it was. She was aged nearly-five, and in Reception—which must be, Coralie worked out, the same as Prep. Her classroom had a giant behaviour chart, and all the students had to 'stay on the happy smile'. She was always so beautifully behaved, merely the idea of being 'on the sad face' made her cry. Adam shook his head. 'Can you imagine? In the end, Marina and I had to go to the school. Marina is Zora's mother.' Coralie had a sudden vivid flash of him adding 'my wife'—she almost gasped. 'My ex,' he said. Coralie soberly inclined her head. 'I think Marina wanted to tear down the charts, sue them for Zora's distress, take her out of there forever, put her in a forest school. I was thinking more like—major charm offensive, maybe asking the teacher to tell Zora she was the best girl ever?'

'What did the teacher say?'

'We were sitting in the little chairs at the back of the class-room. We launched into our speeches, the teacher held up her hand. I know these girls, she said. Perfectionists. Get to secondary and it's top marks, violin, piano, eating disorders, ashamed, anxious, hiding themselves. If Zora ever talks back, or sets a foot wrong, you should throw her a party.'

A shiver ran up Coralie's arm. Until about two years ago, she'd never set a foot wrong either. 'I *know*,' Adam said, though surely he couldn't.

'So where does she live? With both of you?'

19

'Yes, with both of us—separately, obviously. We used to have the nanny, so she'd have a week at one house and then swap. But now, because of school, she's at Marina's, in Camden, during the week.'

'And is that…not as good?'

'It's equally bad for both of us, Marina and I, in different ways. I hate missing out on bedtime. Marina feels like she doesn't get to do anything fun. We make it work.'

'What's Zora doing this weekend, the long weekend?'

'Marina's boyfriend, Tom, is very *family, family, family*. They've gone for a big Easter with his parents.'

'Are you not very *family-family*?' It was the obvious question, but it felt freighted with meaning. Imagine if he said that he wasn't?

'My mum and her partner don't get up to London much.' He paused for a second. 'And my dad died when I was eighteen.'

She knew, from experience, why he had paused. Death, like terminal illness, was a genuine conversation-murderer. 'That's so young, how horrible.' She moved on as naturally as she could. 'And do you have siblings?'

Relieved, he said, 'No. Do you?'

'I have my brother, Daniel.'

'Older or younger?'

'He's only twenty-five.' She pictured him at the hospital, picking up Mum, almost trembling with responsibility.

'And you are…'

'Thirty in September.'

'Thirty, okay!' He seemed relieved; this made her like him. 'But you and your brother, are you close?'

'In some ways—like, I really love him, as a person. But my dad was in the army, and he was posted to Indonesia when I started Year 7, so I boarded at my school in Canberra, and Daniel went with my parents to Jakarta. I hardly ever saw him. We had two separate childhoods.'

'That's crazy,' Adam said.

'I know! My own brother!'

'No, it's crazy because my dad was based in Singapore, and I boarded too! Here though, in England. From age eleven.'

'Eleven! Same as me!'

'Mine was only weekly boarding—I escaped for the weekend. That's why I'm more normal and better adjusted than you.'

'But you were boarding a decade before me...'

'A decade!'

'Mental health wasn't even invented then.'

'Too true. Sadly.'

'Eleven seems so young now.'

'I know,' Adam said. 'I still sucked my thumb. I had two tigers, stuffed tigers from the gift shop at Singapore Zoo. They were balding from being in my bed since I was small. And every night I waited till the other boys fell asleep so I could bring out my tigers and sort of sniff them, stroke their bald patches, get some thumb-sucking going.'

'And do you still do it? When you go to bed?'

'I would! I'd love nothing more. But something awful happened. When my parents split up, my mum moved back here with me. My dad stayed behind, and I spent one holiday a year with him. On the last one, just as I was leaving school, the last holiday before he died, he gave me a huge backpack for

21

Christmas. It had a little smaller bag that clipped on, sort of like a day pack. I had them in there, the tigers.'

'What were their names?'

'Tigey and Cuddles.'

They both laughed for a long time.

'This is already the worst story I've ever heard,' Coralie said. 'It's the saddest, most heartbreaking story ever. I don't think I even want to know what happened.'

'By the time I got to Heathrow, the small pack had come off—gone. They were gone.'

'Awful, awful. But what about your thumb? You still have that.'

They both gazed down at it. 'It's nothing special on its own, though. Not without stroking the missing bits of fur, giving their ears a sniff, you know. The whole experience.'

So he was half an inch taller than the average British male (and fine with it), divorced (and fine with it), outside the iTunes podcast top ten in an obscure category (and fine with it)—and a thumb-sucker. Coralie pushed her wine glass to the side. She rested her palm on the table, close to his. He stretched his hand forward and touched hers. Their fingers gently interlaced. Now they gazed at each other. His pupils were enormous and black. She wished she knew how to draw. She'd love to draw his face. After a moment, he came round to her side of the table. They leaned forward, and she felt for a moment like she'd tip over into him, and join him—inside him. They kissed.

'Wow,' Adam said.

'Wow!'

'If Tigey and Cuddles could see me now!'

2

Outside the pub, she stopped. 'God, why is it so cold? Which way are you going?'

'I live on Wilton Way—up past the park. What about you? Was that your flat next to the Cat and Mutton?'

'Don't tell any murderers, but yes.' They started walking in the same direction. 'It's been awful actually,' she found herself saying. 'I thought British pubs had to close by eleven. But the noise kept me up until one last night. I can't wait to get home to bed.'

She knew if they found themselves alone somewhere private, it would be game over. She didn't have any *The Rules*-ish worries about not seeing him again if they had sex. It was more that she wanted the chatting and laughing to go on forever. Equally, she craved being alone, to take out her memories of their long afternoon and evening together to pore over—she could spend days going over these hours. Weeks. She didn't say any of this out loud, but she saw him take it in, make sense of it, and agree.

They walked, their shoulders touching. As they got closer, Adam groaned. There was an A-frame chalkboard on the pavement in front of her flat.

GOOD FRIDAY?
GREAT FRIDAY!
TUNES TIL LATE

They turned to face each other. She could see their breath hanging in the cold air. 'Why don't you sleep at mine?'

She inspected him carefully. 'But where will you sleep?'

'Um? At yours? I don't care about noise.'

'I don't even know your surname.'

'It's Whiteman. Not Adam John Whiteman who killed his grandmother. I'm Adam *Alexander* Whiteman. That's for when you google me. Do you need anything before I drop you at my house? Toothbrush?'

'Drop me at your house?'

'Oh, is that bad? Are you worried it's a ruse? I lure you in, and then—'

'You Adam John Whiteman me.'

'Ha! This is like the riddle. The fox, the chicken and the sack of grain. They all need to be on the other side of the river. There's a single raft.' He closed his eyes. His face really was so beautiful. 'I've got it,' he said. 'You go up into your flat, get whatever you need, and prop the door open so I can get back up. You keep your keys. I'll give you my keys—my only keys.

24

You go to my place…Have a bath and a lovely sleep…'

'A bath,' she said, almost lustfully.

'A bath. And guess what—I have a guest bed. It's not made up, but there are sheets in the cupboard outside the bathroom. Which has, as I say, a bath.'

'And in the morning, if you survive, we can meet at Climpsons.' She nodded across the street. 'And swap back.'

'Perfect. I need one more thing: tell me your number. Actually.' He pulled his phone from his coat pocket. 'Call your phone from my phone.' The screensaver was a selfie of him and his daughter, squinting, wreathed in sun. 'I'm just going to Sultan to buy a toothbrush,' Adam said. 'Okay?

'Okay!'

'See you soon!'

'See you soon.'

Upstairs she gathered what she needed. She looked around the flat with her eyes and then with his. The landlord had removed every period feature in her Victorian flat. Even the fire-surround had been taken off and the fireplace blocked up. It would be more relaxed, more cool, if it was all a bit less spotless. But it would be artificial to stage the scene. The papers had to go, her notebooks, the drafts of her manuscript she'd printed off at work. She bundled them up, lifted the seat cushion of the sofa, and shoved them out of sight.

On the way out, she propped the door open with Elizabeth Jane Howard's *The Long View*. Abruptly, she turned, pushed back through the door and rushed to the front window. Outside, a black cab drew to a stop. More revellers were disgorged. No sign of Adam. Who was he, anyway? One thing to talk about the fox, the chicken and the sack of grain. What if it was the scorpion and the frog? The scorpion begs the frog to take him across the river. 'Why would I sting you? Then we'd both drown.' The frog believes him, the scorpion climbs on. Halfway across the river, the scorpion stings the frog. 'Why?' the frog sobs. 'I'm a scorpion,' the scorpion says. People hurt other people. Bad things happen, and for no real reason.

The music from the pub was so loud now it made the chimney breast vibrate. Specks of plaster came away and floated onto the books she'd stacked below. She closed her eyes, alone and in hell.

When she looked out of the window again, he was there.

Halfway across the park, she pulled out her new phone with the intention of searching 'Adam Whiteman journalist'. The screen was lit up with an incoming call.

'Is it too loud?' she asked. 'Do you want me to come back?'

'God, no. I can't even hear it.'

'I can hear it through the phone!'

'I have a few questions,' he said. 'If you don't mind?'

'Go ahead.'

'Can I eat two of these eggs and…' She heard the crumple of paper and two loud taps. 'This very appetising brick-hard nub of sourdough?'

'Of course!'

'More questions.' In her flat, the kitchen was at one end of the modest main room. She could sense him turn around and face the blocked-up fireplace at the other end. To his left were the two narrow windows overlooking Broadway Market, beneath them the sofa that hid her (also modest) life's work. To his right was the table with two chairs, and the door through to the narrow hall and small bathroom and bedroom. She'd never sat at that table with someone else in her entire seven months in London. 'The books,' he said. 'Ever heard of shelves?'

'No,' she said wonderingly. 'I'd love you to explain what they are.'

She was smiling and she could tell he was too. 'Are the piles organised in some way?'

'Sort of—can you work it out?'

'Let me put the water on for these eggs. Then I'll crack the code. Where are you now? Is your hand cold from holding the phone?'

'I'm at the Lido—I'm about to walk out past the school. Is that right? I can't look at Maps while I'm talking to you.'

'Go on till you get to Greenwood Road shop and the Spurstowe. Turn left and go past Violet, the cake shop. If you get to the next pub, you've gone too far.'

'Why did you come to the Dove? If you live so close to two pubs?'

'Actually, three pubs.' She heard the clatter of the saucepan on the hob. 'Okay, let's see. We've got Woolf, Virginia. Jean Rhys. Elizabeths—Bowen and Taylor. Barbara Pym. Iris Murdoch. A. S. Byatt. Did you read what A. S. Byatt's children call her? It was in the *Guardian*.'

'Mum? Mummy? Antonia?'

'They call her A. S. Byatt. Those green-spine books by women. Mitfords. Who's Helen Garner?'

Coralie gave a strangled cry.

'We're getting more modern here,' Adam said. 'Ali Smith, Monica Ali—I interviewed her on the podcast! Zadie Smith—my friend snogged her at uni. Allegedly! A bunch of Americans in a clump together. Wow, it's all women, isn't it? No, wait a minute. *The Line of Beauty. A Single Man. Maurice.* Is this a gay pile?'

'It's a gay pile!'

'I see! Girls and gays.'

'That's it! No straight men.'

'Did you bring all of these from Australia? Didn't it cost a fortune?'

'Well.' She sighed. 'It's a long story. I'm outside the shop. Is there anything to eat at yours?'

'Spaghetti, onions, garlic, tinned tomatoes, cheese.'

'Perfect.' She kept walking.

After a while he said, 'Aren't you going to tell me the long story?'

'About the books? Well, it's not really that long or interesting. It's just a bit sad.'

'Go on.'

'I went to boarding school in Canberra, as discussed. Every year, there was a famous book fair put on by a charity called Lifeline, whose number you call if you're depressed. Amazing books. Canberra must have been filled with feminists clearing out their shelves, or maybe their kids doing it when old feminists died—how sad! I didn't think of that before. First-edition hardback Anita Brookners...I got a whole set of the Claudine books, by Colette, amazing pastel covers. I went to uni in

Canberra too, and I kept going to the fair. The books came with me from college to my share house. Then my boyfriend at the time got a job in Melbourne. I've always loved Melbourne; I moved with him. The books came to our flat in Northcote—an area like Stoke Newington, I suppose. Then, when we broke up—when I was twenty-six—I had no idea what to do. I felt so lost and crazy—it was like I didn't want the books to see me like that. I packed them all up and had them freighted to Darwin, where my mum lived, still lives. She put them in her spare room, which she hardly ever used. I moved to Sydney and got on with life, working et cetera. But I always had this idea that the books were my real self, and I'd come back to them when I was ready. Is this boring?'

'It's the opposite. I'm getting the eggs out. This is like my Tigey and Cuddles story, isn't it? What terrible thing happened to the books?'

'Is it past Elrington Road?'

'A few up on the left. Red door.'

'I wish I hadn't started talking about this, but okay. My mum had quite a big cancer operation. She had to go down to Brisbane for it and I flew up from Sydney to help her. It was a week in hospital, then a week in hospital accommodation for lots of check-ups. After that, I had to go back to work, so Daniel, my brother, who was living in Melbourne by then, took her back to Darwin and moved in to Mum's spare room.' She peered at each tall grey Victorian terraced house as she went past. 'I think I'm here. I'll stand on the step, so I don't have to take the story inside.'

'Take it inside, it's so cold. The hall at least.'

'Okay.' His keyring was a leather map of France. She unlocked the top lock with a thin key and the bottom lock with a chunky one. She stood in the dark hall. 'I'm in. So, I was on the phone to my brother, to check up on Mum, and I said, "Sorry about the boxes in the spare room." And he said—'

Adam groaned. 'What boxes?'

'Exactly. You can't get upset with someone who has cancer. Anyway, it wasn't Mum's fault. I forgot about the wet season. It's so tropical. They went mouldy and that was that—no way back. She got the council to collect them and take them to the dump.'

'How ruthless,' Adam said, admiringly.

'When I came over here, I started all over again, ninety-nine pence each at charity shops. Okay, I'm going to turn on the light. Let me call you back, I want to have a look and then ask you about it.'

'I'll just finish my eggs.'

'Great!'

'Great!'

'Bye!'

'Bye!'

Everything was painted the same generic builder's white: walls, skirtings, floorboards, cornices and, at the back of the hall, the stairs. Two bikes leaned against the scuffed wall, one blue adult bike and a small pink one for Zora. The original fireplace was still there in the sitting room, light grey marble with dark grey veins. The alcoves on either side were lined floor to ceiling with ply shelves on heavy-duty industrial metal brackets. One shelf, halfway up on one side, held a record player with an amp and speakers. Records filled the shelves underneath. The rest had books on, all jumbled up.

Ottolenghi, Nigella, Nigel Slater. University reading list-looking books (black-spine Penguins). A selection of novels in French with their distinctive cream covers. Lots of politics and history, post-war British stuff. Diaries: Alistair Campbell, Alan Clark, Chris Mullin, Tony Benn. Politicians' memoirs called things like *My Life* and *A Journey* and *My Life, Our Times*. Extreme levels of Barack Obama: his books and lots of books about him. Adam's sofa was very like her sofa. In the corner was a big TV on an antique trunk, sort of like a pirate's chest. Under the bay window was a giant pink plastic house. Inside, small nude human dolls were taking tea with Sylvanian animals, also nude.

Through double wooden doors there was another small reception, another fireplace. There was nothing in the room apart from a large wooden table. At one end of the table was an open laptop, the screen dark, and two coffee cups, each with an inch of cold black coffee inside. At the other end, a long strip of butchers' paper, sellotaped to the pine, was covered in drawings of animals: orange lions, grey elephants, a black cat. 'ZoRa, ZoRa, ZoRa' Adam's daughter had written. Coralie appreciated the flair of the random capital R. At the top of the page, the sun had a smiling face. The ghost of a childhood compulsion came over her and she put lids back on the uncapped felt-tips. She wondered what Adam was thinking about her long silence. But she couldn't experience his house and process it with him at the same time.

Antoinette, forty-six, lived in a much larger version of this kind of Victorian terrace; her two-decades-older architect husband had replaced the walls at the rear with a futuristic glass cube. (Coralie hadn't personally seen it; one of the top Google results for her boss was a house tour on the website Dezeen.) But Adam's narrow galley kitchen must have been decades old. Wonky pine cabinets ran down both sides, leaving just enough space at the end for a small table and four chairs. There was a window over the sink and narrow French doors leading on to what she presumed was the garden. She peered outside but couldn't see much. In the fridge she found milk in glass bottles, a bag of carrots, a giant slab of cheddar in cling film, tomato ketchup and HP Sauce, half a bottle of supermarket white wine and a phalanx of purple Petits Filous yoghurts.

Upstairs in the big front bedroom that was clearly Adam's room was a bed, made (but the dark grey linen very rumpled), a built-in wardrobe on either side of the fireplace, a bedside table with an industrial-looking task lamp, and a chair with a pair of jeans thrown over the side. The room next to his seemed to have no purpose at all: there were three large packing boxes (stacked, possibly empty), a rolled-up yoga mat and an ironing board. The bathroom did have a bath, a huge freestanding one. Beside it a clear plastic container overflowed with boats, ducks, cups, and a Ken with a plastic mermaid tail in place of his legs.

She clomped up the carpetless wooden stairs, happiness rising within her. When she reached the top landing, she gasped. The big front bedroom was the only one that wasn't white. A nightlight had been left on and a scene of stars and planets gently rotated around walls of a bright sky-blue. Over

32

the single bed hung a red-and-white-striped canopy like a circus tent. A giant wooden toybox was propped open under one of the windows, filled to the brim with silks, feather boas, a spacesuit, a Spiderman costume. Clothes spilled out of two matching chests of drawers on either side of the fireplace. In the unused grate, a collection of stuffed animals huddled together. In front of them, on a Persian rug, was a basket of colourful Easter eggs. The foil was half-removed from each egg and a child's small bite taken out.

Her phone lit up with an incoming call.

'You do have a bath!'

'Have you found anything weird? You've gone all quiet.'

'I've only found nice things. I've just got to Zora's room. It's like a dream.'

'I can't take any credit; she has a granny who's very arty.'

'Your mum?'

'My mum's partner.'

Coralie paused. 'Oh God! Sorry! It's like the riddle.'

'The fox, the chicken and the granny...'

'Father and son are in a horrible car crash that kills the dad. The son is rushed to the hospital—the nurse hands the surgeon a scalpel. "Stop! I can't operate! This boy is my son," the surgeon says.'

'Oh? The dad was gay? Two dads? No! The surgeon was a woman.'

'Sorry it took me so long to work out you could have two grannies together.'

'Don't worry! It took Mum ages too.'

'But where's the guest room? Does it exist?'

'You must be right next to it.'

She walked down the hall to the last door. 'I was right next to it.'

On the double bed was a clean mattress-protector, two fluffy white pillow inners and a duvet with no cover. A chest of drawers stood empty, another task lamp on the top. She clicked on the lamp and hung her tote on one of the drawer handles.

'The stuff is in the cupboard outside the bathroom,' Adam said. 'Towels are in there too.'

'You can change the sheets on mine if you like. They're in an ugly plastic box under the bed. I'm sorry my bathroom doesn't have a window.'

'I'm sorry I only have nine books by women.'

'Wait, is this it? Are you going to bed?'

'Ring me when you've had something to eat and a bath,' Adam said. 'I won't go to bed until you do.'

She didn't make pasta. She found a packet of crackers in the cupboard next to the fridge and sliced some cheddar, which she had with a glass of his wine. Afterwards, she wandered back into the sitting room to find a book to read in the bath. Among the mass of political books was *Recollections of a Bleeding Heart*, Don Watson's classic biography of Australia's charismatic and brooding prime minister, Paul Keating. Truly, no one knew anything about Australian politics in the UK, or anything about Australia at all. But here was a very large paperback all about where she came from, the spine virtually corduroy from avid engagement. Two bits of curled-over paper stuck out from the top, boarding passes for Sydney to Canberra flights in 2004: it must have been the Mark Latham profile trip. He must have been twenty-eight then. She would have been twenty-one, living in a share house with Josh and the other High Court associates, in the final year of her Arts degree and working four days a week on a local magazine. Adam had been in the same city. Now, on the other side of the world, they'd somehow managed to meet—not once, but three times. How could it be this easy?

In a rush of fear, she googled him. *Young Country* did exist. So did the podcast. On YouTube, she watched him amiably review newspaper headlines on a weekend current-affairs show. The Adam of the video was recognisably the Adam of the Dove. She hurried to his bedside table and pulled open the top drawer. Four small marbles and one large one rolled to the front and bounced back. She opened the bottom drawer. It contained a battered, much-read copy of *Meg and Mog*. He was who he said he was. It was real.

In bed, in his clean sheets, in the dark, she went into her call log and saved his number: adam. He answered the call after a few rings. 'I just got into bed,' he said. 'Were you going to tell me about this guy behind the pillow?'

'Brown Bear? It seemed a bit mean after Tigey and Cuddles. Rubbing your nose in it.'

'Is this a boarding-school thing? Stuffed animals?'

'We're profoundly damaged.'

'I've just been dipping in to *The Group*—I found it beside your bed. "Consider yourself kissed"—that's how this bad boy Harald signs off letters to his girlfriend.'

'Later', Coralie said sorrowfully, 'he commits her to an asylum.'

35

'Why are you reading it if you've read it before? That's my question.'

'I can't *believe* you have the Don Watson Paul Keating book. It's such a good book!'

'It's the best political bio I've ever read. I had to write about Prime Minister's Questions once, Question Time I think you call it there. And I watched an incredible video with Paul Keating. The opposition leader, the leader of whatever the Tories are—remind me?'

'The Liberals.'

'The Liberal leader says, "If you're so confident our policies are bad, why don't you just call an early election?" And Keating gets up. "Because, mate," he starts to say. Everyone's hooting, shrieking; the Speaker says to settle down. "Because, because, mate." And then Keating says…'

'Because what?'

'Because, mate.' Adam was quoting, but he was speaking directly to her. His voice came right through the phone and shivered down her spine. 'I wanna do you slowly.'

'So why did you go to the Dove? Rather than the other three pubs?'

'I suppose I can tell you, now I've got you into bed.'

'Tell me.'

'I was hoping you'd be there.'

'And I was.'

'You were.'

In the morning, they remained only a latte-length time in Climpsons before crossing the market to her flat. They spent

36

the whole Easter long weekend together, and almost all the ensuing weeks and months, opening up their individual bodies and minds and knitting them back together, connected—like an operation to separate conjoined twins, only in reverse.

Her happiness made her almost too open, and some things that weren't Adam but shared some DNA with him were let in by mistake, like loose-leaf tea in a pot with a tea cosy, hot puddings (disparaged by the old version of herself as 'second dinners'), listening to Radio 4's *Today* and *PM*, and watching *Channel Four News* and *Newsnight*. Her love, too, overflowed and spilled out, and—having previously not made even the slightest impact—she was suddenly hailed at both her work coffee shop and at Climpsons as an adored and favourite regular.

'I like it,' her boss said one day.

'Oh?' Coralie blushed. 'Like what?'

'Whatever you've done.' Antoinette waved an elegant hand. 'With your' (in a French accent) '*visage*'.

London wasn't unfriendly! London wasn't cold!

'I'm sorry, so sorry to interrupt.' An older woman came up to them on Columbia Road. 'But I just wanted to tell you how beautiful you are—both of you! Together.'

And Adam and Coralie smiled, thanked her, and took it as their due.

The drafts of her manuscript stayed under the seat cushion of the sofa. After a few weeks, she moved them to an IKEA bag. Then she put the bag under the bed. Then she forgot about her writing entirely.

3

Despite being nearly thirty, and a woman, Coralie had always existed in a child-free world. No younger cousins, no babysitting, certainly no peers with kids. As for her own childhood, it was a closed book—one she had no desire to open. She knew from both literature and popular culture that being a mother was all joy and no fun, that the days were long but the years were short, that making art was incompatible with having babies, and that if a man was present in the delivery room and saw you giving birth, your sex life would never recover. ('It was like my favourite pub burning down'—Robbie Williams.)

Being a stepmother was famously even more difficult. You barely heard 'stepmother' without the word 'evil' before it. (*Bzzt!* Getting ahead of herself! She and Adam were *not* married!) Children seemed, on the one hand, a lot of work, and on the other, terrifying: what vulnerabilities might they glimpse? Without the veneer of civility that governed the behaviour of adults, what unpleasant truths might they utter? Before her first planned meeting with Adam's daughter, Coralie found herself studying her face anxiously in the mirror. She had a hormonal blemish on her chin—what if Zora pointed it out?

The first part of the meeting, the coffee (and babyccino), passed by in a haze of politeness and nerves. It was only when they got up on their hind legs and strode out onto the street that Zora assumed her correct proportion in relation to Coralie: not a giant, sinister opponent but a young, small, very appealing person. She had a long plush toy snake lashed to the front of her scooter with a hair ribbon. 'Is that your most special toy?' Coralie enquired.

'Ha,' Zora darkly laughed. 'N-O spells no.'

'We no longer take the most special toys out of the house,' Adam said.

'Because Mummy's boyfriend *Tom* lost my *owl* at the *zoo*.' Zora turned her little face towards Coralie. 'What do you call a snake who works for the government?'

'This was also a present from Tom,' Adam murmured.

Oh, it was a joke. 'What?'

'A civil serpent.' Zora dashed her sneaker on the pavement and scooted off.

Of course, it would've been hard for Zora *not* to be clever. Soon after meeting Adam, Coralie had searched for the barrister profile of his ex, Marina Amin. She was familiar with super-academic legal high-achievers from her time with her ex-boyfriend, Josh. He and his friends never did anything unless it could go on their CVs. Even so, she'd been shocked by Marina's top-tier intellectual credentials: with honours; with distinction; first in year; winner of this, winner of that; her Spanish merely 'conversational', she was fluent in Italian and French. 'Pfff!' Adam had scoffed when she raised this. 'Marina's Spanish is just French in an Italian accent.'

At Hackney City Farm, in its charming cobbled courtyard, Adam slipped on some sort of animal poo. 'Yuck!' he whispered, horrified. 'Yuck, yuck, yuck.'

As he gingerly cleaned his shoes in a puddle, Coralie and Zora wandered over to the pig pen. There, three crossbred Pietrain sows reclined luxuriously as if taking the mud for their health.

'Cora-nee,' Zora said. 'I have a question.'

'Oh, um.' Coralie blanched, preparing for something about feelings, or Adam, or their arrangements, her intentions, or marriage. She would *always* take her seriously, she vowed then. For as long as she knew Zora, she wouldn't lie. 'Go for it!'

'Are pigs waterproof?'

She didn't know what she expected a child to be like, but it was never as great as this.

Not long after, on a beautiful warm day, Coralie and Adam were lying in Coralie's bed in the oblong of sun from the skylight. Adam had collapsed on top of her, still inside her (though not hard), and her hips were aching, but she didn't want to move. 'Half term' was starting soon, whatever that was, and he'd be going to the seaside with Zora. He invited Coralie along, but (from some old instinct about fathers and daughters, entirely gleaned from novels) she said no. Soon the reality of not seeing him for at least seven days overtook her, and she found herself almost in tears.

There had been lots of country boarders at her school, in their chambray shirts and Tiffany heart chains, and one of them had told her a fact about farm dogs. This girl, who was frankly weird, although she had more friends than Coralie, said you should never separate animals who were having sex, because pulling the penis out roughly would bring out all the other animal's insides and guts with it, eviscerating it and killing it. Coralie relayed the memory to Adam. 'That's exactly how I feel,' she said.

She was being serious, almost hysterically so. Adam had a serious face on when he replied: 'Like…a dog?'

'No,' she almost shouted. 'Like, eviscerated and murdered!'

'Oh, thank God,' he said. 'You're the girl dog in this scenario.'

'I don't care which dog I am! I'm telling you how I feel when we're apart!'

'And I'm telling you I feel exactly the same! Completely bereft,' he said. 'Except—with a penis.'

She wanted two children by the time she was thirty-five. She wanted them close in age, unlike her and her brother, and she wanted to keep working, unlike her mum. Adam had always wanted a big family. She didn't care about getting married, but if they did, she'd like a registry-office situation followed by a small formal dinner. He didn't care about getting married, but if they did, he'd like a registry-office situation followed by a big, long honeymoon. Her greatest fears were of being homeless, being in an acid attack, and of angry sounds: sighs, clicks, tsks, grunts, anything that showed she was about to get told off. His were of mice, erectile dysfunction, and of seeing his partner crying and not caring to find out why.

We always have to *talk* to each other, they said. And they were certain, bone certain, they always would.

Her lease came up for renewal, and he didn't ask her to move in with him — he just assumed. They were sitting at Railroad, a restaurant between London Fields and Homerton Hospital. It was small, relaxed, and you could watch the two owners cooking the three or four options on the menu. Adam and Coralie each had a glass of red wine while they shared some salami and pickles. That's when he said it: '*When* you move in...'

She sat for a moment in silence. She hardly registered the rest of the sentence.

'Oh no,' he said. 'You don't want to? Is this a Virginia Woolf thing? Room of one's own, et cetera?'

'God, of course not. I love your house. Besides, I'm not a writer.'

'I'll come back to that and argue with you later. Is it a Zora thing?'

'Oh God! No!'

The question mark stayed on Adam's face. 'It's just,' Coralie said, 'I feel like I've never told you why I moved to London— in the first place.'

'To work on your vitamin D deficiency? Craving Tory austerity? To lower your life expectancy? For the knife crime?'

'Sometimes you make four jokes when one would do.'

'I know,' Adam said. 'It's because I'm short.'

'Now I'm laughing—how can I tell you my bad story?'

He reached around the salami plate for her hand. 'Tell me.'

The break-up with Josh had been bad. Not because she still wanted to be with him, which she hadn't, by the end—but mainly because he'd bought out her share of their Northcote flat. His parents had transferred that money to her bank account with the bleakest description field ever: CORALIE FINAL.

It had been nice to have the money back, equivalent to every dollar she'd saved working since she was nineteen. Still, she would have preferred to have a home.

She packed her stuff, shipped her books to Darwin, and—unable to imagine a new park, a new tram route—moved a few blocks up the hill. The new apartment was small, blank, charmless, but safe. It was late summer when she moved in, and all the trees had leaves. By winter, obviously, many didn't, and she found to her dismay that, from the window in her new living room, she could see her old seventies apartment block. Not into the bedroom! Which Josh by then shared with Lucy! Nothing like that! The way the light played over it at sunset, that sort of thing. No way—she couldn't live there. She found the most lucrative job someone with an English degree could find (in Sydney, in advertising) and paid to break the lease. It really hurt to waste that money. She could never tell her mum.

Adam snorted. 'Sounds perfectly reasonable to me.'

The waiter came over to refill their wine glasses. She started on the next bit of the story, but the waiter returned with their mains. She picked at her pilaf, and wondered if she could go on. It was all so horrible (the story, not the food). It was all so grim (that was an Adam word). So sordid.

'Go on,' Adam said. 'Please.'

She'd googled the agency before the interview and got the sense of its founder as a guru. In his late fifties by then, he was universally considered at his peak. She soon learned first-hand that if there was a rule, or a convention, Richard Pickard broke it. Why meet clients in person when he could kayak across the Harbour shouting at his Bluetooth? Why work in his office when he could be up on the roof terrace tending to his bees? He relished being elusive; he loved being 'off the clock'. Bringing him a pedestrian concern, especially about budget or admin, could ruin his entire day, and ruin the bringer's day too, because of the shouting. So could asking him the wrong question, or not having the right size print-outs of his concepts, or not intuiting that he needed *downtime*, or scheduling him *downtime* when what he needed was a crisis, a conflict, or a compliment (ideally a prize with a trophy).

On the rare occasions he consented to sit in front of his computer, he *tick-tick-tick*ed away like the timer on a bomb. Almost from her first day, Coralie alone could separate out the different coloured wires and defuse him. It was second nature, instinctive: she knew what he needed, how to give it to him and how to manage him. They were a great team, and they won a lot of big jobs, awards and bonuses. At least, he won the bonuses—she was on a salary. He was the boss of the world, and at his feet, on a tiny pedestal engraved RICHARD'S MUSE, sat Coralie.

44

The night outside was stormy and the restaurant very warm; a mist had formed on the window and the lights of passing cars glittered in the drops. Adam nodded at the rest of her lamb and rice. 'Are you going to eat that?'

She was sharing some of the worst parts of her life—and still he wanted her scraps. She gratefully swapped their plates.

In Sydney, her work became her life. Richard was work. Richard was life. She accompanied him everywhere, calming him when he was angry and buoying him when he was low. She helped him with what he called *getting his mind down*: transforming diffuse vibes and insights into something that could be packaged and sold. Or 'Coralie, Coralie,' he'd beg, 'close my tabs.' *Closing his tabs* meant running through his day, his diary and works-in-progress with him and quieting his racing mind. Or *be my sounding board*, he'd say, and she'd make herself available to listen to his riffs, idea after idea based on whatever obsessed him at the time: kintsugi, the ancient art of repairing the cracks in pottery with gold; the way Glenn Gould hummed along to the piano in his *Goldberg Variations*. 'I resonate with that,' he'd say about every piece of stimulus, instead of 'That resonates with me.' He seemed to spend all his time resonating—physically vibrating with his own artistry and passion. Richard was the tuning fork; she was the dull object he tapped to make a sound. She woke every day to five, ten, fifteen texts from him. She kept her phone in the kitchen at night.

When work took them interstate, at first they used dinner to get his mind down. Then he liked Coralie to close his tabs in person, a nightcap at the hotel bar. Then he couldn't go to sleep until she'd put him to bed, which meant going into his room to make sure the space was okay (no overwhelming scents, no strange noises), and closing his tabs in the lounge area of his suite. Then putting him to bed meant being present in the room till he was ready to drop off. Then putting him to bed meant doing all that while stroking his forehead. Then it also meant giving him 'a cuddle'.

'Yes, I have to say,' Adam said mildly, 'I'm really not liking the sound of this guy.'

Her mother had to have her second, much scarier cancer op, and Richard gave Coralie two weeks off work so she could be there. But: *I can't live without you,* he texted. *What are you doing to me? I haven't felt like this in a very long time. No one's done this to me before. I'm utterly entranced by you. I'm totally in your power.* These were the kinds of messages he was sending her—messages she was receiving in recovery, where her mother's staples split and the white sheet that covered her suddenly turned red.

'As I suspected,' Adam said. 'I hate him.'

She returned to find him on the doorstep of her Elizabeth Bay apartment building. He was desperate, out of his mind, in tears; he was dying, he couldn't manage. Terrified, she hustled him into the lobby. Instantly revived, he bounded up eight flights of stairs without becoming breathless. He conducted an energetic and hilarious tour of her small one-bedroom flat, emerging on to her pride and joy, her tiny balcony, with its view of the sparkling azure sea. 'Your own little piece of the harbour,' he exclaimed, reminding her that his own sea-fronted mansion (which he shared with his wife and three kids) had a pool and a jetty for their boat.

Yet despite the mansion, the wife and the three children, it was Coralie he wanted, and as the day grew dark around them, he won from her first a declaration of responsibility, then of care. And attraction? Well, she supposed sometimes attraction. He was ecstatic, she restrained him. He was devastated, she embraced him. Finally, it seemed as though she had achieved the almost-impossible, a triumph of sensitivity and influence: he would depart her house knowing that she *wanted to*, but alas, *couldn't*. His hand was on the door handle. One kiss, he said, and he'd stay forever silent. She kissed him. He tasted like the silt at the bottom of a fish tank. He hauled her towards her bedroom.

'I want to kill this guy,' Adam said. 'I want to murder him.'

She managed it! She solved it! She put a stop to it! But the stopping of it made him cry, then stride around the flat, shouting and hitting himself. He was disgusting, an animal, she was right to hate him. I don't hate you, she said, I care about you. The whole thing started again. After midnight he was on her balcony, threatening to jump off and screaming that she was a cocktease. She sat paralysed on the sofa, sobbing. She found out afterwards the neighbours called the police. Officers banged on the door. Richard was swaggering, charming, joking: 'Don't shoot!' He had everyone laughing as they escorted him down the stairs. But on Monday, he wasn't at work. The day passed in a haze of fear. Richard was in jail, or he was dead—her selfishness had killed him.

That afternoon, as she left the office, a woman rushed up to her, shaking. 'You're ruining his life—my life. Do you under-stand? I've seen your messages to him. You're sick. You're *trash*.' Someone from the office came outside for a smoke. Richard's wife waited for them to move on. Then she leaned in towards Coralie, so close that Coralie could see individual strands of her expensive blonde foils. 'Get your own husband,' she hissed. 'Get your own family.' In spite of herself, with a visceral sense of self-harm, Coralie waited politely for her parting words, which she delivered with pure disgust: *fucking homewrecker.*

It had been a major part of Richard's persona that his agency was *boutique*, a 'shop'. It was also, however, important to him that his work was seen as 'global'. For this reason, he'd cultivated a loose networking arrangement with a similar agency in Portland, Oregon, and another in Clerkenwell, London. It was to this office that human resources suggested she might like to transfer. 'Cultural exchange,' they called it, though there was no talk of her ever returning. They'd pay out her Elizabeth Bay lease. They'd pay for her relocation. Her salary was equivalent, in GBP, to her salary in AUD, and it was made clear just how generous this was, in post-financial-crisis Britain. It was an offer she couldn't refuse! (She didn't have a choice.)

'Coffee? Pudding?' The waiter was back, and keen to talk to Adam about football.

Coralie escaped to the bathroom and cradled her head in her hands. When she thought about that period in her life, she felt repulsive—a worm-like creature, writhing in the mud. She hadn't returned to the office; it had been clear she wasn't welcome. The contents of her desk (her packets of green tea and seaweed crisps, her tampons and her lip balms) had been couriered to her flat. Had Richard cast her out, or had his wife somehow insisted? Did human resources know the truth? What was the truth, actually? She'd inhabited her role as Richard's offsider so intensely that, without him, it was as if she didn't exist. Sometimes she heard her phone ping, but when she checked it, there was nothing. Her Facebook status announcing her 'next adventure' had been a triumph of the copywriter's art. Despite the ninety-seven Likes, she'd closed the door on her third home in under two years with a sense of shame so total it was almost annihilating. And then, once in London, her loneliness had been unspeakable—she felt that now with new force. How had she survived?

When she returned to the dining room, Adam was staring past the condensation on the window to make out the street scene beyond. Two chocolate mousses sat before him, the dark kind with salt and olive oil. He pushed one towards her. 'Please don't let me eat both of these.'

'So that's the story, basically.' Coralie sat down. 'Richard's wife called me a homewrecker, but the only home I wrecked was my own.'

'Now just hold on!' Adam threw down his napkin and joined her on her side of the table. 'You're using some very active verbs here. Coralie.' He took both her hands in his. 'You didn't wreck anything. You didn't do anything. That guy needs his lights punched out!'

The waiter came over with a tea towel. 'Let's see if we can mop this up.' He swept it across the window, clearing up the view.

That was what being with Adam was like. He wiped the slate clean. Everything was new.

And if she felt like a door had closed somewhere, that a complex experience was being tidied away without being fully understood, that she was alone in still interrogating it—that was a small price to pay for his acceptance, his support, his love.

In the Wilton Way house, Coralie took the odd little nothing-room with the boxes and the yoga mat as her own private study. She taped off the skirtings and the window frame and painted the walls in Nancy's Blushes. She let Adam escort her around IKEA, introducing her to the miracle of shelves. They knocked a wall of Billy bookcases together and stacked up her new (old) books. Her desk she found on Parkholme Road: she covered it in paint-stripper and scraped it down to the pine. Once installed in her pink room, she placed a new journal front and centre on the desk, with the intention, finally, of Writing with a capital W. But Zora found the notebook, liked it, stole it and scrawled on the cover

ZORA

PRIVAT

BOOK

—so Coralie let her keep it.

Over the fireplace in the sitting room, she hung *Bowerbird Making a Nest*, a colourful painting by an Indigenous woman artist from South East Arnhem Land. She'd had to unroll the canvas carefully and stretch it; it had spent four years stored in a tube. She'd bought the picture as a present to herself after the break-up with Josh. It wasn't just because her surname was Bower; she liked the birds themselves, so-called because the male builds an intricate, beautiful, perfect home to lure the female.

Adam smiled, satisfied. 'Just like I did for you.'

Well, sort of. Coralie loved the Wilton Way house, but it was not without its flaws. Leaves from the neighbours' tree clogged the kitchen gutters so comprehensively that heavy rain streamed down the inside wall. Multiple split floorboards bounced like trampolines. ('Maybe try to avoid,' Adam said.) Filling the kettle, she found stalagmites and stalactites of limescale. ('Hard water, minerals—good for the hair and teeth!') The cupboard under the sink had a horrible hospital smell (TCP, a liquid antiseptic—Adam's mother, a retired GP, made him gargle it when he was ill). There was also the issue of the Tasmania-shaped sepia stain in the ceiling above the boiler cupboard.

Still, she agreed. 'Exactly like you did for me.'

'I love you,' he said.

'I love you.'

And she did. She had made it. She was home.

4

2014

Adam was a Christmas Eve baby. The first year they were together for his birthday, he was so unexpectedly short with her at Bistrotheque, so passive and enervated and so unlike himself, Coralie asked for the bill early and escaped alone up Mare Street. She was still upset the next day when Adam, dressed only in a Santa hat, brought her up coffee in bed. 'I'm sorry, I'm sorry, I hate my birthday,' he said. 'I never realised how much.' As the next one approached, his thirty-ninth, she cautiously raised the issue of their plans. 'Just time with you, and with Zora,' he said. 'Nothing special. I mean, that *is* special. The *most* special, and exactly what I want, and only that.'

When Zora's term finished, Adam and Coralie picked her up straight from school. Her small rucksack was loaded with important items: five pens, two notebooks, a little skateboard from a set of Lego Friends, a fawn soft toy dog with enormous eyes, some shrivelled conkers, and a slim work of Usborne non-fiction called *Animals at War*. Coralie took a week off work, and none of Boris Johnson's inner circle had time to meet Adam on background for his book, so the three of them chose the tree, made mince pies, and baked little FIMO ornaments with a weird chemical smell. They took Zora to the frigid 'big slide park' in Victoria Park, to ice-skate at Somerset House, and to John Lewis on Oxford Street for a dress to wear to *The Snowman*. All these things only took up a few hours a day. The rest of the time Zora watched *Paw Patrol* or *Ben and Holly*, or was eating, or sometimes even did all three at once, eating while watching *Ben and Holly* on the iPad with *Paw Patrol* on TV.

The dress was a big success, but the musical, a matinee on Christmas Eve Eve, was not. Zora sat bolt upright in her seat as soon as Jack Frost crept on stage, sizeable codpiece jutting problematically, icicle fingers creepily extended. She asked Adam to take her to the toilet, leaving Coralie in the theatre eating Maltesers on her own, mildly gripped by the spectacle. By the time she got the text saying they'd pulled the ripcord, father and daughter were in Pizza Express. Coralie had to catch up, freezing, breathless, stomping along the grey wind tunnels of Holborn, dark already at four in the afternoon. They should have gone to *The Nutcracker*. Whenever an outing with Zora went less than entirely according to plan, she felt tears rise to her eyes, but why? She couldn't exactly say.

Because Zora wasn't just clever and special, she was also loving and sweet: she slipped her hand into Coralie's while waiting to cross the road, and avidly consumed classic books from Coralie's Australian childhood, like *Magic Beach* and *Where the Forest Meets the Sea*. When asked to make a family tree for school, she happily and proactively included Coralie (as well as Marina's new husband, Tory Tom). If she cried, it was because she was tired or injured. When she was clingy or moany, it meant she was getting ill. She could be comforted easily, with a cuddle from Adam, an unnecessary Band-Aid ('sticking plaster') or a snack. Still, there were times, only a few, and she wasn't proud of them, when Coralie felt a creeping exhaustion at the thought of another early dinner, of trying discreetly to communicate adult things to her adult boyfriend over the shiny-haired head of a six-year-old.

In the packed Pizza Express, after the abortive trip to *The Snowman*, she found herself wondering what Stefan from the office and Marcus were doing at that moment. Not a 'Spot the Difference' with crayons on a child's menu, that was for sure. At least (she knew it was bad to look forward to this) Marina was picking Zora up the next day. They'd have a child-friendly birthday lunch together for Adam beforehand—pasta, probably, or sausages. Then they, the grown-ups, The Happy Couple, alone at last, could have a proper adult dinner together. That reminded her, she had to pick up the oysters from Fin and Flounder.

'Look, his bow tie's missing half the bow.' Zora circled it. 'Eight differences.'

'Oh no,' Adam said.

Coralie's heart, already racing, started to pound. 'What?'

'Just something on my phone.'

'Text it to me. Zora, do you want the bathroom? I'm going

before the food comes.'

'I went to the bathroom at *The Snowman*.'

'I wasn't sure if you really did, or if that was your escape plan.'

'It was both. I needed the toilet, and I was too scared of Jack Frost.'

'Okay.' Coralie waved her phone. 'Back in a tick.'

She read his text in the cubicle: *The GGs arrive tomorrow*. It ended with a sad face. She sent a sad face back. When she looked in the mirror afterwards, she found she was doing one for real.

At the table, the pizza had arrived. A bit of basil or something green had been left on Zora's by mistake. Coralie whisked it off before she saw.

'Guess what, sweetheart,' Adam said brightly.

'What?' Zora said.

'Move the glass closer, don't crane your neck for the straw. Lovely news. Granny's coming tomorrow!'

'The GGs? Or Irish granny?'

'The gay grannies!'

'Can I wear this furry dress to show Sally?'

'Sit a bit closer to the table. If there's no pizza on it, of course you can.'

'But are they coming for your birthday, or Christmas, or both?' Coralie was thinking of her menus. The birthday dinner was oysters followed by a fish stew with more than thirty (30) Great British Pounds worth of pre-ordered monkfish. It was a recipe from the Moro restaurant cookbook, with peppers, almonds and saffron. She could double the sauce, divide it into fish and non-fish. Anne and Sally's bit could have chickpeas. (They were vegetarians.) Would that work? But Christmas? It wouldn't be an option to simply make the chicken stretch. She'd have to make all new dishes, unless she just went overboard on the sides. God, Pizza Express was so loud. 'Why didn't they say yes when we invited them in November? Do they know we won't have Zora on Christmas morning?'

'What's it like being so famous?' Adam asked his daughter. 'Everyone wants Zora.' He mimed fighting over her, pulling her one way and then the other. 'My Zora...No, *my* Zora! The GGs would steal you away to Lewes in a heartbeat.'

'Only Sally.' For a moment, Zora's look was pure Marina, penetrating and totally assured. 'Not Granny. May I have my pudding now?'

It became clear, when at eight-thirty Zora was still struggling to get to sleep, that *The Snowman* had been a bigger mistake than they'd realised. The cold made Zora think about Jack Frost, and how the shadows in the room could *be* him. Adam was sitting with his legs stretched across her open bedroom door updating his fantasy football. 'Fucking bloodbath, fucking Reds, ruining my life,' he muttered. 'Lose, lose, lose—I can't hack another season like this. If we don't crush Burnley, I'll off myself.'

All Zora needed was five straight minutes of calm attention. An hour of keyed-up physical presence but mental and emotional absence wasn't cutting it.

'Is that Cora-nee?' It was Zora's voice. She didn't sound the slightest bit tired.

'I'm here.' Coralie stepped over Adam's legs. 'I can't see a thing. Call out to me.'

'Cora-nee, Cor, Corrr...' She trailed off in a funny gargle.

'Zora, Zora, I can hear a pigeon in your room!'

'Coooor!'

'No wonder you can't sleep, look how messy your blankets are. Sit up straight.' She fluffed up the pillows and straightened the duvet. Behind her, she could hear Adam's knees crack as he heaved himself up and lumbered down the stairs. 'Where's Sparebitty?' The special rabbit kept at Marina's was called Rabbitty. Sparebitty had been purchased as a secret back-up in case Rabbitty got lost. Zora got wise to this, and now Rabbitty was kept in Camden, and Wilton Way fell under what Marina called 'Sparebitty's jurisdiction'.

'She slipped behind the bed.'

'Sparebitty! Naughty!' Coralie pulled her out and tucked her under Zora's arm. She sat on the edge of the bed. She could see Zora's eyes glittering at her. Her nose was so sweet and up-turned at the end. 'What's going on in here?'

'I'm not tired.'

'I am. What about you, Sparebitty? God, look at her.' She made the rabbit shake with snores. 'Can you hear that?'

Zora smiled, delighted. 'Like Dada.'

'Turn her on her side, that's what I do to Daddy.' Zora carefully did so. 'What did you mean today, when you said Granny wouldn't want to steal you away?' Zora's face was blank. 'Remember?' Coralie said. 'We were having pizza, and Adam said the GGs wanted to sneak you away with them, and you said Granny wouldn't. What was that about?'

'Granny likes taking me, but she also likes giving me back.'

'You're so interesting, Zora—you should write about that tomorrow.' (Zora maintained a semi-regular diary, where, in perfect cursive, she confided secrets like: 'Today Oscar got 2 blue cards' and 'I do the lessins but I cant relly swim.')

'Tomorrow isn't coming,' she sighed. 'I can't sleep.'

Coralie looked down the corridor of years and saw Zora ending up like her, a lie-in-bed-and-worrier, an awaker-at-four to worry some more. It probably wasn't appropriate that she attempt to influence this child in any way. The spectre of Marina loomed. While rigidly polite, she treated Coralie like Priscilla, her afternoon babysitter: a low-level functionary who nevertheless oversaw an important element of her (Marina's) life. A year earlier, during a Zora handover before Coralie's first Christmas with Adam, Marina had hovered near a stack of Fortnum & Mason champagnes, each in a tasteful wooden box. She handed one to Coralie: 'Something for under the tree.' Sliding it open in summer to chill for Aperol spritz, Coralie would see a card she'd missed. 'Jason—another year of wonderful clerking. What would I do without you? I hope you and the missus enjoy. From your favourite junior and star of the bar—M.A.' She would picture Jason and the missus reading, with confusion, the card that might have been left for her: 'Coralie—thank you for being a bland adjunct to my considerably more interesting life.' Or maybe: 'Coralie—you have given me the greatest gift a new girlfriend can give an ex-wife: being someone I can safely ignore.'

What would Marina want her to say to her sleepless child? This kind of thing was the job of a real mother.

'You had a very big day,' Coralie said. 'And tomorrow is definitely coming. What would you like for breakfast?'

'Flat pancakes?' (Zora's term for crêpes, as opposed to 'fat pancakes').

'You can have flat pancakes. Do you still have Daddy's birthday card hidden?' Zora nodded. 'He's going to love it—your handwriting's so good. I'm going down now, but I'll come up and check on you in ten minutes. I bet you're asleep when I do.'

'What if I'm not?' In the half-dark, Zora looked very worried.

'If you're not, nothing bad will happen, I'll check on you ten minutes after that. Because you know...' She couldn't help it. 'Sometimes people can't sleep. It's perfectly normal and very common. And when you can't, it's important not to lie there making yourself feel bad about it. It's just life.'

'Okay.'

'Okay, sweetheart.' Coralie picked up the rabbit. 'Sparebitty, can you give this kiss to Zora?' She kissed the rabbit's paw, then made the rabbit kiss the girl.

'Night-night.'

'Night.'

Downstairs, Adam was getting gherkins out of the jar with his fingers. 'Do you want some of...all this?' He gestured at his selection of pickles and bits of cheese.

'I'd love some. Pizza Express was a thousand years ago.'

'You know what I'd love.' Adam dealt out some crackers. 'For someone to call me first thing tomorrow and say, "Adam, Adam, there's a huge reporting emergency." And then I could escape for twenty-four hours—to somewhere much more relaxing than my birthday with my mother. A train derailment, maybe. Or a terror attack.'

'It would have to be a pretty big disaster—if they're calling up a podcast host.'

'I'm an author and a broadcaster!'

He was *not* an author yet. The advance for his biography of London's unconventional and popular Tory mayor had been minuscule. The research was arduous, the legal red tape fearsome. Most upsettingly, barely any jokes made by Adam would be as funny as the quotations from Boris. It stung.

'I'm going to pop up to check on Zora again,' Coralie murmured.

'But the snack platter!'

'It'll just take a sec—she'll be asleep.'

She was.

Before she'd gone to bed, Coralie had texted Daniel for any new details about their mother's cancer treatment. Despite never having met any members of Coralie's family, and being a retired GP (with a special interest in sexual health) and *not* a surgeon or a cancer doctor, Anne Whiteman couldn't accept 'No better, no worse' or 'Hanging in there!' as an answer to 'How's your mum?'

Key to defusing Anne's bombardment was giving her a confident, factual early response. So when a knock came at the door before 10 a.m. the next day, hours before the GGs were expected, Coralie was chanting her mother's new chemo mix under her breath: 'FOLFIRINOX, 5FU, cetuximab!

FOLFIRINOX, 5FU, cetuximab!'

'Anne! Sally!' she exclaimed. 'You must have set off at the crack of dawn!'

'Up for hours,' Anne said. 'Did five miles before we set off.'

'Five miles...'

'LSE! Long, slow, easy.'

'But was it a run?' Coralie asked. 'Not a swim or anything?'

'I wouldn't put it past her to swim it.' Sally heaved her bulging tote higher on her shoulder and gestured at a laundry basket full of gifts. 'Sorry, where shall I...? They're for Zora.'

'Come in—sorry. Adam's taken Zora for a hot chocolate.'

Coralie lugged the basket into the front hall. She'd been hoping to get ahead on the little jobs that seemed to fall to her at this time of year as the Woman of the House, like wrapping the presents she'd bought for Zora—the ones from her and the ones 'from' Adam. She'd also bought his present for Anne, a book about the science behind 'extraordinary athletic performance'. Sally had kindly taken her aside the year before: 'Don't worry about anything for me,' she said. 'And I won't get anything for you.' Such a restful presence. Coralie wished for Adam's sake that Sally had been his biological mum—or at least that she'd come into his life a bit earlier.

Anne was wearing wide-legged black wool trousers, a tucked-in grey merino jumper and brogues. She had a sharp short haircut and, courtesy of her orthorexia, a very defined jawline. Her similarity to Adam was quite uncanny. Adam would look great in Anne's glasses. 'Yes, we'll take a tea,' Anne said.

'Come through!' Coralie filled the kettle at the tap. 'But

Anne, it must have been so dark when you went out this morning.'

'Got a running light. For my head. A head-torch.'

Coralie gasped and turned it into a throat-clearing cough.

'And how's your mum doing?'

'Not too bad—thanks, Anne. She's got a new chemo mix...' Coralie took a deep breath.

'And what is it?'

'FOLFIRINOX, 5FU, cetuximab!'

'FOLFIRINOX? I thought that was for pancreatic?'

'I don't know, but I think Mum sort of...has it everywhere now.'

'Strictly speaking,' Anne frowned. 'There's no such thing as cancer of the everywhere.'

'And is your wonderful brother still looking after her?' Sally smoothly moved on.

'He's living with her in Darwin, yes. He's working as a chef—it's so great for Mum; she finds it hard to eat, with the chemo, and all her restrictions...'

She trailed off and let her words become one with the sound of the boiling kettle. Whenever people talked about her mother, it was hard not to hear the question they were carefully not asking: why aren't you with her? But she'd had cancer for, what, nearly four years? Even Daniel hadn't been there the whole time. And unlike Coralie, busy making a living and *building a life*, he had nothing else to do. He was only working casually as a cook—not a chef, she wasn't exactly sure why she'd called him that. Besides, apart from the infrequent crises of her actual operations, her mother always said she was fine. It was patently obvious she wasn't—but, ultimately, she was the boss.

'You must miss home at this time of year,' Sally said.

'I'm still getting used to a cold Christmas—it was all prawns and mangoes for me, growing up. I can't bring myself to do a turkey.' Coralie shuddered. 'It seems so wrong.'

Anne snorted her approval. 'Preaching to the converted.'

'And your family,' Sally courteously persisted. 'Your parents live separately, don't they?'

'My dad is based in Canberra, yes, with his new...' It made her feel a bit sick to say 'girlfriend'. 'Partner? I suppose not that new really, they've been together for a decade. They always have their Christmas lunch in a hotel, for some reason. Mum was the real Christmas-lover.' An image came to her of her mother's festive napkin rings, the holly design she'd painted herself. She packed them up carefully in an egg carton and took them to every house they moved to, to be brought out for one meal a year. Where were they? Where was the cut-glass crystal trifle bowl? Did she still have her puffy red tartan headband from the nineties, and the apron with ALL I WANT FOR CHRISTMAS IS YOU? Coralie glanced at the kitchen clock. Her mother kept a child's bedtime during her chemo cycles. She could possibly catch her if she rang now. *Did* she miss her family? Coralie realised she'd been silent for quite a while. 'Yes...' she said uncertainly.

There came the most beautiful sound in the world: the front door opening.

'Sally!' Zora ran down the hall. 'Look at my dress, it's like fur!'

'Velvet, Zora!' Sally pulled her up for a hug. 'Oh my word!

I would have died for this dress when I was young.'

Adam had taken his scarf off but left his coat on. Coralie realised with a pang that he didn't want Anne to comment on his belly. The last quarter of the year was hard on the waistline; there were the political party conferences, then what Adam called 'shepherd's pie weather', then two or three Christmas functions per week, minimum, all December. She went over and put her arms around him. He rested his cheek against hers. He was beautiful, and she loved him.

'Coralie's made some tea,' Anne said. 'But you've just had a coffee.'

'I'll have a tea.' He kissed Sally on the cheek. 'Hi, Sally.' He kissed Anne on the top of the head. 'Hi, Mum.'

'You don't need your coat on, do you?' Shoulders hunched, Adam sat down, turned sideways, whipped his coat off and draped it over the back of the chair. 'Incredible, isn't it?' Anne went on. 'About Ebola? Eight thousand cases in Sierra Leone. I know someone who's gone over there, a nurse. I'd love to volunteer.'

'What's a bola?' Zora peeped out from the soft folds of Sally's scarf and cardigan.

'A very serious and deadly viral infection. Persists in semen for more than two hundred days, Adam—did you know that?' Adam recrossed his legs to point them away from her. 'Headache, sore throat, coughs, fever, muscle aches, internal bleeding, liver failure.' Zora coughed, twice, her eyes wide. 'It's not in the UK,' Anne said. 'Yet.'

'Oh, Sally!' Coralie said. 'How's Charleston?'

'I've been doing it a bit less frequently, actually. I only guide one afternoon a week. And it doesn't have anything to do with the fact that...' (she lowered her voice) 'a tourist used the loo in Clive Bell's bathroom.'

'No!' Adam finally looked happy.

'True, I'm afraid. We had to call the conservation cleaner. But Zora, guess what I brought?' Sally reached down and lifted her tote.

'The paints!'

'Take me upstairs and show me what you want. Is it still rabbits?'

'No, I've thoughten of something else!'

'And happy birthday!' Anne suddenly exclaimed.

Adam's eyes lost their light. 'Thanks.'

'Daddy's thirty-nine.' Zora turned back from the hall. 'Tom said it's one shoe in the grave.'

Adam smiled. 'Funny girl.'

'One foot,' Anne corrected.

Sally reached back for Zora's hand and led her to the stairs, chatting.

'Anyway, Tom's forty,' Adam said to no one.

Coralie smiled brightly. 'Anne, what are your plans? Staying for Christmas, I hope? We made the bed up for you.'

'No, no.' Anne shook her head. 'We'll take lunch, if you're offering, and be off this afternoon. Tomorrow I'm working on the local LGBT orphans' Christmas dinner. For members of our community who find themselves without family. Sally's cooking. Along with a few others. I'm doing the hall arrangements. The caretaker only opens up for me; I know him from the clinic.' Anne worked for many years at what Adam called the Eastbourne Clap Clinic (not its actual name, Coralie had found to her cost, when she'd used it to Anne's face by mistake).

'An orphans' Christmas lunch!' Adam rolled his eyes after Anne went off to the bathroom. 'The only orphan around here is me.'

Coralie had a strong urge to point out that, far from being dead or even absent, his mother was right there, in the house, visiting him at that moment, on the occasion of his thirty-ninth birthday. Instead, she took out the red onion and peppers and began to prepare the stew. If Anne and Sally were staying for lunch, they could have the special meal then, and for dinner she'd find something else.

'I think it's fairly common for children to prefer food they know at this age,' Adam said mildly. He'd opened a bottle of wine the minute the clock turned twelve. The bottle on the lunch table was their second, even though Anne and Sally weren't drinking.

'We never would have allowed it,' Anne said. 'Or at any rate, we never needed to. You ate like an adult from a very young age. Chicken rice, nasi lemak, laksa. You'd have whatever the amah had.'

'Zora knows we listen to her,' Adam said pointedly. 'She's able to ask for what she wants.'

'I like tomato ketchup next to the rice, and peanut butter next to my carrots,' Zora said. 'But I don't want the carrots to touch the rice. Or the ketchup and peanut butter to touch.'

'Very reasonable.' Sally nodded. 'This lunch is absolutely stunning, Coralie. I mean really superb. The recipe is from

Moro, you said? I'd love to go there myself, one day.'

'Coralie was at Moro recently,' Adam encouraged.

'We were having a work lunch,' Coralie began. 'My boss loves Moro for work things. They have this sort of utility corridor, where there's a coat rack, storage, the bathrooms. I was standing in there gossiping with my colleague Stefan, who's probably about my height, maybe less. Suddenly this man lumbers in with a mountain bike on his shoulder. He's wearing a helmet, and a suit, all wrinkled, the shirt untucked. As he barges past us, his muddy, disgusting bike wheel *scrapes* Stefan's face.'

'Goodness me,' Sally exclaimed.

'Stefan sort of yelps, like "Ow!" But the guy doesn't turn around until he's stored his bike, taken off his helmet, and run his hand through his sweaty hair. Then he tries to rush straight back past us to the restaurant. Stefan says, "Excuse me." The guy looks surprised, and then he puts on a dismissive voice and says, "You're excused." And I say, "You hurt my friend, you hit his face with your bike." Stefan's cheek has a smear of dirt or grease or something on it—so it's really obvious what's happened. And the guy sees it too, he must have, but he says, "I absolutely did not." We start saying he did, he did, and that he should say sorry. Finally, he mutters, "Sorry, okay, fine—are you happy? Sorry." And he walks out.'

'How incredibly rude,' Sally said. 'It wasn't the owner was it? I don't want to go anymore if it was.'

'It was Boris Johnson!'

'How's the book going?' Anne gave Adam a stern look. 'It's due in January.'

'You know.' He winced. 'It's shit.'

At that moment, Zora put her glass of juice down on the edge of her plate by mistake and flipped all the food onto her lap. 'My dress!' she cried.

It would need more than a tea towel. 'Come on, come to the bathroom with me.' Coralie took her hand and escorted her upstairs. 'Give me the dress,' she said on the landing. 'Now run up and grab something else to put on. Don't worry yet, you might still have it for Christmas.'

The bits of peanut butter and rice came off easily, but the ketchup really worried her. She blasted it under warm water until it swirled, bloodlike, down the sink. She turned the tap off and squirted shampoo on the dark area, massaging it on both sides of the grey-blue velvet. When she rinsed off the bubbles, she pressed it dry with a clean towel and gave it a blast with the hair dryer. She'd done it! It was fixed. 'Zora!'

There was no response. A worrying noise was coming from upstairs. She ran up two at a time. Zora was on her bed, in her tights and singlet, or what Coralie had learned, in England, to call a vest. She was curled into a ball and sobbing. 'Oh, no!' Coralie said. 'No need to cry—really, look!'

Zora's face was so wet from tears that her hair was stuck to her cheek. 'I didn't ruin it?'

'You didn't ruin anything.' Coralie wiped Zora's hair out of her eyes. 'First of all, it's only a dress; if cleaning it hadn't worked, we could've bought you another one. Second, an accident is an accident. You never have to worry about stuff like that. And Zora: this is really important. If you're crying up here by yourself, we don't know about it. You should always come down to where the adults are and cry to us. We all want to help you. Everyone loves to look after you if you're sad.'

Zora moved over to the edge of the bed and raised her arms. Coralie slipped the dress back over her head. 'Oh my God!' She was staring at the back of the door. Sally's murals took up four full pine panels, and were all surrounded by very Bloomsbury circles, squiggles and lines. 'It's amazing. Who thought of this? What are these?'

'A dog with a parachute, he's going to help soldiers. That one's a rescue dog, he finds people trapped when a bomb hits their house. A special pigeon? Called Mary? She flew a message with a shooted foot. And that's a bear from Poland who carried heavy things and got a metal.' (She meant medal.)

'How did you come up with this? Was it your idea?'

'It's from my fact book. *Animals at War.*'

'God.' Coralie reeled. 'Where's my phone? Hello, Met Police? I need to report a child. Yes, she's right next to me. It's Zora Whiteman, age six and three-quarters. Yes, *very* dangerous. I'm afraid she's far too clever.'

If there was a better feeling than making Zora laugh, Coralie was yet to find it.

5

Lunch appeared very finished when Coralie and Zora returned to the kitchen. Anne and Sally were sitting back, their napkins on the table. Adam was standing at the stove and lifting the pot lid, a hopeful expression on his face. 'Wait, I want some more of that too!' Coralie said. 'If there is some.'

'That's sad to hear. I could eat that entire meal again.'

'Adam,' Anne warned. 'You shouldn't.'

'By the way, Sally!' Coralie said. 'The door is so beautiful.'

'I've still got a few details to do when it's dry. All Zora's idea. We have quite the young historian here.' Tucked under Sally's arm, Zora glowed.

'Coralie?' Anne was peremptory. 'Adam doesn't have a clue. What are your plans for renovating the house?'

'Oh. Okay. Right.' Coralie turned towards the street and planted her feet. 'At the moment there are the two receptions.

The front faces north. Luckily, the window is quite big and still lets in the light. The back reception, with the big table and chairs, is currently not well used.'

'I use it,' Adam said. 'I work in it.'

Coralie gave him a look that said *Whose side are you on?* 'Every house in this run of terraces', she went on, 'has a blank paved space along the side of the kitchen.' She gestured at the window over the sink, and they all took a moment to gaze at the jasmine and dog rose suffocating the rundown fence shared with their elderly neighbour, Mavis Ballantyne.

'The side return,' Sally said. 'I believe it's known as.'

'Dada? Can I have the iPad to watch *Madagascar 3*?'

Adam got up silently to unplug the iPad from its charger near the fruit bowl.

'Yes, the side return,' Coralie said. 'Almost all the houses have extended the kitchen out sideways to make better use of that space.'

'Not next-door, though,' Anne observed. 'The old Jamaican lady.'

'Miss Mavis is Hackney royalty,' Adam called over his shoulder. 'She's lived there for fifty years.'

Now Anne was staring towards the front door and frowning. 'What happens to the back window of the room with the dining table?'

'The whole wall comes off and steel beams go in for support.' Coralie was pacing and waving her arms around, her movements growing more flowing as Anne's expression remained blank. 'There'll be a couple of steps down into the newly widened kitchen. Glass rooflights all along the sloping side of

71

the ceiling. There'll be room for more storage under the stairs, a small powder room, a pantry.'

'No, I don't understand it.'

'Mum's not a house person.' Adam sat back down at the table. 'I first realised she was with someone new'—he raised his eyebrows at Sally—'when I came home on the weekends and our house was looking *nice.*'

Sally got to her feet. 'I'm going to finish Zora's door. It all sounds beautiful, Coralie, especially the extra light. When will the work start?'

'My boss, Antoinette—her builders have agreed to do it. They'll start as soon as their current job is finished. Maybe as early as January.'

'Great time to take the back off your house,' Anne said.

'Great timing for my book,' Adam said in Anne's voice.

Coralie gave him a long stare.

'Tell me, Coralie,' Anne said in a challenging, BBC *Newsnight* way. 'What's your status here?'

'Here—in the home?'

'No!' Anne laughed, and for a second she looked quite pretty. 'In the UK.'

'My work did all my paperwork. They've just renewed my visa. Next time, I can apply for indefinite leave to remain.'

'And how old are you, remind me?'

'Thirty-one.' She added, in spite of herself, childishly rounding up: 'And a half?'

'Eight years difference.' Anne looked meaningfully at Adam.

'Thirty-one and a half and thirty-nine is nothing like nine-teen and twenty-seven,' Adam said.

This was all new to Coralie. 'Was that the difference between you and Adam's dad?'

'It wasn't the main one,' Anne replied. 'But yes, we were also eight years apart. Planning any children?'

Coralie gaped.

'I ask', Anne said, 'because if so, it's time to start on the folic acid. And Adam, forty isn't young, you know. Everyone knows about *tick-tock*, *tick-tock* for women. Sperm degrades too.'

'Thanks, Mum,' Adam said. 'I'm not quite forty yet. And recovering quite well from my Ebola.'

Who was Anne to snap on her latex gloves, slice and dig into Coralie's chest, yank out her most cherished private dreams, and examine them like an excised tumour? She wished she'd phoned her own mother when she'd had the chance. But that would have left her empty in a different way.

The doorbell rang and she leapt in her seat.

'Zora,' Adam called. 'Marina's here!'

'It's only little old me!' Tory Tom was hale and hearty in the hall. 'Very unlike us to be early! Sorry about that. We've come from a place close to your heart, Anne!'

'Tom, good to see you again,' Anne said. 'How are you and your cronies planning on ruining Eastbourne?'

Tom winked at Coralie. 'You'll have to wait and see!'

'I read what you said about people on benefits.'

'I simply said!' Tom laughed his joyful and infectious laugh. 'That people on benefits move to Eastbourne to be on benefits by the sea! It was a) a joke, and b) a deadly serious fact-based assertion. I mean, if something is funny *and* true—what's the crime? Happy birthday, Adam.' Tom extended his hand and

Adam shook it. 'Do you think my car's safe out there? In Hackney? Murder Mile? Should I bribe a local youth to look after it?'

'Your car's safe in E8, Tom. But I'm not sure you'll get away with those shoes.'

'What?' Tom angled his calf. 'My taupe suede driving loafers?'

'Tom?' Zora called from the sitting room. 'I want to watch the iPad in the car.'

'You can't watch the iPad in the car! You'll do a sick! We have an iPad at home with all the same awful shows on it.'

Anne nodded at the plastic laundry basket near the front door. 'These are our presents for Zora.'

'Oh, that reminds me.' Coralie started up the stairs. 'I've got to finish some wrapping.'

'Gosh,' Tom exclaimed. 'Zora's a lucky girl. You can carry them out to the car, Anne. You're the only one here with biceps.'

As well as being the Conservative candidate for Eastbourne, Tom Dunlop was a police barrister. Coralie had always assumed he was a prosecutor in criminal trials, presenting the case against the accused (the bad guy) on behalf of the good guys (the boys in blue). In fact, he represented police officers against accusations of wrongdoing as various as sexual assault, negligence and murder (or accidental death, as murder was known when police did it). Marina had left Adam, moved to Bartholomew Road, and got together with Tom in suspiciously short order. Coralie and Adam had attended their wedding the previous summer, more to provide childcare for Zora than anything else. During his speech, Tom had spoken wittily about his and Marina's love across the barricades, exchanging flirtatious glances as opponents in the case of the 'accidental death' (by violent police restraint) of a mentally ill person. 'I bet if I looked up the judgment, I'd see it was in 2010,' Adam had said darkly. Coralie had looked up the judgment. The inquest had taken place in 2009, when Zora had been just one. Her parents had still been living together.

Coralie was thinking about all this as she sat in her pink study wrapping a Barbie in a doctor's coat, a plush apricot-coloured onesie with cat ears, a lilac ukulele, a fact book about the *Titanic*, packets of Wizz Fizz and Furry Friends from a UK-based specialist online retailer of Australian foods, some floral cloth bunting with the letters Z O R A, and a child-size full kit from Liverpool FC. Now that Sparebitty was kept at Wilton Way and Rabbitty in Camden, nothing Zora owned had to be urgently transported between houses. Although— they'd picked her up in her school uniform. She dug around in Zora's drawers and added it to her teetering pile.

'Well, send my best to Marina,' Adam was saying as Coralie wobbled down the stairs. 'Zora? Time to jump up, poppet.'

There came three very loud knocks. Coralie dumped the presents in the laundry basket and swung the front door open. 'Sorry, I couldn't last in the car,' Marina said. 'I'm absolutely bursting. Do you mind?'

'Oh God,' Coralie said. 'Of course not!' Marina stomped up the stairs. 'Marina's here,' Coralie announced to the sitting room.

'She must have finished her call,' Tom said. 'What's the deal here, by the way?' He nudged the laundry basket with his foot. 'Are they from you two, Father Christmas, or what?'

'I didn't even think of that.' For a second Coralie was stricken. 'No, she'll recognise the wrapping paper is from us. She'd work it out, I think.'

'It won't be a problem. Marina's bought half of Hamleys, and the Amins have gone quite mad, not to mention my own parents, who've sent down a bloody great trampoline I'll have to put up in the garden. You know how many times she's been on the rocking horse? Once. The trampoline's going to be a very expensive camp mattress for the Camden urban fox.'

'What a relief—whew.' Marina swept down the stairs in her long cashmere coat. 'Thanks, Coralie.'

'Mummy!' Zora ran into the hall.

'Wait, wait till I'm on solid ground.' Marina stepped off the last step. Zora leapt into her arms. 'My beautiful girl.'

When Zora finally slid down to the floor, Marina's coat had come unbuttoned. 'Oh, Marina,' Anne called from the sitting room. 'When are you due?'

It was dark by the time everyone had gone. Shutting the door to her pink room would communicate too obviously that she wanted to be alone. Running a bath would not in and of itself telegraph disturbance; Adam knew she lived a heavily bath-based lifestyle. But what if he did what he sometimes did, swung in with a glass of wine, sat on the toilet with the lid down and gossiped to her? She couldn't face being perceived at that moment, let alone perceived naked. What if she was in the bath and he *didn't* swing by with a glass of wine? Then she'd know he was angry, or disappointed, with her or others, or feeling some other negative emotion (because of, to, at, or around her). She couldn't go down and clean the kitchen because that's what he was doing—from the top of the stairs she could hear the cutlery slotting into the dishwasher. They'd just concluded a full week of Zora-hampered communication. Now she had unlimited time to speak to him and she didn't know what to say.

'Partner's ex is pregnant' she typed into Google on her phone. Immediately the screen filled with first-person accounts of people whose partner's exes were pregnant because the partner themself had impregnated them. Her own shocking jealousy and sudden despair were both too minor *and* too weird to have a relevant search result. Adding to this mess was the issue of Adam's birthday. She was exhausted, and still quite full from her showstopping stew at lunchtime. Only the oysters remained as a birthday-level special food item, unless she wanted to rob Peter to pay Paul (get into the Christmas Day supplies early). Adam would say he didn't want a fuss made. But that was something only someone confident of having a fuss made could say.

'You're standing so still in the dark—are you hiding?' Adam was in the doorway.

'Sort of,' Coralie said. 'Half hiding, half not sure what to do.'

'Yes.' He slid his shoulder around the doorframe and entered. 'What a bombshell.'

'It was very Anne, just coming out with it. Very clap clinic and facts of life.'

'She was always like that.' Adam slumped down to sit on the floor. 'When I had spots, she'd point at my face: "You've got spots." Thanks, I know!'

Coralie hopped up and sat on the desk with her feet on the seat of the chair. 'She was going to tell Zora this week, and then us?'

'Marina?'

'I feel like she should have told us first, before she told Zora—so we could help with it? Becoming a big sister. It's huge.'

'She seemed okay with it—Zora, I mean. She seemed happy.'

'I was fine for a few days when Daniel was born. Then I asked when we'd give him back. Marina's due in April, that's *spring*, that's so soon. Why did she wait so long to tell anyone?'

'I don't know what's going on in Marina's mind.'

'But you know what's going on in her body.'

Suddenly all the air was gone from the room. Adam's voice was tired and distant. 'I had to say congratulations.'

'But you didn't simply say congratulations! How much Nutella this time, Marina? Lock up your Nutella, Tom! Get lots of sleep now, enjoy it while you can!'

'I was trying to be nice. I was trying to show Zora it was fine.'

'You admit it's not fine.'

'It's not not-fine for me, and I'm the one this affects.'

'Oh. I see.' Coralie left the room, but had nowhere to go, and (seeking some kind of solace) rushed up to Zora's bedroom, where she found Sally's lovely artwork had left a paint smell, so she could at least feel useful by opening the window.

Adam staggered up, looking old. 'So—is it not supposed to affect me? Or are you saying it's you this affects?'

She was sobbing. 'Of *course* it affects me—for someone else to get what I want. Merry fucking Christmas, Coralie! "What's your status here?" I don't know, Anne, housekeeper and cook? Adam's back-up prize after Marina left him? I feel like the fucking woman in *Rebecca*!'

'Rebecca?'

'*Rebecca* the book!'

'I know, I'm saying, are you Rebecca?'

'No!' Coralie almost screamed through tears. 'That's the whole point, Marina is Rebecca! I'm the narrator who doesn't have a name!'

It appeared she had breached the anger/sadness barrier. She'd become sad enough for Adam to care about her more than he hated being told off. He walked towards her with his arms out. She fell into them. He murmured into her hair. 'What are you saying? You're envious of Marina?' Coralie nodded. 'I know, it's because she's married to Tory Tom.'

'When Marina was my age, she already had Zora.'

'She was too young when she had Zora, that's all she kept telling me! And I still felt too young, even at thirty-three, and I probably did a terrible job. Any other child, anyone not as perfect as Zora—we would thoroughly have messed them up with what we did.'

'You didn't even slightly mess up, you did amazingly with your divorce, the most mature divorce in England.'

'It was still shit.'

'Okay! But I'm the sad one, by the way! I'm the one getting questioned about my *status*. I'm the one having Christmas away from my family.'

'I'm glad I'm having Christmas away from my family,' Adam said. 'I've never been as glad to say goodbye.'

'Well, me too, to be honest, about my family. And yours. But you're not even having Christmas with me! You walked out on me at *The Snowman*! You're down there clanging the forks in the dishwasher!'

'You hate that,' Adam said, like he'd finally solved a mystery. 'The clanging.'

'And you made fun of the house plans in front of Anne!'

'You know I shut down when Anne's here!'

'It took me ages to make those house plans. Antoinette's husband even helped—he's doing the new flagship store for Yohji Yamamoto! I've had the engineer in about the beam, about the rooflights—they have to be produced to order! It's all signed off by the council, Miss Mavis said yes about the party wall, the builders could start in *January*!'

'Hey…' He put his arms around her again.

'No one gets their plans approved that quickly, it was a full-time job in addition to my actual full-time job! I thought you were excited too!' Suddenly she was crying again. 'All the money I've saved since I was nineteen has gone into that renovation! All of it!'

'I *am*, I am excited about the house plans. And about our life plans!'

'What life plans! That's the whole point! I don't see any life plans at all!'

'Hey…' He leaned back and studied her. 'Where did all this come from?'

'We discussed *all* of this! I thought you wanted it too!'

'Are we still talking about the renovation?'

He was going to make her say the word 'baby'. She couldn't, she couldn't be a woman crying about that. 'We've talked about *all* of it, about everything,' she said. 'Moving in, and then…' She trailed off. 'You added writing a book in the plans, which is fine.'

'You added doing the house up—also fine.'

'But now I'm thirty-one and a half!'

'And a quarter! I let you get away with half to Mum. But not to me! Hey…' Adam reached for her. 'We both want a baby, not just you. It's our future. *Our* future, that we both want.'

He had said it. He'd said the word 'baby'. She was back on solid ground. 'Time's already gone past,' Coralie said. 'The future's suddenly now.'

'I didn't realise it was now.' She had seen him make an effort of comprehension. Now he made an effort of adjustment. 'Okay,' he stoutly said. 'We'll clear the decks and get on with it. Book, get it done. House, get it done. Wedding?'

'No wedding!' Spending a year on planning that was the last thing Coralie needed. Anyway, after the renovation, they wouldn't have the money.

'Modern, unconventional—I like it. No wedding! Book, house, baby.'

It was unclear why *his* book had to be written for *her* to gestate their baby. But it would all be over by May. Five more months. That she could handle. She let out a long, relieved breath. 'Book, house, baby.'

Adam pulled her in to his chest.

'All I have for birthday dinner are the oysters,' she mumbled after a while.

'You wouldn't be allowed to cook anyway. I'm going to run you a bath. You can choose a cup, a duck, a Barbie or a Ken, whatever you like to have in there with you. No? Okay, I'll get you a glass of wine. Then while you're in the bath, I'll cycle to a little place we like to call…'

'Bella Vita.'

'Bella Vita, for pizza, and when I come back, it will be just us, together, no more visitors, no more birthday, nothing left to do. And when we wake up, Christmas is a lovely day with no work emails. It's a No Pressure Day. Okay?'

'Okay.'

He went downstairs to the bathroom. Slowly, she followed him. She heard him wrench on the hot tap. He opened the linen cupboard and got her a fresh towel. He pressed it into her arms and cried in a gently satirical voice: 'He's doing the flag-ship store for Yohji Yamamoto!'

'Stop!'

'I love you so much,' Adam said.

'I love you.'

6

2015

Adam viewed his house as practically and non-judgementally as he viewed his own body. Bit rough around the edges! Does the job! As long as he had one—he was fine with it! He couldn't stand in a three-dimensional space, take stock of it, and visualise something better. He didn't have Coralie's sense of a home as something plastic, dynamic, constantly changing, a delicate ecosystem, responsive to intervention, something alive. (Incidentally, this was not how Coralie viewed her own body. Something to think about!)

By February, she'd packed the entire ground floor of the Wilton Way house into storage, except for the toaster, kettle and one box of kitchen stuff. She'd bought a two-burner electric hob, borrowed a bar fridge from Stefan, and set it all up in her study. Clothes they'd take to Greenwood Road laundromat. The dishes they'd do in the bathroom. The builders shrouded the stairs in diaphanous plastic to keep the dust out. Aside from a week or so when the house had no back, they'd be living on the top two floors till May. May, her perfect house. May, her perfect life!

Adam, however, very regrettably, was hating what he called 'this fucking renovation'. Almost as soon as he'd handed in his Boris bio, he'd landed another book contract, this time embedding with Ed Miliband and Labour to cover the 2015 'GE' (general election—Coralie had to google it). When the campaign kicked off properly, he'd be doing eighteen-hour days to capture it minute-by-minute. Before then, he was trying to focus on what his editor termed 'backfill': pre-prepared chunks of well-reported background to be distributed throughout the book. Coralie had *not* planned for another book to take over Adam's (and by extension, her) entire life. Everything Adam said he needed was in storage—the paper copy of Labour's 2010 manifesto; Ed Miliband's father's books; the giant pine dining table that was revealed (in its absence) to be the 'lynchpin' of Adam's 'writing life'. Coralie had bought him a membership to the London Library, which he liked for quiet work, but every time a source phoned, he had to run outside to call them back. 'If only there was somewhere I could write, talk, make a coffee and take a shit whenever I wanted,' Adam said. 'Oh yeah, there was—my fucking house!'

That 'my' really stung. She didn't mention it, but neither could she forget it.

Unfair of him to complain, because the renovation was going as well as it was possible for a horrifically expensive and disruptive project to go. By the time Coralie left for the office each morning, Oneal and his core team of builders had arrived, four nearly-silent men of large stature and mature years. The tallest and most silent one made them all a cup of tea with their own kettle. Then they gathered round the camp table so Oneal, like a general, could lead them through his plans for the day. Coralie was beginning to think she would miss them when they left. Unlike Adam, they at least seemed happy to see her.

'Just got to get through it,' Adam would say, through gritted teeth, about the renovation and his book.

'Just got to get through it!' Coralie agreed, meaning his book, delaying her dreams, and his attitude.

One day, before the formal beginning of the election campaign, Ed Miliband was pictured with his wife in a charmless fluorescently-lit grey prison cell or psych ward. Staring awkwardly beyond each other, they seemed on the verge of divorce.

'Don't say anything boring like "I wish I had a kitchen," but...' Coralie angled her phone towards Adam in bed. 'Look at Ed's shit kitchen.'

'I wish I had a kitchen.' He searched for it on his own phone. 'Oh dear, the *Daily Mail*'s on to it.'

Coralie found the article. 'Not much prospect of a decent meal emanating from that mean, sterile, little box inside Ed Miliband's home,' she read out loud. 'Miliband's kitchen is as bland, functional and humourless as a communist housing block in Minsk.'

'That's so odd,' Adam said. 'I've been to their house, and I was sure they had a big kitchen in the basement.'

Coralie sighed. 'I wish I had a kitchen.'

The next day, she was working late in the office when she received a subjectless email from Adam. It contained a link to a tweet from a journalist and Miliband family friend: *Ed Miliband's kitchen is lovely.* The *Daily Mail* pictures, she'd clarified, were of *the functional kitchenette by sitting room* which was *for tea and quick snacks.*

TWO KITCHENS! another journalist had immediately replied.

I wish I had two kitchens, Coralie wrote back to Adam.

This will be a massive prob, he gloomily replied.

It was unfortunate, because obviously Coralie wanted Labour to win. First, because she wasn't a bad person; and second (well—equal first), so Adam would sell more books.

But soon after, by the time of Zora's seventh birthday party, Labour appeared to be gently, marginally, taking the lead. In the garden at Bartholomew Road, Tory Tom struggled to keep up with hordes of frenzied Year 2s, all screaming for water as though ten minutes bouncing on a trampoline had dehydrated them to the point of death.

'Did you see YouGov?' Adam nudged him. 'Cameron's down four per cent.'

'God, I wouldn't mind losing at this point.' Tom dabbed his damp brow with his sleeve. 'Court five days a week is a holiday compared with everything I'm doing in Eastbourne.'

'Despoiling its environment? Taking food from the mouths of its babies?'

Tom gave Anne a cheery thumbs-up. 'Lovely to see you too!'

Part of the myth, the *legend* of the Whiteman–Amin divorce, 'the most mature divorce in England', was that any Zora-related event, from nativities to gymnastics displays, was open to all family members from both sides. Coralie had been dreading seeing Marina's dad again, the Hon. Mr Justice Amin, retired now and working on a compendious history of cricket. ('And are you a barrister too?' he'd asked at Marina's wedding. Coralie had admitted she was not. 'Oh,' he'd replied mournfully. 'That's a shame.') Fortunately, the Amins spent most of their time in St Helen's Bay, where Marina's Northern Irish mother, Geraldine, had spent idyllic, if rainy, childhood summers. They'd be down for weeks when the baby arrived, Tom had explained, so they were giving Zora's birthday a miss.

'Tom: the baby,' Anne said. 'When's it due?'

'Ten days to go. Zora came on her due date, apparently.' He shot a look at Adam, who nodded. 'And second babies are supposed to be quicker. Could be any minute.'

'Hopefully *not* on Zora's birthday,' Adam murmured. 'Therapy bills dot com.'

Although Coralie wouldn't put it past her, Anne wasn't being rude by calling the baby 'it'. Tom and Marina didn't want to know if it was a boy or a girl in advance. One of the things that hurt Coralie most about Marina being pregnant was her seemingly endless casualness about it. The gap between having a baby and not having one yawned so large. Not having one: your longing made you silly, at the mercy of fate, a clichéd figure of fun, mockable. Having one: unassailable right to a baby, demanding of respect, instantly A Mother. When had she crossed from normal life into constant painful yearning? A few years earlier she'd been entirely ambivalent and fine.

Marina had made the party a drop-off but had invited the parents to join for cake. Coralie watched as she spun elegantly around the garden, a word of greeting for each person, or a joke. She almost looked like a beautiful actor playing a pregnant woman, as if she could reach under her elegant, roomy man's business shirt, unclip a fake belly and walk away. Soon she brought out the cake, four store-bought caterpillars with ghostly white chocolate faces, all laid out on a large oak chopping board. As Zora took her place in front of them, surrounded by her schoolfriends, her face lit up by the candles, Coralie saw with a pang that the little girl she'd come to know was gone forever. In the space of a few months, she'd grown up. No dresses anymore, not even the velvet one from Christmas. Leggings only, no pink. She refused to do ballet on Saturdays, or to eat sausages 'made of pig'. ('What did you think they were made of before?' Adam had asked. 'Ingredients!' Zora had replied.) Marina was videoing the singing—Coralie should have offered, so Marina could be in the footage too. It was too late now. She was suddenly overwhelmed by the noise, the shouts, the people, and the terrible feeling of time having gone by. Tears almost came to her eyes—God, what was wrong with her?

'I'm going to eat some cake and then we'll go straightaway,' Adam said. 'Remember last year at ours? They left on the dot of four. They're the hosts this time—cleaning up is their problem!'

Coralie ducked back into the house for the loo. In the big family bathroom upstairs, she took her time having a wee, scrolling her phone, washing her hands, and taking a peek in the mirrored cabinet. (Marina used Clarins skincare and Chanel make up? She was thirty-seven—not sixty.) The Bartholomew Road terrace had been redecorated, before Marina had bought it, by someone who'd made it look modern. It wasn't Coralie's style, but she could tell there were no water pressure problems or sudden heating failures in the luxe, all-white bathroom. Like in a hotel, there was even a shaver socket.

The only other room on the first floor was the big main bedroom. The door had been closed on her way up. Now it was half open. As she crept past, she caught a sudden glimpse of Marina. Sitting on the end of the bed, slumped, eyes closed, her face was grey and haggard with exhaustion.

Downstairs, Coralie located the plastic bag filled with other plastic bags under the sink. She found one that didn't have a hole in it and went out to clear up the garden.

Despite Tom's talk about the baby arriving early, the due date approached with no action. On Thursday, Adam was planning to pick up Zora for Easter holidays, drop her at Coralie's office, and catch the train up to Salford for the leaders' debate. But after lunch, he texted to say that, if she could pick up Zora, he'd head to the debate early. Ed, or Ed's team, had invited him to join the run-throughs.

In the big corner office of the agency's Clerkenwell building, Coralie's boss was writing in a Moleskine at her £1,200 marble Tulip table. 'Antoinette? Knock, knock.'

'Mmm?'

'Oh, you had it framed!' Coralie nodded at her boss's cherished photograph of herself with Idris Elba, marking the occasion of Antoinette being named number 89 on a list of the most influential Black Britons. (Idris Elba had been number 5.)

'Yes, soon I'll have to…' Antoinette trailed off modestly as she gestured towards an open copy of *The Gentlewoman*, where, above a profile of herself as a ground-breaking creative director, she'd been pictured wearing Look 3 from Céline's 2015 ready-to-wear collection, months before it came available to the public.

'Oh yes, you have to,' Coralie said.

'And what can I do for you?'

'I think I have to leave early today. To pick up Zora from school? But Stefan has everything he needs.'

Antoinette put her pen between two pages of her notebook and gently closed it. 'How's the renovation?'

'Good, I'm about to do the lighting plan.'

'Light switches ninety centimetres above the floor,' Antoinette said. 'Any higher, they interfere with the hang.'

'The hang…of what?'

'The picture hang? When the art goes up.'

'Ah,' Coralie said. 'Of course.'

'And by the way.'

Coralie poked her head back round the door.

'I'm not going to complain about you leaving early,' Antoinette said. 'I rely on you to manage your time, and I know you often work outside formal working hours to get the job done. Of course, in a creative role, such as the one you hold, it's not simply enough to produce your own deliverables. Part of the job is to be available for teamwork, for bouncing off colleagues, for taking old elements and combining them in

90

a way that's new—the *essence* of being creative.'

Coralie felt herself run hot then freezing cold. She was being told off.

'No, my real concern', Antoinette went on, 'is for your self-worth, your standing in your intimate relationship. I hope you don't mind if I offer you some personal advice.'

'No, please.'

Antoinette bent her head and gently pressed her index fingers to her temples. 'It's one thing running around after your own child.' She looked back up. 'It's quite another to do it for someone else's.'

It was a shock. As recently as Christmas, Antoinette had wrapped up a copy of Sheryl Sandberg's *Lean In* for Coralie and inscribed it: 'From your mentor.' Her own builders were right that minute toiling on Wilton Way. Did Antoinette even like her? Was her job in danger? Coralie had transferred straight to London without taking a break. Tuesday morning 5 a.m., her plane had landed. Wednesday morning eight-thirty, she'd reported for duty in the Clerkenwell office, an hour and a half before Antoinette had even arrived! What more could she *give*? She was thinking about all this, or catastrophising (as thinking unfounded dark thoughts was sometimes known) as she strode up to Angel for the Northern line. When she arrived, sweating, to Zora's pick-up area, she saw only five children left, and none of them were Zora. Panic ballooned inside her.

'Coralie!'

Thank God. She turned to find Zora. Behind her was Marina, with an open-hipped, rolling walk she hadn't had less than a week ago at the party. 'Did I...' Coralie began. 'Weren't we supposed to...'

But to her surprise, Marina looked a little sheepish. 'Sorry to be confusing. You and Adam do have her. I've done all my work, and I'm officially on mat leave, but Tom's in Eastbourne until tonight. My mum won't get on the plane until I start contractions because my first labour took so long. I...Sorry.' Marina blinked up at the sky.

That was intriguing new information. (The only thing Adam had told her about Marina's pregnancy with Zora was that Adam had put on weight. 'No offence,' Marina had apparently said, 'but you're getting really fat.' Adam had responded gently that this caused him to feel offended. 'I said,' Marina had screamed, 'NO OFFENCE!')

'Can I go to Poppy's for a play date?' Zora leapt up to grab Marina's arm. 'Can Poppy *come* for a play date?' The child who must be Poppy stood back a little, smiling a shy smile and blinking behind purple glasses.

'Zora, please, don't yank me, I can't balance, I'll fall over.'

'Let's ask *your* mum instead.' Zora pulled Poppy's hand and they ran off together.

'Argh.' Marina pressed her fingertips briefly on top of her closed eyes. 'I just wanted to see her.'

'Oh, don't worry,' Coralie said. 'We could go to the park with her, or you could take her to yours—I could get a coffee, do some work in a cafe?'

Marina's eyes sprang open instantly. She seemed to elongate from the spine. 'She's not going to Poppy's, that's for sure. Zora!'

After a while, Zora skipped back. 'I don't want to get the

train, Mummy—I want to go home with you.'

Coralie's heart sank. It was truly beyond her to assert any power over Zora's movements. She didn't have any power to assert.

But Marina held Zora's hands and spoke in a kind, firm voice. 'Sweetheart, I came to give you a kiss. I can't keep you this week, Daddy and Coralie would be too sad.'

'It's true,' Coralie said. 'I don't want to see your daddy crying, sobbing like a baby—do you?'

'Boo-hoo!' Marina said surprisingly. 'Boo-hoo-hoo!'

Zora laughed.

'And if we get on the train now,' Coralie said, 'we'll be in time for a Violet cupcake.'

'I didn't hear that!' Marina threw up her hands. 'Well, I suppose someone who's about to be a big sister should have lots and lots of treats. It's a very special time.'

Smiling, dodging running boys with untucked shirts, they made their way together to the gate.

Coralie had to admit, it was not ideal to bring a seven-year-old into a building site, even though Oneal and his men were meticulous about their tools and swept up as they went. She served Zora brown pasta and baked beans (separate) and ate her own brown pasta, peas and cheese (mixed). At the desk in the pink study, Zora was watching *All Hail King Julien*, a Netflix animated comedy about a party-boy lemur's unlikely rise to power. 'This is just so funny,' Coralie kept murmuring, until Zora asked her if they didn't have funny shows in 'the olden days'.

After she put Zora to bed, Coralie half listened to the leaders' debate on her laptop, while searching for what Oneal had taught her to call 'door furniture'—knobs and latches, et cetera. Seven leaders was too many to have on one stage. Ed Miliband had drawn the middle lectern—nice and central. He was wearing a good suit and fizzed with almost manic energy. But as she browsed and weighed up between lacquered and unlacquered brass, between bronze and cast iron, something began to worry her, from her new perspective as a Labour supporter: she only mentally tuned in when it was David Cameron's turn to speak. A member of the audience asked a question about the National Health Service. To her surprise, Cameron replied with a tremor of emotion in his voice. 'I'll never forget, as the dad of a desperately disabled child, what I got when I took him to hospital every night worrying about his health. I got unbelievable care, and I just want that for every family and everyone in our country.'

She opened Google. There was a *Guardian* article from 2009 about the death of six-year-old Ivan, who'd had severe epilepsy and cerebral palsy. 'I know that the whole house will want to express their sorrow at the death of Ivan Cameron,' then-prime minister Gordon Brown had said in Parliament. 'He brought joy to all those around him. Every child is precious and irreplaceable.'

'His parents lived with the knowledge for a long time that he could die young, but this has made their loss no less heartbreaking,' the Tories' William Hague had said in reply. 'He will always be their beautiful boy.'

'Jesus fucking Christ,' Coralie moaned out loud and began

to cry. Maybe she shouldn't have come off the Pill. She was nuts.

Ed was on fire! Adam texted later. *Did you watch?*

He did a great job! Coralie wrote back.

Was it a lie? No. Ed seemed like the type of guy who could do pretty badly. Not doing badly meant he had done well.

For Easter break, they'd booked Zora into a performing arts club in Islington so they could keep some semblance of a working life. Signing her in took such a long time, Coralie didn't get to Clerkenwell until ten. Antoinette cruised by her and Stefan's office and stared in, the *Jaws* music almost audibly playing.

She shivered. 'Does Antoinette know I only just arrived?'

'I don't think so.'

'What if she saw me walk past in my coat?'

'Why do you care? She's your CD, not your parole officer.'

This was a bit rich from Stefan, who used to beg her to jiggle his mouse so his screen stayed on when he went downstairs for a smoke. But he'd quit now, and had replaced milk in his coffee with *butter*, and had started 'bullet-journalling' too (thanks, Marcus).

All week Coralie felt her boss's eyes on her, not only judging her competence as a worker, but her status as a 'creative', a 'career woman', as a feminist, and even her worth as a human being.

On Friday, Adam received a surprise text about the holiday club concert. He couldn't attend—could Coralie? Coralie messaged Tom and asked if he was free. Tom wasn't; he was in court. She wrote to Marina, but didn't get a response till she'd raced to the community hall and slid into the last seat: *So sorry,* Marina wrote. *I was in acupuncture.*

'Don't worry, Mum's here now,' she heard one of the instructors say. And without wanting to hear it, despite closing her ears through an effort of will, she heard Zora respond, 'She's not my mum.'

After the concert, Zora was low-energy, even sullen, before starting to cry, ostensibly at the inadequacy of Coralie's snack, a popcorn bar she'd bought at Pret that morning (for herself). 'Did you wish Daddy could've come?' Coralie had to say, and Zora nodded, tears rolling down her face. It was hard for Coralie not to cry that she wished that too. All the while, she was conscious of an argument going on inside her, between the part of her that loved Zora and would do anything for her, and the part that hated being taken for granted by the adults in Zora's life.

On the bus home, an email arrived from Antoinette. *I seem to have missed you* the subject line read. Sinisterly, the body of the email was blank.

When she and Zora arrived at Wilton Way, they found a bumptious young electrician touring the ground floor, the lighting plan in his hand and a frown on his face. Everything Coralie had chosen was 'really not normal' and 'sorry, not being funny, but just wrong'. People usually had spotlights in the kitchen, recessed. Pendants were for living rooms, not above kitchen islands. Nobody would look for a light switch at a height of ninety centimetres. (The electrician mimed sweeping the wall for a switch in the dark.) For a 'property of this nature', he'd expect something fancier than the basic white switches she'd chosen, like brass or even gold. (Gold?!) Towards the end of his whirlwind tour through all her mistakes, her face was red, and she was trembling. 'I want what I've said I want,' she almost shouted.

There was a long pause. 'Well, okay, but I can't do the work if you're going to be here.'

Coralie laughed from shock. 'I live here.'

'I mean,' he said slowly, as if to a stupid person, 'normally the house is empty. When I'm working? I'm going to be turning the power off, replacing the consumer unit, all that.'

'We'll be out of the house all week. Also working.' (She'd be staying late in the office every single day and making sure Antoinette knew about it.) 'This has all been arranged with Oneal!'

'Your choice,' he said grimly. 'Your choice!'

Over the course of the weekend, she realised once and for all how pivotal the shape of a dwelling was for making the people inside it feel okay. With her pointless mocked-up, temporary first-floor half-kitchen there could be no long luxurious stirring of onions in a pan, where she could complete a discrete task (gaining a sense of achievement), simultaneously zoning out as Zora drew or played on the iPad (feeling pleasantly companion-able), while also producing 'the family meal' (the fact of it benefitting others placing her beyond reproach). There was nowhere to simply *be*. When Zora came into their room, she felt self-conscious and smothered. When she went into Zora's room, she felt dominant and overweening, as though her physical presence was promising a level of personalised attention and face-to-face engagement on which she couldn't follow through. Adam seemed to have adopted the top floor spare room as his own, reams of research and transcripts spread out across the bed. 'Less than a month till the election, less than two months till deadline,' he muttered again and again. When she brought him a cup of tea he said, 'Thanks.' When she paused, waiting for a more effusive response, he said 'Just leave it there.'

'Okay, Tolstoy,' she said in a nasty voice.

Just got to get through it!

On Saturday evening, late enough for Coralie to be in her pyjamas, Adam received a call from the *Spectator*. Someone from the *New Statesman* had dropped out of a podcast live-record. Could Adam please come on as the Labour-leaning guy? There'd be great promo in it for the *Young Country* pod, and his books—and a case of Pol Roger? It would take up the entire Sunday morning she'd hoped to spend sourcing taps. 'Of course you must,' she said dully, as he set his alarm for seven.

By lunch, he still wasn't back. They were due to drop Zora off at four. She couldn't be in the house a moment longer. 'Let's go for a walk!' She could hear her own desperation. 'We'll go to Victoria Park Village! We'll have some fish and chips! Adam's on his bike, he'll meet us there!'

'I don't want to walk.' Zora was mutinous. 'Walks are for adults and creatures.'

'What then?'

'Stay inside. I know, I'll FaceTime Mummy and Tom!'

Coralie was too beleaguered to interface with those two. 'You're going to see them this afternoon.'

'Please.'

'Okay.' She couldn't come between a child and her mother. 'I'll text.'

By the time Tom replied, Adam had returned, packed up Zora's bags, and headed out towards the station, promising hot chocolate on the way.

Change of plan! Tom's message to Coralie said. *Marina's contractions have started and we're on our way to hospital! Can you keep Zora? Geraldine's flight was cancelled and we don't have back-ups. Perhaps you can extend the drama club? With thanks, Tom.*

Change of plan! With thanks, Tom!

She rang Adam in the hope he hadn't got on the train. 'Where are you?'

'Outside the Iceland at Hackney Central.'

'Good. Well, change of plan. The baby's coming. Tom says can we keep Zora for a while?'

'Zora!' she heard Adam call. 'Stop!'

'Love to get a bit of notice.'

'I know,' Adam said. 'And I'm off to Manchester tomorrow.'

'What?'

'I'm off to Manchester tomorrow? Manchester? For the Labour manifesto launch?'

'And when do you think you'll be back?'

'I don't know, Wednesday? I didn't think it mattered. I was going to see what Ed was doing.'

Coralie hung up.

*

That night, as Zora cuddled Sparebitty, too excited to sleep till she knew whether she was getting a brother or a sister, Coralie and Adam whispered one of the worst fights in the two years they'd spent together. 'You chose to go to the concert—nobody made you!' Adam said. 'You knew I had a book to finish. What am I supposed to do, not write the book?' He was passive, sullen. He refused to meet her eye. 'I have a *contract* to write the book. Should I give the money back?' She became hysterical; she sobbed that he was ruining her life. 'It's good to know you feel this way before we try and have a kid,' he said. 'If we're ruining each other's lives, we should stop.' What do you mean? she almost screamed. Tell me what you mean! 'Coralie,' he said blankly. 'You can decide what I mean.' He was a stranger.

At 3 a.m. she stopped crying. At 4 a.m. they had sex. At five, Adam left to catch the train to Manchester. At six, she got a text from Tom with a picture of Zora's new brother, Rupert, to be known as Rup. At seven, she promised a very excited Zora to take her to the hospital to see him. Immediately after she emailed in sick, a full complement of builders arrived, reminding her she'd be without power for much of the day. By nine, Antoinette sent back a scary one-word reply: *Noted*.

But just as she and Zora were getting ready to leave, there came a knock on the door. It was Sally. Behind her, in the car, Anne sat looking annoyed. Adam had issued a pre-dawn SOS and they'd come to take Zora off her hands. Coralie surprised all of them, and herself, by bursting into sobs of despair.

At a week old, Rup was already too big for his white John Lewis newborn sleepsuit. He lay stretched across Marina's lap like a witchetty grub. 'He's lovely and relaxed,' Coralie said.

Tom gave her an anguished look, and Marina actually snorted.

In the corner, Geraldine Amin glanced up from her sudoku. 'He's *not* like this in the night.'

Adam looked around for Zora. 'Are you ready, poppet?' She was: her backpack was on.

'Have a lovely weekend,' Coralie said.

'Don't worry,' Marina replied, 'we won't.'

'Oh?'

'Tom's campaigning in Eastbourne. Totally exhausting politics. An absolute waste of my time.'

'Hormones. Don't worry, sweetheart.' Tom squeezed her hand. 'I'm probably going to lose.'

'Oh, don't worry.' Marina was grim. 'You will.'

On the train, Zora said she'd always imagined feeding the baby with a bottle, but Granny Geraldine wouldn't allow it. She wanted to read to him, but if he ever 'got awake', he just wanted to eat or cry. He couldn't talk, he couldn't play, and did they know he didn't have teeth? 'Granny Geraldine says I love Rupey really.'

'And do you?' Adam asked.

Zora put on Marina's face and mangled one of her phrases. 'Let me get back on you to that.'

Adam was on the road most of the time. On the rare occasions he was at home, they huddled close, almost wordless, recovering from the fight. They had made up, they were *in love*, but Coralie had been so harrowed she seemed to have lost part of her brain. It was the part she normally liked best, the companionable bit, jollying the rest of her along with observations, witticisms, analysis and—sure!—a bit of overthinking. To lose it was depressing, but helpful in a way. She became a person who did one thing at a time. At work, she was at work. Antoinette was pleased with her. At home, she was at home. The bespoke glazing was installed, the renovation not even late. She felt confident to schedule the redelivery of the books, kitchen things and ground-floor stuff that had languished for months in storage. Their lives would be back to normal after the election, almost to the day.

And thank God, because towards the end of April the campaign had gone what Adam would call a bit 'bonkers'. David Cameron caused an outcry by forgetting he supported Aston Villa. *This has to cost Cameron the election, surely? How can anyone 'forget' which football team they support? Unforgivable,* Piers Morgan had tweeted. Meanwhile, Ed Miliband had some unlikely support from teenage girls, who called him 'Milibae' and themselves 'Milifans'. With fewer than two weeks to go, the word on the street was that the nation was heading for a hung Parliament, and another coalition government—but whether Labour or the Conservatives would be the larger party, nobody really knew.

Ultimately, however, the fate of the UK's democracy turned out not to be her problem. In the first week of May, just as life was as close as possible to normality, Coralie's brother summoned her home.

Sorry, Cor, Daniel's email said. *Mum's in the Last Chance Saloon.*

7

She emerged from Darwin airport in a daze. The air hummed with insects. Everywhere birds were calling. Her first flight home in nearly three years. Had it existed the whole time— Australia? All this warmth? The early-morning sun was an affront.

'Cor? You look shocking.' Daniel took the handle of her suitcase. 'Get in the car quick, I don't want to pay for parking.'

Dan told her the story driving with one hand on the steering wheel. Their mother had gone into chemo like any other day. She'd got new bloods done. The doctor had checked the scans, then checked them with someone more senior. The nurses had been whispering and staring. Mum had realised, once they'd mentioned it, she wasn't feeling that great. They'd admitted her to the ward for pain relief and fluids. After a few days, the surgeon (her personal hero, Dr Ainslie) 'went in' to make 'a few minor adjustments'.

'What does that mean?' Coralie asked.

'Major stomach surgery,' Dan said. 'Her fourth. Dr Ainslie reckoned it would be a small job. A bit of untangling—that's what he said. That's why I didn't tell you before.'

There was a high-pitched tone in Coralie's ear. She leaned her head against the window. 'So Mum didn't think anything was wrong. But something *was* wrong. And now it's been fixed?'

'Sorry, am I telling the story badly?' Dan's anxious eyes roamed the wide empty road lined with palm trees. He got all the luck—lashes that stayed dark until the ends, not fading to blonde like her own.

'No, you're telling it fine. It's like I'm hoping I'll find a loophole. A flaw in the logic that will mean she isn't sick.'

'Well, she's sick all right. It's a disaster in there.'

'Can't they just give her a bag? Forgot the stomach, go round it.'

'You know she'd rather die.'

'God forbid her insides be visible from the outside.'

Dan gave a tired sigh. 'Dr Ainslie's trying to persuade her. He says anything's better than getting a blockage. But she's running out of time. She's getting weaker by the day, and the op itself could kill her.'

'So do nothing, which is bad. Or something—which is bad.'

'Yeah,' Dan glanced at her, pleased to be understood. 'Two options, both bad. That's why I sent you the message.'

'You did exactly the right thing.' When she closed her eyes, she could still see the psychedelic airport carpet from her layover in Singapore. The pattern twisted and danced. She tapped her phone to see the time. Nearly 8 a.m.

'What do you want to do first?' Dan said. 'She's got her own room, but we're not allowed to visit this early.'

'What day is it?'

'Good question.' Dan paused for a while. 'It's Sunday.'

'Can we go to the market? I'm starving.'

He put the indicator on. 'I suppose we can.'

'Just tell me one thing,' Coralie said. 'Does Mum know I'm coming?'

'She does, yeah.'

'She knows it's a real emergency?'

'She does.'

During the week, Nightcliff's small shopping precinct was home to a supermarket, a pawn shop, a betting shop, a payday lender, and a massage parlour that might or might not have been a sex one. But on Sundays, it transformed into a lush oasis, with stalls for fresh fruit and vegetables, plants, bits of hippie tat, souvenirs made of or depicting crocodiles, boxes of cut mango with lime and papaya with chilli, sugarcane juice (in fact, all kinds of juice), laksas, Vietnamese coffee and crêpes. Coralie loved it.

'I had a massive crush on someone at the market,' she said as they parked the car.

'Is he bald? I knew it,' Dan said. 'Well, he's still there. His operation has expanded. Three burners now. Lots of staff. He just stands in the background, overseeing his empire.' And there he was, Ben of Ben's Crêpes, looking perhaps more portly than he had fifteen years earlier, and with some unfortunate mirrored sunglasses. 'Are you going to have one, a crêpe?'

'I'm such a mess. My body thinks it's dinnertime. I'm getting a laksa. This is bad, but what I want most is a beer.'

'You know Darwin. There are no limits.'

They found seats at a communal table. It was the dry season. The weather would be perfect for months, thirty beautiful degrees a day. Men with giant beer bellies sauntered past in battered Akubra hats. Women screeched with laughter like birds, freckled shoulders shaking. His long limbs cool in tiny football shorts and a singlet, Dan sipped his watermelon juice like an elegant woodland creature. With her lank aeroplane hair and heavy London clothes, Coralie felt haggard and gross. 'It's been cold in London since Halloween. It's crazy to see people's bodies,' she said. 'Help, this beer's gone to my head.'

'Did you sleep on the plane?'

'Not at all. God.' She rubbed her eyes. 'I'm so tired I thought I saw a snake on that man.'

Daniel turned around. 'There *is* a snake on that man. It's the Nightcliff Snake Man. Don't you remember him? The Snake Man?'

'Jesus Christ.'

After a bit, she nodded towards the public bathroom. 'Remember once I went in there? And there were green tree frogs in the toilet?'

'I don't,' Dan said. 'But I wouldn't put it past them…frogs.'

As they approached the hospital, she could feel herself regressing to a childish state, laughing hysterically at what her brother had said in earnest. 'I wouldn't put it past them…frogs,' she kept saying. They got out of the car and began to cross the lawn to the big glass front doors. 'I wouldn't put it past them…frogs.' Suddenly she was on the ground, laughing so much she was crying. She'd fallen in a shallow hole. 'I'm not drunk, I swear.'

Dan reached out to help her up. 'You might be, but don't worry, I'm not.' As Coralie brushed cut grass off her knees, he put his hand up to shield his eyes. 'Hang on—is that Mum?'

On a large concrete terrace there was a lean grey stick in a nightie, waving.

Coralie's family had been based in Darwin from 1999. Before then, they'd been in Jakarta, where her father was a brigadier in the army. For both those far-distant tropical postings, the Australian taxpayer subsidised her school fees and paid for her travel home. She experienced these breaks as an achingly long period of exile from her real life. Too hot to leave the house after 8 a.m., she could be drenched in seconds by ferocious monsoon rain the same temperature as blood. Bush stone-curlews curdled the air with frankly terrifying shrieks. Overripe mangoes dropped from the trees and stank to high heaven in the blazing sun. Three days a week she caught the bus to an air-conditioned mall to work at a children's shoe shop. The rest of the time, she read books. How fortunate she'd had so much practice as a teen, biding her time in the tropics at one careful remove from reality. How did people who actually existed in the world cope with the dramatic enfeeblement of their mothers?

In her private room, Judith Bower held the sheet up over

her nose. Her sweet brown eyes peeped marsupially over the top. Coralie gave her cool forehead a kiss.

'Flight must have cost you a fortune,' Judith whispered.

'How are you feeling?' Coralie ventured.

'Better than you look.'

For the first couple of days, Coralie was so jetlagged and so shocked by her mother's condition that she couldn't tell up from down or what was real and what was not. There existed a constant low-level fever of expectation around the next operation: if it would happen, when, and how soon afterwards their mother could reasonably go home. They all three spent most of their time waiting for Dr Ainslie to 'pop in'. He did this once a day. It was painful to observe their waiting mother's eagerness. It was a glimpse of what she'd been like as a child.

In the evenings, after a long day in the hospital, brother and sister dined at Asian Gateway or Taj Curry Indian. Later, Dan went for a long late-night run along Casuarina Beach, and Coralie sat on her mother's balcony to look out over the dark sea, composing sprawling, mordant emails to Adam about her macabre and otherworldly hospital-based life. He replied in the same vein about the campaign. Ed Miliband had unveiled a three-metre-tall stone tablet upon which Labour's key election pledges had been carved. The idea was that, if Labour won, the stone tablet would be placed in the Downing Street rose garden. There it would remind Miliband daily of the solemn duty he owed the British people. In the *Telegraph*, Boris Johnson called it 'some weird Commie slab'. Someone called it 'the heaviest suicide note in history'. Everyone else called it the EdStone. It seemed Coralie's mother was not the only one dying a slow death.

I wish I was with you, I miss you so much, I love you so much, CYK, Adam's emails ended.

Consider yourself kissed. That was a blast from the past.

CYK, she wrote back. *CYK!*

But Adam always sent the final CYK, one more than she'd think to expect, and that made her feel glad, and safe.

One day, Dr Ainslie popped in very early, before ten. This was unfortunate, as there was still a lot of the day to get through, and now there'd be nothing to look forward to.

There was a long pause as doctor and patient stared at each other. It was as though Dan and Coralie were not in the room. 'Well now, Judith,' Dr Ainslie said. 'Eating?'

'Oh yes, white toast.' (A lie—she'd had a mouthful.)

'And the nights?'

Their mum had been routinely ill and in distress every night from seven onwards. She called it her 'witching hour'.

'Still the same.'

'Not worse?'

Hopeful face: 'No?'

'Very good. Well, Judith. Got to get going. Got a few sick people to see.' (His inveterate farewell. Satire? Helping Mum feel others had it worse? Simply a statement of his to-do list?)

This time, Coralie pursued him down the corridor. He couldn't be further from her idea of a venerated, superhuman cancer surgeon. With his strange orthopaedic loafers or slippers, and tufty grey hair sticking out of his ears, he looked like an old-age pensioner off to place a few bets on the dogs. 'How will you decide if you'll do the operation? Are you waiting for her to get stronger?'

'Every day she's getting weaker. If it happens, it'll be soon.'

'And when will you know?'

'Tomorrow. Scan.'

It was Friday. In the morning, she used the fourteen-day free trial of a VPN to tune in to the UK news. Surely there was no hope Labour could win outright. Yet Adam had told her about the legal experts the party had assembled and briefed—the meeting rooms (even the catering) pre-booked for long days of coalition negotiations. It was still possible for Labour to end up the biggest party, and Ed Miliband the next PM.

The stirring music of the BBC's election coverage blared out from her laptop. She felt a sudden homesickness for London, watching the high-speed footage of the city by night: the Thames, Parliament, the tower of Big Ben, all lit up. In four minutes, David Dimbleby said, he could reveal the contents of his envelope, the results of the BBC's exit poll: 'Tantalising.'

'Exit pohle,' Dan mimicked.

'Exit powl,' Coralie said in her flattest, broadest Australian accent.

'If neither David Cameron nor Ed Miliband can command a majority on their own, is there going to be a place for the Liberal Democrats at the Cabinet table?' Dimbleby wondered. 'Or for Nicola Sturgeon's SNP? Or Nigel Farage and UKIP?'

'Dickhead,' Dan said.

Big Ben chimed. 'Here it is, ten o'clock.' Dimbleby turned

to a giant screen. On it, David Cameron looked like a sock puppet with googly eyes, or a boiled egg with a face drawn on. 'And we are saying the Conservatives are the largest party. And here are the figures which we have. Quite remarkable, this exit poll. The Conservatives on 316. That's up nine…Ed Miliband, for Labour: seventy-seven behind him at 239.'

'Okay.' Coralie shut her laptop. 'Fuck you too.'

When they got into hospital later that morning, the room looked different. The blinds were still down, and the sheets were in disarray. Their mum was not in the bed. The door to her bathroom was slid across, closed. Jerome, the stocky nurse from the Philippines, came in with a trolley. 'Morning.'

'Morning, Jerome,' Dan said.

At the bed, Jerome whipped off the disposable protective undersheet and quickly put on a new one. Coralie lowered her voice as quiet as it could get. 'Did she have a bad night?'

'Listen, she was running to the bathroom that fast…' He shook his head. 'She can't run, okay? No matter what. I will clear up any accident. Any! But I can't fix a broken hip. Okay? No running.'

'We'll tell her,' Dan said. 'Thanks, Jerome.'

'She's a lovely lady.'

'You're a very good man.'

Jerome nodded on his way out. 'Safety first.'

The door to the bathroom slid open and their mum crept through. She was a skeleton, so small her cotton gown had been sent over from the children's ward. Coralie felt like calling the police. The murderer was inside her mum's body.

'Hi, Mum.' She put on an upbeat voice. 'What time's your boyfriend coming to see you?'

'Dr Ainslie,' Dan translated.

'Natasha's taking me to the scan,' their mum whispered. 'Pop down to the nurse's desk and tell her I'm ready to go.'

Without the presence of their mum and the pressure to be cheerful for her, the room seemed more scary, and the situation more bleak. Coralie opened the blinds.

'It's so fucked up.' Dan frowned, his eyes welling.

Coralie remembered how, when he was young, he'd cried so much, and so passionately, tears had almost bounced off his cheeks. Their father had told him that if he wanted to cry like that, he could do it in someone else's house. Once, when they'd lived in Canberra, they'd lost him—five-year-old Dan. He'd gone to cry at the neighbour's. 'Have you told Dad about all this?'

'I haven't spoken to him,' Dan said. 'Have you?'

'No! Has Mum?'

'I doubt it.'

A little while after the scan, there was a gentle tap at the door. Dr Ainslie shuffled in. 'And how's Judith?'

Before Coralie could say she was asleep, a soft voice piped up from the bed. 'I'm okay.'

'Had a bad night?'

'A bit.'

They were talking so quietly Coralie had to inch forward. 'Scan looked good,' Dr Ainslie murmured. 'Less distended.'

He had said if it looked good, he'd do the op. Here he was,

seeming to say it looked good. Coralie cleared her throat, a loud sound in the quiet room. 'So that's good?'

'It's all doing what it's meant to down there. Moving around. No, she's doing well.'

'What does that mean for the surgery?'

'I'm inclined to leave it. Operation…Complex, isn't it? Might work. Might be worse. Not saying we might not do it. But yes, no—not now.'

None of that made sense, but his watery-eyed frown made one thing crystal clear: Coralie had overstepped. A miasma of ambiguity swirled around her mother's condition and care, and that was the way it had to be. It had been the height of bad manners for her to seek to bring in facts.

Dr Ainslie shuffled out.

'Parking's running low. I might just move the car.' Dan left too.

'Mum?' Coralie said. 'Are you disappointed?' (*In me?* she might have added.)

Judith Bower turned her face to the wall and drew up her thin legs like a Pompeii victim. 'I'm not thinking very much.'

It seemed to be the limit of her talking, too.

Whenever it was that they were supposed to cry, to love, to say what they meant to say—that time had passed. It had probably been decades ago, maybe in childhood, maybe when Coralie had been born.

In 2004, Coralie's father had been posted to Iraq. It had been a fairly major role in operations to support the Coalition forces. There had been a few profiles of him in the right-wing newspapers, a source of keen embarrassment for her. It was a shock when, a year later, straight off the plane from Baghdad, he'd moved in to a serviced apartment in Canberra, just as Mum and Dan were loyally waiting for him back him Darwin, Dan with an elaborate homemade banner featuring a kangaroo fighting an upright crocodile, both in red boxing gloves, and a speech bubble saying welcome back dad. 'Probably lucky he didn't see it,' Dan said. 'I was just asking to be called a homo.' (At seventeen, he wasn't out at school, or to Roger, who greeted the rare same-sex couples in his orbit with a chilly 'In some parts of Indonesia, you'd get one hundred lashings for that.')

The mystery had been solved when Coralie had seen photos of Roger on Facebook with his younger (though not young) girlfriend, Jenny, a Chinese-Australian single mother who was high up in Australia Post. Their mother stayed in the big family home in Fannie Bay until Dan finished Year 12. At that point, letters from Dad's solicitors forced her to move on. She could have gone anywhere—back to Hobart where she'd grown up, or to any of the fourteen places and bases her husband had dragged her over the course of his career. But her mother had been in Jakarta and then Darwin since 1996. It would have been hard to get used to the tropics, but harder to leave them behind. She decamped ten minutes up the road to Nightcliff.

When, a decade ago, Coralie had first seen her mother's new house, she'd thought it was nothing special. Now, after so long in London, she could easily grasp its appeal. Made of dark wood, it was up on stilts in case of flooding, and so the Volvo could be parked underneath. The garden grew thick with tall trees and jungle. The scent of frangipani filled the air. Tiny finches flitted around, in and out of the louvre windows. Cockatoos strutted along the balcony, overlooking the eroding dingo-coloured coastline and the light grey seas of Beagle Gulf. Deceptively calm on the surface, the waters teemed with deadly jellyfish and saltwater crocs.

But inside, her mother's interiors had the charm of a suburban bookkeeper's office or a law firm. The bottom shelf of her main bookcase held a row of files labelled, in her neat handwriting, will and legal, warranties, bank, car, identity, bills. The top shelf was home to a plastic fern, two elephants carved from a smooth beige stone, and plate of ceramic tropical fruit. The absence of utility or beauty in the ornaments was so poignant that Coralie had to despite them so they wouldn't break her heart. Some of her mother's personality, or at least personal history, was evident in the bamboo furnishings (cushions covered with batik fabric) and, on the wall, a trio of Balinese masks. The television was distressingly large, the choice of a lonely person.

It would have upset their mother no end to see what her living room looked like after weeks of her children camping in it. When she'd first arrived, Dan had kindly given Coralie the 'spare room' (his room) with its king-single bed. Now there was no hope of their mother returning home anytime soon, it seemed right to reconsider the arrangement. The afternoon of the unpleasantly ambiguous operation verdict, they opened the door to their mother's bedroom, and with a visceral sense of trespass, went inside.

The room was 'neat as a pin' (her mother had always been

a very 'neat as a pin' person). The bed was immaculate, with beautifully laundered sheets of white waffle cotton. On the bedside table was a Rosamund Pilcher novel with a Nightcliff Public Library bookmark a quarter of the way in. It was two weeks overdue. The short-sleeve blouses she'd had tailored in Jakarta hung neatly pressed in her wardrobe. Her pearls and delicate gold watch lay in a dish on the dresser. Next to it was a picture of Dan and Mum in a rickshaw (rickshaws only carried two passengers). The en suite was scented with the lavender soap Judith Bower unaccountably hoarded. 'I don't think I can sleep in here.' Tears were streaming down Dan's face.

'I will,' Coralie said. 'You can move back into your room.'

They changed the sheets on both beds and moved their things around. Afterwards, Dan went to the garden to smoke a cigarette. Coralie tackled the kitchen. In the fridge, the milk was off. Dirty dishes were piled up in the sink from the few ad-hoc meals they'd managed. She eyed them with her mother's critical gaze, then eyed herself with that gaze too. She'd had such a long break from it, that gaze. Being with Adam had been one long holiday from shame. Now she cringed, shrivelled inside, and raised one shoulder as if warding off a blow. How interesting.

She filled one half of the stainless-steel sink with hot water and added a toxic green squirt of Morning Fresh. She slipped her hands (her mother's hands) into her mother's yellow washing-up gloves. A perfect fit. She washed and rinsed every plate, and would have dried them too, but Dan joined her with a tea towel, and stacked them all away.

Afterwards, they took some beers down to the foreshore to check up on the Miracle Tree. Coralie remembered it from years ago. It was right on the edge of the slowly eroding cliff, its roots now fully exposed. 'It's really clinging on for dear life,' Dan said.

'For dear life,' Coralie repeated. 'I've never paid attention to those words before.'

'To dear life.' He held out his beer, and they clinked.

'Why do you think you're crying so much, and I can hardly cry at all? Maybe it's because...' *Mum never really loved me*, Coralie was going to say.

'...I'm a massive poof?' Dan said, and (as the sun set dramatically around them) she found she couldn't stop laughing.

She couldn't remember her childhood before him. She could hardly remember it after. What if they'd been able to grow up together? How much better it might have been.

They didn't have the air con on at night, just fans. Through the open windows, in their separate rooms, they could smell frangipani, hear geckos clicking, and the sea.

As Darwin became more real, London seemed further away. She woke to a long and funny email from Adam about how awful the election had been. Worst of all, Tom had won Eastbourne, and people on Twitter were saying they quite fancied him.

Coralie couldn't reply. She didn't want to write about what was happening, and not happening, in the hospital. Just like her mother, she didn't want to think too much.

Dan drove her to Chemist Warehouse at Casuarina.

'What kind does she like?' Coralie asked. 'Adult nappies.'

'They're called, like…I don't know. Reliability pants, or Be Safes or something. Back-ups. Something like that.'

'She's so discreet, isn't she? Never a hint of what's going on inside.'

'She's just a tiny, tidy little bird.'

She bought four extra-large packs of Depends, enough for two weeks or more.

Dan watched as she threw them on the back seat. 'Optimistic.'

There was a beep on Coralie's phone. 'Oh, it's Mum.' She slid into the passenger seat and read out the message: *Cor, Palliative Care have called. A room is available. They're moving me up this afternoon. C U soon.*

Dan got out of the car and slammed the door.

'Palliative Cor,' she couldn't help joke to no one.

After five minutes, Dan came back with a pink face.

They drove back to the hospital in silence.

Coralie busied herself wrapping her mother's flowers in pages of the *NT News*. There was a funny story about a juvenile crocodile who got into Parap Pool. She took a photo of it. 'I'm just sending this to Adam for Zora,' she narrated.

'Who?' her mother grunted, or perhaps 'Why?'

'Zora? Adam's daughter? My, sort of, stepdaughter? I miss her so much.'

Her mother murmured something into the pillow.

'What's that, Mum?'

'You're not married,' her mother said. 'She's not your anything.'

'But', Coralie said, her eyes filling with tears, 'I do love her.'

'Easy to be lovey-dovey about someone else's child,' her mother said. 'Wait till you have one of your own.'

'What do you mean?' Coralie said. 'Mum, what do you mean?'

But there was no reply.

'Mum?' Coralie said later.

'Mmm.'

'Don't you think it's unfair?'

'What?'

Coralie gestured around the room. 'All this.'

The words were spoken, they were in the air. They hung there. With no one to catch them, they drifted away, lost.

Soon after, Jerome came with the wheelchair. 'Judith, your chariot.'

They all piled into a car for the short journey. It was just a regular car, without hospital branding. Was it Jerome's? There was nothing of Mum to put the seatbelt over. She was two-dimensional, like a T-shirt drying on the line.

Outside the hospital cafe, a willowy Aboriginal woman pulled down one side of her colourful sundress to breastfeed a roly-poly baby. The baby's hand rose and waved. The mother looked down and the baby cupped her chin. The mother kissed the baby's palm.

Coralie looked away.

'Judith,' Jerome said at the hospice, 'you were a wonderful patient.'

Coralie wondered if the past tense struck a wrong note. But

their mother gave a gracious tilt of the head, a celeb impor-
tuned by a fan.

That night, Dan went on a longer run than usual, and the next
day, when Coralie got up early, she saw Jerome in her mother's
living room, putting on his backpack and tiptoeing out the
door.

Back in London, the stuff from storage had been re-delivered,
a surprise to the builders and Adam (and to Coralie, who'd
forgotten). Oneal sent her a picture of the newly painted sitting
room, filled to chest height with box after box of books, all
jumbled with boxes of kitchen things. The sofa was, for some
reason, on its side. The person who had packed those boxes,
herself of four months earlier, no longer seemed to exist.

When Stefan sent her gossip from the office, she couldn't
quite picture the scene.

I wish I could be with you! Adam emailed every day. *CYK,
CYK, CYK.* He *could* be with her. By getting on a plane. Oh
well.

Her mother hadn't eaten since being transferred to the
hospice, and neither, Coralie suddenly realised after a week,
had she.

She sat by the bed reading Rachel Cusk, feeling as blank as
the narrator in *Outline*. When her mother woke, she put the
book down. 'Mum? Did you say something? Do you need me?'

Her mother's face contorted. She was repelled. 'No!'

Dan went in at night, jogging along the Dripstone Cliffs.
Coralie came in early each morning to relieve him. He was

broken, his face a mask of horror. 'She gets so scared. She's terrified, lying there alone in the dark. Sometimes she's calling for me: "Dan, Dan." She doesn't realise—I'm right here holding her hand.'

One morning, she woke to a question from human resources. How much longer would she be 'on leave'? On leave? They made it sound like a holiday.

At the hospice, she poked her head around the door to the manager's office. She was at her desk, eating a bircher muesli and watching highlights of Formula 1. Coralie suddenly understood the meaning of the phrase 'in rude health'. 'Katherine? How much longer does my mum have?'

'She's not drinking much?'

'Not really.'

'I'd say we're in the home straight.'

She went into her mother's room. The colourful blanket, crocheted by volunteers, had slid half off the bed. Coralie adjusted it, and smoothed her mother's hair away from her face. Her skin was waxy like a candle. These weeks had been very cruel.

In the vinyl recliner at the back of the room, Dan startled awake. 'Oh, Cor,' he said. 'The morning.'

'Was it a bad night?'

'No, a lot better. Quieter. Maybe they have the drugs right. She gave my hand a squeeze. I think she knew it was me.'

'She definitely knew.' Dan put his headphones in. 'Have a nice jog,' Coralie said. He gave her a gently ironic salute.

She leaned over the bed and spoke in a clear, soft voice.

'Mum? It's me, Coralie. Don't worry, ignore me. I'll just be sitting next to you.'

She wrote to HR, telling them she'd be back at her desk in two weeks. She felt an uncommon feeling of 'take it or leave it'. They could stop her pay. They could end her employment, undermining the whole basis of her visa, and her right to live in the UK. She could wave goodbye to Wilton Way, to Adam and to Zora. Would that be so bad? Her mother was dying, and Coralie was on the other side of the world, alone. Should she have specifically asked Adam to come? *Please be with me instead of writing your election book.* She couldn't do that. She shouldn't have to. It struck her she'd invested her life savings into renovating a house she didn't own: a non-feminist and life-ruining error of almost comical proportion. On the plus side, most of her stuff was already packed—Adam could just ship it. But to where? Perhaps she'd be here forever, sitting at a deathbed in a hospice.

When she looked up, she realised she hadn't heard any breaths for a while. She waited for a minute, and then another minute. There were none.

She rang Adam, but her call went straight to voicemail.

She thought of Dan, running home through the bush. She thought of ringing him, so he could turn around and come back. But that would mean he'd hear the news on his own. She told Katherine on the way out to the car. Then she drove the short way back to Nightcliff.

When Dan saw her in the driveway, he burst into tears, and stayed crying all the way back.

122

Hi Dad,
Just thought I'd let you know that Mum died this morning. We're having the funeral next Tuesday here in Darwin.
Coralie

Hi Coralie,
Nice to hear from you. Any chance you'll make it down to Canberra on this trip? Jenny and I can't offer to put you up, but we could recommend you a hotel. Have a think.
Best wishes,
Roger

After the *Roger*, he'd added, in brackets, *Dad*.

That night, Dan disappeared when the sun set. Coralie walked alone to Taj Curry Indian. She'd never taken in her mother's voice, so she didn't have anyone or anything inside her saying, in a kind way, 'You need to eat.' But if a couple of weeks at the hospital had shown her anything, it was that not eating resulted in death. She ordered butter chicken, basmati rice, raita and a white wine. *Just a bite will do*, she made a voice inside her say. She felt self-conscious, like Zora as a five-year-old giving dialogue to her dollies. Saying something like 'You must eat', or 'Take a rest', or 'That sounds hard, poor you'—all that felt natural when she said it to Zora.

When would she have a baby of her own, someone who began inside herself and then came into the world, separate and real, someone she could look after and love, someone she was responsible for, and who needed her? Had her mother felt that way about having her? She'd never know. Tears were streaming down her face. The waiter walked up and, without saying

123

anything, put down an inch-thick pile of red paper napkins.

It was the morning but still dark when she heard a small commotion outside. Someone was rattling the flyscreen, and not loudly, but persistently, repeating 'Coralie! Coralie!' No one in Darwin knew her except Dan. Had he locked himself out? She pressed her phone to see the time. Nearly six. She saw she had some texts from Adam. *If this sends, I've landed in Singapore!* Then another, from 5.15 a.m., *I don't know if you'll get this, but I've landed! CYK!* She ran to the door. He was there— Adam. He looked ghastly, with dark circles under his eyes. He smelled like a Pot Noodle. His face, and the V of his chest, gleamed with sweat. But he was there, and smiling at her. He had come!

After the funeral, Adam borrowed the car and drove them to a mystery destination two hours out of the city. It was a mild surprise to Coralie when the sleek multi-lane main roads became narrower, more bumpy, and lined with a thick red dust. Before them, all around them, the sky was wide, blue and unlimited. She had existed in the hospital and the hospice for what felt like all her life. Seeing so much sky almost hurt.

Adam pointed. 'What are these beautiful trees?'

'Who cares?'

'Good question.'

'I'm not an Australian author. Do people who know the names of trees become writers? Or do writers feel like...' She took a deep breath to carry on. '...they have to learn names of trees?'

'Fuck knows.' Adam nodded out the window. 'Fuck you, trees.'

She fell into a pit of silence for a few kilometres. After a while, she said, 'Obviously they're better than English trees.'

'Obviously. I'm just going to check my phone—Dan wrote me some notes. Oh, we're so close, hold on.' He pulled off the road and they bumped and crunched along a track, first gravel and then dirt. 'Here we are.'

'Can you take a photo and bring it to me in the car?'

'Let's walk very slowly. Come on.'

She thought they were in the middle of nothing and nowhere. But, as they kept walking, the track turned into a boardwalk and a wide green space opened up—that vast blue sky again, almost eerie—and soon there loomed into view something even spookier, a mass of tall sand-coloured shapes that could hardly be part of nature, being evenly spread over a large distance and all facing the same direction.

'Like your books—in the Broadway Market flat, remember?' Adam said. 'Termite mounds.'

'They're so big.'

'Two metres tall.' He looked at her slyly. 'My height.'

She laughed out loud, just briefly, for the first time since her mother had died.

'Have some water,' he said back in the car. 'We're going to one other place.'

'Are you going to be watching me? For my reaction? I don't think I can act surprised.'

'You don't have to be, or do, or say anything at all.'

After a while, they pulled in to a car park. As she readied

herself for the effort of getting up, she could sense him hustling and fussing in the boot for whatever he had stowed there. 'A little walk—it's worth it,' he said. 'According to Dan, and Google.'

The path became a raised boardwalk taking them down, down, deep into thick green rainforest. 'I don't think I'll be able to get back up.'

'I'll help you. We're nearly there. Look.' In the thickest part of the monsoon forest, water plummeted down a sandstone gorge. 'Florence Falls. That's where we're going, where the water ends.'

She leaned over the safety barrier and gazed down to where, far away, through the canopy, there was a hint of navy blue.

'I've got your swimmers in the bag,' Adam said. 'And my swimmers. And some for any crocodiles who'd like to join us. Don't worry, there aren't any around here. That's a fact.'

At the bottom of the gorge, she nearly cried at the beauty of the water. Almost all in shade, and so clean it smelled like rain. Only a few other people were swimming, slowly breast-stroking to the misty haze where the waterfall met the pool. Coralie and Adam changed into their swimmers and piled their stuff behind a tree. Closer to the water it seemed to change from navy to green. The sandstone in the shallows glowed gold. They crept carefully to the edge, holding hands to balance on the rocks. They sat down, dangled their legs, and pushed off into the pool.

Afterwards, she couldn't remember what they'd talked about in the water, or if they'd talked at all. But after their swim, she was able to smile, and to eat a bit again, and (when they got back to London) unpack her bags, place an Ocado order for groceries, to inhabit the new kitchen, cook and properly eat. She could touch Adam, be touched, kiss again, have sex, laugh.

She had to remember—it was her mother who'd died, not Coralie. Coralie was still alive.

It was strange, though, to empty all the boxes in the sitting room and make order from their jumbled contents, to flatten them out, and to line them up for Adam to take to the big recycling bins near the cake shop, because the box (inside) where she kept her feelings about her mother also felt empty, and had felt empty for a long time, and if she weighed it, it felt like nothing, and if she looked inside (this was all metaphorical) it *looked* like nothing, but still the box refused to be broken down or gotten rid of, it remained a fucking useless void in a box, so she did what any normal person would do: put it in the attic (still a metaphor) to deal with it some other time.

8

2015–2016

She impulse-booked a gender scan on Ultrasound Direct as soon as her pregnancy app said 'Baby' was sixteen weeks.

'See those three lines?' the sonographer said.

Adam was beaming.

'What do they *mean*?' Coralie almost shouted.

'It's the vagina!' the woman said. 'It's a girl.'

It was a beautiful summer's day. They walked for a while, elated, then went for ramen in a chain restaurant near Bank. In the bathroom, she took out the printed scans to look at them in private. Inky black, a ghostly-white outline, her daughter's perfect nose. Then she cried, because her dream had come true. Her baby, her girl. Florence, like Florence Falls—they decided the name before they'd finished their lunch. Walking back from the tube that afternoon, they stopped off at Cotters' Yard, the most highly reviewed nursery in London Fields for ages six months to five, and put the baby down to start in March 2017, the week she was due to turn one.

Hubris? Choosing a name at sixteen weeks? Putting a foetus down for childcare? Already it seemed astounding that *sex* had resulted in a pregnancy. For a pregnancy to result in a baby, so much had to go right, and nothing could afford to go wrong. Was it true she should buy different brands of kale, all grown in different locations, to mix up her consumption of pesticide? 'In 1997, before the election,' Adam said, 'people all used the same phrase about Labour's huge lead in the polls.'

'Okay.' She sighed. 'What?'

'Blair was like a man carrying a priceless Ming vase across a highly polished floor.'

Actually, it was exactly how Coralie felt.

She made the mistake of confiding in Adam's mother, who was a doctor after all, and so might've had something to offer: if not emotionally, scientifically. 'It'll be fine,' Anne briskly said.

And was it fine? Was *she*? She was in nesting mode, warm bath mode, cossetted by Adam, stood up for on the tube. Popping into hospital for her scans, or the community centre for her midwife appointments, she felt like a VIP, albeit one of many VIPs in an overcrowded waiting room. She transformed her pink study into a tranquil yellow nursery. From Dalston Oxfam, for £20, she found a chest of drawers exactly the right size and height for a changing table. The top drawer she filled with minuscule newborn nappies. In the other drawers, she stored cotton squares for wiping, muslin cloths for burping, a brush with the softest bristles, a floating bath thermometer in the shape of a flower, sleepsuits, nipple cream, little hats, scratch mitts—yes, she had everything (except a baby).

'I miss your pink room,' Zora said.

Coralie didn't. She hadn't done any of the work she'd expected to do there. Letting go had been a relief.

Eighteen months on, Zora's relationship with her new brother remained boundaried and courteous. (Coralie imagined a bottle of champagne in a wooden gift box: 'Rup, it has been a pleasure getting to know you. I look forward to many more years of fruitful association—Z.') Now that she read a minimum of two parenting books a week, Coralie could see that none of the adults in Zora's life had properly 'made space' for her feelings after Rup's birth. She took Zora to Violet for a banana muffin and a chocolate milk. 'I wonder if you're worried about things changing—when your baby sister comes?'

'They will,' Zora said.

'How?'

'Grown-ups get tired and stressed. No one reads to me at night. Rabbitty doesn't like it.'

Keep reading to Zora, Coralie mentally noted.

When she wiped and saw her mucus plug, a formless splodge at first, then (upon more wiping) something as solid as a creature washed up on a beach, she thought, with happiness, and not even a flicker of stress: *This is it. She's coming.* But then she went into labour. Far from something natural, it was like a sinkhole swallowing a car, the Boxing Day tsunami, an air-raid siren, a car skidding off the road, a bomb blast, an emergency. Her mind simply *went*, she became not Coralie, a mother-to-be with a girl inside her, but some other fucked-up mixture: a wild creature craving the woods, desperate to run, to hide, and to die; her mother waiting for Dr Ainslie, the sheet pulled up to her chin; a gif she'd once seen by accident of a man getting run over by a truck.

A full night, a full day, and half a night at home. A journey to the hospital, where she was probed in a cubicle, the curtain half-drawn. 'I can offer you paracetamol,' the midwife said. Adam's face ashen in the taxi back home.

Another journey, examined again, only three centimetres dilated, but running a temp, better to be safe than sorry, we'll have to find you a room. Gas and air: everything turned white. She saw the boxes of books she'd gathered since she was a child, transported from boarding school, to uni, to her flat with Josh in Melbourne, the freight company picking them up. She saw them as if she'd been there, watching her mother take delivery of them, storing them not in the spare room, where she'd promised, but *under* the house, uncared for and exposed. 'Otherwise,' she said urgently to Adam, 'why *would* they...?' Get mouldy otherwise, she meant; carted off to the dump. 'No,' she moaned. 'Stop!'

Adam's worried face as he whispered with a midwife. The gas and air was taken away. Pethidine (she spewed on the floor). Curl over, that's right. Hug the pillow. Blissful needle in the spine. Reunited with her mind. God, how she'd missed it, and those other dear companions, her thoughts.

Alert, sitting up, she monitored Florence's heartbeat bouncing on the screen, as if she herself were a doctor. It didn't look great. 'Baby' was 'finding it stressful', the doctors said. Would Coralie agree to a caesarean? The risk-assessment document warned of paralysis, cardiac failure, death. *Surgery*—her mother waking up in Brisbane with half her insides gone. Still, it was time for this baby to be (in the words of the influencers she'd ill-advisedly followed on Instagram) 'earthside'! On the last page of the consent form she wrote (seeing her own handwriting was like seeing an old friend): 'Do NOT remove any organs no matter what you find inside.' She double-underlined the 'NOT', signed her name, and was wheeled away.

When Florence was placed on her chest, vast black eyes staring up at her, Coralie became Coralie again (broken, yes, but no longer mad) and something new, altogether—a mother.

9

2017

Viewing Cotters' Yard in high summer and signing Florence up on a whim had not given them an accurate picture of the profoundly depressing space under a railway arch that received no natural light for three hundred days of the year.

They'd also completely messed up their timing.

On Coralie's side, Antoinette had communicated clearly through word and deed that twelve months was too long a mat leave and that nine months would be more suitable for the agency *and* Coralie. What could she say to that?

On Adam's side, his 2015 campaign book had been number 8 on the *Sunday Times* Bestseller list for one week and his Boris book number 10. David Cameron's majority government wouldn't go to the polls until 2020. For a brief, shining period early in Coralie's pregnancy, Adam had been able to construct a touching fantasy that his overwhelming lust for status, attention and success was all behind him, and that when Coralie returned to the office, Florence could do short days at nursery from ten till four, and Adam could do drop-off and pick-up, perhaps with a swim in the Lido. Jogging, maybe? He might even jog?

Then came Brexit: the in/out referendum on Britain's membership of the European Union. His workload as a political commentator doubled. His stress trebled. The morning after the Brexit vote, Coralie rolled over to her bedside table and, still with her eyes closed, reached out to pick up her phone. To her surprise, Adam prised it from her hand. 'Don't look,' he said. 'Stay not knowing as long as you can.'

Breastfeeding had been hard for Coralie: whether it was the angle, or a special sensitivity, or Florence's 'latch,' or bad luck, her left breast couldn't hack it, even with a nipple shield, and she'd had to feed the baby on the right while milking her left into a bottle with a machine, before topping up Florence with the bottle if she wanted it or filing the contents away in a sachet to freeze with the date on. Engaged in this complex multi-step operation the morning of 24 June, she'd only half watched the BBC as the pound plunged and David Cameron resigned.

The dream of 'short days with a Lido swim' was over. 'Great, so now my baby's starting nursery in January, *and* she'll be doing long days.'

'Not long days,' Adam protested. 'Just *days*!'

In the first week of January, Coralie and Adam were encouraged to sit on the sidelines for an hour and observe Florence 'settling in', which she appeared to do instantly, sprawling on the carpet in the Baby Room and gnawing her plastic giraffe as, around her, her peers crept or wriggled, coughing like barking seals. A staff member swooped to wipe a child's nose with a torn-off piece of blue industrial hand towel. It was the hand towel that got Coralie, and she cried in Climpsons afterwards, burying her face in her daughter's silky hair and breathing in her lovely smell. It was *so* rough, she tried to explain, the towel and the gesture; she'd never put something so rough on her girl's beautiful face, and do it—the wiping—so *roughly.*

'But we'd also never lie on the floor to build and rebuild a block tower,' Adam said. 'Or play Peepo for more than a minute. Or read a book in that slow, sing-song voice, or have other kids her own age around, and so many nice toys. She'll have *so* much stimulus in that nursery, so much to think about, and do.'

It was true Coralie couldn't see herself doing that kind of stuff. She read, of course—various Mogs, *Totally Wonderful Miss Plumberry, Possum Magic, Koala Lou*: books of a vintage that could almost have been read to her (though she only remembered reading alone). But playing: no. Crying had been the order of the day for the first two months of Florence's life, for both of them. Then their world had become more predictable. Nappies, always. Sleeping, sometimes. The laborious breast-feeding stuff. In between, they enjoyed companionable parallel lives: Florence on her soft sheepskin sent by Elspeth from Australia, grasping for the toys on the wooden arch; Coralie cooking and tidying, always keeping an eye on her in her small playpen in the kitchen. They listened to audiobooks over the Bluetooth speaker, *Wolf Hall* first, and *Bring Up the Bodies*, and all the P. D. Jameses and John le Carrés, all narrated by the same man, so that the happiest time in her life would be forever linked with the voice of Michael Jayston. Zero conference calls. No client emails. No one bothered her. She was exactly the right amount of alone.

And on the weekends, when Zora came round, Coralie had the ongoing marvel and good fortune of watching her girls fall in love. Aged eight, having not cared about dolls since she was five, Zora rediscovered baby Layla from the toybox. She gently bathed the plastic parts of Layla's body (the middle was made of cloth). She changed her nappy (a tea towel) and swaddled her (also in a tea towel). On walks, Layla was strapped to her chest in Adam's Liverpool Football Club scarf. At the end of Year 3 assembly, Coralie found herself swamped by Zora's peers, all stroking the soft top of Florence's head with eager, gentle hands.

She enjoyed it too much, loved it too much, for it to be *good mothering*.

Adam was right: the baby needed someone who'd sit on the floor with her and gasp 'Oh no!' when a tower fell down. Coralie had never heard of the songs the staff performed in the circle on the carpet. (*Pull, pull, clap, clap, clap.*) Soon, too soon, the jig was up. She re-downloaded Outlook on her phone. Florence would be handed over to the reliable care of professionals.

The Baby Room manager talked a big game about accommodating expressed milk for bottle feeds. For day two, when 'settling in' was longer and would include 'snack', Coralie defrosted a sachet from her dwindling stockpile. Her milk had dried up a few weeks before she was due to return to work, and because it had not been her choice to stop breastfeeding, and because breastfeeding had been so complicated and hard-won, she didn't feel that sense of liberation other women described at getting their 'body back'. Florence could have Coralie's body as long as she wanted. In fact, if Coralie could have, she'd have carried her around in a pouch, or slid her back into the womb for naps. The nursery provided 'snack' ('hand-made organic vegetable purées and finger foods') but she'd kept the milk as a connection between mother and baby, to help Florence cope with her absence, and herself cope with the absence of Florence.

'She didn't take her bottle, mama!' Liliana reported at pick-up.

'Oh no—what did you do with the leftover milk?'

'I put it out, in the bin? For good hygiene.'

The logic couldn't be faulted, but that milk was *of her body* and now it was in the *bin*. Florence, that other precious product of her body, was safe in Coralie's arms, but an air of threat enveloped her, as well as a bad new smell of other children's nappies. Even her toy cat, Catty, smelled like the nursery. For this they'd be paying £1,650 a month.

That night, after Florence's bedtime, Coralie cried and couldn't stop.

'It's only hard for you *because* you love her,' Adam said. '*Because* you're such a good mother.'

'I feel bad because I *am* bad,' Coralie sobbed.

It was possible some hormones were at play. There hadn't been much breastfeeding or pumping towards the end, but

137

stopping completely was a big shock for the body. There was anxiety too, about leaving the home, which she'd made perfect, and was in charge of, and going back into the impersonal office, to be at the mercy of others. Everything about her was vulnerable and soft. Her trousers still had an elastic waist. What if she was the scared one, not Florence, and Florence was actually fine?

Either way, by the second week of January, her darling baby was a full-time inmate at a lightless germ prison with borderline strangers as guards. Sitting on a crowded 55 bus, Coralie could either collapse crying from missing her, or vow to one day brutally exact her revenge on Adam. (Why Adam? Why not? Somehow, she knew he was to blame.)

Florence, Flossie, Floss-Floss, Rennie, Wren, Birdy, Cheep-Cheep. Crying and missing was too painful, so revenge it would have to be.

10

Before Florence turned one, Coralie started to joke. 'This time last year, I got my first contraction.' Much later: 'Ah yes, this time last year was when the hospital turned me away!' But after a while, the enormity of what she'd gone through hit her, and she cried about it properly for the first time.

The Sunday after Florence's birthday, they hosted a small party for her at home: Anne and Sally were there, up from Lewes. So was Stefan from work, 'on a break' from Marcus and pretending to be fine; Daniel, now twenty-eight, who'd just moved to London on a Youth Mobility Visa. Zora was there, of course, with Layla; Tory Tom came early with Rup. Nearly two, Rup seemed a giant, running around in a collared shirt, a thick nappy under his bulky jeans. In the space of ten seconds, he climbed to the top of the sofa, rolled onto the seat, then onto the floor with a thump.

'I never knew this, Adam—did you?' Tom dragged his sobbing son onto his lap. 'But boys who are tall for their age have rather a hard time. Everyone expects Rup to behave like a three- or four-year-old.'

'No,' Anne said. 'Adam didn't have that problem.'

Tom gave Adam a sympathetic glance. Then—'Tell me, Daniel,' he said. 'How are you finding London? Where do you live?'

'Tottenham,' Dan said. 'In a warehouse with thirteen house-mates.'

'Ooh, edgy.'

'Where do you live, Tom? I don't know London well enough to make a joke.'

'Clapham?' Stefan guessed. 'Putney?'

'Camden, actually—surprise! It's my wife, she's liberal intelligentsia.'

Zora made a comically puzzled face she had learned from a tween comedy on Netflix.

'I don't think that's a rude thing to say,' Coralie assured her.

'When people call *me* a liberal, they do mean to be rude,' Adam said. 'Trust me.'

'I saw a clip of you on that show,' Daniel said. 'What's your problem with Jeremy Corbyn? Too nice to the poor? Not enough bomb-dropping on Iraqis? Doesn't look good in a suit?'

'Daniel, please!' Adam held up his hands in defence. 'It's hard enough having a Tory in my home.'

'What do you do here in London, Daniel?' Stefan asked politely. 'Coralie says you're a chef?'

Seeing with Stefan's eyes, Coralie suddenly realised anew

how handsome her brother was. His creamy skin and delicate features made sense in London in a way they hadn't back in Darwin. His hair was long, down to his shoulders. It was elegant. She saw Stefan as Daniel might see him too, tanned from a trip to Mexico, his physique newly honed from his regular CrossFit WODs (that meant 'workouts of the day'—he posted them on his Instagram). It had been quite a long time since she had attracted anyone or been attracted to anyone new. She'd almost forgotten it was part of life.

'Stef, mate, I'm a cook. I work in a place near Mare Street? Called Junkyard? Yeah, it used to be a junkyard. The mains are thirty pounds each. But we have a weekday lunch that's a bit cheaper.'

'I'm trapped in Clerkenwell during the week,' Stefan said.

'And he doesn't eat,' Coralie said.

'Protein shakes are nutrition.'

'Maybe! They're not food.'

'I thought it was all about Moro for you two,' Sally said. 'Wining and dining, Stefan.'

'We took a hit after Brexit,' Stefan said. 'The agency, I mean. Our big campaign for Eurostar, remember how much work we did?'

Daniel elbowed Tom with a smile. 'Your fault, mate.'

Now Tom raised his hands. 'I voted Remain! Unlike your friend Corbyn.'

'Woah, woah!' Coralie said. 'This is a birthday, not a panel show.'

'I don't understand why Theresa May hasn't called an election,' Adam said. 'Twenty points ahead in the polls. Or is it thirty? You could put Labour out of business for a decade just with a snap GE.'

'No need to sound so happy about it,' Dan said.

Tom grimaced. 'I'm in the most marginal of marginals. And Marina's only just forgiven me for the last one.'

'Anyway, Tom,' Coralie said, 'aren't *you* liberal intelligentsia?'

Stefan made a little moue. 'Not in that quilted gilet.'

There was a single long cry from upstairs. Sally clapped her hands. 'She's awake!'

Anne darted to the door. 'I'll get her.'

One thing Coralie loved to do was cuddle Florence after a nap, her golden hair all tousled. She gave Adam a wounded look. He nodded towards the door: she should go up too, if she wanted. Coralie could feel Sally watching; she'd almost certainly seen the exchange. Partly from embarrassment, she made a dash for it. But she was walking quietly, and when she reached the landing, she saw something that surprised her. Hard Anne, all angles, was holding Florence to her chest. Florence's head was leaning on Anne's shoulder, eyelashes fanned out above her pink cheeks, utterly relaxed. Anne swayed, humming. Coralie tiptoed back down the stairs.

As she reached the hall the doorbell rang. 'It must be Alice and Beauty,' she called into the sitting room.

'Flo's little best friend from nursery,' Adam announced.

Sally was enchanted. 'Is her name really Beauty?'

Coralie opened the door. 'Hi!'

'Hiiiiii!' Alice jumped up on the front step and swept Coralie into an elegant cloud of blonde hair and fragrance.

142

'You smell nice. Where's Beauty?'

'Ugh! She only napped for five minutes. Nicky has her in the buggy. But it won't work.'

'It never works. Well, come in, I have quite an assortment of oddballs for you.'

Anne was standing on the stairs with Florence, looking amused.

'Hi, Florrie!' Alice cried. 'Happy birthday, gorgeous girl!'

'That's Anne, Adam's mum.' Coralie swept Alice into the sitting room. 'This is Alice, Alice, this is Tory Tom...'

'*Conservative* Tom.' He shook her hand. 'Florence's half-sister's brother's dad.'

'Stefan from work, my brother, Daniel, Florence's other granny, Sally, who volunteers at Charleston.'

'Ooh,' Alice said. 'Lovely. Bloomsbury, very cool.'

'Zora you've already met.'

Alice nodded. 'What are you reading, Zora?' Zora held up her graphic novel, a Sherlock Holmes rewritten for kids. 'Someone once told me I was *so thick*,' Alice said, 'I thought Sherlock Holmes was a block of flats.'

'No, it's Holmes, with an L,' Zora said.

'Well, I know that *now*!'

'That's a lovely dress,' Stefan said. 'Is it RIXO?'

'Sorry, it's Portobello,' Alice said. 'People hate it when I say that! Vintage!'

'It's lovely,' Sally approved. 'So how do you two know each other, or is it really the babies who are friends?'

'Oh, no!' Alice grasped Coralie's arm. 'We're friends!'

They were, against all odds, despite Alice being a literal 10 who hadn't read a book since school, and Coralie being a charmless Australian who commuted on the bus, had a dull winter complexion, and *still* wore Uniqlo elastic-waist trousers. They'd met when they'd both picked up their daughters late on the same day. In the shed, they struggled with their buggies, both with burning faces, until Alice said, 'I hate being told off, don't you?' They walked home together through the park. Alice paid for three days a week of nursery by renting her flat out as a photoshoot set. It was on a corner above a former pub in Dalston and got the light from 'three aspects'. Alice revamped it seemingly every month, repainting, tiling, putting up shelves. She also made lampshades, wall hangings and tapestries, which she got bored with after a short time and sold through her Instagram. Ever since that first meeting, they messaged each other to walk to nursery together. Sometimes, when Nicky was away, and Coralie was in the bath, she and Alice texted for an hour straight. So yes—they were friends.

Anne put Florence down so she could pull herself up and try to walk. Immediately all the adults crouched to encourage her, while Adam made the tea. The doorbell rang. Tory Tom went to open it. 'Florence,' he called. 'It's your little pal.'

After a dramatic pause, a small girl toddled in. Seeing the large group, she stopped in her tracks, before running back to clutch the baggy corduroy trousers of her tall and diffident father. 'Look, Beauty, there's Mama.' Nicky pointed to Alice on the sofa. Beauty ran over and climbed into her lap.

'Hi, Nicky,' Coralie said. She noticed Stefan stare towards the kitchen at Adam, who raised his eyebrows above the tea tray. 'Wait.' She jogged over to him. 'Let's have it all in the kitchen—we can do the cake now and have it with the tea.'

'Cor,' Adam said urgently. 'You didn't tell me Nicky was Nicky Adebayo.'

'I didn't really know he was Nicky anyone?'

'I thought you were the Google fiend?'

'Not about men! Anyway, I knew who he was from Alice. I just didn't think *you* would know him. What were you saying to Tom before? There won't be an election, will there?'

'No. No, no. Nicky, hi!' Adam stretched out his hand. 'Adam!'

'Nicky,' Nicky said.

'That's lucky,' Anne said. Everyone turned to her. 'That Beauty is beautiful. You know—that name's a real gamble.'

Nicky laughed. 'We chose it after she was born, when it was safe.'

'Well, well done.'

'Tea?' Adam said. 'Coffee? Cake time? Flossie, is it cake time?'

Florence made a happy noise. Everyone exclaimed that she'd clearly said 'Cake time', and it felt natural after the applause to go straight into 'Happy Birthday', while processing in a group to the kitchen. Adam lit the 1-shaped candle and picked up Florence so she could blow it out, and Coralie took a lovely candid photo of them together, illuminated by the bespoke glazing. There were no lovely candid photos of her (at all) and especially none of her with Florence. A few times, in the park, or once on mat leave when they'd gone to Charleston and Coralie had just had her hair done, she'd asked Adam to take a photo of her and the baby. He'd gamely agreed, straddled his legs, leaned back from the waist, pointed the camera up her nose and counted down loudly from five. By two, there were tears in her eyes. She'd deleted the photos without looking. 'Happy birthday, dear Florence,' the group sang, at which point they all became aware of a single stand-out voice: Nicky Adebayo singing like an actual cello.

'Mate,' Dan said, after the candle was out and everyone was waiting for a slice. 'Have you thought of singing professionally?'

'Ahh, stop!' Nicky covered his ears and backed towards the pantry.

'He does! He does sing professionally!' Stefan said. 'I saw him at Glasto, 2015! It was amazing—you were amazing!'

'That's so nice,' Nicky mumbled. 'Normally when I meet new people, they go *out of their way* to say they've never heard my stuff.'

'Glastonbury 2015,' Coralie raised an eyebrow to Alice.

'Where the magic happened,' Alice murmured back. (Beauty had been conceived in a yurt.)

'Went back the year after—shocking.' Nicky shook his head. 'Woke up and it was Brexit.'

'Not my fault!' Tory Tom said.

'What are you, David Cameron or something?' Nicky laughed. 'Why would it be your fault?'

'Funny you should say—'

'Tom, Tom,' Zora called from the sofa, where she'd retreated to have her cake. 'Rup's doing a poo in his nappy.'

'Where is he?'

'Hiding between the sofa and the window.'

'He does this.' Tom shrugged. 'He likes to skulk. Sorry, do

146

you mind if I use the changing table?'

Coralie shuddered inwardly at the thought of that giant boy in her tiny girl's space. 'No, please, of course!'

'And how old is Beauty?' Sally asked in her gentle way. Beauty, her hair in bunches, was tapping a wooden lemon against the play kitchen.

'She turned one a few weeks ago,' Alice said. 'We had the loveliest weekend away, didn't we?'

'We did,' Nicky said. 'My mum took her; we went to Paris.'

'Happy birthday to *you*,' Stefan said. 'You don't get out much, do you, Cor? You haven't had a night out in a year.'

'Oh!' Coralie said. 'Well, the baby had so much to get used to. Being born.' Everyone laughed, although she hadn't been joking. 'Then she goes to nursery for such long hours. Home is kind of her safe space—I would feel bad if she woke up at night and a stranger had to comfort her.'

'Cor.' Alice pulled her aside. 'Do you have any...' She trailed off with a meaningful face.

'Valium? Cyanide?'

'Pads? A tampon? I'm on my period, I can feel it.'

'Come up, I'll find some for you.'

They jogged up the stairs together with the relief and joy of cutting class. 'I loved not bothering with this when I was pregnant,' Alice said.

'I quite like having mine. Everything's ticking along, that's what a period says to me.'

'Getting mine tells me Nicky managed to pull out.'

'You don't want to...?'

'I do want to, but the flat only has one room.'

'I want to, but my boss would probably sack me.'

'Who cares about your boss!'

'I do! A bit. For some reason.'

In the next room, they became aware of Tory Tom, droning as he changed Rup's nappy. 'And on that *farm* there was a *shark*, E-I-E-I-O!'

'Not exactly Nicky Adebayo,' Coralie whispered.

'Not exactly,' Alice agreed.

In the kitchen, after everyone had gone, Adam loaded the dishwasher with mugs and cake plates. 'Nicky Adebayo! Even I know him. He won the Mercury Prize. What's he working on? He wouldn't say.'

'He's in a fallow period. Are you starstruck by a nursery dad?'

'No!'

'You and Tom think you're the famous ones.'

'Tom's not famous.'

'Okay!'

He opened his arms and she relaxed into him, her forehead on his shoulder.

'Another great weekend being the world's best parents.' Adam looked over to the play kitchen. Florence appeared to be climbing into the oven. 'Floss, Flossie? Stop trying to Sylvia Plath. Did you have the best time ever?'

'Soh,' Flossie said. 'Soh-Soh?'

'Zora's gone to Camden, Cheep-Cheep,' Coralie said. 'She'll be back next weekend.'

'Do you want the park, Wrennie-Wren? Park time?' Florence

gave Adam an interested look, or at least didn't start to cry.

'Did Tom take Rup's shit out with him,' Coralie murmured, 'or did he leave it upstairs?'

'He left it for the shit fairy. That's me, I suppose. I'll take it to the park bin.'

'Thank you.' Coralie leaned back into the hug. 'It's nice Tom wants Rup in Flossie's life, isn't it? Or is it weird?'

'Nice, I think? He had to pick up Zora, anyway. Might as well have some cake.'

'Daniel was on good form, I thought.'

'Very good form,' Adam said. 'For a Trot who lives in a squat. A squat Trot. Hang on, who's texting me. Oh, it's Sally. What the hell?' He held out his phone.

We'd love to come up one weekend soon so you and Coralie can get away, Sally had written, *and we can have some Florence time. Give us a few dates and we'll make it happen. This is an offer from both of us. Love the GGs.*

'Praise be,' Coralie said. 'It's a miracle.'

Soon after, Antoinette announced she was leaving the agency to join Edward Enninful's *Vogue*. Stefan was appointed the agency's new creative director. He moved into Antoinette's old office. Sadly, she took the Tulip table with her.

'I hope you understand, Coralie,' Antoinette said. 'And that you're not too disappointed. A big job like this requires commitment. Commitment *and* sacrifice.'

'Cor,' Stefan begged, 'please can nothing change?'

Apart from their long partnership, his title, his salary and his status?

Of course, and there were no hard feelings, and she was proud of Stefan, and wouldn't have wanted the job anyway— but Florence had just taken her first steps at nursery, and Coralie hadn't been there to see them.

It was a bit rich to talk about sacrifice.

11

'Come inside me,' Coralie told Adam, in the stimulating anonymity of the vinegar-scented all-white bed in a boutique Paris hotel.

Adam paused, still inside her. They heard the distinctive *nee-no nee-no* of a French police siren. 'Shit, it's the pigs.'

'They're arresting me for my bad choices.' She meant not using a condom.

'It can't be bad to do something so good,' he breathed into her ear. 'I want a thousand babies with you.'

'I'd love that too, it's just *hard*.'

He leaned down until their noses touched. 'It'll be different this time.'

'Promise me it'll be different,' she said. 'I don't want it to be the same.' Her mind had played tricks on her when Florence was a baby. When things were good, she'd thought they were good. Then she'd woken as if from a trance. Work guilt, home guilt, C-section scar still numb, clumps from post-partum hair loss still clogging up the drain. Having a baby was lovely if that was *all* you had. Anything else in the mix—forget it.

'It'll be different.' Adam started to thrust again. 'So different, so different, even better.'

Two weeks later, Theresa May called a snap election, and Adam was instantly offered a contract for another book. When it arrived, a few days later, Coralie's period was the most operatically dramatic it had been since giving birth. *Hell no*, her body seemed to say. If Brexit had made things more difficult on Wilton Way, a long election campaign (and another book project) would smash what little amity remained.

Adam seemed not to sense the danger. His admiration for Ed Miliband had made his first book a torment—that was how he remembered it. He didn't have the same inner conflict about Labour's new leader, Jeremy Corbyn, whom like many of his colleagues he viewed as an allotment-dwelling, strategy-free, kindly but irrelevant kook. And he simply *revelled* in his new insight into the Conservative Party, which this time he was also contracted to cover.

One day, early in the campaign, Coralie came home late from work and nursery pick-up. The buggy groaned under the weight of Florence, binders of printed-out longform web copy requiring urgent review, and last-minute supplies for dinner. Adam, lounging on the sofa in his socks, hung up his call and padded to the door, giggling. 'Guess what the Australian pollsters just called the chancellor—off the record till publication?

Coralie? You know, Philip Hammond? I said guess!'

'Could you get the shopping from under the buggy?'

'Fine, I'll just tell you.' He was laughing so much she could hardly understand him. 'A *fucking cheesedick*!'

Theresa May was a diabetic, apparently, and owned more than 150 cookbooks. She gave up crisps for Lent. She didn't have children, which was something she was sad about. On a rare evening when Adam was home with her on the sofa, Coralie watched the Mays' first joint appearance on a BBC chat show. The husband seemed quite sweet. The PM looked sick with nerves. Was it a fucked-up feminist impulse, trauma maybe from Clinton in 2016? Whatever it was, Coralie found herself full of pity. 'Oh dear, really?' Adam said. 'This is a woman who once made an entire conference hall of Conservatives boo the Human Rights Act.'

'Okay, but you know who else is awful? Men in her own party who insist on calling her Te-ray-sa. She's said it's Ta-ree-sa. Her husband's saying Ta-ree-sa right now! And still they do it. Do they think they know better?'

'It's likely they think they do.'

'Well, they *don't*.'

'I know!' Adam said. 'Why are you cross with *me*? I'm not them! I'm me!'

'You're bad enough,' Coralie muttered.

He looked puzzled, then hurt, then annoyed.

Princess Diana voice: 'There were three of us in this marriage'— Adam, Coralie, and Adam's *bloody* book. For the duration of the seven-week campaign, she did drop-off, pick-up, bathtime, bedtime and Zora's Saturday circus school almost entirely on her own. There could not have been a worse time to add a pregnancy into the mix. Luckily, she'd put her dreams of a second baby on ice. Along with all her other dreams! But Adam was achieving his! So that was great! For him!

'But what other dreams do you have?' Adam asked her in a kindly voice.

What a cunt!

Close to election day, Daniel texted and asked if she'd like to campaign with him for Labour in Chingford. *If power is lying in the streets,* he wrote, *pick it up!*

I'd love to effect some political change, she bitterly replied. *Sadly, I have the girls and a full-time job.*

May won the election but lost her majority. It was a huge embarrassment for her (and by extension, all women—or maybe only Coralie felt that). Jeremy Corbyn was jubilant, and so were all his supporters. So close—they were *so close.* If the campaign had run one week longer, they would have won.

Tom lost his seat to his Lib Dem rival. One day he was an MP, the next day he wasn't. 'I keep thinking WhatsApp's broken,' he marvelled. 'But I've just been kicked off the groups.'

For the rest of the UK, at least those who visited the *Guardian*'s website compulsively, there was no post-election *exhale.* The shocking closeness of the result meant nobody could relax. At fever pitch since the Brexit referendum, at fever pitch they remained. The days were boiling, too—record high temperatures for June. Heat shimmered from the pavements, and even people with seats stood up on the bus to suck in air from the windows. Reaching for her phone one morning, Coralie discovered a large tower block in one of London's richest areas had been entirely consumed by a fire. Residents had foreseen the disaster: no one had listened. People calling for help had been told to stay inside. Twelve people died, no, a hundred; actually, no one knew. Theresa May didn't dare visit the homeless and bereaved. ('In office,' Adam said in his quoting voice, 'but not in power.')

Whatever 'the room' was, it was clear there were no adults in it. It wasn't a safe way to live.

One Saturday, waiting at the bus stop after circus school, the back of Coralie's throat ached from pollution, while Zora visibly wilted. In the buggy, Florence was down to her nappy, passed out beneath a muslin shroud. At Greenwood Road shop, Coralie bought juice boxes and ice lollies. Back home in the garden, she dragged the paddling pool into the shade of the bay tree and filled it with the hose. She achieved five minutes of peace, sitting on the back steps scrolling her phone, before Adam appeared, stirred up the girls with horseplay, stole an ice lolly, and returned to work upstairs.

'Girls? Zora?' Coralie said. 'Could you sit back down in the pool?'

'Cara Lee?' A voice came from the garden next-door.

She got to her feet. 'Hello, Miss Mavis. Are the girls disturbing you?'

Shrewd eyes were visible through the fence slats. 'Aren't you worried they'll burn themselves up?'

'They've got sun cream on, and they're in the shade, but you're right, it's time to go in soon.'

'Miss Mavis?' Zora had known their elderly neighbour since she was little. 'Can I have a Jammie Dodger?'

'I've just seen you have two ice lollies, am I right?'

'She *is* right,' Coralie told Zora.

'That baby's going to slip on the pavers,' Miss Mavis observed, as Florence did indeed slip, landing hard on her little bum. Her appalled cries brought down Adam, who scooped her up, but not before giving a baleful look at Coralie.

'You fucking do it then,' she hissed and stomped off.

She'd just locked the door, sat down on the loo, and mindlessly reopened Instagram when a text popped up from Daniel. He was at Glastonbury, and had filmed a clip from deep within a crowd. 'Oh, *Jeremy* Corbyn,' everyone roared, over and over. After a bit, before she'd decided on her reply, he sent another. This time his camera was focused on a huge screen next to the festival's biggest stage. The Labour leader looked spritely in a blue open-necked shirt. His snaggle tooth and lopsided eyes lent him a friendly vibe, like one of Jim Henson's Muppets, or more specifically (and showing her age) a Fraggle. 'If I may, I'd like to quote one of my favourite poets, Percy Bysshe Shelley,' Corbyn said.

A shadow appeared below the door. 'Mama, Mama.' Florence rattled the handle. Had Coralie forgotten to close the stair gate? Had Adam just let her roam free?

Back on the screen, the Labour leader was reciting:

'Rise like Lions after slumber
In unvanquishable number—

156

Shake your chains to earth like dew
Which in sleep had fallen on you—
Ye are many—they are few.'

Another world is possible, Daniel wrote.

Still on the toilet, her beloved daughter wailing outside, Coralie broke down and sobbed. How could the world with all its inequalities be made fair—when two people who loved each other couldn't even manage a *life*?

Adam submitted the first draft of his manuscript one Friday in late July. They spent the weekend with Zora as usual, circus school (together this time) and two drop-off parties. On Sunday afternoon, Marina came to collect her. 'How's the book? Finished?'

'Done!' Adam said. 'Exhausting—insane deadlines. But now I'm a free man!'

'Zora, poppet, go and get your bag,' Marina said. 'I've got Rup asleep in the car.'

Coralie, who was sitting on the stairs, moved to the side to make space. 'Tiptoe past the baby,' she murmured.

Adam leaned on the banister. 'How's Tom?'

'Put it this way,' Marina said. 'He now lives in one house, has one job, has his weekends back, sees the kids, earns proper money, and doesn't talk about Brexit all the time.'

'That sounds—good?'

'Happy wife,' Marina said darkly. 'Happy life.'

'Oh, trouble in paradise!' Adam said when he closed the door. 'Tensions high in Bartholomew Road!'

'I wouldn't be laughing if I were you.'

'Are you all right?'

Coralie was suddenly shaking. 'Those were the worst four months of my life. Running from pillar to post, working, not a minute to myself, but *you're* the stressed one, you're the one with "deadlines". Deadlines! Five a.m., Florence is up; nine a.m., nursery drop-off; fifteen minutes later, I'm on the bus to spend all day doing *pointless* bullshit for Stefan, who used to be my colleague and is somehow now my boss? I have to *run* to get Florence by six—or pay a late fee! Six-thirty, dinner—or Florence loses her shit! Seven: Florence's bath, alone. Seven-thirty: Florence's bedtime, ALONE! It's all hopeless, I feel *absolutely* hopeless!'

'I do some baths! I do some bedtimes! What about last week: I picked up twice! You don't do all the drop-offs!'

'*Some* baths! *Some* bedtimes! *Some* pick-ups! And who gets up when she calls out in the night? Not you, me—you don't even hear her! And then I'm awake, looking at my phone, watching my sleep time tick down, down, down until it's gone, and another day starts, as awful as the last!'

'I know it's been bad, but it's over, it's done!'

'*I'm* over. *I'm* done.' Coralie was shaking. 'I'm moving out. You can have two kids on your own every weekend. Two days a week, a hundred days a year, I'll finally have a fucking break!'

She stormed out of the house. Two hundred yards down the road, she stopped for tea and cake, and spent ninety minutes on Rightmove, furiously shortlisting two-bed flats.

Adam did drop-off and pick-up for three days in a row. On the third night, Coralie briefly lay on Florence's experimental new big-girl bed while Adam was reading, and together they cuddled their daughter, though not each other. But afterwards, she ran a bath, lay in it for half an hour, got dressed in the bathroom and once more went up to sleep in what used to be called the spare room, but which (somehow) over the previous two years, had become 'Adam's study'.

Is there anything I can do to make it up to you? Adam texted after a while.

This sounded like a sext, like he thought sex would fix it. *No thanks,* she texted back.

I don't mean in a sex sense, I mean in a practical one. I'll do anything to make things better.

She didn't reply.

Anything, he wrote. *Please.*

Why do you get to write books when that's always been my dream? she typed and erased. *Having a baby is the nice bit,* she typed. *It's having a husband I can't stand.* She erased it. For one thing, they weren't married.

Come down and tell me, he wrote. *Tell me anything and I'll listen. Please?*

'I'm a shit parent, and shit at my job, and a shit person,' she cried when she got downstairs. 'I feel shit, and I hate myself, and my life.'

Adam pulled her into bed. 'Beautiful Coralie. *Beautiful* Cor. You're the best mother, the cleverest at your job. I love you so much, I would die if you left me. I would *die*.'

'I can't keep the whole house quiet so you can be free. I can't work full-time so you can post all day on Twitter!'

'Tweeting is sort of w— Okay! I know what you mean! I

159

need to organise my time better.'

'You know where I am *every* minute of every day. I'm either in the office, on the bus, or at home. You just do whatever you want, whenever you want, and trust that I'm there to cover it! And the pathetic thing is, I am! I always am!'

'I'm sorry. It's bad. I'm so, so sorry.'

'Everyone matters more than me. No one cares about me. I was alone when my mum died. I was alone!'

'I'm so sorry. Cor, Coralie, I'm sorry. I came as fast as I could. I didn't sleep for sixty hours. I finished that book on the plane!'

'I was alone then, and I'm still alone. I look after everyone else! No one looks after me!'

'I'll look after you! I will!'

'How will we ever have another baby? We can't even manage Flo.'

'We are, we can, we will!' He wrapped his whole body around her, even, somehow, his legs. 'Coralie—I love you. *Please.*'

Luckily for their relationship, all the Rightmove flats had been shit.

Adam's third book came out in October. He didn't savour the process quite as much this time round. The people who provided him with blurbs were more prominent (good), but the blurbs were correspondingly more measured (bad). The BBC's Nick Robinson, who'd released a competing history of the last campaign, called the new book a 'madcap dash'. 'It's rushed', Adam said. 'He's saying I rushed it!' ITV's Robert Peston, whose book on the referendum was its direct competitor, called it 'a fine first draft of history'. 'Fine?' Adam moaned. 'First draft?!' Emily Maitlis, whom he knew socially, called it 'whip-smart'. 'Whip-smart? That's a girl adjective! Maitlis knows *exactly* what she's doing!'

'It's everyone's dream to write a book,' Coralie said reasonably. 'Have you considered just enjoying it?'

'No!' Adam said. 'I have *not*.'

It was worse than his birthday! (He was turning forty-two in December, what he grumpily called a 'stupid nothing-age'.)

'If you're not going to celebrate your book, or your birthday, can I at least do something I like?'

For five years in a row, Coralie had been tortured by watching the Great Australian Summer unfold on her phone through Instagram. She didn't want to miss out again. Florence, who had Australian citizenship, had never set foot on her homeland. Soon she'd be too big for the fold-down Qantas bassinet. Soon, as well (hopefully, if they could manage it), they'd have another baby, making the pilgrimage even harder. Adam mumbled something about key Brexit votes. Coralie said she'd go by herself. He backed down.

When the plane touched down in Sydney, she cried and couldn't stop. It was a huge sensory rush: the smell of sun cream on warm skin, the sound of the birds and the button at the pedestrian crossings, the shrieking and cackling of the Botanic Gardens' bats, swooping in lilac skies. The towering ferns, the salt of the sea, the reliable daily benediction of the sun. She wanted to stop people in the street: *Do you know how lucky you are?* Walking along with Adam (sunburnt) and Florence (in the carrier) she was shocked people weren't shouting it back.

161

Because Australia might be the same, but *she* wasn't. She loved and was loved in return!

They had pancakes at Bills and took Florence to Taronga Zoo. They had Bourke Street Bakery sausage rolls, yum cha in Chinatown, and fish and chips after a swim at Bondi. They caught the ferry from Circular Quay to Wendy Whiteley's Secret Garden. They walked to Elizabeth Bay. 'And here's the park and the koi pond,' she narrated into her iPhone to send to Zora. 'And this is my old flat…' She trailed off and ended the video. Suddenly, the elements of the Richard Pickard story rearranged and fell into place. What would she say to Zora if, in her twenties, her boss chased her around her own bed begging her for sex? *Gross, Zora—you're gross. How did you get yourself into that mess?* As if! No, the boss was a creep! God! She was almost winded by the scale of revelation. What had happened to her wasn't right. She stopped worrying about bumping into Richard. She began to hope that she might.

In Melbourne, they went to Marios for double avocado on toast, and swam in Fitzroy pool under the AQUA PROFONDA sign made famous by Helen Garner's *Monkey Grip*. Afterwards, she rushed to the big Officeworks and bought a stack of yellow-covered Spirax notebooks and a box of Artline pens. As a jet-lagged Adam napped with Florence every afternoon, Coralie rushed to get down the jumble of memory and impressions stirred up by the trip. It became a daily ritual: 'Shh, Mummy's writing,' she heard Adam say to Flo. In Brunswick Street Bookstore, he gestured wide at shelves of books: 'This will be you one day.'

It wouldn't, but it was kind for him to say.

162

Perhaps because their bodies were reliably warm, or because the air smelled so nice, or because most of the people who caused them stress were asleep on the other side of the world—whatever the reason, they had sex almost every day until Canberra, the last stop on their trip, when something gave Coralie a temporary eye-twitch and a sore shoulder, and the passion trailed off, then stopped.

Coralie and her childhood friend Elspeth gossiped in the shade in Elspeth's Red Hill back yard, five minutes away from where they'd both gone to school. Adam pretended he knew how to barbeque with Elspeth's husband, Jack. Florence ran nude under the sprinklers. Elspeth was pregnant. In March, she'd be having a boy. It was incredible to think they hadn't seen each other in seven years. School felt only yesterday. The ice in Elspeth's ginger ale tinkled. 'And are you seeing your dad for Christmas?'

'Yes, ugh!' Darkness moved across Coralie's field of vision as though a cloud had blocked out the sun. 'Don't ask!'

But reality had intruded. The holiday was over.

The days with Roger passed in a haze of horror, obligation and good manners. Coralie cried as the plane took off and didn't stop for more than an hour. She sobbed into Adam's shoulder, all the while thinking, *I want to go home.*

But did she mean onwards, towards London? Or back the way she'd come?

12

2018

She'd had her period on the flight out. A week after they returned, she was late. Had she conceived an Australian baby? She was ready to dream that she had.

On their first Saturday back, Adam did circus school with both girls. Coralie layered up with thermals, a jumper, a padded vest and her biggest puffer to walk across the park and buy a pregnancy test. At Broadway Market, she wove through the crowds browsing Scotch eggs, Gujarati thali, cheeses, flowers, and old black-and-white photos of Hackney. As usual, there was a clear divide between locals (rushing, annoyed) and people who'd put on their fanciest outfits to travel in from somewhere else. She didn't feel like a coffee. That could be a good sign.

On her way out of the pharmacy, she spotted a familiar face. 'Dan!' Her brother's hair had grown very long since Coralie had last seen him. 'How do you get your ponytail so sleek?'

'I don't do anything.' He embraced her. 'My hair's just oilier than yours. I keep it back when I cook. I was using the thin elastics from Boots, but they kept breaking.'

'No, you'd need the thick ones. What are you doing now? Do you want a bagel with me?'

'I've literally come here for a bagel! I always have one before work!'

The bagel lady, who had inch-long acrylic nails, laid out the meat with care. 'Gherkin and mustard?'

'Yes, please, for both of us,' Dan said. 'I love your nails.' The lady smiled, delighted.

'I can never do this with Zora around,' Coralie said. 'She makes sick noises about the salt beef.'

'That's nice that she's a vego. I hardly cook meat at home.'

'Florence doesn't eat meat, either. I'm thinking of not forcing her.'

'Do you remember the chops? When we were young?'

'Stop,' Coralie said. 'Disgusting.'

'Dad made me finish them before I could get down from the table. Once he found where I'd left all the chewed-up bits. In the wooden bowl, hidden in the pinecones—do you remember?'

'I don't. Was he angry?'

'No, he was really relaxed and easy-going, just the greatest, kindest dad ever.'

They both laughed.

'I put a bit of extra gherkin on for you,' the lady said. 'Have a lovely day, yeah?'

They pushed through the crowds. 'Would you want nails like that if you didn't have to cook?'

'Nah,' Dan said. 'I like them though.'

'You know what else is cute about Zora? When she talks about being grown-up, she says "my husband or wife". Isn't that nice?'

'That's so nice. Lucky little kid. Be free.'

They left the main market to sit on a low wall. They were shivering. 'Brr,' Dan said. 'It's frigid. What was Australia like?'

'Heaven on earth. How was your Christmas? What did you do?'

'I worked, of course, on Christmas Eve. But on the actual day, I...' He fluttered his eyelashes. '...went to my boyfriend's house.'

'Your what?'

'Yes, I have a boyfriend.'

'No, I mean, of course you do, you're a very eligible man, but your boyfriend—has a house?'

'Oh, very funny. I didn't choose to live in poverty. We're not all hobnobbing with Tories and centrist dads.'

'What's his name then?'

'I just want to keep it to myself for a bit. You can meet him soon. Or...at some point.'

'But is he wonderful?'

'Yeah!' Dan's jacket started buzzing. He pulled his phone out. 'Speak of the devil.'

The name on the screen, in all caps, was BIG MAN. Dan cancelled him coyly and put the phone back in his pocket. They both paid attention to their bagels.

'Put me out of my misery,' Dan said after a bit. 'How was Roger?'

166

Coralie swallowed her last mouthful. 'Ugh!'

'I know. Did you do hotel Christmas with Jenny?'

'We weren't invited!'

Dan gasped. 'You went to Canberra to see them!'

'We had Boxing Day together, at Ruby Chinese Restaurant. In Dickson, remember?'

'I hardly remember Canberra.'

'Well, the food was really nice. We saw Edwin, Jenny's son, who's also *nice*. He works for Deloitte. They both speak Mandarin, so they ordered for us. I've met Jenny once before, but have you ever met her?'

Dan looked away. 'Nope.'

'I was struck by how she managed Dad. She had a little more wriggle room. Mum wouldn't dream of taking liberties!'

'Liberties like what?'

'Jenny still works at Australia Post—she has a job. But mainly it was the fact that she laughed at him. Just a tiny bit. She rolled her eyes when he wiped his chopsticks down with a napkin.'

'I forgot he always did that.'

'And Florence was doing her best, but she was jetlagged and exhausted, and squashed into a high chair, which she hates. Dad gritted his teeth—you could see his jaw actually clenching. He asked if I could "sort her out". Jenny gently put her hand on his arm. And after a second, he shook it off, but he didn't say anything else.'

'Yeah, you better sort that baby out.' Dan rolled his eyes. 'Did he ask you any questions?'

'Only why we didn't visit more, and why we weren't staying any longer.'

'Hmm, I wonder why?'

'I guess we'll never know!'

'Did he mention Mum?'

'He didn't,' Coralie said.

'Did he mention me?'

She didn't know which answer he'd like best, so she just told the truth. 'No.'

'Well, as long as he doesn't come here.' Dan stared off into the distance. 'Everything should be fine.'

At home, she unwrapped the pregnancy test and placed it next to her on the sink.

But when she pulled down her underwear, she found it was stained with blood.

13

Adam was doing the newspaper round-up on Andrew Marr's curvy orange sofa at the BBC's new Broadcasting House. 'Back me or get Jeremy Corbyn and no Brexit,' he read from the *Mail on Sunday*. 'Prime Minister Theresa May warns MPs against voting down her EU withdrawal deal—as she reveals how she keeps calm by eating *peanut butter* out of the jar.'

'Peanut bupper?'

'That's right, Cheep-Cheep.' Coralie turned back to the television as Florence, still in her pyjamas, ran off towards the pantry.

'Mrs May has told the *Mail* she hopes the Commons will sign off on her Brexit deal on Tuesday, so she can enjoy her goose and a glass of red wine this Christmas,' Adam told Marr on TV. 'She warns that failing to sign off on her deal could see Jeremy Corbyn in Number Ten, or even no Brexit at all.'

'But with hardline Brexiteers already vowing to vote against her withdrawal agreement,' Marr said, 'will it be Mrs May's goose who's cooked?' He turned to the camera. 'To his critics he's the man whose blithe, airy promises have landed us in a Brexit nightmare, and a thoroughly embarrassing foreign secretary. To his admirers he's one of the very few truly rousing Tory politicians of the age and a shoo-in, surely, as the party's next leader. He is, of course, Boris Johnson.'

On screen, Boris Johnson smiled. 'Good morning.'

Coralie snorted. 'Good morning, you fat twat.'

She glanced back down to the kitchen. Fortunately, Zora was watching her iPad with headphones on. The problem wasn't the T word, but the F one. Coralie was absolutely ruthless about not engaging in what the experts called 'body talk' in front of the girls. No staring into the mirror smoothing her thighs with a disgusted face. No 'I feel bloated', no 'I earned this treat', no gossip about people's appearances, none of it. Years ago, she'd spent ages carefully live-editing Roald Dahl while reading aloud to Zora, and soon she'd do the same for Flo. So why couldn't she help herself when she saw Boris Johnson?

Little footsteps approached. 'Where's Dada?' Florence's face crumpled. She'd brought him the peanut butter from the breakfast table.

'Oh, Wrennie, you're so clever! He's not on the screen anymore. Here, let me take a photo for Daddy. Show me the jar?'

She sent the photo to Adam. *Flo thought you wanted this*. She added a heart emoji and four CYKs.

He replied instantly with five heart emojis. *Beautiful girl. How was I? Any feedy-b?*

By 'feedy-b' he meant feedback, and it was Coralie's job to pass it along.

Attention of all kinds had significantly increased since he'd been offered a staff job on *The Times*, a sprawling, high-profile role involving some Parliamentary sketch pieces, helming its gossipy daily email, and setting up a chatty new podcast. At a time when politics was life and death, he would be paid to try and be funny. He'd tweeted the announcement with a self-effacing *Some personal news.* The resulting storm of mentions was the 'best day' of his life. ('On Twitter!' he'd quickly clarified to a horrified Coralie. 'The best day of my life on *the platform.*')

A WhatsApp arrived from Sabine, a Cotters' Yard nursery mum: *Jonas wants to know if Adam's jumper is from Cos?*

Coralie forwarded it to Adam. *It's from Folk!* he wrote back. *Anything else?*

She searched Twitter for 'Adam Whiteman'. In the most recent tweet, someone had called him a *groan-worthy remoaner chubster.*

That wasn't suitable. She searched 'Adam Marr'.

The top result: *Dreamboat Adam's back on Marr #yesplease.* It had been liked four times. With a sigh, Coralie shared it.

Now we're talking! Adam was delighted.

Was it awkward with Boris in the green room? (Three years on, Adam's biography remained unacknowledged publicly by its subject.)

No! Adam replied. *A polite hello. But I can't really be sure he*

171

knew I was me. Breakfast will be the test.

The breakfasts after the Marr show were the stuff of legend. Or maybe Adam only said that to get out of childcare for hours.

Marr's voice broke through to her from the TV. 'Can you give me an absolute categorical promise here and now', the journalist said, 'that you will not stand against Theresa May?'

'I'll give you an absolute categorical promise', Johnson craftily replied, 'that I'll continue to advocate what I think is the most sensible plan.'

'Horrible man.' Coralie pointed the remote like a gun and shot him.

Upstairs, she tried to lie Florence down on her back, but was not surprised when she stiffened, struggled, and firmly announced, 'Stand up.' Coralie gave her the cheap plastic calculator they kept by the changing table as a distraction. With a comedy frown on her perfect face, Florence raised it to her ear. 'Hello? Phone?'

'Are you being Daddy, funny bunny?' Coralie unpopped the top popper on her sleep suit and ripped open the rest in one go. Florence wriggled and jumped, delighted. '*Brr!*' Coralie blew kisses into her neck, chest and belly. Florence shrieked and laughed.

Zora looked up from her copy of *The Week Junior* ('TOUCHDOWN! scientists celebrate the successful landing of a new spacecraft on mars'). 'What if she was just learning proper maths on that calculator and you disturbed her?'

'We can't have two genius girls in the family,' Coralie said. 'I won't be able to cope.' Zora smiled and went back to reading.

'Flo–Flo. Do you want to sit on the potty?'

'No,' Flo said, disgusted.

'Do you want to wear a nappy?'

'No,' Flo said, appalled.

'Then why don't you have a try on the potty? Just a little try? And then I can put your knickers on.'

'I'll pud dem on!'

'That's a good idea, you go to the potty—and then you can put your knickers on!'

Florence launched herself off the table and into Coralie's arms. 'Flo! Be careful!' She tipped her backwards to cradle her. 'You can't fly!'

They smiled at each other, and Florence reached out a hand for Coralie to kiss. How she loved her little girl.

And yet, just as passionately, Coralie longed once again to be pregnant. It was scary to be back in the wanting place, the almost desperate place, craving a second baby while her beautiful existing baby was there before her. To justify wanting more when she had everything, she had to tell herself it was for Florence: a sibling close in age, a built-in best friend, something both she and Adam felt they'd missed out on. They'd been 'trying' for almost a year; she had a private fertility appointment booked for January. Nothing seemed to be working. Why?

In the bathroom, Coralie squatted on the floor, and tried not to look impatient as Flo scrabbled in the bath toybox instead of doing a wee.

Florence had been born before Brexit, before Trump. Since then, a crazed right-winger had shot *and* stabbed a woman MP to death during the Brexit referendum campaign, shouting, 'Britain first!' Donald Trump's 'zero-tolerance' policy to separate any families entering the US across the Mexican border had seen thousands of children, even nursing babies, locked away in camps with no one to take care of them. When public outcry caused the policy to be stopped, they hadn't been able to reunite with their parents because their records were messed up. In Australia, the prime minister was a total dipshit, a global warming-denying embarrassment: 'This is coal,' Scott Morrison had said in 2017, brandishing a black lump of it on the floor of Parliament. 'Don't be afraid. Don't be scared. It won't hurt you.' Meanwhile, in October, the world's leading climate scientists had said the last remaining best-case scenarios were already barely manageable. Sweeping wholesale changes had to be made within the next twelve years. Nothing was okay anymore, everything was bad, and even if she was able to bring another child into the world (and it felt like an 'if' at that point)—was it moral to do so? Was it right?

Florence had produced something in the potty. Coralie exclaimed over it, wiped her bum, took out the green plastic insert, tipped the contents into the toilet, swilled out the bottom of the potty with some clean water, and poured it on top of everything else. Why was she craving more of this? Was she mad?

At least she could put Flo in knickers now, and have two clear hours before starting to ask, at first casually, then with more urgency, and then with an anxious sheen of sweat above her lip: 'Flo, Flo—*do you need the toilet?*'

'Can I choose her clothes?' Back in the nursery, Zora laid

down her magazine.

'Yes, but something the snowsuit can go over. I'm hoping Adam will take her out.'

'He only ever goes out for coffee. He would've had coffee with Andrew Marr.'

'If he doesn't go out, *I'll* have to go out. I want to get some writing done.'

'Where do you go when you go out and write?'

'If I have an hour, Violet, the cake shop. If I have two, the library.'

'What if you have longer than that?'

'Oh, Zora!' Coralie said. 'I'll let you know when that happens.'

Downstairs, the front door burst open. 'I'm home!' Adam heaved and clattered his bike through the kitchen to shove it outside in the bike store. Coralie and the girls were down to meet him by the time he came back in. 'Whew,' he said. 'My fingers have frozen off. Who wants to feel my hands? Zora, come here.'

Zora screamed. 'No!'

'No, no!' Flo began running too.

Adam chased them into the sitting room. Coralie put the kettle on and waited to hear her fate.

After a little while, Adam returned. 'Bad news, I'm afraid. Zora says she'll get a blue card in PE if she doesn't take plimsolls in to school.'

'We'll have to buy some. We'll have to go to M and S.' Zora looked levelly at Coralie. 'In Stratford.'

Stratford! My God, she was looking at two, two and a half hours alone! She could sit and write in the kitchen where the heating properly worked. She was free!

'Tell me if you want anything from Westfield,' Adam said on the front step, resigned, as Flo kicked her snowsuited legs in the buggy. It had taken them twenty minutes to get ready.

'Nothing, I need nothing!' She kissed Zora on the head and whispered, 'Thank you.'

There was nothing 'creative' in her job as 'a creative'. She'd spent ten years codifying tones of voice for brands. When Antoinette, and now Stefan, presented designs, they were filled with Lorem ipsum. Her own text came later, ignored if the client was illiterate, picked over—massacred!—if they weren't. Everything she wrote for work, she viewed through a single lens: *How will this cause me trouble?* It wasn't a training ground for art, it was antithetical to it. The mindsets were not compatible. When she opened her social media feeds, competing voices overwhelmed her and she couldn't hear her own. 'I like to write first thing in the morning,' authors said in profiles. Coralie was lucky if Flo slept later than five.

She came to the page a broken woman. If she waited to be fixed, she'd never start.

Now she brought her laptop down from upstairs and sat at the kitchen table. Without the girls and Adam, the house was silent, uncannily so. She opened her long document and started reading from the top. It was a story about someone like her. But it wasn't her, and so far it wasn't a story. The father. What should she call him? She clicked into the paragraph and started typing: 'Robert was capable of great charm.'

The floodgate of impressions opened. Her mind was overrun. The problem with having a warm kitchen was that it sometimes became too hot. She stood to remove her jumper. The moment it covered her eyes, she felt the presence of an assailant, someone sneaking up behind her to attack. Her heart was pounding. She couldn't sit back down. Oh look, the washing machine had finished its cycle. It was very, very dangerous to write even a sentence. Housework would keep her safe.

Coralie and Alice had comprehensively lost consent for the buggy. Where before they could meet for a relaxed walk through London Fields and have a nice chat at adult level, they now had to muster the girls on foot, drag them or even chase them to get to Cotter's Yard on time. On Monday morning, after running wild for a while, Flo and Beauty squatted to inspect some muddy rocks. 'Anything good on for the weekend?' Alice said.

'We're meeting Daniel's new boyfriend on Friday.'

'*Oh là là!* Beauty, no!' Alice grabbed her daughter by the hood to stop her toppling over. 'Beauty, can you hop up? Hop up?'

'Flo? Can you hop up? We've got to get to nursery!'

When they made it to the Big Puddle, a permanent fixture of the park for the rainiest six months of the year, they were confronted by an unwelcome sight. Their friend Sabine watched proudly as her son Luka splashed in water up to his hips.

'Hi, Sabine,' Alice said.

'I won do go in the puddle,' Beauty said.

'Florence, Beauty, girls,' Coralie said. 'No one's going in the puddle.'

'There is no bad weather!' Sabine announced proudly. 'Only incorrect outerwear!' Luka was dressed in a full-body waterproof suit, wellies up to his knees, like a Scandi noir policeman dragging the pond for a corpse. 'Coralie, did you hear?' Sabine said. 'The ruling from the European Court? Article 50 can be revoked and Brexit cancelled. Unilaterally! With no penalty! Maybe all our problems can be solved.'

At that point, Coralie's main problem was Luka, who was shouting, 'Florence W! Florence W!' (There were two Florences in the Duckling Room.) 'Get wet! Get wet!' She felt anguish and fury rise within her, as if Sabine, a perfectly nice woman, and Luka, a perfectly nice boy, had been placed in her path expressly to make her late for work. It was this bubbling, rising heat feeling, this panic, that she *knew* was keeping her from getting pregnant.

Alice reached into her tote bag. 'Anyone who's *not* in the puddle can have a jam tart.'

Luka splashed out immediately.

'Genius,' Coralie said.

At work she was dealing with an unpleasant hangover from Antoinette's time at the agency. Somehow a Norwegian fossil-fuels company called Futurum had decided it was good and relevant comms to sponsor a major exhibition and events program at Vanessa Andorra, a woman-helmed contemporary

178

art gallery in a vast warehouse on Regent's Canal. The deal was worth a spectacular £2 million over three years. The first year, under Antoinette, most of the money had been spent on a series of sumptuous summer parties. The second year, after Antoinette moved on, Stefan and Coralie had sub-contracted an events team to run an outdoor cinema showing important documentaries. In 2018, planning for the final year of the sponsorship contract had been unavoidably hampered by Greta Thunberg in her yellow raincoat holding up a homemade sign reading skolstrejk för klimatet.

'We would have got away with it,' as Stefan said, 'if it wasn't for those pesky kids.'

For Coralie, it was a hard one. On the one hand: they were supporting contemporary art (good). A show at the gallery could make a woman artist or an artist of colour a star. On the other hand, per multiple experts, there were just twelve years left to save the world (bad). When she got in to the office that morning, Stefan was distraught. Someone had started an Instagram account called Andorra's No Tomorrow. It called on artists and patrons to boycott the gallery until such time as its relationship with Futurum was renounced. The campaign's points were well researched and trenchant. Perhaps most deadly of all, and especially wounding to Stefan, the design was very elegant.

Caught up in the crisis, Coralie didn't check Twitter until elevenses (Pret white filter and a popcorn bar). There she discovered Theresa May was locked in an emergency conference call with her cabinet. Ten minutes later, the vote on May's Brexit withdrawal agreement had been called off.

Coralie googled 'How many days until 29 March 2019'. That was when the UK, unless the withdrawal agreement was passed, would crash out of the EU without a deal. The answer was 109. The prospect gave her a brief apocalyptic thrill. Sure, she was culture-washing a fossil fuel company on a dying planet! But if people couldn't get fresh food or cancer medicine, she was less likely to be personally cancelled.

Nursery had sent several texts pleading for all Duckling Room occupants to be sent in with a complete change of clothes. On Wednesday morning, Coralie was scrambling to get it all together when Adam whooped from inside the bathroom. She paused outside the door. 'What?'

'There's a vote of confidence in Theresa May tonight!'

'Poor old thing,' Coralie said.

Adam came down when she was trying fruitlessly to persuade Flo into her coat. 'It's all happening!' He was quite giddy. 'What a week!'

Coralie narrowed her eyes. 'Please don't forget we're going to Daniel's boyfriend's.'

Adam froze. 'Tonight?'

'Oh my God,' Coralie cried. 'On Friday!'

'I won't forget!'

'You already had!'

'Silly old Cor.' Adam gave a superior smile. 'I mean I won't forget it *now*!'

She didn't find this as annoying as usual. Was it possible she was ovulating?

*

That day, at lunch, Coralie ate a Pret tuna sandwich at her desk and watched Prime Minister's Questions on her laptop. It was sad but sort of sweet to see Philip May in the Commons to watch his wife. In 2017, after she'd lost her majority in the election, Theresa May had been profoundly humiliated during her speech at Tory conference. A prankster had run up to her to make a joke, the set had collapsed around her, and she'd coughed a horrible dry anxiety cough for what seemed like minutes at a time. After that, apparently, May had gone offline for five hours, and no colleagues or advisers could reach her. According to Adam, Philip had 'talked her off the ledge'. (The 'quitting as prime minister' ledge? Or the *ledge* ledge?)

Coralie drank her cup of tea and studied the Tory leader. She was elegant and profoundly unusual. It was dreadful that this practical, dutiful woman, with awful Tory politics, but a firm hold on reality, was being hounded by her colleagues (mainly men) who were living in a fantasy world, where the UK should be able to leave the EU with no penalties—only rewards! Even Florence, at two and almost three-quarters, could grasp the sad fact that if you ate a cake, you no longer had it.

Well, it was not Coralie's problem. She squashed her apple core into her sandwich box and tossed it in the bin.

That night, Coralie and Adam sat on the sofa together to watch the results of the confidence vote. Immediately afterwards, Adam would have to repair to the spare room to record an 'emergency podcast' (under a blanket to boost the sound quality). Now he looked up from his phone with a grimace.

'Apparently May had to swear she wouldn't fight the next election as leader. Apparently MPs were crying.' On the screen, a group of men and one woman trooped into the room and stared out solemnly from a splendid Westminster backdrop. 'Oh—turn it up.'

'The Parliamentary party *does* have confidence in Theresa May,' a tall man proclaimed. Tory cheers rang out, a complex mix of 'Ooh', and 'Wahey!' as well as a bit of 'Hyar, hyar, hyar!'

'Oh, good!' Coralie said.

Twitter had the figures. Only 200 Tory MPs had voted for her; 117 had voted against. 'She won, but it's *not* a win,' Adam explained. 'Thatcher got two hundred and four, and she still had to resign. May just can't catch a break.'

'They won't rest until she's sobbing on the floor,' Coralie said. 'I hate them.'

Parliament wouldn't vote for the withdrawal agreement, the Tories wouldn't change the leader, and the EU wouldn't change the deal. Two and a half years after the shock referendum result, Brexit had hit a brick wall.

14

On Friday night, Miss Camilla from the Duckling Room came round to mind the girls and earn some cash-in-hand. Before she arrived, Coralie had given Florence her bath and dressed her in pyjamas. (Miss Camilla had been so proud when Flo had 'moved on' from nappies. She didn't need to know she still wore pull-ups in the night.) Zora was lying on the sofa reading *My Story: Suffragette*.

'We're off, sweetheart,' Coralie said.

Zora lowered her book. 'What's Daniel's boyfriend like?'

'That's what I'm hoping to find out.'

'Okay. Well.' Zora raised it up again. 'Report back.'

Coralie straightened her back and saluted. 'I will.'

Outside, the cold air smelled deliciously of other people's wood stoves, pumping out fine particulate matter injurious to human health. All week she'd been bracing for Adam to let her down and not come because of work. But there he was, next to her. 'I feel like we're on an adventure,' he said. 'Bravely setting off to *Casa Millennial*—a whole new world.'

'You know, I was born in 1983,' Coralie said. '*I'm* a millennial.'

'A geriatric one—no offence. Daniel's a real one. What do you think we'll find when we get to Amhurst Road? Another squat? A flat above a chicken shop? A sort of Sally Rooney scenario: thin brunettes eating a single orange, messaging each other about socialism?'

'I've read those books. I love those books! *You* haven't read a novel the entire time I've known you.'

'Yes, but I've read *about* them! That's called being cultured.'

'You're a charlatan, a hack, an articulate Oxbridge fraud!' Coralie screamed as he wrapped his arms around her and lifted her off the ground. 'You're everything that's wrong with this country!'

Outside Borough Wines, Adam set her on her feet. 'Let's give them a little treat. *Two* bottles.'

They strolled up Amhurst Road towards the wide green space of Hackney Downs.

'Do we know anything at all about this guy?'

'The boyfriend?' Coralie said. 'We don't. Big Man, he'd saved the number as, all in capital letters.'

'Big Man,' Adam mused. 'I'll be the judge of that.'

To their surprise, the address Daniel had texted her corresponded to an entire four-storey Victorian terrace. 'Surely not,' Coralie muttered, as she got out her phone to check.

They rang the doorbell and hovered on the vast porch. A lantern turned on above them. The door creaked open, and Dan was there in a woolly jumper, shorts and socks. He looked pink-cheeked and princely in the extra-wide hall, in which a row of sconces was illuminated and reflected in heavy gilt-framed antique mirrors. He stood back and gestured, aware of the dazzling effect. 'Please come in.'

'Sorry...' Coralie embraced him. 'What the *fuck* is this?'

'I thought we'd be dumping our coats on your mattress on the floor,' Adam said. 'Not hanging them up in Versailles.'

'I don't really know what *Versailles* is,' Dan admitted. 'But you'll love the house, Cor. It's all old stuff, right up your alley.'

'Big Man,' Coralie said. 'Big house.'

'Oh, I forgot I used to call him that. Being in love is so embarrassing. Please don't call him Big Man, especially you, Adam. You can call him Ian—or Barbie, people sometimes call him.'

'I promise, Dan, I won't. And who's this?' Adam bent to pat a skeletal and ancient black poodle who tottered into the hall.

'That's Madonna,' Dan said. 'I'm glad you didn't bring the girls, she's terrified of children.'

'So she should be,' Adam said. 'Hello, tiny one. You're a sweet little thing, aren't you?'

'Come into the kitchen, I've got some stuff on the go.' Instead of leading them downstairs to the basement, where she'd expect a kitchen to be, Dan took them through the first door off the hall. What would originally have been the vast double reception had been turned into a kitchen and dining room. Wide wooden floorboards lined the entire space. All the intricate cornicing had been kept, swags of roses and egg shapes and bows. An antique dining table ran the whole length of the front room to the huge, shuttered bay window. Dan saw her staring at it. 'It had to be winched in.'

'You could cook me on a spit in that fireplace,' Adam said. 'Enormous.'

The fireplace in the rear reception had been removed. Inside the chimney breast was a brass-knobbed range cooker with about eight burners. The ceramic sink must have been a metre wide. The standalone fridge was double-doored. Over the kitchen island, a bronze pot rack hung on chains, loaded with pans of all sizes on sturdy industrial hooks. 'It's like a fairytale,' Coralie said. 'A giant's house.'

'That's funny,' Dan said. 'Because—'

'Fee-fi-fo-fum!' came the cry behind them. An actual giant had entered, pulling a jumper down over his T-shirt. 'Sorry, I was in the shower. Ian Barbagallo.' He lunged for Adam's hand.

'Adam!' Adam said.

'She's the important one,' Dan murmured.

'Of course, Coralie! Finally! Now you can tell me the story of how you got your name.'

'Oh—' Coralie started to say.

'But a drink first!' The giant strode over to a cabinet.

'We brought some, didn't we, Coralie?' Adam darted out into the hallway and came back with his two bottles, now revealed in this setting to be only moderately nice or generous. The giant ignored them in favour of his own much better wine. After a moment, Dan took them out of Adam's hands with a murmur of polite thanks.

Yes, Ian was tall, and he was much older than Dan. Fifty-five? He was almost bald, and what hair remained was shaved. He was big, really big, with a physique like a held breath. Coralie glanced over at Dan, tending to something bubbling in a pot, at peace with the world and his choices. The cork popped out of Ian's wine. He took down four cut-glass crystal goblets and filled them to the brim. 'Your good health!' He gestured at the chairs. 'Please! Sit!'

Coralie and Adam obeyed. As Big Man strode over to deliver Dan his wine, they shared a long, neutral glance to convey their mutual surprise.

Ian was back. 'Dan says you're on the telly?'

'Sometimes, sometimes,' Adam said. (*Don't say 'For my sins,'* Coralie silently begged.) 'For my sins!'

'And what do you do, Ian?' she asked.

'Nothing.' From the stove, Daniel tutted. 'I used to be in the talent business,' Ian said. 'Now I just keep myself busy.' He appeared momentarily inscrutable. 'Bits and pieces.' (What did he mean? Crime?) 'What about you, Coralie?'

'Oh, I work for an agency,' she began.

'Am I going to have to ask again about the name?' He gave her a sudden and very charming smile.

If she started telling the story of her name, which she hated, and she was interrupted again, which she hated, she would start to cry, and the night would be a failure. 'Oh—' she began.

'Dan?' Ian interrupted. 'Don't forget the radicchio or whatever. The pink lettuce.'

'I won't.'

'I might just...' Coralie got to her feet. 'Is there...?'

'There's like, four,' Dan said. 'Go to the one on this floor: you'll like it.'

She escaped, gladly. At the back of the hall was a big door with coloured glass, probably leading out to the garden. The bathroom was tucked under the stairs. Inside, the wallpaper was black with an intricate design of insects travelling between, perhaps pollinating, vaguely sexual flowers, all generously endowed in the stamen department. The lighting was sophisticated and made her look beautiful. But the full wall of photographs, framed and unframed, was surely what Dan had been directing her to—she inspected them from her position on the loo. Big Man, back when he had hair, his arms around the Three Tenors. With Pete Sampras and Andre Agassi. With Madonna—the singer, not the poodle. Amy Winehouse like a little doll. Rappers, girl groups, the Coldplay guy?

Alice, she WhatsApped urgently. *Ask Nicky, does he know Ian Barbagallo? I'm at his crazy house.*

By the time she'd washed her hands, Alice had written back. *OMG. Barbie? Nicky says he's a full recluse.*

Nicky was himself extremely shy. If *he* thought Barbie was a recluse…

She'd been away from the table for too long. She slid her phone into her pocket and returned. Daniel was still at the stove, stirring. Adam and Barbie were hunched over a platter arrayed with various cold vegetables: slim carrots, both orange and purple; the promised radicchio; half-moons of roasted delicata squash, the skin still on; courgettes quartered lengthwise with stripes seared on from the grill. The men were hungrily dipping them into, and scooping them out of, a large

188

bowl of yellow stuff: aioli.

'Yum,' she said. No one paid any attention.

'I just find that incredibly patronising,' Barbie said.

'It's the truth, I'm sorry to say.' Adam spread his hands. 'It's thoroughly irrational from start to finish. The sad fact is most Leave voters are the very people who will be hurt most by leaving without a Brexit deal.'

'You seem like a well-off guy. Author. *The Times.* Telly, and so on. You've got a home of your own, don't you?'

'Not as big as this one.'

'But you're still a homeowner in London, that's top ten per cent stuff. Have you voted Labour in the past?'

'I have. Obviously.'

'Then you were voting to pay more tax. Is that rational?'

Adam gave a quick laugh. 'I suppose not. It's about values, though, isn't it?'

'Exactly,' Barbie said. 'And it's the same for Leavers. Unless you're saying that only *some* groups of people get to live by their values?'

'Barbie,' Adam said, 'I'm not saying anything. I have no thoughts. After this week, I'm officially braindead.'

'Here.' Barbie refilled his goblet. 'This'll help.'

Coralie pushed her chair back quietly and tiptoed over to the stove. 'They're like two silverback gorillas.'

'Barbie voted Remain, by the way,' Daniel said. 'He loves a good debate. I try to...float above.'

'What's in the pot?'

'Risotto.'

'This is by far the nicest kitchen I've ever been in. It's

actually murdering me—the next time I see mine it's going to feel all shrunken and cheap.' She opened a floor-to-ceiling cupboard built into the alcove next to the stove. Jar upon jar of dried grains and pulses, expensive tins of Italian whole tomatoes, herbs and spices, rice and pasta, pickles, crackers, slabs of dark chocolate, olive oil, vinegar, mustards, Heinz ketchup, and tin after tin of baked beans. 'Aladdin's cave,' she said. 'What *is* this—No Deal stockpiling?'

'Normal stockpiling,' Dan said. 'A cook's pantry.'

'A cook's pantry!' Coralie scoffed. 'When you lived at Mum's, I was lucky to find spaghetti.'

'That was different. She didn't eat what I made. She hardly ate at all.'

'Not like me.' Barbie was up on his hind legs and rubbing his own belly. 'I love everything Dan makes.' He wrapped his arms around Coralie's brother and kissed him on the top of his head. In spite of herself, she blushed. Her eyes focused on a glittery magnet on the fridge. In glamorous scrolly writing, it said:

It's not a whorehouse
It's a whorehome

'Coralie, your name?' Barbie said. 'Go on. Tell me.'

'I want Dan to take me on a tour, show me round the house. Is that okay?'

'It's his house too, love. Go for it.'

'Let me put the last of this in.' Dan ladled in the dregs of his stock, turned off the burner and put the lid on. 'It'll be perfect when we get back.'

They ducked into the hall. 'Sorry he's so *massive*,' Dan said. 'I was thinking I should somehow warn you.'

'He's like someone out of a Guy Ritchie film—a loveable gangster.'

'An armed robber with a heart of gold. I won't bother with downstairs, it's all modern and boring. It's the zone for his sons and their wives—the guest rooms and bathroom and a little kitchen for when they stay. That's hardly ever—they live in Brooklyn. Come upstairs.'

'What's this, another reception?' Coralie pushed open the door. 'God, it's massive, it's stunning, it's beautiful.' The double doors between the two rooms were open. Every surface was painted red. Red walls, red ceilings, even the frames and shutters of the big bay window—surely unusual to have bay windows on two floors. The cornicing and ceiling roses had been left white. Unavoidably, the clear comparison was to the womb (if the womb was filled with wall-to-wall books, thick Persian rugs, and giant sofas on tall turned wooden legs). It made her own tasteful paint job—Farrow & Ball Mizzle—feel ludicrously drab.

'It's sort of like a library, and a study, and we can pull a big screen down and watch movies on the projector,' Dan said. 'Barbie did it all, long before I got here.'

'Who reads the books?'

'That's a bit offensive, Cor.'

'It's not you though, is it?'

'I read! You're not the only reader.'

'Fine, who *buys* the books?'

'Yeah, it's Barbie. He's one of those guys who walks into

Donlon Books, you know, that shop on Broadway Market? Throws down his black Amex and gets anything that catches his eye. And he does read them, just not in any order. Literally sometimes he's flipping between two or three at a time. A paragraph here, a chapter there. Like a book jukebox.'

'Dan!' a man's voice bellowed up the stairs.

Brother and sister both jumped.

'I've asked him not to do that,' Dan said.

They ran down the stairs together. Barbie was at the kitchen door. 'Danny, I'm worried about the risotto. Should it just be sitting on the stove like that?'

'I turned the hob off. But you're right, it's time to eat.'

Dan served it at the stove, then brought cheese to grate at the table. He shook up a dressing in a jam jar and splashed it over a salad. He elbowed Coralie. 'Why are you staring at me?'

She shrugged, because she was a bit drunk by then, and it was hard to admit that she was seeing him in a whole new light, just because now he was cherished and rich. It made her seem shallow. She *was* shallow.

The risotto was lovely: yellow from saffron, creamy, buttery, very rich and cheesy. 'It's delicious,' Coralie kept saying.

Barbie took the compliments as his own. 'I keep telling him he should open his own place.'

'But then you'd never see me,' Dan said.

'Okay, Coralie. I insist.' Barbie set down his fork. 'The name.'

'It's boring, really.' She paused to check he was listening. 'Coralie. It's just a small town in the middle of nowhere in Queensland. My dad grew up in a bigger town nearby. Not that big, really. Not that nearby.'

'Where was the bigger town?'

'Cairns? If you know it.'

'I don't, but I've been up north—to Darwin, with Danny.'

It was a betrayal. 'When?'

'After we…' Dan took a breath. 'Got married,' he said. 'We went to visit Mum's ashes. In October.'

Adam looked from Dan to Barbie. 'Married?'

'It was a visa thing,' Dan mumbled.

'Maybe for him it was!' Barbie rolled his eyes.

'Okay, no, it was a love thing, but my visa was going to run out, you know, Cor. I was on the youth one. You only get two years.'

'We should have brought champagne,' Adam said. 'Or at least more expensive wine. Well, congratulations, you two. Wow!' He dropped his spoon on the table and rushed around to hug Barbie. When it was Daniel's turn, he gave him a kiss on the cheek.

Daniel was watching Coralie. 'I hope you don't mind.'

'Did you have a party? And not invite me?'

'No, no. We had a Hackney Town Hall wedding. The witnesses were our neighbours.'

'Hackney Town Hall,' Adam said. 'That's what we're going to do.'

'At some point,' Coralie said.

Barbie hunched over his bowl. 'You haven't put a ring on it?'

The question was for Adam, but Coralie shook her head. 'I mean, my visa was from work—they did it for me. We didn't have to get married—for me to stay.'

But why hadn't they? They'd become a couple so easily, so

193

quickly, so romantically! She had moved in—an instant family with Zora. The renovation, even—making Adam's house ('my fucking house') into both their houses, with an investment of her care and money. And then Flo. All these things were bigger than a ceremony, they were the momentous daily commitment of *life*.

'Excuse me for a second, would you?' Adam did a funny stork-like walk to mime searching for a bathroom.

'Just in the hall, at the back,' Coralie said.

Barbie refilled Coralie's goblet. 'Why didn't you want to tell me where your name was from?'

'First, because you were doing something I fear and hate—asking me a question but not waiting for the answer.'

'Oh, sorry, I do care. It's my ADHD, I just—bounce around. Okay, go on, you said 'first'. What was second?'

'I don't like being attached to a town I know nothing about, and that no one knows anything about.'

'And?'

'And?' She was three goblets deep. 'I suppose I don't like my dad that much.'

Barbie looked at Dan. 'I see.'

'That's the reason we haven't got married,' she found herself saying. 'I can't imagine having him at the wedding.'

'Well,' Dan said. 'Same.'

'You didn't catch up with Roger when you went over?'

'God, no.'

'What's wrong with him?' Barbie's tone was pleasant and his facial expression, as he gazed at Coralie, seemed interested. 'I know what Dan says, but what do you say?'

194

'Ah.' She shrugged. 'I can't even remember now, really.'

'You were the good one,' Barbie said. 'And Dan was the bad one.'

'I don't think…'

'Enough, enough.' Barbie dusted off his hands. 'Enough of the hard questions from me. You're a writer, Dan tells me. How's the writing going?'

Coralie dropped her head into her hands and moaned.

'Look at you!' Barbie laughed. 'You're like an oyster when the lemon is squirted on. Don't shrivel away! Just tell me!'

'Ugh,' Coralie said. 'It's fine.'

'Writer's block? No ideas?'

'I have ideas!' Tears of protest rose to her eyes. 'The world is…' She mimed being dizzy. 'What's the point?' Of reading, she meant as well, not just of writing, when no one had time to think.

'You need to get your shit together,' Barbie said.

'He's being kind,' Dan quickly clarified.

Before she could reply, Adam was back. 'Barbie, bloody hell, what's the story with the lav gallery? Those are some total A-listers.'

'The talent—my talent business. I was a manager, a fixer, that's how I made a crust.'

With a waiter's discretion, Dan cleared up around them, as Barbie told the story of how he made and lost his fortune. He was a Londoner by birth, and grew up around Clerkenwell and Farringdon.

'That's near…' Where Coralie worked, she was going to say, but Barbie wasn't listening.

His parents were from Sicily. When they moved to London, his mother worked as a seamstress, and his father in one of the Italian cafes on Clerkenwell Road. Barbie was smart, and everyone could see it, but he did shit at school and got himself into trouble, beating up anyone who called him thick. Left school early, got into music, made himself useful, good at all the practical things: venues, tickets, merch, security. Made himself more and more useful to the more and more famous.

'Anyway,' he said, 'that was how I became a success. But it wasn't easy. My wife was American, my little sons were settled in New York. Every time I came to London, I went for these huge, long walks when I was jetlagged, along all the big main roads, looking for the same kind of place where I grew up, where I could feel the road rumbling and the traffic kept me company. When I found them, I bought them. Mare Street, Old Ford Road, Graham Road, this place—you can hear the traffic now.'

They all paused to listen. Something huge drove by. The chandelier crystals shimmered.

His whole life had been based between London and New York but what had happened next was that he'd stopped being able to fly—scared to death, crying like a child, bundled off the plane in a wheelchair—unless he was knocked out like an elephant being airlifted from the savannah, 'and I *was* an elephant by then, too, twice the size I am now.' He rubbed his ribs and belly. 'The talent didn't like it, they need their guy on the ground, they want to feel like they're the only one with problems. The wife didn't like it, having me at home all the time. I drank more, I ate more, I stopped going out. The boys were getting to the end of their schooling, it was time to choose where to die. I chose England. I sold the business, gave the money to the boys, said goodbye to the wife and moved into this place.' He had tears in his long black lashes.

'But you didn't die, did you?' Daniel said sweetly.

Barbie passed the back of his hand over his eyes. 'Nope! Fifty-six now. Fit and well. Married to the love of my life. I never thought I'd see it.'

He clasped Dan's hand, and they leaned their heads together.

Humbled, Coralie and Adam held hands too.

'How did you manage the flight to Australia?' Adam asked.

'Drugged to my fuckin' gills.'

'Speaking of...' Dan murmured.

Coralie pulled her phone out of her pocket. Well past ten. They'd told Miss Camilla they'd be back no later than eleven. 'Oh, we should—'

'I've made something lovely and special,' Dan said.

'You'll *love* this,' Barbie said.

Dan went over to the drinks cabinet and returned carrying a silver salver with ten perfect chocolate balls balanced on top. 'I'm still experimenting...' he started to say.

The little poodle, who'd been snoozing on a kilim cushion, trembled, arched her back, sprang to her feet, whined and spun in a circle. 'Ah,' Barbie said. 'Madonna needs to cut a record. I'll take her out the back. Don't wait for me. Come on, luvvie. Come on.' Madonna followed him into the hall. They could hear the bolts on the back door click and slide.

'Dan,' Adam said. 'I mean, what a triumph. The meal, the house, the love story. But we still don't know how you met?'

'He kept coming into the restaurant and asking for the chef's table. That's when you sit in the kitchen with me, and I feed you bits and bobs. After a while, I said it might be easier, and cheaper, just to ask me on a date. So he did.'

'You're a great cook, it must be said.' With a single fluid motion, Adam flipped a chocolate into his mouth.

Daniel started to speak but his words were drowned out by a horrifying cry, a guttural roar of fear and outrage. They all leapt to their feet. 'Barbie!' Dan cried.

At the back of the hall, they were confronted by a ghastly sight. Barbie was cradling a shivering Madonna in his arms, blood pouring down his face and even into his eyes from a long, deep scratch on his bald head. 'She's okay,' Barbie said. 'She's okay.'

Daniel burst into tears.

Barbie lowered Madonna to the floor. She put her nose down and ran back towards her kilim. 'A fuckin' fox in the garden. Got the dog in his jaws, right around her neck. I had to prise them open like...' He wildly mimed pulling them apart. 'She's okay, she's okay, that's my blood, not hers.'

'Did he bite you? Barbie,' Coralie said. 'You'll get rabies.'

Barbie leaned over with his hands on his knees. 'It's all from my head. The fox ran away, then I stood up and scalped myself on a fuckin' tree. Jesus Christ. Oh, hey.' Daniel fell into his embrace. 'Hey.'

'I'm going to make tea.' Coralie took Adam by the elbow. 'Come on, we'll make the tea.'

'We'll go upstairs and clean up. Won't we?' Barbie said gently to Dan, who nodded.

In the kitchen, Adam brought the chocs over to where Coralie was boiling the kettle. He leaned back against the bench and ate another one with a groan of intense pleasure. 'Have some,' he said. 'Your brother's amazing.'

Coralie bit into one. It was hard on the outside but soft inside. There was a strange quality to the taste. 'Remember when we bought that coffee blend from Climpsons? The one that we hated?'

'The tasting notes said *vegetal*,' Adam said. 'It was like drinking the canal.'

'That's what this tastes like, but in a nice way. Is it bad to have another one?'

'I don't think so? There were ten, and four of us?'

She popped another choc in her mouth and pushed the silver tray away. 'That blood was the scariest thing I've ever seen in a private home.'

'I never want to hear a scream like that for the rest of my days.'

'I kept trying to see how deep the scalping had been. Was it a flap?'

'It wasn't a *flap*,' Adam said. 'A flap!' he suddenly operatically sang. 'Head wounds bleed like mad, I found that out at school when I walked into a fence.'

Coralie poured hot water over the leaves in the teapot. They made a crinkling sound, then were drowned. Weird, she felt a bit sorry for them. 'Poor Barbie's the injured one, and he's up there having to look after Dan,' she said. 'He should be in hospital, getting stitches and a tetanus shot.'

'Maybe we should leave them to it,' Adam said. 'I wouldn't mind a tea though.'

They started their teas. No sign of their hosts. Coralie checked her phone. 'Eleven, poor Miss Camilla. I'm going to creep up and say goodbye.'

'Dan?' she called in the hall. 'Barbie?'

They weren't in the library. In the hall, she mounted the stairs to the top floor, the floor she hadn't seen yet. She became aware of a low murmur, a deep rumbling sound, that could only be intimate and private, but something drove her to find its source. In the acid-green front bedroom, Barbie lay on the massive bed like a pharaoh, towel around his waist like a skirt. The long scrape on his bald head was clean but looked quite sore. Dan was cuddled up to him, his eyes closed, face resting on Big Man's rising and falling chest.

'To come to the end of a time of anxiety and fear!' Barbie said. 'To feel the cloud that hung over us lift and disperse—the cloud that dulled the heart and made happiness no more than a memory! This at least is one joy that must have been known by almost every living creature.'

He was reading from *Watership Down*.

Coralie backed out silently and tiptoed down the stairs.

The walk home was strange, like she was inside Google Maps, clicking herself further and further down the road. 'Don't you feel like you're in Street View?' She turned to Adam. 'Clicking along the road.'

'But on Street View you don't see the stars.'

'No, you're right, I *can* see them,' she said. 'In the sky.'

Inside, Miss Camilla had the vacant eyes and messed-up hair of someone on a long-haul flight. Coralie pressed a wad of cash into her hand. 'You're wonderful,' she urged. 'You're a wonderful person.'

Upstairs, Flo was on her tummy, her mouth a perfect O where her thumb had slipped out.

On the top floor, Zora had fallen asleep with her nightlight on. It had been years since she'd seen the stars and planets slowly revolving on the ceiling. Coralie stared up. A tremor of pure delight ran through her at the shadows made by her hands in the flickering light: flowers, birds, bees, just like the insect wallpaper at Big Man's house.

She ran a bath, undressed, and watched the water pour from the taps. Steam billowed; the mirror fogged over. The window at Railroad, when she'd first told Adam about Richard. The waterfall plunging to the pool at Florence Falls. She sent a picture to Adam, to see if he remembered too. Before the two ticks had turned blue, he was in the bathroom with her.

'Did you see it,' she said. 'Did you get it?'

'Your sext? I certainly did.'

It wasn't a sext, but she could see how he'd made that mistake—she could see everything, and suddenly realised there were no mistakes, that nothing and no one was inherently wrong, and nothing and no one was inherently bad. 'So funny,' she said. 'I love you.'

She lay on the bed in her towel. Adam unwrapped her like a present. After a while, a realisation dawned on her, literally rose in her mind like the sun: what if *she* could penetrate *him*? On top, she incorporated his penis inside her, where it became part of her body, and as she moved she focused on the sensation she imagined at the base, roots like tree roots, where the forest

201

meets the sea, all the nerve fibres, electrical pulses, phospho-rescent sea creatures, tendrils trailing. 'You're inside me,' he said. 'You're stirring me.'

They came, but she didn't want to separate. 'Don't pull out,' she said. 'You're part of me.' They rolled extremely carefully onto their sides, still attached, facing one another.

'Why did you bring Zora's nightlight in?' she asked after a while.

'I didn't,' he said. 'Where has the roof gone?'

Weeks later, Daniel still felt bad about the shroom truffles. But Coralie didn't. She was pregnant.

15

2019

It was probably a bit of a tragedy she hadn't done an NCT class the first time around. Or was it an NCT *group*? The National Childbirth Trust groups or classes were a rite of passage for middle-class mums—it was where they learned that having a C-section meant they'd failed birth, and using a bottle meant they'd failed their baby (Coralie had to work that out for herself!).

They were also a matchmaking service for women who lived locally with similar due dates. Alice had made two close friends in hers: one who worked in art PR, and one (on Navarino Road) who was so rich she had a utility-room shower for her dogs. The three of them went to Clissold leisure centre every week for dippy eggs and soft play. Coralie'd had no friends on her first mat leave—aside from Florence. But beyond the fact she was an immigrant who hadn't known about NCT, why hadn't she joined a mothers' group? 'You're a cat who walks alone,' Adam said. 'Anyway, you were reading it all in books.'

At the time of Coralie's first pregnancy, her own mother had recently died of a gruesome abdominal illness. There had therefore been no question of *optimising* birth; it was simply something to survive. Perhaps there'd been a little feeling inside her too that, as a stepmother, she wasn't having a pure first-baby experience. Unlike other new mums, if she didn't know how to change a nappy, she could ask Adam.

But with this second baby (last baby) she had a craving to do everything better and properly. She had googled 'Hackney birth classes' to discover the Thursday-night classes on Eleanor Road. Birth, breastfeeding and parenting were covered, and there was gentle pregnancy yoga too. Unlike most courses, which went on for the whole final trimester, this one took place over three ninety-minute sessions, which was good, because as the first Thursday approached she began to feel sick at the thought of missing Florence's bedtime.

I wish I wasn't doing this, she messaged both Adam and Alice.

It will be brilliant, Adam wrote back. *Think how fun it'll be to google all the mums.*

You have to do it, Alice replied. *You need a new local Mom Friend. I feel like a dead wife in a romance movie...finding her husband a new love from ~ beyond the grave ~* (Nicky had hit a hot streak producing other artists. They were spending most of the year in LA.)

After work, on the second Thursday in July, she carried on past the nursery bus stop on Mare Street. While she ached to see her daughter and cuddle her, it was a relief not to have to sprint after Florence on the scooter, living in fear that either of them (or both) would fall and knock their teeth out. At thirty-two weeks, Coralie was too massive to run, and doing the sideways lean to drag the scooter along was even worse. These days her entire rib cage creaked as it strained above what she hated calling her 'bump'. When she lay on her left side in bed—this was what the books seemed to recommend—her pelvis was so wide that her right leg sloped down like Mount Fuji, which made her hip joint painfully burn. If she rolled on her back in her sleep, she had nightmares about being choked or crushed. If she ate after 8 p.m., she woke at midnight, her throat corroded by reflux. Florence now slept through (thank God). Coralie still woke at five.

There was something slightly zombie film about getting to the end of Reading Lane and seeing pregnant women lumber from three directions. Coralie stayed on the other side of Eleanor Road so she didn't have to chat, but sped up to enter the front gate with the others so she didn't have to knock. An enormous lavender bush spread across the front fence of the compact three-storey terrace. She'd brought Florence past it scores of times on the way to the park. As the other women chatted, she studied the facade of grey bricks. The intricate stained-glass windows looked original.

'Shoes off, up to the top floor, bathroom on the first floor,' came a confident voice from behind the open door. (It was a kind of voice she thrilled to; she was instantly back at school: 'Girls! Take out *Medieval Women* and turn to page fifteen!') Too shy to look around, Coralie inspected the floorboards. The varnish had been ruined by decades of traffic. She longed to get a sander and tackle them herself. (It was still her cherished ambition to have the white paint buffed off the boards on Wilton Way). At the first-floor landing, she found a queue for the bathroom. She checked her phone and, with the focused air of someone responding to an urgent work task, WhatsApped Adam that she was freaking out.

If you hate it, just leave, he replied. *But I promise you won't hate it! CYK!*

Upstairs, the top floor was a surprise, a church hall-like space with no dividing walls. The ceiling had been removed between it and the attic, revealing the contours of the pitched roof. As well as the front and back windows, four skylights let in the burnished early-evening sun. Dust motes danced and shimmered. Coralie sneezed.

'Take a cushion, take a place! Don't be shy, you're all new, form a circle, find a patch of carpet, sit down and stretch out, lean right over, touch your ankles if you can, your knees if you can't. If you watch a baby, the baby's toes are never just a big block or lump, but each one is separated out. Free each toe. Wriggle-wriggle!'

Finally, from the safety of her own little patch of carpet, she was able to look at people's faces. There was Fiona Doherty, the birth teacher, in her sixties perhaps, muscled calves in leggings, a long chambray shirt over the top, the sleeves rolled up to her elbows. A bandana held back her thick grey curls. Her tanned, expressive face had wrinkles of all kinds: laughter lines, frown lines, diagonal quizzical ones above each eyebrow. 'Draw your knees up to make a bridge,' Fiona cried. 'Reach up! Look at the ceiling! Deep breath! Ahh! Now stretch out one leg, draw the other up in a triangle shape. Roll around, loosen the hip!'

Coralie peeped around at the others. One woman, with her eyes closed, looked to be Coralie's age. Her face was normal size, but her features (all beautiful) were enormous, like a movie star crossed with a frog. Her huge eyes snapped open, catching Coralie mid-stare. She grimaced in sympathy. Coralie smiled with relief.

'We'll go around the circle,' Fiona said. 'Your name, how many weeks, journey to conception, was it easy, hard? Is it your first baby, any complications, and, finally, one hope and one fear.'

Jesus! Coralie's mind went blank. She missed the first woman's introduction almost entirely. 'And I suppose my biggest fear is that I'll have to have a caesarean,' the woman said. 'I don't want that kind of start for my baby. And my hope is, um, that I'll have a girl.'

'Thank you, Charlotte,' Fiona said. 'I'm noticing that you're not in control of either of those things, are you? Whether you'll need a medicalised birth, or whether the baby's a boy or a girl. Well, during the course, we'll talk about things you can control, so I hope you'll find that helpful. Next?'

(*Hi, I'm Coralie*, Coralie started practising silently.)

'Hi, I'm Sam,' the next person said. 'In my normal life, I'm a man.' He shrugged and waved a hand in front of his face and torso. 'But my wife can't get pregnant, it took us years to find out, and the only option was for me to carry. I'm thirty-two weeks, I cry every day, it's worse than puberty for messing with my head. My biggest fear is that the midwives call me 'Mum'.

Actually, my biggest fear is that they'll call the trainees in to stare at me. I'm having a C-section, it's already scheduled. Sorry if that's anyone's worst nightmare.' He rolled his eyes, but not *at* Charlotte.

'Sam, the birthing parent's in charge at the hospital. Anyone extra who wants to come in needs your permission. That's one thing I want all of you to take with you when you leave. And your hope?'

Sam had taken off his cap to rearrange his hair. For a moment he kept it over his face. 'I just hope it works,' he said. 'It took so long, and it was so, so hard. If something happens to the baby, my wife's heart will be broken, and I'll die.'

Fiona nodded. 'Thirty-two weeks, that baby is already cooked. You could give birth tonight and odds are they'd make it. But try and last the distance if you can: they're laying down lots of lovely fat.'

Sam nodded, grateful.

'Next?'

'I'm Lydia.' It was woman with the big eyes and smile. 'I'm thirty-four weeks, and this is my first baby. I'm having her on my own, using the sperm of a donor.' *The sperm of a donor.* What a precise way to put it. Coralie regarded her with respect.

'Yes,' Lydia went on quietly, almost to herself. 'I was a writer first, freelance. Journalism, essays. But then, when I was thirty-five, I suddenly thought, *Someone needs to take charge here, or I will* not *be having a baby.* Spreadsheets, I had to work out how to make them. I chose teaching, for the mat leave and school holidays. And the pension, I *love* having a pension; I check it every day on my phone.'

Sam gave an emphatic nod. The whole group was leaning forward.

'Two Novembers in a row I tried to conceive, and both times I missed the window. I needed an August baby, to save me a year of paid childcare. I'm forty now. Last November was probably my last chance, that's what it felt like, anyway.' Lydia placed a long, elegant hand on her bump. 'And it worked. My hope is that everything goes okay, medically. My fear is that a part of my child will always be a stranger to me, and they'll grow up feeling like a science experiment, rather than the product of love.'

'Swap legs, circle around the other hip. Anyone here a lesbian?' Everyone glanced around. No one raised their hands. 'That's funny—Hackney? Normally quite a few. Well, one thing you find with same sex-parents. The baby comes to resemble them both, bio and non-bio. How? Expressions. You don't just have genes in common, it's that daily face-to-face contact. Even if you share *no* genes, they become like you. Baby mirrors you, you mirror baby. There will be nothing about your baby that's strange. You longed for her, even before she was conceived, and did everything to make it happen. It's the greatest love story in the world. Next!'

Tears had come to Coralie's eyes from 'the greatest love story in the world'. 'Um.' She blinked them away. 'I'm Coralie? I'm turning thirty-six pretty soon. Oh, the baby! Thirty-two weeks. This is my second baby, I have a little girl, and I'm missing her bedtime right now.' She cleared her throat. 'Sorry! My first birth wasn't that great, I found myself getting scared. My hope is that this one's better.'

'And your fear?'

'Umm—everything else.'

There was a comforting sound, a quiet, warm swelling of group laughter.

'It's a very scary time,' Fiona said. 'Next!'

Back home, Adam had made spaghetti bolognese. The kitchen smelled of burnt garlic. The outline of each piece of onion was clearly visible, which meant they hadn't been cooked long enough. The tinned tomatoes were still chunky and vivid red. But the meat was properly brown, and he'd grated a lot of cheddar. Starving, she asked for seconds. He served it to her, gratified.

She waved her phone. 'Just updating Alice.'

'Did you find your new Hackney wife?'

'A woman called Lydia, maybe? A single mum. Hang on, who's that?'

There was a tiny TV in the kitchen, which Adam used to watch *Newsnight* when he was 'doing the dishwasher' (his main item of housework, much mentioned by him). On screen, a beefy white man was pushing through throngs of other beefy white men. He was wearing a homemade T-shirt that said, in white letters on a black background: CONVICTED OF JOURNALISM.

'That's Tommy Robinson.' Adam turned the volume up on *Sky News*. 'The far-right guy.'

'To the judges at the Old Bailey, he's Stephen Yaxley-Lennon, and they've already found him to be in contempt of court...' the journalist said over the footage. 'Arrested outside

Leeds Crown Court last year, he was broadcasting live on social media about a sex abuse case.'

On the screen, the reporter held the microphone up to Robinson in the crowd. 'I'm telling you!' His face was red with fury: 'I am being sent to jail for doing what you just done!'

Adam pressed the mute button. 'He's asked Donald Trump for asylum.'

'Um, why?'

'He's says he's being persecuted as a citizen journalist.'

Coralie put her arms around him. 'I'm getting you that shirt for your birthday.'

Adam laughed, and they hugged for a long time, but, when they separated, he looked rueful, grey and tired. When he opened the dishwasher, it was with the grunt he used to signal that something was not okay, and that it was probably her fault, or at least required her attention.

She paused on her way up to the bath. 'Do you want to talk to me about anything?'

Adam was blank.

'Because you've got your blank face on and you're making your little resentful grunts.'

Adam grunted. 'I'm not resentful,' he said in a resentful voice.

'Is it the dishwasher? You hate it?'

He wedged the pasta pot into the bottom tray. 'No one *likes* doing the dishwasher.'

'This is your last chance...' She was walking backwards. 'To reveal your emotions...' She had reached the pantry. 'Or stay forever silent.'

'Journalism,' Adam said. 'I don't really feel like I do it. Bits and bobs. The newsletter. The podcast. It's not exactly Woodward and Bernstein.'

'You write *books*,' Coralie said. 'People would kill for your career.'

'It doesn't seem very *serious*.'

Coralie had read lots of novels about this—Updikes, Roths, that one where Leonardo DiCaprio couldn't move to Paris because Kate Winslet got knocked up (at least, that was the movie version). She could all too easily inhabit the mind of a man in his forties, one who felt disappointed, stymied perhaps—cockblocked. Men were supposed to pursue, hunt, fight and excel. Cooking for his pregnant wife, loading the dishwasher—constraints on his freedom, any at all, restrictions on his God-given rights and ability to go out and do anything he wanted, at any time. It lowered his testosterone, made him less of a man, could actually *kill him*. Domesticity! That was to blame, that was behind the so-called stalling of his career, that was what his tsks and sighs were conveying to her in the kitchen. Nothing to do with the changing media landscape, that all the old certainties had been torn away, and that unprecedented access to behind-the-scenes info had revealed every job in the world to be shit. It was *her* fault, that's what he was saying.

'Actually,' she said, 'I think you're doing really well.'

He shrugged, but not angrily.

And it was a measure of some new maturity, as well as how tired she was, that she simply left it at that.

*

Upstairs, Florence was sleeping like a baby (on her back, with her arms in a triangle above her head).

In bed, Adam folded himself around Coralie, both of them lying on their sides. 'I can't believe tomorrow's the last normal pick-up.'

It would be the last Friday of Zora's primary-school life, although school continued till Wednesday of the following week. After the summer holidays, they'd agreed with Marina that she'd catch the train to Wilton Way each weekend on her own. The change couldn't be more significant.

'I don't want to think about it,' Coralie said. 'She has to stop growing right now.'

Inside her, her new baby kicked and swirled. A boy this time. His face had been perfect in the sonogram, pointy-nosed and elegant like Dan's. She still had years of children being children in her house. Decades. Sometimes it was a terrifying thought. But that night she found it a comfort.

The weekend was so fucking horrible it was a relief to drop Florence at nursery on Monday and get the bus to work. Coralie had never seen Zora act like that before. A friend's party had been in the diary for weeks, and the present (lip balms in four flavours and a book token) was wrapped and ready on the mantelpiece. But when the time had come, Zora had refused to go. She'd screamed at Coralie and Adam, stomped up the stairs, and slammed the door. Just as they thought they'd calmed her down, some other little thing had set her off. She'd been unrecognisable—either shouting or in tears for two days. She was due to be at Wilton Way for the first two weeks of the school holidays. Coralie was starting to dread it.

At work, perhaps fortunately, there was no time to think about Zora. Stefan nabbed her before she had time to put her bag down: 'Vanessa Andorra's having second thoughts.'

She hadn't wanted to waste any maternity leave before a baby, but thirty-two weeks, on the cusp of thirty-three, was far too far along to still be expected to work. It was inhumane. She wished she'd never had the shrooms by mistake. In the days that followed, before she knew she was pregnant, something else was also gestating, an answer to a problem: the three-year sponsorship deal signed by Futurum, the gallery, and the agency under Antoinette. It was inconceivable the parties would renew the agreement when it ended this summer. Per the contract, however, the final event still had to be held. In those heady post-shroom days, when parts of her brain lit up and connected in new ways, Coralie had come up with what she believed could be a solution: Feel Tank. Get it? Like riffing on a think tank? (Sadly, when she googled it, she found it was not original.) Anyway, Futurum would be paying for a weekend festival of interactive exhibitions, workshops and public events on the topic of emotional dynamics in public life.

It hadn't been difficult to persuade high-minded intellectuals and principled activists to speak, for a large fee, at a much-admired contemporary art gallery in N1. It had been a lot harder once it was revealed that the event's sponsor was Futurum. The agency promised zero interference, no topic off the table, no restrictions on what might be said about climate, fossil fuels, even the company itself. Slowly, the programme

214

built up and filled out into something she could almost be proud of. The merch was also great. Tote bags, patches, badges, posters—all covered in the word FEELINGS. The launch on Friday night would be catered by a Syrian refugee charity kitchen (the food was stunning; Coralie had tested it). So what was Vanessa's fucking problem?

Stefan was walking and talking like someone on *The West Wing*. 'We're doing this in my office.'

My office.

Stefan's iPhone was on his desk. He took it off mute. 'Vanessa, I've got Coralie.'

'Hi, Vanessa,' Coralie said, in a way that was polite but also mildly puzzled, because the launch was this coming Friday, and everything was in the can.

'I don't know about this, Coralie,' Vanessa said. 'I didn't think it would be so big.'

'Seven hundred thousand pounds,' Coralie said. 'Seven months' work. Ha-ha! Yes, it's quite big.'

'People on Instagram are annoyed. And so are my friends. Look at the programme, I say. All that left-wing, Goldsmiths, hipster academic shit! But they can't get behind the sponsor. I'm getting emails. My niece says I'm the problem!'

The baby kicked high up near Coralie's heart. For a moment, it mimicked the feeling of fear, her heartbeat ratcheting up a notch. But she didn't feel scared, not really. The event would be over on Sunday. In two weeks, she'd be on mat leave. Nothing mattered as much as her baby, not even, for the moment, the fate of the earth. (Let alone Vanessa's finer feelings about a problem of her own making.)

'Let's think about where we were in December,' Coralie said in a soothing voice. 'Locked into the Futurum contract, unable to pull the pin. But we chose to focus on what the gallery does best, sparking conversations and transforming culture. That's the path we chose together. Now you have a programme of events that embraces complexity, ambiguity, the grey areas of life—where art happens! Art *and* change.'

This was easy for her to say as a copywriter for a brand agency solving a comms problem. There's no way she'd boldly advocate for this approach as *herself*. She'd stopped posting on Twitter altogether, so great was her fear she'd be seen as too radical, not radical enough, or (this was also bad now) too *medium*.

Vanessa gave an anxious moan. 'But what if protestors show up?'

'Let them! Discuss it! Invite them in!'

The chat went on for a few minutes, but Vanessa's wobble was over. Stefan hung up with a sigh of relief. 'Well,' he said in a loud voice, 'what do you think of *that*?'

As Coralie stared at him in surprise, a funny sound came from the work landline on his desk. *Clap, clap, clap.*

'Brava,' came a familiar voice on speaker. 'Coralie! Brava.'

Her chest was an ice shelf, and a crack ran through the middle.

'Your protégé, Richard,' Stefan said.

'Well,' Richard purred down the line from Sydney. 'She certainly learned from the best.'

Coralie didn't hear anything else. She walked to her desk, unplugged her laptop, picked up her bag, and left.

She wasn't faking it, the thermometer said thirty-eight degrees. She didn't go into work on Tuesday or Wednesday, and missed Zora's final pick-up from school. When Zora crashed into the house and rushed up the stairs, she felt each stomp like a punch. '*Zora*,' she called from her dark bedroom. 'Please!'

'Please *what?*' Zora stood in the doorway, a frown on her beautiful face.

'Please don't storm around, I have a headache.'

'Fine!' Then she did something Coralie would never have guessed in a million years. She slammed the door behind her.

I've asked Marina, Adam WhatsApped from downstairs. *She doesn't know what's wrong.*

One of their strategies for not buying Zora a phone was letting her text on her iPad. She could use it to message Adam from Marina's, and Marina from Adam's, but if she wanted to be in touch with her friends, she had to ask an adult to text her friend's adults. This would all change when she went to secondary. *Everyone* was getting a phone. But now she composed a text to Zora's iPad, relieved not to brave the dragon in its den. *Raspberry sorbet in the freezer,* she wrote. *What do you have planned for tomorrow? Do you want me to ask if you can visit Daniel and Madonna?*

(Daniel had hosted Adam's birthday at Barbie's last Christmas Eve, and let Zora flame the pudding with his lighter. She loved watching movies far too old for her on the big screen in their red sitting room: *Mean Girls*, *Titanic* and *Clueless*.

The grey dots showed up, bounced, and disappeared. Left

on read by an eleven-year-old?

Then a one-word reply appeared. *Yes.*

The next day, Daniel appeared after breakfast with the poodle tucked under his arm. Coralie looked at him meaningfully as he escorted Zora out the door. He shrugged, and she wasn't sure if he was saying *I'll see what I can do,* or *I refuse your mission to find out what's wrong.*

Coralie was going in to work for the first time since Richard Pickard had spoken to her on the landline at work.

At the office, she leaned round Stefan's door. 'Banh mi today?'

He gestured regretfully to the little fridge under his desk. 'I'm on a juice cleanse.'

'Okay.'

'Coralie!'

She turned back.

'Maybe just half,' he said. 'Tofu.'

Later, they took their lunch to the lavender-scented green space of Spa Fields.

She stumbled through the story.

'I'm sorry that happened to you,' Stefan said formally.

Maybe she hadn't told the story well enough. 'It's confusing,' she empathised with Stefan. 'The not-actually-having-sex part. But I think that's what we're all working out now, or I am. It's not about sex, but power.'

'He's a very powerful man. Hey, listen. Coralie. Richard got excited about the idea—about Feel Tank. He's coming for the press day.'

'But it's my thing.'

'Our thing.'

'But can't you stop him?'

Stefan pressed the side of his phone to make it light up. 'He landed seven hours ago. He's napping at Dean Street Townhouse. He's coming to the office at three. He wants to go over the materials.'

'My materials,' Coralie said.

'The agency's materials.'

She looked down at the bench between them, where Stefan's banh mi lay still in its wrapper. 'I don't think my cold is better,' she said. 'I came back from sick leave too early.'

'Yes,' Stefan said. 'You don't look very well.'

She got up, waiting for him to say *Stop, stop*, that he'd talk to Richard, he'd send him home.

'Take it easy,' he said instead.

She blundered back to the office with tears in her eyes. The Richard stuff had been nothing compared with her first friend in London *not caring*. They had started off the same, two twenty-nine-year-olds knocking back wine, gossiping, tip-toeing around Antoinette and having a laugh. Now Stefan wore Raf Simons suits to client events and was named industry organ *Campaign*'s 'Creative Leader of the Year'. If he was a monster, Coralie had helped create him: she'd ghost-written all his guest columns. She wanted to run back to Spa Fields, to make him understand and fix things. But she was too pregnant for that sort of thing, too tired and too sad.

Before she left, she took her fancy tea bags, her spare make-up, the gym kit she hadn't used in about three years, the pen holder Zora had made her, and all of Florence's nursery art. Incredible. Two and half years her darling daughter had been at nursery. So—why? So she could clock in at the brand factory? Unvalued by her colleagues (even her so-called friend), or by society (grappling, or more accurately, not grappling, with the existential problems of inequality and climate change)? Taking the *fucking* piss.

She spread the rest of her stuff out so her desk still looked occupied (because what would it do to her mat leave if they thought she'd left for good?). But she knew she'd never set foot in the agency again. It was seven years since the first time Richard had forced her out, almost to the day.

16

'Take a cushion, find a square of carpet, stretch out, touch your ankles if you can. No—you're too far along for that. Touch your knees instead. Wriggle the toes, spread them out, baby toes. Who remembers last week? In pregnancy, some of us bundle up all the fear and danger, and what do we do? Project it onto the medical professionals, those nasty people trying to control us, and our bodies! Who's having a home birth?'

Charlotte and one other woman raised their hands.

'Some of us think the call is coming from inside the house!' Fiona said. 'The danger is *within*, something will go wrong with our bodies, and the only thing that can help is a nice doctor in clogs and scrubs! Hospital?'

Coralie, Sam, Lydia and two other women raised their hands.

'Surely the truth lies in the middle! Midwives, doctors,

drugs, they're there to help. But you, the birthing parent, you have your own strength too. Intuition! A mother's knowledge! Parental instinct, I mean. Sorry, Sam.'

'It's fine.'

'We talked about the baby, going from its beautiful, warm, perfectly regulated kingdom, out into this horrible world, where Boris Johnson will be prime minister; our world with its loud noises, bright lights, and cold winds, although not today, this heat is rather womb-like. Leg up in a triangle, lean forward, round and round, massaging the hip. The baby will be disturbed by the change, and, after giving birth—so will you. Two disturbed people. Is that a disaster? Do they take away your parent badge?'

'No, no,' the pregnant people murmured.

'No, they don't, and while I don't wish discombobulation on anyone, bone tiredness, the kind of sleep deprivation that leads to hallucinations—no one wants any of that, but is it bad? Is it the end of the world? It's not, because by being in that state, disintegrated, you get a sense of how the baby's feeling. Slowly, slowly, you build yourselves back up, together. Change legs!'

Coralie and Lydia had both worn Birkenstocks, so they avoided the pile-up of women (and Sam) sitting on the stairs to put their shoes on. Outside on the pavement, Coralie gestured towards Fiona's house. 'Maybe *too* helpful?'

'Mmm,' Lydia agreed. 'Learning too many new things at once is bad for my self-esteem.'

'I feel a bit ripped off. Fiona's obviously the expert; why can't *she* deliver my baby?'

'Maybe she could raise it as well. We can collect them when they're eighteen. Surprise! It's me, your mother.'

'Where are you going, are you nearby?'

Lydia pointed at a tall tower-block at the end of the street. 'I'm up there, tenth floor.'

'Do you overlook the park?'

'I do!'

'Lucky. Will you have a maternity leave?'

'Yeah—you?'

'Yep.' Coralie looked down and pointed one sandalled toe. 'Maybe we'll…'

'I'd like that!'

She was halfway down Wilton Way, thrilled, before she remembered Zora.

'Yes?' Dan answered the phone in a pretend impatient way.

'Yes, Dan, okay! How's Zora?'

'Tell her I want to sleep over,' she heard Zora say in the background.

'I'll say no if it's too much,' Coralie said quietly. 'I don't mind being the bad guy.'

'I want her to stay, and she wants to stay!'

'Then I'll get her in the morning.'

'What about work?'

'I can't say strongly enough: fuck work.'

'Okay!'

'I've got to do something after the nursery run. I'll come and get her at eleven.'

One crazy thing about where they lived was that, despite Hackney being miles from the sea, flocks of seagulls regularly flew over, shrieking. It was Ridley Road Market, all the fish laid out on ice at the stalls. The birds couldn't resist. With the warmth on her face, the seagulls screaming, Zora in safe hands, her boy gently kicking inside her—everything felt like it could be okay.

At home, dinner wasn't made. Adam was full of apologies. He'd done Florence's pick-up, and given *her* dinner, obviously! *And* put her to bed! But then he'd got a call from the journalist Boris Johnson had once planned to kneecap.

'Hang on,' Coralie said. 'What?'

'But I can go on my bike and get Turkish?'

It was already after eight. Having a mixed grill was begging for a sleepless night. She found herself near tears.

'Ah, the reflux thing,' Adam said.

'It's the reflux thing, the tiredness thing, starvation, and being let down. You don't even know what my day was like!'

'I'll make toast,' he said. 'Right now.'

Darius Guppy (seemingly his real name) was an Eton-educated ne'er-do-well, at one point—could this be right?—jailed for faking a jewellery heist. He'd been caught on tape asking his schoolfriend Boris Johnson for the address of a journalist he wanted to bash. As she ate her toast at the kitchen table, Adam read out the transcript of a secretly recorded phone call.

JOHNSON: How badly hurt will he be?

GUPPY: He will not have a broken limb or broken arm, and he will not be put into intensive care or anything like that. He will probably get a couple of black eyes and a cracked rib.

JOHNSON: A cracked rib.

GUPPY: Nothing which you didn't suffer in rugby, OK? But he'll get scared and that's what I want him to do. I want him to get scared.

(They went on in this vein for a bit longer.)

JOHNSON: OK, Darry, I've said I'll do it. I'll do it, don't worry.

GUPPY: Boris, I really mean it, I love you and I will owe you this.

'That's mental,' Coralie said. 'Did the journalist get bashed?'

'No, but I'm getting him on the pod to talk about how scared he was, and how sickening it is that Boris will be PM next week, et cetera.'

'I feel like other things he's done have been worse. But when *was* all this, when was the secret tape from?'

'1990.'

'Oh.'

'News is news! Do you still have to go in early for the Feel Thing press thing?'

'No,' Coralie said. 'I don't.'

'Good, because I've got an early record tomorrow.'

And then his phone rang, and he answered it, and that was the end of that.

Later, in the bath, she was glad he hadn't followed up about her day. It meant she could carry out her plans without discussion.

At first, she wondered if she'd come to the wrong place. Tucked around the Haggerston side of Broadway Market, it looked like any other community hall. Through the security grilles on the high windows, she spotted paper cut-outs in the shape of children's hands. This was it. She rang the bell. Not a sound came from inside. She knocked. After a full minute, a small woman (grey hair cut short like an acorn cap) came to the door, an expression of polite curiosity on her face.

'Sorry,' Coralie said.

'No need to apologise.'

'I just, sort of, urgently need to enrol my daughter in the school.'

'We don't really do things *urgently*,' the woman said. 'How old is your daughter?' She peered around, as if Florence should have come. Coralie hadn't even thought to bring her.

'Three and a bit? She turned three in March?'

'And is she at a Montessori currently?'

'No?'

'Ha-ha! It's not a test, you can't fail. Come in. This is my horrible office, with my horrible computer, ignore the mess. Sit down. Tell me the story.'

'It's just that I've wasted the past two and half years of her life,' Coralie burst out. 'She's in nursery nine hours a day, in the dark. She's really loved there, she knows everyone, she can talk so well, and point to the letters in her name. But it's just not what I want, for her life and for mine.'

'I don't think her life has been wasted. And what do you think we do here?'

'Um? Nothing urgent.' They both smiled. 'I like the idea of doing things slowly, and the children having little tasks that they do by themselves, and the day being shorter. And you have a garden.'

'You've read about Montessori?'

Coralie had read about it on Instagram. But she didn't need to know that. 'I have.'

'I was just about to go home, you know. Term finished yesterday. The classrooms are all packed up. And now you want me to turn on my big, ugly computer?'

'Yes please,' Coralie said. 'And thank you.'

At Daniel's, the poodle sensed her approach. Coralie could hear her thin paws scrabbling at the back of the door. 'Madonna,' she called through the letterbox. 'It's me!'

'She's here!' It was Zora's voice.

'Get in position,' Daniel hissed. 'Hello, welcome.' He pulled the door wide. 'Please come in.'

'Are you playing a trick?' Coralie stepped cautiously into the hall. Zora was at the foot of the stairs, posing with Daniel's big curve-handled dog-walking umbrella. She was wearing what looked like a white linen bathrobe, belted at the waist, over a trailing white skirt or dress. Her long dark hair was pouffed up and tied into a long plait. Her face looked exquisite, blush on her cheeks, her eyebrows groomed into an elegant shape.

'Lucy Honeychurch,' Daniel whispered, just as Coralie exclaimed, '*A Room with a View!*'

'She got it!' Daniel said.

'Holy moly. Don't move. Stay right there.' Coralie pulled out her phone to take photos. 'How did you manage this! Helena Bonham Carter dot com! What's under the bathrobe?'

'It's petticoats and a slip. We made them out of sheets! We watched the movie on the projector!' Zora jumped off the

227

bottom step and became a child again. 'We saw the naked men!'

'Oh, I remember them,' Coralie said. 'We always pressed pause on that bit when we watched it at school.'

'I love that movie. *Beauty! Joy! Love!*' Daniel shouted to the back of the house.

Zora gave an indulgent smile. 'He's saying his creed.'

Daniel put out his arm to Coralie. 'Care for some tea, Mr Beebe?'

'I'm not Mr fucking Beebe! But thank you, Mr Emerson.'

It had been the Year 7 taster day, Daniel explained while Zora was downstairs getting her things. 'It's like a practice run for high school.'

'I know what it is, she had one a few weeks ago.'

'Some horrible bully with bad taste said her eyebrows were too thick.'

'What!'

'She asked me if she could get her eyebrows threaded! I said no way.'

'Her beautiful face,' Coralie said. 'God.'

'Anyway, Barbie had the idea about the movie. He loves Helena Bonham Carter, he calls her HBC. Zora likes her eyebrows now. And, by the way, she wants to do piano.'

'She quit piano!'

Daniel shrugged. 'What are your plans, anyway? For the girls, when the baby comes. Because we'd be happy to have Zora anytime.'

'But not Florence,' Coralie said.

'Of course we'd have Florence! She's just not really interested in what I can provide. If she cries, *I* want to cry.'

'Anne and Sally are threatening to come up. I'd love to see Sally. Anne I can take or leave…It would be good to have them nearby, to look after the girls when the time comes. I want the help, but I don't want to pressure them. But I also don't want them to think I'm inviting them to stay.'

'Why don't I ask Barbie if they can have the Graham Road flat?'

Coralie mimed holding on to the counter for support. 'What do you mean, the Graham Road flat?'

'Don't be a pain about this, or I'll take the offer back. It's one of Barbie's flats. I've been managing it for Airbnb. I'm sure it's free, or if it's not, I can make it free. Cancel someone's booking.'

'Daniel the Corbynista landlord,' Coralie mused. 'Ol' multiple houses Barbie. Well, if it's available, and it's okay, I would really love that, Dan—thanks.'

Coralie and Zora (no longer in her Edwardian garb) picked up Florence early and took her to Hackney City Farm. The Farm cafe was teeming with mothers and under-fives. Coralie had thought almost everyone worked. Now it seemed no one did. It was a shock.

'Why do you look like that?' Zora asked. 'Is the baby making you sick?'

'No, I'm just thinking about how I'm taking Florence out of nursery. Not just today—all the time.'

'To do what?'

'There's a Montessori school behind the market, where they take their shoes off and put on slippers to start the day, and call their playing "work", and they learn to put their own coats on by flipping them off the floor. I thought I'd put her in there.'

'That sounds cool.'

'You're the cool one, you look so great with your hair like that.'

'Daniel learned to plait by making bread.' Zora studied her. 'He told you what I told him, didn't he? Okay. That's okay.'

'*Sorry*. I really am. I made him find out. I was freaking!'

'It's not your job to freak out about me!'

'It's not my job,' Coralie admitted. 'It's a hobby. And I know you're getting older, and you need your privacy, and you will have secrets. But always remember. You have so many people in your life who care about you. Who love you.'

'Okay,' Zora scoffed.

'Including me,' Coralie said. 'Do you remember we came here the first time we properly met?'

'Soh-Soh?' Florence tugged at Zora's sleeve. 'I want to see the piggies!'

'Let's go and see the piggies.' Zora stood and helped Florence down from the table. They walked towards the door, holding hands. Coralie reached for her phone. She almost didn't hear Zora rush back. 'And Coralie?' She looked up. 'I do remember. And I love you, too.'

Sooner or later, she'd have to move Flo upstairs into the spare room so the baby could have the nursery. Then where would she sleep on nights like this when she couldn't bear sleeping with Adam?

He'd cycled to Mangal for Turkish takeaway, claiming they'd eat 'well before eight', which would be fine for Coralie's sleep. At seven forty-nine, he served mixed dips and mixed grill at the small table in the garden, a tablecloth over the bird poo. He had a beer, and Coralie had a sip. Where should she start? Zora was first, the eyebrow thing. The offer of Barbie's flat, which Barbie had approved, and reserved for the last week of August and first ten days of September. She told him about Richard Pickard attending the press day, and how Stefan didn't care. 'So I'm going to be off work next week, with my cold,' she concluded. 'Then I'll start my mat leave.'

'Good! Fuck him, and fuck them. Honestly!' He was sincere, but after a second, he picked up his phone and swiped to check his WhatsApp.

'And I don't think I can go back after mat leave.'

'Yes, okay, wow.' He put his phone on the table, face-down. 'What are you thinking? Not that you *must* have a plan.'

'I'll think of something. But I was also thinking—of giving notice at nursery. Holidays are coming up. But then I thought— why send her back? I'll be off with the baby anyway.'

'You want to look after two pre-schoolers? Full-time?' His eyes looked wild, bloodshot from tiredness. 'Are you mad?'

'No! God! No, I've enrolled Flo at Montessori. You know, the one behind the market. Nine till three-thirty every day. Half-days on Friday. It costs a lot less than nursery.'

'You've enrolled her?'

'The office closed today, I had to rush.'

'I'm surprised you didn't discuss it? Or even mention it?'

'Surprised I didn't ask for permission?'

'I didn't say or mean that, *at all.*'

'But you thought it,' Coralie said. 'Thanks for dinner!'

She stormed off towards the house, stumbling a little on the steps and giving her ankle a painful twist. 'Ow!' she shouted back at Adam, as if he'd tripped her over.

'What did I…' He started laughing, expecting her to laugh too.

But after a bath, she took Brown Bear and her pillow into the spare room, where she remembered all the ways he'd let her down. 'My fucking house', he'd said. Well, that was exactly how she felt about her children! Florence might have half his DNA (actually, she had no idea if that was how DNA worked), and she might have his surname. But she was still Coralie's. And so was the son inside her. And she would decide how they lived.

My babies, she cried silently, her teeth clenched. *Mine, mine, mine.*

The next morning, Adam brought up breakfast for her in bed. 'You can have this very special breakfast no matter what.' He put the toast and tea down next to her. 'But I'm just wondering if you're still angry with me?'

'Are you still angry with *me*?'

'I wasn't angry with you.' He sat on the bed. 'I was just caught by surprise.'

'I wasn't angry with you,' Coralie said. 'I just didn't appreciate how you made me fall over.'

'I'm *really* sorry about that,' he said sincerely, even though it was clear she meant it as a joke. 'I also have something to show you before you see it yourself.'

She sat up. 'What?'

He handed her his phone. What was she looking at? Vanessa Andorra, Stefan, Richard—each standing (at a weird 'arty' angle) on three bollards outside the gallery. The headline of the article was when life gives you fossil fuels. The sub-head read: 'Vanessa Andorra's compelling new programme engages with and subverts its problematic source of sponsorship.'

'What the hell? Oh, it's in the Culture section. I thought it was in the *news*.' She handed him back his phone. 'Vanessa will be pleased, I think. Not that I care. Futurum probably will be too. Anytime they're allowed in polite society, the big polluters win!' She was grinning and trying to be funny, but she felt insane and very near tears.

'I'm sorry that awful man is standing on a bollard in your town,' Adam said. 'And taking credit for your work. He's a total, and utter, *cunt*.'

'Which awful man? Stefan was my friend!'

'I'm sorry to say it,' Adam said. 'But he's a cunt as well.'

And Coralie felt that beautiful feeling, the feeling she'd longed for all her life, that the outside world didn't matter, and that no one could hurt her, because she had everything and everyone she needed, *right there* in her home.

On 23 July 2019, as everyone had known would happen for weeks, if not years, Boris Johnson won the Conservative Party leadership race and became the new prime minister. It was 100 days before the second Brexit extension would expire. The thirty-first of October was the new 'do or die' date to leave the EU with or without a deal. 'Do or die' was Johnson's own phrasing. What about people who didn't want to leave the EU—*or* die? People like Coralie Bower?

She resented having to add No Deal planning to her already packed to-do list of nesting and baby prep. In addition to months of nappies, wipes and some tubs of emergency baby formula, she had a cupboard full of Heinz ketchups, recycled toilet roll, Mutti tinned tomatoes, jars of peanut butter, curry pastes, basmati rice and the nice Barilla pasta, all bought on offer over a period of months. Closer to the deadline she'd add paracetamol, ibuprofen, pulses, fish fingers and frozen peas. The night after Boris Johnson moved in to Downing Street, she woke up thinking, *Salt!* It made any meal nicer, and was good to trade in an emergency. Actually, so was sugar. At 2 a.m., as if it were totally normal, she added four boxes of Maldon and six slabs of Lindt to her Ocado.

The final Eleanor Road birth class took place on the hottest July day ever recorded in the UK. Well, at that point! Presumably it was just the first of many thirty-eight degree-plus days as mankind cruised through the planet's habitable threshold! Thirty-eight degrees was nothing in Australia. But in London, everything and everyone ground to a halt in shock. On her way out, she popped to the neighbouring terrace to call upon Miss Mavis.

She took a long time to come to the door. 'Are you checking on me because I'm elderly?'

'No!' Coralie lied.

They both laughed. Miss Mavis tutted. 'You should rest in this weather, in your condition.'

'I'm going to a birth class.'

'A birth class! Teaching you pain, is it?' Miss Mavis shook her head. 'Foolishness!'

'You *poor* thing!' a posh old white lady called to Coralie from across the street. 'I carried *all* my children in high summer *too!*'

Coralie had to get the impression down as quickly as she could. 'You *poor* thing!' She exclaimed the whole exchange into a WhatsApp voicenote and sent it straight to Alice.

Gathering in Fiona's hallway, the women and Sam were moaning and fanning themselves.

Upstairs, the skylight blinds and curtains had been closed. Two fans raged in opposite corners. 'Cushions, patch of carpet,' Fiona ordered. 'Now let's get on our knees and vocalise!'

Coralie and Lydia swapped glances. It was the part they hated the most.

'I know it's not comfortable,' Fiona said. 'To take up space and make a noise. But when you're giving birth, making noises freely opens *everything* up, the lips up the top, *and* the lips down below! *Brrrr!*' She blew a dry raspberry, and the circle copied her. 'Buh, buh, buh!' While everyone was still saying 'Buh, buh, buh,' Fiona cried: 'Let's moo!'

'Moo!' everyone lowed. 'Moo!'

'Good,' Fiona said. 'There's nothing embarrassing about *any* noise you make in labour. Who's pooed their pants before, as an adult?'

Sam raised his hand. 'Food poisoning in Morocco.'

'Mortifying!' Fiona said. 'Fantastic! You know you can

235

survive! Now we're standing, we're rolling our ankles, loosening them up. If you lose your balance, steady yourself and start again. We'll go round the circle: say how many weeks you are, and let's talk about our mothers. If you didn't grow up with your mother, make it your main carer instead. Lydia!'

'Thirty-five weeks,' Lydia said. 'I can only have this baby because of my mother. She showed me a single mum can provide everything a child needs. And she's coming down for the first month to help. Um, Fiona, I hope that's what you meant.'

'Wonderful,' Fiona said. 'Coralie?'

Coralie had just taken a gulp of water from her flask. She choked and coughed. Red in the face, she waved an apology. Fiona nodded. 'We'll come back! Charlotte?'

'Thirty-three weeks, not enjoying this heat, ha-ha! To put it simply, my mother's my best friend.' Charlotte had that beauty-queen delivery Coralie found triggering in other women. She paused after every sentence as if waiting for applause. 'We can share anything.' (Triumphant pause.) 'I just know she'd do anything for me.' (Triumphant pause.) 'She can't *wait* to be a granny!' (Thrilled smile, wave at crowd.)

'Thank you, Charlotte.'

With her instinct for a leader's feelings, Coralie knew this shallow analysis of the maternal bond had not gone down well with Fiona.

'Coralie,' Fiona said. 'Are you ready?'

'Um, I'm thirty-four weeks.' Normally she experienced thoughts and feelings as a flowing stream, and even when put on the spot in public, she could dip in her cup and get something out. The stream appeared to have dried up. 'My mum picked me up when she said she'd pick me up. My clean school uniforms were always hanging in the cupboard. Um…' She trailed off. The cup was empty. So was her mind.

'And does she take an active role with your daughter now, or is she in Australia?'

'Sorry, Fiona. I should have mentioned,' Coralie said. 'She's dead.'

'Oh!' Charlotte gasped, as if Coralie had shot *her* mother.

Fiona ignored Charlotte. 'I'm sad to hear that,' she said sincerely. 'We're getting on the floor, we're drawing one leg up and rolling around. When we give birth and have a vulnerable infant in our care, we can access quite primitive states and memories that have been closed off to us for years,' Fiona said. 'It can be disturbing to go back in time and feel as you did back then. Greet the feelings when you see them, pause and take a note. What's happening now, and what's a ghost from the past? Important distinction, keep it in mind. Mothering—parenting (sorry, Sam)—it takes it right out of you. It can leave you empty, running on fumes. Not enough care to go round. Someone has to be there to hold you in their mind as you are holding the baby. It doesn't have to be your mother. It doesn't have to be a partner. But someone. You need to be looked after too.'

That night, Coralie had a strange dream. She was hiking in a jungle. She was alone and it was hard going. Up ahead there was a cupboard. When she opened it, her mother toppled towards her, straight and stiff as an ironing board. Coralie caught her, alarmed, and tried to angle her back in, but it was difficult, because she was mixed up with a mop, a broom, and a vacuum cleaner. At her touch, her mother began to unfreeze (that was why she was stiff: she was frozen). Life came back into her eyes, which searched Coralie's face, and her mother's mouth moved as if she was about to say something. *I'm sorry? I love you?* Why had everything always been so empty between them? Even the fact Coralie was paying attention meant she was too conscious to dream. Reality rushed in. Her mother faded away. She was alone, awake, and crying.

17

On 4 May 2015, David Cameron had tweeted: *Britain faces a simple and inescapable choice—stability and strong Government with me, or chaos with Ed Miliband.* Coralie looked back fondly on that election, her first in the UK, and (she hadn't realised this at the time) the last that could credibly be called normal. Those were the days! By the end of summer 2019, she was thirty-nine weeks pregnant and living in a failed state.

Somehow it was no longer enough for the UK to exit the European Union. Every former tie and mutual obligation had to be expunged. No deal was better than a bad deal, Tories repeated on every news round. In a little over two months, the country looked likely to crash out of the EU, without arrangements in place for not just medicines and food but transport, national security, toilet roll or the chemicals needed for clean water. But did Boris want No Deal—or did he want a better deal from Europe that only the threat of No Deal could deliver?

Coralie couldn't help thinking of Adam trying to get the girls to circus school on the weekend. Only at the last minute— when every water bottle, shoe and raincoat was lost, when missing the bus was all but assured, when Zora had stormed out, Flo was crying and Coralie was bathed in anxiety sweat— could Adam finally rouse himself to leave the house. All he required was chaos. He had that in common with Boris.

On the last Sunday in August, the *Observer* revealed that the prime minister was considering proroguing Parliament. Everyone suddenly learned what proroguing meant—it meant a total shutdown. All politicians would be sent home at the end of the week. Westminster would stand empty. There would be no political debate or scrutiny of the government's plans before the final summit in Europe. The stage for No Deal would be set.

While Coralie had hoped for some help with Florence's dinners and baths, Anne and Sally rushed straight from Barbie's flat to 10 Downing Street. There they joined thousands of others chanting 'Stop the coup! Stop the coup!' Adam, for his part, cycled into Westminster at eight in the morning and didn't return until Coralie was in bed. In the first week of September, the baby was due, Florence was starting Montessori, and Zora would have her first day at secondary. There could not have been a worse time for the entire political system to explode.

On the plus side, Lydia's very overdue baby, Nancy, was born in the birth centre at Homerton Hospital in the dying minutes of 31 August. Had she delayed her arrival any further,

her school start date would have been pushed back an entire year, leaving Lydia on the hook for an impossible £20,000 worth of extra childcare costs. *She's a very, very good girl,* Lydia WhatsApped the birth class group. The first photo showed a pink frog sprawled on her back in a minuscule newborn nappy. The second was a close-up of the baby's shoulder, which had a sprinkling of fine blonde hairs. Coralie felt something weird inside her bra. Pulling her top down to inspect her nipple, she found tiny, shimmering golden bubbles: milk.

What was the birth like? Sam wrote. (His had gone fine. His son looked exactly like him.)

BESTIAL, Lydia replied.

Coralie had found her first birth more shattering than bestial. Her mind had fragmented the instant she'd felt pain. This time, she *prayed* for bestial. She wanted to howl at the moon. It would be all about her body! Her mind wouldn't even come in to it! She'd breathe, in a yogic way. She'd stay at home for twice as long, three times as long as she did with Florence. When she got to the hospital, being examined wouldn't hurt or embarrass her, and would reveal that she was extremely dilated, possibly even six centimetres, and everyone would be excited, not cutting their eyes away in dismay. Rather than screaming at Adam to stop eating *fucking crisps*, she'd let him cuddle her and be nice to her and bring her water and cups of ice. Afterwards he'd be grinning, ecstatic, and bragging about his wife being a warrior, instead of going off in private to be sick in a plastic bag. All she wanted to do was to be able to *let go*. Buh! Buh! Loose lips up the top, loose lips down below!

*

241

All summer Coralie talked non-stop about 'big nursery', the new nursery Florence would go to for 'big kids'. Florence scooted (Coralie walked) down Malvern Road, practising the new route. They journeyed to Westfield Stratford to pick out a lunch box, a water bottle, a rucksack and some lilac Crocs for slippers. florence w, read the extra-adhesive dishwasher-safe nametags they put on everything. Once, when she was talking about 'big nursery', and Adam muttered, 'Query: what was wrong with *old nursery*?', Coralie rushed up, cornered him in the open pantry, angled the door so Florence wouldn't see, and hissed, 'Get on board or shut the fuck up!' And because she was so pregnant by then, and he was a largely absent deadbeat dad in thrall to his mistress, Journalism, he backed away, looking sheepish. 'Sorry, sorry, okay? Sorry.'

Anne and Sally kindly offered to drop Florence off for her first day, but Coralie said she'd do it herself.

'Florence.' Miss Sarah, the Montessori teacher with the acorn hair, reached for Florence's hand to shake it.

Coralie cringed as Florence slapped Miss Sarah's hand, clearly presuming it was some kind of 'side five'.

'So, you're going to be a big sister,' Miss Sarah said. 'Do you know if it will be a boy or girl?'

'It's a brudda,' Florence said. 'What's in that?' She pointed at a large fishtank.

Miss Sarah looked coyly over her shoulder. 'An axolotl. Have you ever seen one? He looks like he wears a crown, or a head-dress. But they're really his feathery gills. Shall we go and meet him?'

And Florence, tiny, dwarfed by the smallest Kånken rucksack, walked in happily without saying goodbye.

Back at home, Anne and Sally had set up camp in the sitting room.

'Staggeringly hypocritical,' Anne scoffed at the television.

'Tea?' Coralie offered. 'Coffee?'

'Oh, I'll make the tea,' Sally said. 'And what's that you have? Sourdough? I'll make you some toast with it. You sit down and enjoy some rolling news.'

Coralie collapsed on the sofa next to Anne. 'What's the latest?'

'Crunch time,' Anne said. 'Parliament's prorogued from the end of the week. Will they have the time, and the numbers, to outlaw a No Deal Brexit? Some senior Tories might cross the floor. Boris will expel them all if they do. Hypocrite! He's obviously the only one who's allowed to rebel.'

Coralie remembered getting the train out to Croydon to take the compulsory 'Life in the UK' test in order to stay in the country. How seriously the UK took itself as a nation, historically and in the present day, as the centre of civilisation and the world, the mother of all parliaments and the inventors of 'the rule of law'. 'Who built the Tower of London?' was one of the simpler questions on the test. (It was William the Conqueror, after he became king in 1066.) And, confusingly:

What is <u>NOT</u> a fundamental principle of British life?
- Looking after the environment
- Driving a car
- Treating others with fairness
- Looking after yourself and family

And, almost satirically:

On his escape from the Battle of Worcester, Charles II famous-ly hid inside what?

- A cellar
- A forest
- An oak tree
- None of the above

God! Like, who cared? Who the fuck cared? Talk about self-obsessed! How long had Indigenous people inhabited what became known as Australia before the British gave them small-pox? In which episode does [redacted] die in the classic Australian TV drama *Love My Way*? What's the acceptable ratio of blue-sky days to desaturated white or grey? Because, you see, Coralie also came from somewhere! Somewhere that was, in some ways, shit—and in others, really quite good? Why did she have to learn all these so-called facts about the UK, when the only thing British people knew about Australia was *snakes*?

She loved the UK, she really did: lunch at Towpath cafe, a tube carriage full of passengers ignoring a mad person talk about the Bible, Lahore Kebab House, Falcon Enamelware, Stormzy at Glastonbury in a Union Jack stab-vest, Popbitch and the Cazalets.

But now these tin-pot chumps were breathlessly livestreaming their own slow-motion societal collapse, pausing only to zoom in on Boris Johnson's new rescue dog, Dilyn, who (trembling) was being carried into Number Ten in a see-through pet bag.

'A puppy?' Anne said. 'How can a puppy that young be a rescue?'

Well, Coralie didn't have anything on until Montessori pick-up at three-thirty. And she couldn't give birth until after Zora started secondary the next day. And Sally had just made her buttery toast with marmalade. She tucked her feet up on the sofa, took a sip of her tea, and relaxed to enjoy the show.

For her first day at Camden Girls, Zora wore a white broderie-anglaise nightie she'd bought on eBay using her birthday money, and a generic black M&S school blazer from a charity shop. Underneath, for modesty, she had a white T-shirt and black bike shorts. On her feet were white socks and the very scuffed Doc Martens she'd worn throughout Year 6 as school shoes. Her hair was tied back, Lucy Honeychurch-style, with a black grosgrain ribbon. At Bartholomew Road, Marina, Tom, Rupert (aged five), Adam, Anne, Daniel and Madonna (and Coralie) all assembled at eight-fifteen to see her off.

'And Florence sent this for you,' Coralie said. 'Sally's taken her to nursery.'

It was a drawing of two smiling balls on sticks.

Zora studied it tenderly. 'Is that us?'

'I think so,' Coralie said. 'She's not very gifted.'

'Coralie!' Tom protested.

'In *that* area!'

'Zora.' Marina put her coffee cup in the sink. 'Are you sure you don't want to wear something normal?'

Daniel gasped. 'Don't listen, Zora. What do you think, Madonna?'

'There's no such thing as normal,' he made the poodle say in a funny voice.

'Well, there is,' Tory Tom said. 'It's me, and things that I like. But you're not normal, Zora, you're far too special.'

'She's far too beautiful,' Adam said.

'Stop!' Zora covered her ears. 'Cringe!'

Coralie waved her phone. 'Where will we do the photos? We need some natural light.'

'Come onto the stairs,' Marina said. 'Out the front.'

They did Zora by herself; then Zora with Rup; then Zora with Marina and Adam; then with Tom as well, and Coralie. (Daniel took that one.) Then Zora with Anne, and Zora with Anne and Adam. Finally, they did Zora on her own with Madonna in her lap. More and more girls walked past, streaming towards the school.

'This is actually getting embarrassing,' Zora said. 'And the whole point of secondary is that I go to school alone.'

'Not on your first day,' Marina said.

'*Yes* on my first day!' She descended the stairs, looking like a child one second and an ancient, intimidating queen the next.

How could this be? Zora Whiteman going to secondary school? Tears were forming in Coralie's eyes. Marina was openly crying.

'Stop growing up!' Anne said.

They all watched silently as she walked to the end of the street.

Marina sniffed. 'Is she not going to turn around?'

Zora turned, waved, then disappeared.

Tom put his arm around Marina, and punched Adam softly on the shoulder. 'You did it.'

'We did it,' Adam said. 'Whew. Well, I'm off. Big day

covering the Tory civil war.'

'A disgrace.' Anne frowned at Tom.

'But not my fault, in this instance,' Tom said. (Back at the Bar since 2017, he'd marched for a People's Vote with an EU flag knotted over his gilet.)

Adam held Coralie to his chest. 'If there's even a hint of the baby coming, or you feel like a hint is potentially imminent, or you just need *me* specifically to make you a tea, or you need anything at all, just call me. And I'll leave whatever I'm doing, and come. Straightaway.'

'She'll be fine!' Anne briskly said.

Back home on Wilton Way, Sally presided over a perfectly tidy kitchen. Exhausted by the emotions of the morning, Coralie retreated to her room for a nap. When she woke up, there was a scary tweet at the top of her feed. It was from the journalist who'd broken the news about Parliament being shut down. *I remember the poll tax riots sweeping through central London,* he wrote. *Cars overturned with drivers in them. Shops smashed up. Terrifying. Atmosphere outside parliament today similar and very tense. Just needs a spark,* the journalist concluded, with a sinisterly long ellipsis.

Coralie shivered, and the shiver extended deep into her pelvis, tightening into an electric shock. A contraction? Not quite. She lay there for a few minutes, wondering if she'd feel another one. She didn't, but when she wiped after the loo, she saw a single drop of blood.

Downstairs, Anne was seething in front of rolling BBC news coverage while Sally folded laundry on the rug. 'That was a nice rest,' Sally said. 'I've made soup, and there's eggs, or pasta. There's bread from yesterday, too. When was the last time you had a boiled egg and soldiers? That's what I'll make you, don't you think?' She bustled into the kitchen and got started.

'Oof.' Just as Coralie was about to sit down, the jagged feeling came back in her pelvis. She stood, half bent over, holding the bottom of her bump. She needed the bathroom again, very badly. She didn't think she'd make it upstairs. She lumbered to the small powder room mere metres from Sally, slammed the door shut behind her and wrenched on the tap, desperate for some white noise. She made it onto the toilet in time for a complete and violent evacuation. In Fiona's class, she'd prepared herself as much as possible to bravely shit in front of a midwife. Rubbing it in Sally's face just seemed like bad manners.

After a few wipes, she looked down at her fourth crumpled handful of loo roll. In the middle, quivering like gelatinous homemade chicken stock, although lighter in colour, and with a few flecks of blood, was her mucus plug.

She emerged, pale. 'I think it might be happening.'

'Oh, Coralie.' Sally beamed. 'Well done.'

Was she comfortable calling them contractions? As she ate her toast and drank her tea, two further instances of pelvic tightening left her gasping. She had two more as she watched Anne watching TV.

Later, in the afternoon, Sally poked her head in. 'I really enjoyed seeing Florence's school this morning. I'd love to collect her, if that's okay with you.'

What a triumph of sensitivity to frame a favour in that way, so Coralie could feel like the helper, rather than the helped.

'Oh!' Anne was looking at her phone. 'The legal appeal against prorogation might be heard in the Supreme Court. Now if you don't mind, Coralie—I'll turn on BBC Parliament. The prime minister's making a statement.'

Actually, he didn't stand up for a further twenty minutes, during which two long contractions (surely she could call them that?) left her breathless.

At the dispatch box, Boris began by noting it was the eightieth anniversary of the date the UK entered the Second World War. 'This country still stands—then as now—for democracy, for the rule of law.'

'Ha!' Anne bitterly laughed.

Coralie could never follow Parliament, just as she could never follow football. She had to zone out, let the action blur, and pay attention to the soundtrack, the roars and emotion of the crowd. Suddenly, the noise in the Chamber was cacophonous, hooting, derisive. 'I wish my hon—' Boris stumbled. 'I wish my honourable friend—all the best!' She had to go on Twitter to understand what had happened. A Tory MP had crossed the floor to sit with the Lib Dems. On his feet as PM for fewer than five minutes, Boris Johnson had lost his majority.

'Oh-ho!' Anne crowed. 'Buffoon.'

'Yesterday, a Bill was published—a Bill that the leader of the opposition has spent all summer working on,' Boris said darkly, as if working in summer was the most shameful thing a person could do. 'It is a Bill that, if passed, would *force me* to go to Brussels and *beg* for an extension. It would force me to accept the terms offered. It would destroy any chance of negotiation for a new deal! It would *destroy* it. Indeed, it would enable our friends in Brussels to dictate the terms of the negotiation. That is what it would do. There is only one way to describe the Bill: it is Jeremy Corbyn's surrender Bill!' The camera cut to the Labour leader, rolling his eyes in tired disgust. 'I therefore urge this House to reject the Bill tonight, so that we can get the right deal for our country, deliver Brexit, and take the whole country forward!'

The Speaker jumped up amid the tumult. 'For the avoidance of doubt! There is no vote on a *Bill* tonight. There is a vote on a *motion*, and if that motion is successful, there will be a Bill tomorrow.'

The camera cut to Boris. He was murderous.

'He *loves* being corrected,' Anne said. 'As you can see.'

It was past three-thirty. Coralie texted Zora. *How was your first day? I know you'll have a lot on, but please send me your verdict when you have time. An emoji will do!*

Anne eyed her beadily. 'Are you texting Zora about school?'

'I said an emoji would do. Oh, she's typing!'

An emoji popped up. It was a skull.

Does that mean bad? Coralie replied.

It means better than good, Zora wrote back. *It means it was so good, I died.*

'She says it was so good, she died,' Coralie reported.

'*Right,*' Anne said.

Jeremy Corbyn got to his feet. Coralie felt another unmistakable tightening. Back on her phone, she downloaded a contraction timer from the App Store. It took an age to get it working. Another contraction had come, and Corbyn was ending his remarks. 'The prime minister is not winning friends in Europe; he is losing friends at home. His is a government with no mandate, no morals and—as of today—no majority!'

'That's clever,' Anne said. 'He must have ad-libbed that.'

'Are you a Corbyn fan?' Coralie asked curiously.

'We have *a lot* of Jewish friends,' Anne said. 'So *no*.'

On and on the debate went. After a while, Coralie took herself upstairs to the bedroom, planning a short lie-down before Florence came home. She woke two hours later when a terrible pain entered her consciousness. For the first time, she began to get scared, and cried to herself as she restarted her contraction timer history (she didn't want her average to be affected by her sleep). She'd missed two calls and several messages from Adam. She envied other women the boring jobs of their partners. Coralie could see what he was dealing with just by tuning in to the news. In a perfect world, he'd be with her, but Brexit was *do or die*. How could she summon him home for a *twinge*? Last time she'd taken so long to dilate that a doctor had called her cervix 'recalcitrant'. (Rude!)

She wandered into the yellow nursery and picked up Flo's toy cat, Catty. Tears once more came to her eyes. What a fool she was; worse—a criminal. For ruining a perfect life, with her one perfect child, by taking a punt on another. She could die in childbirth, or the baby could. Even if all went well, Flo's life would be destroyed. And what about Zora? What if it took her two years to enjoy her half-brother, as long as it had taken with Rup? Coralie had wasted the past ten months of her life, distracted by pregnancy. Wasted ages before that by trying to get pregnant. Ages before that, by leaving her baby girl in nursery so she could work her stupid job. She wasn't a good person, a good mother, or a writer. It was all a complete disaster.

She heard Florence in the kitchen, banging her enamel dinner plate with the sippy cup she insisted on using. Thank goodness Coralie hadn't slept through bedtime.

'Mama,' Florence said when she went in. 'Axe the lottle comes from Mexico.'

'The axolotl, I think,' Sally murmured.

'The axolotl! Did you find out its name?'

'David!'

Coralie laughed until tears came to her eyes. 'Of course. David. Oof.' She held the table for support.

'Breathe.' In a louder voice, Sally said 'Flo? Maybe you'd like a Sally bath?'

'Sally bath!' Flo cheered. 'Yeah!'

In the sitting room, Anne was drinking a glass of red wine and crunching an abstemious Barack Obama portion of almonds, her chiselled jaw cracking.

On the screen, live in the House of Commons, a scruffy Tory was speaking from the backbench. 'The prime minister,' he said, 'is much in the position of someone standing on one side of a canyon shouting to people on the *other* side of the canyon that if they do not do as he wishes, he will throw himself into the abyss.'

Titters in the Chamber, and the Wilton Way sitting room (Anne).

'Oh, it's seven—Coralie, do you mind?' Without waiting for an answer, Anne switched the channel.

From the screen there came the propulsive strains of the *Channel 4 News* theme, which brought Coralie almost to tears again with its energy and forward motion, as though the news was somehow pioneering, brave and free, rather than a bleak and disingenuous round up of the lives and times of malignant show-offs. Jon Snow was crossing live outside Westminster in a zany airport-shop tie and flesh-coloured *X Factor* headset. Behind him, the Elizabeth Tower (which housed Big Ben) was clad in a sinister scaffolding exoskeleton. Beneath it, a carnival of mainly white middle-aged people waved EU or Brexit flags and shouted in each other's faces.

'MPs have returned from their summer break straight into a defining moment for Brexit,' Jon Snow said. 'They will vote this evening on whether to seize control of the Parliamentary agenda from the government. If they win, Tory rebels and other parties could then introduce a law to force a Brexit extension. In theory, that would stop us leaving without a deal at the end of October. Boris Johnson has said *that* will result in his calling a general election—but to achieve that, he needs two-thirds of MPs to vote for one.'

'Ow.' Coralie clutched the sofa's armrest.

'You seem to be saying that quite often,' Anne said. 'Are you timing?'

'I'm trying to use my app…'

Anne stood and walked towards the kitchen. She returned with a piece of Florence's drawing paper and a crayon. 'Let's do it the old-fashioned way.'

'Mama!' Florence called down.

Upstairs, Flo had been bamboozled by Sally into wearing

sweet little pyjamas she normally refused to wear, a gingham shirt and trousers. Coralie got into her big-girl bed with her and kissed her: her cheek, her chin, her delicate temple. She breathed in her hair and traced the tip of her upturned nose. 'Eat me up,' Flo said.

'No, I can't...' Coralie tried not to devour her daughter before bed. It made Flo overstimulated.

'Eat me up, Mama!'

Coralie squashed her tiny chest, growled and snapped her teeth near her ear and neck. 'Yum, yum, my little girl, will you be my dinner?'

Flo writhed. 'No!' she shrieked. 'No, no!'

Coralie stopped. (She had read this was how you 'modelled consent'.)

'Maybe a bit,' Flo said.

'Rarrr!' Coralie nibbled her ear.

Florence was laughing so much she had hiccups. 'I've gorten hick-pups,' she reported soberly.

'Why don't I tell you a story tonight, instead of reading? I'll turn off the light but stay in your bed.'

'Okay.'

'Okay, once upon a time. There was a girl, the most beautiful girl in the world.'

'Me,' Florence said.

'*You...*'

Downstairs, on a stool next to the sofa, Sally had arranged bowls of crisps, olives, smoked almonds, cut-up cucumbers and a herby Greek yoghurt dip. She stood like a waiter. 'Small glass of wine?'

Coralie hadn't felt like wine or coffee the whole time she'd been pregnant, but with the night air at body temperature, and a breeze blowing through the big bay window, she suddenly did. She snacked, and sipped her white wine, and as the sky turned navy blue, she zoned out, only the occasional shout of 'Order!' recalling her to the television, the room and reality.

'There's one,' she said when the pain began, or just grunted if it was awful. 'Finished now,' she'd say, and Anne would mark it on the page, hardly taking her eyes from the BBC.

The candles on the mantlepiece were really just ornamental, but no one had told Sally that, and rather than put the lamps on, she'd lit them. Still half in her dream, Coralie checked her phone, and saw Adam had Whatsapped: *CYK.*

She had the absurd thought she should name her baby boy CYK. (Could they be his initials? Claude was on the list.)

'Sit up,' Anne shouted.

Coralie, who had been lolling to the side, shot upright.

'Silly,' Anne said. 'No, look on the TV—Jacob Rees-Mogg.'

The insufferable Tory languidly reclined across three seats on the front bench. He was a poor person's idea of a rich person (a snob had once told her at a party), and Boris a thick person's idea of a clever one.

'Sit up,' MPs shouted. 'Sit up, man!'

'Ow!' Coralie gasped.

Anne glanced at her watch and made a note. Soon, the whole page of drawing paper was full of scribbled figures. 'Almost a minute each, every five minutes. You're really getting there.'

'Wonderful, Coralie,' Sally said.

A wave of wellbeing swept over her, so powerful she felt she could almost fly up to the ceiling.

On TV, shouts interrupted someone speaking. Out of nowhere, the Speaker called a vote. 'Division!' he howled. 'Clear the lobby!'

The audio feed to the Chamber was cut. MPs got to their feet and milled about.

'So old-fashioned, to have to use their bodies to vote,' Sally mused. 'It takes forever. Use phones, screens or buttons or something.'

'The Russians, you know,' Anne said. 'Hacking.'

Slowly they drifted back in. Men in suits. A Sikh in a red turban. 'Those old biddies with their handbags,' Anne muttered, as women MPs slid to the back of the green benches and hunched over their phones. Clerks lined up to share the results. 'The ayes to the right—328,' one called. There was a sharp intake of breath. 'The nos to the left—301.'

Was that good or bad? Once more she found herself at sea. 'Oh-ooh!' everyone in Parliament chorused. Scattered laughter and a few slow claps. Someone called out chidingly. 'Not a good start, Boris!'

Good, he must have lost.

The prime minister rose. 'Thank you, Mr Speaker.'

'His hair is quite golden,' Sally said. 'He's genuinely tow-headed.'

Boris had on a humorous face, as though he'd made a joke. Jeers filled the Chamber as he spoke. 'I do not want an election, but if MPs vote tomorrow to stop negotiations and to compel another pointless delay to Brexit, potentially for years, that would be the only way to resolve this! And I can confirm that

256

we are tonight tabling a motion under the Fixed-term Parliaments Act 2011.'

A motion for what? Another election?

Another campaign. Another of Adam's *books*.

Suddenly realising what this meant for her 'fourth trimester', her mat leave, her mental health and her life, Coralie started to cry, and her contractions slowed down, and stopped.

Adam didn't get home until almost midnight. She listened as he showered and used his electric toothbrush for what seemed like forever. He scrabbled for his charger cord, plugged in his phone, slid into bed and moulded himself around her. 'Clomping and clattering,' she said. 'Lucky I wasn't asleep!'

'Oh no! Cor! Sally said you were asleep. I thought you were getting a good rest!'

'Is Sally still here?'

'She was, when I came home, in case you needed her. I told her she should stay the night upstairs, but she said Anne "liked her to be there" when she woke up.'

'Weird.'

'I know, Anne doesn't *like* anything, as far as I know. I walked her round to the flat. It's nice.'

'Barbie owns the whole house,' Coralie yawned.

He cradled her belly. 'Any more…developments? Sally said it was quite exciting?'

'Actually, no!' She propped herself on her elbow to turn and whisper-shout at him. 'It may surprise you! But guess what! Your absence, and finding out there's another election coming, so you can abandon me—and ruin my life—is not *conducive*, is it! To relaxing! And contracting!'

'There won't be an election for months. Everyone's too worried there'll be a No Deal. Labour will oppose it, everyone will.' He sat up and studied her. 'Do you mean it's slowed down? All the action? Or stopped?'

'I don't know!' She was tearful in the dark.

He leaned down and spoke to the bump. 'What are you up to in there, little boy?'

Inside her, the baby elbowed her and kicked out with his foot. 'Did you see that? He heard you.'

'He's telling us he's okay. Do you think you can sleep? Maybe he's giving you a break on purpose, so you can rest.'

'That's a nice way to think about it.' She turned back over onto her left side. 'Rather than me failing at birth, again.'

'What would Fiona say, your guru from Eleanor Road? How would she view this kind of negative self-talk?'

'I can't remember, I'm too stupid and exhausted.'

'Oh Cor, beautiful Cor.'

They lay there for a long time.

'Boris expelled twenty-one Tories for voting against him,' Adam murmured.

Coralie didn't reply. Like a boat slipping its mooring, she drifted off, asleep.

By 6 a.m. the next day, she was walking around the hidden green space in the middle of a Hackney estate. There were two conker trees—what was their real name? Horse chestnut. She was trying to have an 'active birth' this time, and active meant *walking,* not lazing on the sofa while Anne made snide remarks about the news. She was back on the timer app, a contraction for a full minute every five. Even as she walked laps and breathed through the pain, part of her was eagerly anticipating Adam waking up and finding her gone. At seven, she received a video call. The screen opened up, but all it showed was darkness. 'Flo.' She could hear Adam's voice. 'Flo. You can't eat it.'

'Send Mama a kiss-kiss,' Flo said.

Adam seized control of the phone and held it at arm's length. They were in bed. 'Where are you?'

Her labour couldn't be serious if she was still trying to achieve a good angle on FaceTime. She sighed. 'I'm out near the school. Hello, Flo-Flo. I love you. I miss you.'

'Oh, she's run off,' Adam said. 'Are you coming home for breakfast?'

'I suppose so.'

'Should I put the tea on?'

'I suppose so.'

'You're doing so well, my darling.'

Tears filled her eyes. 'I don't think I can do this, not much longer. I should have booked a C-section.'

'Come home,' Adam said. 'We'll be here.'

As she trudged up to Wilton Way, she heard someone running behind her. She struggled to stow her phone in the pocket of her ASOS leopard print maternity dress. Not now, she couldn't afford to be mugged *now*.

'Coralie!'

'Anne!' Coralie held on to a fence for balance, partly from exhaustion, but also from shock—Anne was wearing toe-shoes,

259

those running shoes like gloves for feet. As she reeled, Anne beeped her sports watch and walked in a circle, hands on her hips. She was very trim in her black leggings. *The toe shoes! God, don't look.*

'I see you're admiring my Vibrams,' Anne said. 'Closest thing to barefoot running! I don't use them all the time. Just sometimes, to keep all the muscles toned and the bones, especially my arches, very strong.'

'Ow.' Coralie buckled over. For a moment she thought she'd be sick.

Anne put her hand on Coralie's shoulder. 'Coralie?'

When she was young, and living in Canberra, her parents had given in to her pleas for a pet, allowing her a goldfish, because by the time her father got a new posting, it would probably be dead. They drove to the pet shop in Woden, where she picked out a black fish with googly eyes. The pet-shop man caught it in a net and plopped it into a thick plastic bag full of water. She kept the plastic bag, about the size of a basketball, on her lap for the drive home, marvelling at the fish, which belonged only to her. She set up the small bowl (with the coloured stones, two special weeds, and a treasure-chest ornament) on her desk, so the fish could keep her company while she was doing her homework. Concentrating, she sat down, forgetting that the fish, in its bag, was on her chair. *Pop!* The bag burst open, the water flooded out, and the fish was a metre away, flapping on the carpet.

He was fine. Her father heard her screaming, ran in and saved the day. He was great in a crisis, always happy when life was hanging in the balance, actually angry when it was *not*.

260

And that great pop, and splash, and shock, was exactly what it was like when Coralie's waters broke on Lansdowne Drive.

'Coralie!' Anne cried, looking down at her soaked left toe shoe. 'These cost a hundred pounds!'

What was there to say? Some people just couldn't give birth. She arrived at hospital contracting like mad, refused all pain relief except gas and air, was four centimetres when examined (not too bad), and dilated to ten *full* centimetres over the course of nine hours, but the baby was floating off somewhere like an astronaut in space.

'Baby's not there,' she heard someone say, and a huge shame engulfed her. She wasn't even pregnant. She had wasted everyone's time. But what about the kicks she'd felt, and the printed-off sonogram photos on the fridge, his perfect nose pointed upwards like a puppy in *101 Dalmations*?

Someone had to say something, she should advocate for herself. Or maybe that was Adam's job. He was huddled next to the bed wearing the baby blanket she'd packed in the hospital bag. It got very cold in the hospital, as anyone could have told him. God forbid he dress adequately and look after himself!

'There *is* a baby,' she said. 'I'm going to be sick.' A papier-mâché bowl reached her just in time. Afterwards, the midwife discreetly wiped her arse. She'd done it. Shat herself! Bestial!

But somehow the baby hadn't descended enough to be sucked out with a vacuum or levered out with forceps. Compression socks, gown, the spinal. She was wheeled in to the operating room, a curtain set up across her. '*Señorita*' played on Kiss FM. The anaesthetist stroked Coralie's hair from her forehead with a delicate gloved hand.

A chorus of *ahs* as a long thin creature was held aloft over the curtain. Coralie's gown was pulled down and the creature was deposited on her chest, warm and slimy like her own heart or entrails. Beside her, forgetting to take photos as usual, Adam wept.

The miracle of her new boy's alert black eyes. He craned up, tap-tap-tapped his little chin, and fastened his mouth on her breast.

18

It was the day before Christmas, and in the Wilton Way house, everyone was stirring, even a mouse. That morning, at breakfast, a half-empty box of Rice Pops toppled on its side in the pantry. A small brown shape streaked from the open door, zigzagged past the playpen, and disappeared under the fridge. Luckily, Adam was still upstairs, having a lie-in for his forty-fourth birthday. Florence was swinging her legs at the table and watching *Peppa Pig* on the iPad. She hadn't noticed.

'That didn't happen,' Coralie said. 'Zora? Hannah? That didn't happen.'

Zora's friend Hannah had slept over the night before. 'I honestly didn't see anything,' she said. 'I just worked it out from the sound, and your faces.'

'Zora? It'll ruin his whole birthday, and Christmas.'

'Oh, totally,' Zora said. 'It didn't happen.'

Barbie overslept and almost missed his plane to New York, meaning Daniel was late, and so was Adam's birthday lunch, which Dan was meant to cook. Madonna was unsettled by the rush; she sat trembling in Dan's market basket, then staggered round Coralie's kitchen, barking at the pedal bin. Dan jettisoned the slow-cooked lentil lasagne in favour of a much quicker pasta, but they still didn't sit down at the table (extended by an Amazon trestle) until after two. Just as well Coralie, who'd been up four times during the night with the baby, had already eaten three breakfasts.

At Montessori, a week earlier, Florence's friend Anatole had stuck a pomegranate seed up his nose. Pressed by Adam to relate the story in the high-stakes environment of this large family lunch, a tongue-tied Florence demonstrated by putting a raisin up her own nose, where it immediately got stuck; Anne seized her, blocked the other nostril, and blew sharply into Florence's mouth. The raisin dropped onto the kitchen floor. As everyone else applauded, Adam knelt to pick it up, muttering crossly about 'tempting rodents'.

Over the top of his head, Coralie and Zora shared a long, silent gaze.

(Putting a raisin up her nose was something a young Zora Whiteman would never do. That was *all* Bower. Embarrassing.)

And worst of all: Boris Johnson had decisively won the 12 December election. His majority in Parliament was huge. The Tories released a triumphant Christmas video of him making mince pies with his father. Surrounded by the detritus of the birthday lunch, Adam played it on his phone at the table. Someone once bet Boris he couldn't eat a 'scalding' mince pie in five seconds flat, Stanley Johnson said. But 'I got that mince pie...*done!*' Boris replied. He was clearly still in election mode, saying 'Get Brexit Done' every five seconds. Well, Brexit *was* done. On 20 December, the withdrawal agreement had passed in the Commons. The UK would leave the EU on 31 January. But it would *not* be Coralie's problem. She'd been on a news and social media break since election day. Nobody could make her hear that man's voice without her consent. 'Mmm,' she hummed. 'La, la, la!'

'The YouTube comments are quite deranged,' Adam said. 'Whether you like the Conservatives or not,' he read out, 'Boris does make you smile, and brings a bit of optimism, unlike Corbyn, who made me feel suicidal!'

'Very cool and normal,' Coralie said. 'A cool and normal thing to say in a cool and normal country. Can we try to have a Boris-free day?'

'You can't hide from reality,' Anne said. 'Boris Johnson will be the prime minister until 2024—at the very least. Perhaps longer! It's our duty, as citizens, to engage with rising tides of authoritarianism in Europe and the US. We can't just turn away!'

'I agree,' Hannah said.

'Actually,' Coralie said (under her breath). 'I already have.' She used to reread Virginia Woolf's *Diaries* every year, a tradition she'd started at school, but had stopped when she'd shipped her books off and moved to Sydney to work in advertising, which was also when she'd got Twitter. Coincidence? Well, no more. She'd just bought another full set of the *Diaries* from AbeBooks. Twitter, gone. Instagram, gone. The *Guardian* app—*so* gone. Anne could be ever-vigilant, a bulwark of liberal democracy. Coralie'd had enough.

'Show it to me?' Daniel surprised them all by saying. He was rolling out pastry for his own mince pies.

'Yes, chef.' Adam pressed play and leaned the phone against a candlestick.

'Oh, stop,' Daniel said, as soon as he glanced at the screen. 'Stop!'

Coralie stretched over and paused the video.

'His father hates him,' Daniel said. 'Can't you see? God, someone tell Boris. He's in danger.'

Adam raised his eyebrows as he pocketed his phone.

'We're the ones in danger,' Anne said. 'From him.'

In the playpen in the corner, Max kissed the air above his shoulders. 'I'm going upstairs to feed the baby.' Coralie escaped.

She would never, ever take a full house and her Amazon trestle table for granted. Her childhood Christmases had been so bleak—her parents, in opposite armchairs, watching Coralie and Daniel open one present at a time, every expression and utterance scrutinised for the correct amount of gratitude. Invariably, having been 'given so much', Daniel would commit the crime of wanting more, or something different. He would cry, their father would shout, their mother would sob as she ironed in the spare room, and Coralie would read, alone. Throughout university, she'd been a guest at her ex-boyfriend Josh's family Christmases, an outsider in a foreign world of cousins, dogs, boisterous games and water fights. By the time they'd broken up, so had her own family, and she didn't have the money, the annual leave or the inclination to catch a plane to her mother's place in Darwin. She spent the day with friends, and didn't put up a tree. But even having tasted loneliness, and knowing on a bone-deep level that what she had was special, she was still glad Maxi needed feeding at least every two hours so she could take a little break.

Stretched out on the soft cloud of the winter duvet, she gazed down at his silky blond hair, and distracted him by stroking him, squeezing his earlobe, and craning to kiss his head, until he broke off and gave her an enormous smile. He was a perfect boy and her best friend.

'You know the nicest birthday present you could give me,' Adam had said that morning. 'A night without this Coralie-hog in the room.' That was a bit rich, coming from him—if he didn't insist on having a study to write his election books, Florence could sleep in it, and Maxi would move into a beautifully redecorated nursery next-door. The Pinterest board was ready! But, to be fair to Adam, not that he deserved it, she was on the fence about moving Maxi too. If it was up to her, Maxi would stay a baby and remain in her bed for *life*. And if Adam had to move out, that was *his* problem! 'Isn't it, Minnie?' She kissed his cheeks until he was trembling with delight. 'It is!'

'Cor?'

'Zor? Come in.'

'When's Hannah's dad picking her up?'

'Five, I thought. Any minute now.'

Zora sat on the bed. 'Coralie?'

'Mmm?'

'Do I have to go to Tom's?'

It was Marina's turn to have Zora for Christmas Day. They'd be spending it, as usual, at Tom's family home in Sevenoaks. Zora probably didn't want to endure the drive. Since attending a big climate march in late September, she'd stuck an adhesive skull on Tom's Range Rover, and had threatened to let down his tyres. 'Oh?' Coralie tried to keep it light. 'Why?'

'It's not my family, it's Tom's.'

'They're okay though, aren't they?'

'Zor? Zor?' They could hear Hannah calling.

'Let's talk more about this,' Coralie said. 'Tom and your mum aren't coming till six.'

Zora nodded at her feeding half-brother. 'That looks a bit gross. Is it gross?'

'I thought the whole idea of it was gross—until I was about thirty. But now, no. I love it.'

'Freak,' Zora said on her way out.

'You're the freak.'

'Bye, freak.'

Maxi had nodded off. Coralie moved him to the centre of the bed. With a nap this late, he'd be up till nine or ten. Then he'd still expect his midnight feed. *And* his feeds at 3 and 5 a.m. She owed her tenuous grip on sanity to breastfeeding hormones and a packet of biscuits a day.

Upstairs, the door to Zora's room was ajar. 'It's not exactly a good look,' Hannah was saying. She was inclined, occasionally, to be bossy.

'It's not what I would choose for myself,' she heard Zora say.

'Why shouldn't you choose? It's your name.'

They must be working on their novel. It was a sprawling,

complex work called *Seven Sisters*. There were seven main characters (all sisters), and it was set in Seven Sisters, a part of London that, to Coralie's knowledge, neither author had actually visited. She tapped on the door and pushed it open a few inches. 'Hannah, your dad must be due any minute. Don't forget your toothbrush.'

Adam was trudging up the stairs as Coralie was on her way down. 'Where are the girls?'

'Upstairs, plotting.'

'Hmm...' He kept walking.

'Does Zora have to go to Tom's family tonight?'

Adam shrugged tiredly. 'It's their turn.'

'I know.' *Are you okay*, she wanted to ask. He'd only lie and say yes, but in a way that showed he wasn't. Or if he said no, he wasn't okay, then what was she supposed to do? She had a house full of people and a fifteen-week-old baby. It would have to wait till everyone went home. But when everyone went home, he'd have to work on his book about the last election campaign, due on 6 March. So when would they talk? Never.

The doorbell rang. 'Hannah!' she called.

But when she opened the door, she found Tom. 'Bit early, sorry! Rup was asleep in the car, so we just packed up and left. Zora!'

'Come in,' Coralie said. 'She's got Hannah over.'

'Thanks, it's okay. We're in a rush.'

'I'll shut the door at least.'

Tom stepped inside. 'Sorry, yes.'

'It's freezing. Adam! Tom's here for Zora.'

'Get Brexit done,' Daniel boomed from the kitchen.

'Well, indeed.' Tom was once again an MP, having run for Eastbourne again a few weeks earlier and unexpectedly won, swept in on a tide of Boris.

'Tom, you're too early,' Anne called from the sitting room.

'Oh, hello, Tom,' Sally said sweetly.

'Hello to *you*, Sally. Merry Christmas. Hello, Hannah— merry Christmas.'

Hannah was carrying her things down the stairs. 'Oh, I thought it was my dad. We don't do Christmas! But thanks.'

'*Happy Holidays*,' Tom said in an American accent. 'Zora!'

'I'm not coming!' Zora shouted.

Tom pretended he hadn't heard. 'Mum and Rup are in the car. We're a *little* bit worried about traffic.'

'Well, I'm a little bit *not coming*.' Zora sat on the stairs with a bump. Hannah glanced back and sat down too.

'I see,' Tom said. 'We shall, we shall not be moved. Extinction Rebellion in the house. Gluing yourself to the bannister.'

'But seriously,' Daniel said. 'Tom? Zora's got a performance to do on the keyboard.'

It was 'Old Town Road' by Lil Nas X. She'd taught herself to play it from a YouTube tutorial. Only Daniel and Barbie had seen it so far. Coralie had heard her singing it in the shower in a surprisingly clear and tuneful voice.

'Tom doesn't give a shit,' Zora said.

'Zora!' At the top of the stairs, Adam's legs appeared.

'Don't worry, I can handle it, I'm a big boy,' Tom said. 'Happy birthday, Adam. Look, Zora, I'm really sorry about being early. Do you want me to get Rup in from the car, and Marina? We can all watch your song.'

'I'm not doing my stupid song!' Zora's lip was trembling. It was a tantrum she never threw as a child. 'I don't want to go to stupid Sevenoaks!'

Holding Sally's hand in the hall, Florence gazed up at Zora in surprise.

'I see.' Tom realised the limit of his authority. 'I'll fetch Marina.'

The hall filled with frigid air as Tom opened the door, then slammed it.

'Zora, sweetheart,' Coralie began.

Upstairs, there was a long wail. Max had woken up. 'Thanks, Tom,' Adam muttered.

'I'll get him.' Daniel slipped up past the girls towards the bedroom. He didn't like to be around conflict, even of a restrained and English kind.

Another knock on the front door. Coralie swung it open, expecting Tom.

'Dad!' Hannah said.

But Hannah's dad was looking out towards Wilton Way, where Tom was carrying a drowsy Rup and frowning. 'Oh look, it's Mr Brexit!' Hannah's dad said. 'Boris's boy in Camden. I hope you're proud of yourself.'

'Politely,' Tom said rudely, 'give me a break.'

'You give *us* a break,' Anne popped out of the sitting room. 'You should be ashamed of what you've done.'

'What exactly?' Tom said. 'I didn't vote for Brexit, but the majority of people did; certainly, some fifty-seven per cent of Eastbourne. It's called democracy.'

At least three people made a disgusted sound: Anne, Adam

and Hannah's dad.

'You voted for it this time,' Anne said. 'Waving through the withdrawal agreement…Shameful, Tom. Why are you in this conman's government? No one forced you to be an MP.'

'She's not wrong.' Marina was on the doorstep. 'Hi, Jonathan.'

Hannah's dad raised his hand in greeting. 'Hannah? Time to go, sweetheart. We'll leave these guys to their important Christmas ritual of having a huge argument.'

'We're *not* having an argument,' Tom said stiffly.

'All righty!' Jonathan gave another little wave. 'Hannah, say thanks for having me.'

'Thanks for having me,' Hannah said in a robot voice.

Rup had wriggled to the ground and slipped into the front hall. Marina and Tom were still shivering on the doorstep. 'It would be great if you could come inside,' Coralie said. 'Our central heating's not very good.'

Marina swept in and sat in front of Zora on the stairs.

'Wrennie, Rupey.' Sally led them back towards the kitchen. 'Shall we cut up some carrots for the reindeer?'

Adam sat down on the step behind Zora. 'Sweetheart, what's going on?'

Zora laid her head on his knee and burst into tears. 'I don't want to go to Sevenoaks, it's *so* far, and *so* boring, and I can't even walk to the shops. Tom's dad makes me call him Mr Dunlop, like we're people from the olden days! They use the same cutting board and serving spoons for my food and the meat. And last time I went, Tom said we were going to move there!'

Everyone turned to stare at Tom. 'I said I wouldn't mind sending Rup to school there,' he said. 'For secondary! He's only just started primary!'

'We would never make you leave school or move,' Marina said firmly.

'I'm always moving,' Zora sobbed. 'I've always got a bag packed. *Got your bag, poppet?* I'm sick of it! I want to be in charge of who I'm with and where I go.'

'But we all want you,' Coralie said. 'We'd all keep you with us all the time, if we could.'

'It's true,' Marina said. 'We share you so it's fair.'

'Fair for *you*,' Zora said. 'Anyway, you don't want me! You all have new children, your real children, and I'm just boring old leftovers in the fridge.'

Marina and Adam closed over Zora like a clamshell.

Coralie looked at Tom. 'Let's have a cup of tea.'

In the playpen, Florence and Rup wriggled on their backs, pretending to be babies. Tom slumped at the kitchen table.

'Has it been very tiring in the Parliament?' Sally asked.

'He's been an MP again for two weeks,' Anne scoffed.

'Anne, it's none of your business,' Tom said, 'but when they asked me to run again in Eastbourne, I thought I was going to lose. My seat was so marginal, why would I think I'd win? I was doing Conservative HQ a favour. And—shoot me if you wish—I didn't think Jeremy Corbyn could be trusted with public money and the nuclear deterrent. Is Boris perfect? No, but he's better than the alternative. It's very tiring, yes, *even* after two weeks, and Marina's furious, and everyone hates me.'

'You're playing with fire putting a known liar in as leader. Boris lied his way to Brexit, and he lied his way to Number Ten,' Anne said. 'Twice.'

Tom raised his hands. 'I give up.'

'You seem to expect to be comfortable everywhere you go,' Anne said. 'But the things you do and say have consequences, for the nation generally, and for you and for your family. And when that impacts Zora, that means *my* family.'

'For—' Tom pushed his chair back. 'For heaven's sake, Anne!'

Anne sat impassive as Tom stormed out of the room.

Coralie looked over at Tom's son, giggling in the playpen. 'Maybe Rup belongs to us now.'

'Don't be silly, Coralie.'

'Tom's out in the car.' Marina came in looking stunned. 'And Zora wants to change her surname to Amin.'

'Good,' Anne said. 'I don't care. Whiteman was never my name. She should!'

'Marina?' Coralie said. 'What's happening with Zora?'

'We're letting her choose where to be, at least for tonight and tomorrow.'

Anne shot out into the hallway, presumably to make her case.

Rup wouldn't leave the playpen until Coralie gave Marina a mince pie to use as bait. 'Embarrassing to give him a bribe,' Marina said.

'I want a bribe,' Florence cried, so Coralie gave her one too.

Finally, Marina and Rup left. Sally and Florence left. Alone for the first time in the entire day, Coralie lowered her head to the table. That was where Daniel found her when he came in with Max.

'Are you dead?'

'No, unfortunately.' Coralie sighed. 'Hello, Maxi! Hello, Moo!' Max leaned out of Daniel's arms and into Coralie's. 'Was that the first time you've had Max alone?'

'It was. It was crazy.'

'What was crazy about it?'

'I lay on the bed next to him and watched him. He wasn't crying or anything. He was looking at me, looking at my mouth, my eyes, my whole face. I gave him Brown Bear, which you have in your bed still, like a loser.'

'You're the loser,' she said automatically.

'And it was crazy to see him study it, look at Brown Bear's fur, his eyes...'

'Why was it crazy?'

'I never realised babies had a *mind*. That time worked on them, the same way it works on us. He was conscious. The seconds ticked by, the same for him as for me.'

Coralie stared at him, puzzled.

'She's staying,' Anne announced from the door. 'Zora's staying with us!'

In the pantry, there was a rustling noise. 'Oh no,' Coralie said.

A small brown shape was at the playpen, the table, the sink, then under the fridge. Coralie screamed.

Adam poked his head in. 'What's going on?'

'We're extremely excited to have Zora,' Anne said.

'Yes,' Coralie said. 'Exactly!'

Daniel baked the leftover pasta and lentil bolognese with béchamel.

'Isn't it awful about the bushfires,' Sally said halfway through dinner.

Under the table, Coralie crossed her fingers, hoping that would be the end of it.

'Five million hectares,' Anne said. 'Nine people dead.'

Coralie's Instagram had been full of Australian friends wearing surgical masks to go to work. Smoke was so bad you couldn't see the Sydney Harbour Bridge. In Canberra, Elspeth couldn't sleep—during the bushfires of 2003, her childhood horse had died, trapped in its stable. Sometimes Coralie thought of koalas, stuck in the top of burning trees. She thought of a giant scoreboard, measuring parts per million of atmospheric carbon dioxide. What would Maxi's life be like? Would Australia even exist? 'Climate Change and the End of Australia': there'd been a piece about it in *Rolling Stone*. 'Yes…' She trailed off. 'Not good.'

'All that smoke is like a packet of cigarettes a day,' Anne said. 'For the lungs. And you can see it in placentas. Climate change, of course.'

Everyone murmured their agreement.

'Still, you must miss it,' Sally said. 'Australia. And will you two be FaceTiming your father tonight? It must be Christmas there already. Or are *we* ahead? I can't remember. Coralie, what does Florence call your dad?'

Coralie didn't know what to say.

'Mr Bower,' Zora joked.

'When I was a teenager,' Daniel said, 'he made me call him sir.'

'Maybe we'll FaceTime him?' Coralie looked at Daniel, who made a generous 'go right ahead' gesture, implying that he, of course, would not.

'It's somebody you know's bedtime,' Adam said.

Florence was lying in his lap, her eyes half shut. She realised everyone was looking at her. 'I want a *bribe*.'

'She means a mince pie,' Coralie murmured.

'And I want a *Sally bath*,' Flo said.

Sally got up immediately. 'I mean—if it's okay with you...'

Adam made the same gesture Daniel had made moments earlier. When Sally led Flo out by the hand, Zora became the child, and lay her head on Adam's shoulder.

'It's nice to have you here,' Coralie said.

'Very nice,' Anne said.

How had Marina responded to Zora's choice? Maybe the surname thing had taken out some of the sting. Coralie was glad not to be in that Range Rover, speeding Zora-less towards an awkward Sevenoaks Christmas. Of course, Marina had known Tom was a Conservative when they'd met; they'd joked about it at the wedding. But being a Tory in 2009 was somehow different from being one now—or was it? It had always been pretty grim. It *was* nice to have Zora, but breaking long-held arrangements, with none in place for the future, was frightening. Did they want to be in a child custody dispute with two barristers? It seemed foolhardy.

As if he was reading Coralie's thoughts, Adam cupped Zora's chin. 'The name stuff I don't mind. But I would die if you didn't want to see me anymore,' he said. 'Zora? You always have to see me. Do you promise?'

'I promise,' Zora said.

Anne sat back in her chair like a patriarch as Daniel and Adam cleared the dinner. Coralie fed Maxi at the table, self-conscious in front of Anne, not about her exposed breast ('I've seen it all before,' Anne grimly claimed) but about her habitual murmured endearments, and the baby's smiles and laughs. 'Maybe just let him get on with it,' she'd once admonished. She often said that kind of thing, along with 'You're making a rod for your own back.'

'I might go up and read to Wrennie,' Zora said. 'Cor, that's your phone.'

In the middle of the table, Coralie's screen was flashing with a video call. 'Oh, it's Roger,' Coralie said.

Daniel turned, shocked.

'I'll get it!' Before Coralie could stop her, Zora accepted the call and propped the phone against a wine glass.

Roger, no greeting, peremptory: 'What's that you're doing?'

'Hi, Dad. This is Max,' Coralie shrugged. 'You know!'

'Big unit, isn't he? Rugby guy. He gets that from our side.'

'My father was tall, actually,' Anne said.

'Who's that?'

Anne picked up the phone and scrutinised it.

'Oh, you must be Adam's dad,' Roger said. 'Hello, mate.'

'Adam's mother.' Anne was amused. 'Anne Whiteman.'

'No offence intended! It's a compliment being mistaken for a man!'

'What's your background there, Roger? Trees?'

'Yes, it's my walk. I'm on the bush track. Here in Canberra. Look, Princess loves it.'

Coralie, who had buried her face in the baby, took a cautious glance at the phone. A ratty creature was prancing along; its tail, a long plume, swayed from side to side.

'What a funny little dog,' Anne said. 'A Chihuahua or something?'

'Pomchi. Pomeranian Chihuahua cross. A ladies' dog, she was Jenny's—but now she prefers me. Routine. A firm hand. Dogs are like children. They like to know who's boss.'

Zora, who had paused in the doorway, looked horrified and escaped.

'Hi, Roger,' Adam called over his shoulder from the sink. Anne held out the phone so Roger could see him.

'The man himself!' Roger said. 'I've been reading your stuff. Merry Christmas to you, mate.'

'Merry Christmas to *you*, mate.'

'And who's that next to you with the ponytail?'

Daniel turned around slowly. Anne was still holding the phone up. There was no escape. 'Hi, Dad.'

'Good grief, Daniel. That's new!'

'Oh, it's…good in the kitchen. For my work. When I cook.'

'And how's that going over there?'

As far as Coralie knew, Daniel hadn't worked in a professional kitchen since the day he'd married Barbie. 'Great,' Daniel said. 'Thanks!'

'Isn't it *awful* about the fires,' Anne enunciated very clearly as she replaced the phone on the table.

'Awful!'

'That's climate change for you,' Anne said.

Coralie's shoulders touched her ears.

'Actually...' Roger began.

Danger! If Coralie could have squirted ink like a squid, she would have. 'What are you and Jenny up to today?'

'Hotel, roast, watch TV with the air con on, walking Princess nice and early before the bushfire smoke gets too bad. We'll go round to Edwin's later—you know, Jenny's son. He's had a kid, a boy.' Coralie didn't know. 'Nice little guy. No trouble yet—but he will be! Ask Daniel! Boys ruin your life!'

'How old is Edwin's son?'

'That's a question for Jenny. Hang on, he was born when I was watching the AFL Grand Final—so that was about three months ago.'

This at least was firmer ground. 'Oh! Max is fifteen weeks!'

'Fifteen weeks! It's been too long,' Roger said. 'Time for me to meet him. Jenny wants Paris in the springtime. We're getting there through London. Week or two, war museum, Churchill War Rooms, love to see this young fella. Tickets are booked for March.'

March? Adam's deadline was the sixth. Out of sight of the phone, at the sink, Adam's face was the murderer's mask from *Scream*.

'You should stay in Daniel's Airbnb,' Anne said. 'Lovely place. Nothing fancy, but well located. They've done a lovely job on it.'

Now Daniel's face was the mask from *Scream*.

'Tell me everything, Dad!' Coralie frantically squid-inked.

'All your plans! Email me! Itineraries! Ideas! We can't wait! Florence will be so happy to meet you.' She had a sudden horror her father would say *Who's Florence?* Squid squid squid! 'This must be costing you a fortune! We'll let you get back to Jenny!'

'Bye, Dad!' Daniel shouted.

Coralie lunged for her phone and pressed the end-call button.

'I wonder why he thought the catastrophically unprecedented fire season was unrelated to the changing climate,' Adam mused.

'Best not to open all that up.'

'A charming man,' Anne surprisingly said.

Daniel made an ill face. In the corner by the pantry, Madonna leapt to her feet and spun in a circle. 'Oh, she needs to go out.' He charged towards the front door.

'I'll kiss Florence goodnight,' Coralie said. 'Then join you.'

'Give Max to me,' Anne demanded.

Coralie complied.

Up in the yellow nursery, Zora cuddled Florence while Sally sat very upright next to them, reading *The Paper Dolls*. 'And...'

They all waited for Florence to shout, *Flo with the bow!* She didn't. She was asleep.

'Night, Flo.' Zora wiggled off the end of the bed.

Coralie turned off the lamp. 'Goodnight, little Cheep-Cheep.'

'Wrennie, my little girl,' Adam said. 'Night-night, sweetheart.'

'Night-night, Floss.' On the way out, Sally murmured, 'You

know what they say.'

'What?' Coralie said.

'A loved child has many names.'

Outside, the air reeked of cigarettes. Coralie pulled her coat tighter. 'Yuck.'

Dan nodded down towards the shop. 'Just did an emergency dash.'

'Gross. What does Madonna think? Her lovely ringlets stinking.'

They looked down at the poodle, snuffling blindly around a council-maintained street tree. 'Imagine if his dog was a boy-dog,' Daniel said. 'And he let it be called Princess.'

There was no need to ask who the 'he' was. He had been *he*, if not He with a capital-H, for the whole of both their childhoods.

'I can't square that guy on the phone with the Roger we used to know. Anne thought he was charming. Maybe he wasn't that bad?'

'He let me choose what he'd hit me with, a ruler or a belt,' Daniel said. 'In Jakarta, he hit me with a badminton racquet. That was in front of the gardener, and Alan.' He must have realised Coralie didn't know who Alan was. 'My friend from school. Who didn't come back, or talk to me, ever again. But didn't he do it to you too?'

She remembered running away from smacks, but never actual smacks. Maybe she'd always been fast enough?

Daniel turned to blow smoke away from her. 'Which was the house where we had the pool?'

'Brisbane?'

'I saw you get slapped with a rolled-up towel.'

'Oh, on my...' She laughed, embarrassed. 'Face?'

'No, legs. I remember seeing you running.'

'If it was Brisbane, I would have been, what—eight? You would have been three and a bit.'

'Florence's age.'

They stared at each other for a long time.

'I remember reading Boris Johnson's sister once, in a column. She said they were smacked.' She swiped her phone open and searched. 'Yes, look. When they filled the family wellies with water, they got beaten with a stick. It's in the *Daily Mail*.'

Daniel blew out a long stream of smoke. 'The *family wellies.*'

'Like Wellington boots. Gumboots.'

'I know what they are. What do the commenters say?'

'Stop those three-year-old tantrums before they begin! First time. Then you never have to do it again,' Coralie read out. 'Wow, lots of all-caps: It is necessary to prevent future problems, this person says. Children are like dogs, they need discipline, and a spank does not have to be hard to get the message home. That sounds familiar.'

Daniel bent over and tickled Madonna's tiny rib cage. She jumped into his hand. He stood up with her cuddled to his chest. 'Search Boris Johnson and smacking.'

'All right.' Coralie searched. 'Also in the *Daily Mail*, from 2012: Parents must have the right to smack their children to instil discipline, says Boris. Okay then.'

'We're the losers for not liking it. Maybe it was actually *good*. I wonder if Roger will hit us when he comes in March?'

'I wonder if we'll hit him?'

'I FaceTimed Barbie,' Daniel said. 'He was at lunch with his sons in Brooklyn. *They* have a nice dad.'

'You didn't want to go with him?'

'Ugh, I did, and it would have been fine, but I didn't, for some reason. I couldn't face it.'

'Stay here tonight,' Coralie said. 'Anne and Sally are in the spare room. You can have the sofa.'

'I've got the keys for the Graham Road flat. It's more my size when I'm on my own.'

'Nice to be a property mogul.'

'It is, I have to say.'

'Come as early as you want in the morning. Florence will be up from six.'

'I won't be.'

'I will,' Coralie said sadly.

'Isn't that your neighbour?'

Miss Mavis rounded the corner, walking with a stick. 'Merry Christmas to you, Cara Lee,' she said. 'Thank you for the cards. Come in, come in, I have something for the girls.'

They followed her into her front garden, paved over and empty except for her bins and a narrow strip of dirt where two giant camellias grew, their drooping petals scarlet in the security light. In the hall, Miss Mavis leaned her stick against a tall walnut console table. On it was a crocheted doily and a brass dish. In the brass dish was an envelope from British Gas. Capital letters shouted from a big blue oblong: DO NOT DISREGARD THIS LETTER. PAYMENT DUE. Above the table, hanging from the picture rail, was a framed piece of delicate cross-stich:

CHRIST is the HEAD
of the house
THE UNSEEN GUEST
at every meal
THE SILENT LISTENER
to every conversation

Daniel was staring at it, his face pale. 'Like Roger.'

'What did Barbie mean that time,' Coralie said urgently, 'when he said I was the good one and you were the bad one?'

'Here we are.' Miss Mavis shuffled back in with two envelopes and a packet of Jammie Dodgers. 'One for Florence. One for Miss Zora. She's not too old to get a card and her biscuits.'

'She'll love them, thank you, Miss Mavis. They both will. What are you doing for Christmas?'

'Church for me. Busy all day. And who is this?'

'It's me, Miss Mavis. Daniel. I'm Coralie's brother, we met before.'

'Nice to see you again,' she said with great formality.

'Nice to see you again,' Daniel laughed as they went back next-door. 'She definitely forgot me.'

'So clever, so polite, she sounds like a politician. Like Tory Tom. Oh no.' She could hear Maxi wailing through the closed front door.

'Eek, that's a lot of crying. I'll head off.' Daniel embraced her. 'Say bye to everyone, and happy birthday to Adam. I'll see you tomorrow for lunch.'

'You will, because you're cooking it.'

'Oh, 'e's the best at cooking,' Dan made Madonna say in a Cockney accent, gently holding her tennis ball skull. 'The best li'l boy in the weald.'

Inside, the real best little boy in the world was waiting for her in his new nappy and clean pyjamas. She arranged herself in the semi-dark, propped up against the bedhead with a pillow across her lap. For this part of bedtime, they kept the door open and only the bathroom light on, just enough to see by. Maxi was sucking his thumb with an intensity that meant he had recently been in tears, was probably about to be so again, and was very hungry. Adam tossed the wormaid onto the bed and ceremoniously laid Max in and zipped him up. (The 'wormaid' was their name for his sleeping bag: it made him half a worm and half a mermaid.) Transformation complete, he was handed over to Coralie for milk. 'Night-night.' Adam kissed him gently. 'Little baby boy. I'm going to work in the kitchen tonight. Not too late, maybe midnight.'

'Do you think we'll ever get to talk,' Coralie asked quietly.

'What, you and me? Alone, as adults? Probably not.'

'It seems unlikely.'

'A far-off dream.'

'Happy birthday,' she said.

He slipped out.

Maxi's hair was damp from his bath. She tried not to chat to him during his last feed of the day. Night-time was supposed to be night-time, that's what all the books said. They also said not to feed a baby to sleep, but his eyes soon shut, and his fists flopped back to his ears. She blew on his long eyelashes. They fluttered, but he didn't wake up. When she got to her feet, she couldn't hear any milk inside him. (Usually he sloshed like a hot water bottle.) Her left breast was still full; if he didn't wake up in a few hours, she'd be in pain and have to hook up to the dreaded pump. But Max always knew what to do. They were a team. She laid him in the cot. He looked enormous in it, dwarfing his toy sheep. She leaned down to kiss him and tiptoed out, pulling the door shut softly behind her.

As she stood in the hallway, her ear to the door, her father came to her, and the black hole of growing up. She felt herself sitting to attention in her bedrooms in Brisbane, Canberra, Jakarta, Darwin, waiting to be given her orders for the day; tiptoeing around, always silent and ideally invisible; arranging her face to be attentive, alert, polite. Never sad, never angry, never happy; it wasn't worth it. To have an emotion (bad or good) was to make yourself a parent's problem. To make yourself a parent's problem was begging for trouble. She learned the lesson of The Look. The Look was all it took with Coralie, but Daniel never learned it, he had to have the smack (that must have been what Barbie had meant, about the good one and the bad one). All this still churned inside her. But it wouldn't touch her children. She was the wall, between the past and the future, and they were safe on the other side.

For as long as she was alive, she would protect them.

Swept up in *Untitled 2019 Campaign Book*, Adam nonetheless devoted three days over the New Year's break to record test radio shows for *The Times* and the *Sunday Times*. Partly based on the popularity of his podcast, the idea was to launch an 'audio product' to drive print subscriptions for the paper. The spontaneity of radio appeared to suit him (less slogging, more blagging). Now he was the front-runner to get his own politics variety show: a mix of hard and breaking news, light-hearted

287

quizzes, pre-made packages, interviews long and short, and a potential phone-in segment. It would go out live, between 5 p. m. and 8 p.m. Monday to Thursday, from the studio in London Bridge. If it went ahead (the launch date was late spring) Coralie would be dealing with at least four pick-ups, children's dinners and solo double bath and bedtimes minimum every week. She'd be a widow without the sympathy.

But Lydia was an actual single mother. And when Nicky went away, or was busy at the studio, Alice was on her own for months at a time. Coralie couldn't trouble them with her despair.

When she complained to Adam, he immediately said he'd turn it down—'You're the boss! Just say the word!' An easy offer to make, since he knew she'd never do it. Ask an ambitious show-off to refuse high-status work? She wasn't *mad*.

Besides, there were other things to worry about. A third person in Britain was diagnosed with the novel coronavirus, and (getting a packet of custard creams from the pantry) Adam had seen the mouse.

19

Pandemic

Brexit, Donald Trump, even climate change—aside from the very hot days when she was pregnant, so far not a single catastrophe had befallen her personally as a result of these apocalyptic harbingers. Privilege alert! But it was true. All the stress and psychic energy of monitoring their daily developments had been an absolute waste of time. The fact was, no amount of vigilance about 'the news' did anything to alter or control it. That was the hard-won insight she'd been left with. She was reluctant to give it up.

Sadly, developments in 2020 meant she had to.

In February, her father had cancelled his trip to what he called 'Europe' (London and Paris). *Observe, Orient, Decide, Act (OODA)* read the subject line of the email he sent to both Coralie and a Hotmail address Daniel hadn't used since he was twenty. The body of the email was devoted to what he called his 'sitrep'. The upshot was that he didn't want Jenny exposed to 'the virus, now formally designated Covid-19' as they transited through Singapore, where eight new cases had been reported, bringing the total to fifty-eight. *I realise that this may be a disappointing email to receive, but I must act decisively given the available data. Regards, Roger,'* he concluded, helpfully adding, in brackets, *Dad.*

Roger's cancelled his visit because of the coronavirus, Coralie WhatsApped Dan, adding a restrained seven thumb emojis.

Pussy! her brother replied.

But Coralie redownloaded Twitter and followed every journalist she could think of.

She had her Brexit stockpile still—the pasta and so on, and began adding to it every week. She wasn't some kind of *freak*, like a prepper! She was *strategically forward-purchasing* things she had planned to buy anyway. What difference did it make if it was stored it in her pantry (and the spare room) instead of the Ocado customer fulfilment centre? She imagined, sometimes, a sparkly magnet, like Daniel and Barbie's:

It's not a warehouse
It's a warehome

'Got any Vitamin C in the stocky-p?' Adam asked one day. A forwarded message had gone round both his university friends WhatsApp group *and* his Liverpool Football Club WhatsApp group (aka 'The KopTwats') saying it was clinically proven to halt progression of the disease. 'That's directly from doctors in Lombardy,' he said. (The news at that time was dominated by footage of overflowing Italian hospital wards where older people, mainly men, lay on their fronts hooked up to machines.)

At Montessori, the children were playing Corona, a version of tag where, if someone breathed on you, you lay on the ground and 'died'. In the second week of March, a parent in the pick-up line said it was time to shut the schools. The words resounded in her head like a hit gong. She swayed, faint. Disease she could handle, sickness, even death. But *no school*? No drop-off and pick-up, nine and three-thirty, the unalterable rhythm of her days? The unknowns were so vast, and the terror suddenly so great, that—on the pavement, at the front gate, with Florence's scooter ready, and Maxi sleeping in the buggy—she found herself flying into the air; for a moment, she was a ghost, or an angel, weightless, shimmering, a vapour of pure fear. Then she dropped back down to earth, Coralie again, a mother in a puffer coat with a tote bag full of snacks.

On 18 March, a day when thirty-three people died of Covid in Britain, bringing the death toll to 104, it was announced that the schools would close on Friday. Glastonbury was cancelled. Forty tube stations were shut down. *Just confirmed at lobby briefing,* Adam texted. *London won't be sealed off.* That was good to know!

On Friday, New York and California residents were ordered to 'shelter in place'. When Coralie picked up Florence for the last time, the teachers handed over a pile of her (bad) art, as well as her Crocs, and all her spare knickers and clothes. 'She might have grown out of them by the time we see her again,' Miss Sarah said. Coralie cried silently all the way home.

Adam, meanwhile, his draft finished and nothing to do until

the edits came back, or his *Times* show started, urgently texted colleagues and spads to work out who was taller, him or the chancellor, Rishi Sunak? A chilling official message from a hospital in Harrow went viral on UK WhatsApp: *We currently do not have enough space for patients requiring critical care.* Finally, at 5 p,m., the prime minister declared all pubs, gyms, theatres and restaurants were to close.

Over the weekend, which was sunny, Broadway Market and Columbia Road Flower Market were both heaving. Angry people posted pictures of the crowds on Twitter: it was okay for them to be there, breathe the air and take crowd pictures— but it was *not* okay for others to be there, breathe the air, and be IGNORANT of the danger the nation faced.

There was huge support for the formal lockdown, announced by Boris Johnson in his most serious gravelly voice on 23 March. It seemed to make people feel good to know that no one in the United Kingdom could enjoy themselves. Members of the new Wilton Way WhatsApp group (description field: IN A WORLD WHERE YOU CAN BE ANYTHING, BE KIND) competed with each other to be the *least* free. *My dog needs walking twice a day for his arthritis. Do you think I can take him on my government-sanctioned exercise, and my government-sanctioned shop?* In what world would that *not* be okay? Why ask? Even so, a few people gently tut-tutted, one stating they'd 'erected an agility course' for their 'doggo' in their garden, using low-cost environmentally friendly materials available from Argos.

'Doggo,' Coralie muttered on the sofa.

'Erected,' Adam replied.

'Agility course.'

But neither of them was laughing the next morning. A cabinet minister went on *Good Morning Britain* to say children of separated parents had to stay in one house for lockdown. Zora was in Camden. They might not see her for weeks!

Adam found the clip on Twitter and sent it on to Tom: *Exactly what is your pathetic government playing at?* Ten minutes later, on a different show, the cabinet minister said that he'd misspoken: children of separation were allowed to see and stay with both parents. Adam tried to delete the message, but there were already two blue ticks. Fortunately (or worryingly), Tom did not reply. When Boris Johnson, the health secretary, and the chief medical officer were all diagnosed with Covid on the same day, Adam messaged that he hoped Tom was all right. Tom replied with an italicised red 100 emoji. That seemed to be an English thing, operating on a small emotional chessboard with only four main moves: Jolly, Polite, Withdrawn, Cold. What was a 100 emoji? Polite/Withdrawn cusp? At least Tom still drove Zora between their two houses, so she didn't have to catch the train.

At the beginning of lockdown, they'd started a tradition of family lunch, sitting down together at half past twelve every day. But it was a chaotic and loud affair: Maxi in his highchair, throwing or mashing finger food, and Florence tapping her feet against the chair, knocking her glass off the table with her elbow, sliding down onto the floor. Zora looked more and more stressed every mealtime, the food on her plate untouched.

Coralie offered to bring up meals to her room. But that shone a spotlight on her, only highlighting that most of the food came back down again. Zora washed her knives and forks and plates separately from the rest of the household's, and dried them on paper towel, in case any meat (or meat steam from the dishwasher) had touched them, or meat water from the washing machine had touched the dishcloth. Even after Coralie stopped cooking meat altogether, Zora still said she could smell it.

Coralie had never had a regular one-on-one text correspondence with Marina, but from the beginning of lockdown they shared, without small talk, what was working. *Fage Greek yoghurt full fat, plastic spoon not metal. Waitrose blueberries organic, soaked to get rid of white stuff. Broadway Market kefir, plain not fruit, I'll send two bottles home with her. Peanut butter crunchy, not smooth, glass jar better than plastic tub.* Calories were going into Zora; she certainly wasn't starving. But if there was any tension or noise in the room when she eating, her throat closed over and she could hardly swallow or breathe.

Coralie had read so many books when she was young, because to read was to enter a different, and private, world, one her parents might have been suspicious of, but ultimately had to respect. She often wondered why Zora (with her clearly superior intellect, and almost unlimited access to books) didn't read as much as she had. Perhaps it was because, unlike Coralie, Zora didn't have anything to escape. She was content to exist in real life, and didn't need to be swept away for entire days at a time. It was sad, then, when the trauma of the global pandemic plunged Zora into constant, insatiable, dissociative reading, all day and half the night. Coralie spent Maxi's naptime taking down favourite novels from the alcove shelves in the sitting room, dusting them, and arranging them to make them attractive and accessible to Zora: *Love in a Cold Climate, I Capture the Castle, Bonjour Tristesse, Prep.* It felt odd to touch books again because she had barely read a chapter since the start of the pandemic. And as for writing—ha! Scrolling the news was all she could do.

Having written four full-length books of non-fiction on crash schedules, Adam thought he knew what it was to be confined to his desk. But he'd still been able to record his pods, go into the newsroom and Westminster, have lunches and coffees with colleagues and sources, and swim (only rarely) at the Lido. Locked down for weeks on end, his show on Times Radio not starting till June, he withered from lack of connection, spending endless hours on Twitter reading #longreads from American science communicators about how even mild cases of Covid led to chronic brain damage. Because the events had taken place in a different universe, no one cared about his December 2019 election book, scheduled for publication after Easter. He wasn't happy about that, and he was nervous about the radio show, whether he'd be good enough, whether anyone would listen. But he didn't express his anxiety in a way that Coralie could deal with, empathise over and try to soothe. It came out instead as *tsk*-ing irritation, minor explosions, or he'd zone out for half a conversation, then come to with a scathing 'What?'

He tried to impose order in a world where there was none, by controlling what he could: namely, the twice- or three-times-daily stacking of the dishwasher in a precise way and to a precise schedule known only to himself. Often Coralie would be at the chopping board, preparing yet another elaborate vegetarian meal (meals being the main way of marking the passage of time) only to find Adam hovering behind her, waiting to slot her knife into the cutlery basket.

One Sunday night, Coralie, Adam and Zora watched the Queen's national address from the sofa. 'Republic now,' Coralie murmured. 'And not just Australia—here.' But that old lady had really lived through a lot, including (unlike most people fulminating about the Blitz spirit) actual World War Two. For a moment, her mere existence seemed to say that everything would one day be okay. 'Okay, republic soon,' Coralie backed down. 'At least before we get William. Oh, Anne's on FaceTime. Anne? Did you watch the Queen? Quite moving, I thought.'

'Silly,' Anne said.

'What exercises should I do in the house, Granny?'

'Zora? Do Yoga with Adriene.'

'What did you ring for?' Adam was scrolling his phone. 'Shit! Boris Johnson's been taken to hospital!'

Well, anyone could have foreseen that! He was clearly so fat and unfit! Anne was still on FaceTime, so Coralie rushed to get her laptop and search Twitter. But as she watched the news spreading through the Westminster hacks, through Boris's supporters and his many enemies, she found herself unable to feel gleeful, or even to keep blaming the victim. Her heart was racing. She was scared.

'Yes, it must be day eight, or thereabouts,' Anne was saying. 'That's when it takes a turn for the worse. Well, as long as it's not pneumonia.'

'What would happen then?' Zora's face was pale. Was it

296

wrong to let her hear all this? Were they like those parents who let their kids watch 9/11 on the news?

Lots of doctors were on Adam's Liverpool WhatsApp. One of them said it was well known in 'medic circles' that Boris was already 'prone and vented'.

Prone and vented! Fucking hell.

She thought about the prime minister's body, and joined what she knew of it with the images she'd seen from Italy of old men lying on their fronts, their vulnerable white folds of back skin exposed—weren't they cold? Would Boris's back have bristles, like the hair sometimes left on roast pork, which she no longer cooked because Zora's revulsion had infected her? Would he have rough skin with inflamed follicles, or soft baby skin, untouched by the sun after years of justifiable embarrassment about taking his shirt off?

All this was rushing through Coralie's mind as she contemplated the prime minister's death. As a plot development it was dramatic, a season 1 finale-level shock. Who would be in charge if he was in a coma? If he died now, and she was given the option (was God-like in some way, or a showrunner) would she go back in time and make him die before Brexit? Yes, if he had to die, and she was given the choice, she would opt for 2015. But if he could stay alive? Maybe weakened—perhaps even bald? She found that she would prefer it.

A few days later, somewhat anticlimactically, Rishi Sunak reported that the prime minister was 'sitting up in bed and engaging positively with the clinical team', raising the intriguing prospect he'd previously been lying down and engaging negatively. Little bitch, getting Coralie all worried—

297

the ultimate selfish act from the ultimate selfish man!

Ever since she was a child, she'd made sense of her life by looking forward. As soon as she'd known Maxi's due date, she'd created a spreadsheet in her Dropbox labelled life plan, with columns for her, Adam, Zora, Flo and Maxi. In September 2020, Florence was due to start Reception at the primary school next to the park. Maxi would start Montessori in September 2021, just as Zora was starting Year 9. When Coralie was forty-one, in 2024, both her children would be in primary school. Would any of that happen? What was life if you couldn't rely on LifePlan.xls?

As lockdown spring unfolded, sunnier and more beautiful than any London spring she could remember, Coralie realised that her old full-time job at the agency had allowed her to dream of more time with Florence with no prospect of it coming true. Then, the nine-to-three-thirty Montessori schedule had left so many remaining hours of the day for parenting, she'd briefly (for the six shining months Florence had attended in-person classes) felt like a capital G, capital M Good Mother. Now, having no Montessori, or any childcare at all, and a baby boy who was beginning to assert himself, she was in the unusual (for her) position of wanting *less* time with the children—much less. It was bad enough to be a personal chef, food source, bum-wiper, teacher and entertainer for fifteen hours a day plus night feeds; it also felt bad to feel bad about hating it. It was perhaps unwise to have spent so much time reading about gentle parenting and attachment, about childhood trauma and 'breaking the cycle'. If she knew anything, it was the impact a parent had upon a child.

Overwhelmed, stymied, resentful to the point of break-down, she targeted Adam with all the anger it was otherwise unsafe to express, snapping at him to get off the sofa, to leave the house, to get over his dishwasher fixation and to *man up* (where did that come from?) about starting his new job. She snarled at him to get off her side of the bed ('an invisible line, running down the mattress—don't cross it'), stop polluting her air with his flatulence, stop laughing loudly on the phone, stop moaning about his book, stop talking to her, stop looking at her, and give her some fucking space! She was like a sandcastle, and Adam and the kids were like the sea, eroding her and flattening her with their proximity and demands. If she went for a walk, or listened to a podcast, she could begin rebuilding her ramparts, only to get knocked down again by wave after wave of *needs*.

But all this time, NHS staff and key workers were out there risking their lives daily. Black people and people of colour were getting murdered by the police, an injustice that was not new, but suddenly became the pressing and public concern of white people. Coralie herself posted a black square on Instagram, only to remove it a day later when activists said it messed up results for the Black Lives Matter hashtag. (Alice said Nicky's white accountant had asked how he was 'holding up'. 'Financially?' Nicky was confused. 'You tell me.' White people who didn't know he was famous winced apologetically at his Blackness in the street. White people who did know he was famous gave him solemn and respectful fist-bumps.) Some elderly people were so lonely they could die of isolation; some houses and flats were so packed with multiple generations of the same family it was impossible to shield the vulnerable. When single people said they were going mad with boredom, parents bitterly suggested they try looking after some kids. Parents of kids with special needs were too overwhelmed to compete about whose lockdown was the worst.

During the pandemic, Zadie Smith wrote that while privilege can be conceptualised and 'atoned for through transformative action', all suffering was uniquely personalised, 'absolute', and equally awful for the sufferer. She was such a good writer she could make anything sound true. With a small garden, the occasional Ocado slot, and a grumpy but alive husband, Coralie didn't feel able to complain.

In September 2020, after a summer they could almost pretend was normal, Florence started school. On the first day, they lined up at the gate, standing on yellow footsteps sprayed two metres apart. As Florence skipped in, they slimed her hands with sanitiser. She made it to Halloween before multiple positive tests shut down the class.

Home-schooling a four-year-old was a maddening waste of time. On the days Adam had his radio show, he took the kids from eight-thirty till ten and, however bitter the cold and rain, Coralie went out to Victoria Park, or Haggerston, or Hackney Downs, anywhere that wasn't home. These were called 'Mummy's walks', and she steeled herself to insist on them.

'You don't see me getting time for *self-care*,' Adam said.

'You don't see me getting to cycle in to London Bridge and be made a fuss of,' Coralie replied.

'I wouldn't call doing my job *being made a fuss of.*'

'I wouldn't call an hour away from my kids an especially special treat.'

'An hour and a half,' Adam muttered.

Then somehow a fight bloomed, and she was saying that every single choice about their life was a choice that was made by him. Where they lived, having Florence later than Coralie had wanted so she was starting school in a global pandemic, the way he simply missed the hardest part of parenting for the majority of every day, how he'd used their eight years together to grow professionally, produce lauded work and become famous, and she'd used their eight years together to run her body into the ground with two pregnancies, go backwards intellectually, and become a pathetic household drudge.

'Everything we do is your choice!' Adam was incredulous. 'The renovation, Florence's nursery, you quitting—none of that was my choice at all!'

Those were just surface things—why couldn't he see? She made surface-level changes, had a surface-level say, but he was the tectonic plates, his was the selfish core. Superficially accommodating, up to his neck in rinse-aid and nappies, it was nonetheless the bedrock of Adam, Adam's career and Adam's needs that underpinned and structured every aspect of their lives. His Times Radio work was the best he'd had in terms of profile and income, but by far the most inflexible. There was no satisfying, worthwhile job Coralie could take that would a) bring in enough money for Maxi's childcare, and b) allow her to drop everything the next time schools were shut on a whim.

And what if she didn't want to be in the UK at all? What if

she wanted to raise their children in Australia? That was an option they never entertained, even as the NHS collapsed around them, life expectancy fell off a cliff, and raw sewage bubbled into the sea. For most of her near-decade away, 'moving back to Australia' had functioned as a ripcord for Coralie. Jump—pull—float gently back to safety. But back home, the devastating fires had been followed by raging floods, and the right-wing Liberal government looked like it was there to stay. There was no escape, no alternative, and no dreams left to dream.

Even Lydia, a single mother in full-time work, was managing the global pandemic better than she could. Four short stories finished, one published in *The Stinging Fly*! In her house, there were two important people, a mother and a daughter. They both had needs, the needs were balanced. In Coralie's house, there were the kids and Adam—and they sucked her completely dry!

'Sweetheart?' Adam's tenderness broke her heart. 'What about your book? Why don't you use this time to write?'

This time? Which time did he mean exactly? The hour between the kids finally falling asleep and Adam arriving home expecting a hot meal? Maybe the hour between her waking up at four to worry and Maxi waking up at five to start his day?

Fridays, Adam said. He could work from home on Fridays, she could take the whole day to write—she must!

But it wasn't a *time* thing. The problem was the emptiness. All of life had drained from her, and she had no thoughts beyond the house.

*

Somehow two years had passed. Easter 2022 was 'the end' of the pandemic—well, that was when they took the Perspex screens down from the checkouts in the Hackney Marks & Spencer. It was also when the police issued more than fifty fines for illegal parties that took place in Downing Street during the pandemic. Having been so comprehensively flouted by the people in charge of making them, it was clear than no further Covid restrictions could ever be imposed, even if a deadly new variant emerged, or one that targeted children.

Alice and Nicky moved back to Hackney from LA to find they'd been priced out. Their old flat above the pub was for sale again, for nearly three times as much as they'd paid. They rented a one-bed on Cecilia Road to save up for a bigger deposit—a two-bed was pointless, because after two years of lockdown, Beauty refused to sleep away from them. Nicky felt like all his success had been for nothing. Alice tried to keep him cheerful but she hated everything about the flat. She had a hundred ideas for improvements, but the landlord wouldn't allow paint, minor repairs, or even nails to put up art. It was like a racehorse forbidden to run.

Coralie marked 'the end' of the pandemic by seeking rec-ommendations from her Instagram friends for an affordable holiday somewhere warm enough to swim. The votes had come back for Lanzarote, in the Canary Islands, four hours away on EasyJet. She hadn't slept anywhere except her own bed since Max was born, and she couldn't sleep at all at the resort. As Max wailed from his blue synthetic collapsible cot, she felt like doing the same. The heavy door between their interconnecting rooms was propped open with a wastepaper basket. Maxi dislodged it on the first night, causing the door to close on Florence's finger. Max's sleep, and probably Coralie's, could have been improved if Coralie had slept with him in the double bed and Adam and Florence slept in the other room in the two singles. But Adam refused, and used 'the finger thing' as a reason to keep the interconnecting door shut.

The countdown timer started ticking for holiday sex.

Max was too young for the kids' club. Florence refused to go alone. Neither of them knew how to swim, so the four pools felt less like luxury oases and more like chlorine deathtraps. When she held a laughing Max in the water, or pushed Florence around on her blow-up doughnut, Coralie felt briefly strong, maternal, radiant with love. When she lay by the pool and watched Adam take his turn with them, she felt painfully self-conscious about her lockdown body—pallid, no muscles to speak of, neck and (somehow) wrist pain.

The second night passed with no sex.

Lanzarote (Coralie hadn't really realised this) was just a browny-black rock in the middle of the ocean. Fresh food might have arrived on its shores (and surely there were fish out there to be had) but none showed up at their all-inclusive buffet. How fortunate Zora had chosen Marina and Tom's luxury trip to the Maldives. No way was Marina washing Rup's underpants in the sink and eating two to three ice creams a day.

On the third night, when silence finally descended on the kids' room, they gingerly attempted some intimacy.

Soon they heard a strange accompaniment to, almost an echo of, their cautious, arrhythmic thumps. 'Just ignore it,'

Adam said. Coralie jumped up, wrapped herself in a towel, and opened the door out to the hallway. It was Florence, who'd escaped the children's room and was wandering towards the pool in tears. 'I'll fetch her,' Adam said. 'Don't go anywhere.'

('The intercourse will continue until morale improves,' she darkly joked to no one.)

As she lay on the bed in her towel, trying to empty her mind and exist, if not in a sexual mindset, at least not a stressful one, Maxi also started to cry.

'My mummy,' he sobbed. 'My mummy.'

Quietly, illegally, she opened the interconnecting door.

'No,' she heard Adam say, in a tone of infinitely weary stubbornness, '*my* mummy.'

She got dressed and went in to comfort her son. Adam left without a word. When she crept back into their room, he was asleep, his face towards the wall.

Two further nights passed. Then it was time to go home.

She almost cried with relief when they flew into Gatwick, with its small M&S full of expensive environment-destroying plastic pots of fresh fruit. But as they rode the crowded train, more broken after the holiday than before it, her blissful return was ruined by a text.

Coralie, it read, *arriving London Heathrow this Thursday 0500 hours. I will drop bags at my accommodation and arrive your place 0800. Jenny is not with me. We have parted ways. Please share with Daniel, as I do not have his UK number. Best wishes, Roger.*

After a moment, a second text arrived: *(Dad).*

20

2022

Christmas 2017 had been the last time she'd seen him, tanned and vigorous in his belted slacks and tucked-in navy-blue polo shirt, his remaining hair white and close-cropped, the very model of a retired major-general. He was now seventy-three, an old man. Coralie was nearly thirty-nine, a grown adult with a home and family of her own. There was no need to wake before 5 a.m. every day, trembling and breathless, dreading her father's reappearance in her life. Yet that was what she found herself doing. Her shoulder was so high from the stress she gasped when she caught a glimpse of her reflection. Her eyelid began to twitch.

In some magical world, the world of text-based Instagram therapy posts, Coralie could have said: *0800 hours, or eight am as normal people say, doesn't suit me or my young family to receive you, as that is just before our finely calibrated Montessori and school double drop-off where every second counts.* But honesty, negotiation, and compromise take place between *people.* In the beginning was the word, and the word was Roger: her father wasn't a person, he was the law. At precisely 0800 hours on Thursday, she heard the rumble of a black cab and the crunch of footsteps up the path. The bell rang. He had arrived.

Coralie opened the door, but it was Adam he greeted first, lunging forward with a handshake so firm it made his sinewy bicep perceptibly bulge. Over his checked shirt he was wearing what she always thought of as a right-wing jumper (lambswool, with a quarter zip and a ribbed collar; Tory Tom always wore one). Instead of his old R.M.Williams boots, he'd actioned a smart travelling sneaker in a soft brown leather. ('Your father has no problem spending money on himself,' she remembered her mother saying once.)

'Bloody awful,' he was saying as they embraced.

'Oh, the flight?'

'Coughing and spluttering up and down the plane. If I didn't have Covid before, I do now. Gosh, London's changed, hasn't it?'

'Oh?' This was almost certainly a comment about racial and ethnic diversity. 'Well, how long has it been since—'

'Hello,' Roger cut her off. 'And who's this?'

Florence, flushed and giggling, was peeping through the open door to the sitting room.

'This is Florence, isn't it, Flo-Flo?' Adam held out his arm. 'Come and say hello to Grandad.'

'Florence. Well, aren't you a looker? What a stunner. Where did that come from?' He scrutinised Coralie and Adam, searching for the source of her beauty and evidently not finding it.

Florence faltered, unable to match up what sounded like a compliment with Roger's accusatorial tone. Where was Max? 'Minnie!' Coralie called.

Roger stared at her. 'Who's Minnie?'

'Max? Maxi? It's a nickname.'

'Why?'

'Oh, because—'

'Max! There you are, mate!' Max was bouncing in the hall on his tiptoes. 'Hold on.' Her father stared at him. 'Are you a boy or a girl? He's a boy, isn't he?'

'He's a boy!' Florence said.

'I just thought, because of the hair…'

Coralie had never had her son's now-shoulder-length hair cut, first because he was a pandemic baby, and then because he looked so pretty. While Flo's had matured into a light brown, Maxi's hair was still shiny and gold. She had clipped it back at breakfast so he could eat his Weetabix. 'Oh, no, it's just that—'

Roger snatched the sparkly clip from Maxi's hair, pulling several flaxen strands out along with it. 'We'll get rid of that, at least!'

Max stared at him, astonished.

'Well, Roger!' Adam stepped into the aghast silence. 'How are you feeling about beverages? Tea, coffee? We've got time for a quick one before we get these guys off to school.'

'You don't need school, do you? Stay home with Grandad.'

'Oh!' Coralie laughed. She'd just had the children home (and in Lanzarote) for three weeks over Easter. Before that they'd been home for *two years*. 'He's joking! Grandad's joking. Flo, did you know Grandad has a dog? A tiny dog, and do you know her name? Princess!'

'Not anymore,' her father said. 'Jenny kept her.'

'Sorry to hear about that,' Adam said.

'Jenny? Her loss. I'll take a coffee, since you're offering. And where's that other big girl's blouse?' Roger barked as he strode to the kitchen.

'Oh,' Coralie said faintly. 'Daniel, you mean. He's hoping to cook dinner for us tonight.'

'Tonight?' Her father pulled back the chair at the head of the table. 'I won't be around. No, I'll make it to four, five maybe. And then I'll be in bed. Won't I,' he growled at Florence, who looked flattered to be addressed, although unsure how to respond.

'Grandad,' Flo began.

'What's all this?' He gestured at the array of pleasingly realistic Schleich animals that accompanied Maxi everywhere and were presently clustered around his toast plate.

'Tiger!' Maxi said. 'Lion, *rar!*'

Roger picked up the largest of the animals. 'And here is a heffalump.'

'Heffalump?' Flo repeated, confused. 'No, no, Grandad, it's an elephant.'

'Enna-phant,' Max said charmingly. 'Fuh-fah!' His trunk sound.

'Oh dear,' Roger said. 'You don't know what a heffalump is. Well, in that case, children, I can't help you!'

She had forgotten this aspect of her father's character, a

fantastical strain barely compatible with his self-presentation as a fact-based, strategic military man.

'I think a heffalump is from a famous book from the olden days,' she explained. 'Called *Winnie-the-Pooh*.'

'Winnie-the-*Pooh*?' Flo repeated, astonished.

'He wasn't a poo,' Coralie said. 'He was a bear.'

'A poo who was a bear?'

'That's enough of the toilet talk,' Roger said with a frown. 'It's not polite, is it?'

Coralie stood up. 'I'm just going to…' She trailed off. 'We have to leave in a couple of minutes for nursery drop-off. Are you going to come, Dad?'

Florence was stunned. 'Dad!'

'Yes, Roger—*Grandad*—is my dad.'

Florence shook her head in disbelief. Coralie couldn't quite believe it either.

'I'll come,' Roger said. 'How far's the drive?'

'It's just a walk through the park.'

'A walk through the park,' he mused. '*Okay*. What about you, Adam? You'll be too busy, I suppose?' He was genial, comradely—one tireless world leader to another.

'I often do the school run.' Adam caught Coralie's eye and carefully added, 'In the mornings.'

'But he has meetings this morning,' Coralie said. 'Don't you?'

'I do,' he said. 'Sadly.'

'I read your election book,' Roger said. 'The Boris one. Now, he's a real character, Boris. Someone I'd have a beer with.'

'He's in trouble at the moment for doing exactly that,' Adam said. 'During the pandemic. You've read about Partygate?'

'Pfft,' Roger said. 'Britain won't know what it's got till it's gone.'

'We actually have to get moving,' Coralie apologised. 'Maxi's drop-off is before Florence's.'

But by the time they managed to farewell Adam and leave the house, it was already twenty to nine. They would have to do Florence first, and then ring the bell at Montessori and cringingly insinuate Max into class. Miss Sarah didn't like the children to miss their handshake.

Out in the street, Florence trotted next to Roger. 'What's your favourite subject at school?' he quizzed. 'Physics? Geography? Advanced mathematics?'

'I like reading? And—' (*And gymnastics*, Coralie knew she was going to say. Flo adored Marley, her gymnastics teacher.)

But her father didn't let her finish. 'Reading, eh! That sounds familiar. Your mother loved sitting on her backside with a book.' As Coralie digested this, Maxi gave a little shriek from the buggy. Roger wheeled around as if he'd been punched. 'What's *your* problem?'

They had reached the wall Max liked to walk along, holding hands with Coralie, and then getting what she called a 'tall kiss' at the end, because the wall made him the same height as she was. 'Sorry, Maxi, there isn't time,' she said.

He beat his legs and feet against the buggy and squirmed against the straps. Viewing her beloved boy's behaviour through the judgemental eyes of her father, she was shocked to find herself wanting to shake him—not her father, Max. She checked the time on her phone. 'Okay, a quick one.'

Maxi's tear-stained face was all smiles as he leapt up. 'He's a very good balancer,' she narrated, as he stepped nimbly along the wall with just the lightest touch of her hand.

'He's got you wrapped around his little finger,' Roger said darkly.

It was time for Maxi's tall kiss. Coralie tried to get away with a quick one, kissing his soft cheek before wrapping her arms around him and imperilling her pelvic floor as she hauled him bodily back into the buggy. He started wailing again; she buckled him in, her flesh crawling from embarrassment as everyone on the street was left in no doubt about her maternal incapability. She dug out the emergency squeezy tube of pureed fruit in her bag, clicked the lid off and gave it to him.

'That's right,' Roger told Max. 'Get some pure sugar into you. You bloody cry-baby.' He said it wittily, roguishly, almost like an inside joke.

'Grandad...' Flo tried again.

Roger strode off in the lead, despite not knowing the way.

She lost him for a bit in the crowds doing drop-off. Only children in Year 3 and above were allowed to run into the school building under their own steam. All the younger years lined up in the playground then processed in with their teacher, parents grouped around to wave farewell. As usual, a significant number of children were crying, causing delays. It was hard to keep her buggy out of the way, and to navigate around the buggies of other people. Often she didn't get out of there until ten past nine, and so it was that day. Her father was waiting outside the gate, pacing, a haunted look on his face.

'Very hectic,' she empathised.

'Battle of Basra in there. Where's my AS-90 self-propelled howitzer? Joking! Of course, I didn't see action myself in Iraq. I was merely a...'—he pronounced the words with relish—'*desk jockey.* Good grief, now where are we going?'

It would be a very painful visit if he was bored after only an hour. 'Maxi's nursery, through the park and behind the market.'

'This is what you do, is it? Walk around all day with a pram? Yummy mummy?'

'Oh!' Coralie said. 'I suppose—'

'Hi Coralie,' one of a pair of mums called. They were in their activewear. Coralie would have given a limb to be striding out for a walk with a friend, unencumbered. Lydia dropped Nancy at nursery and went to work. Beauty went to a different school nearby but was on the waiting list to transfer. *Alice, Lydia, Adam, my children, home.* She drew strength from the thought of them. Roger might be her father, but she wasn't a child. Things were different now.

'So tell me,' she said. These types of pauses were dangerous around her father; he invariably hijacked them. 'What are your plans while you're here?' she quickly finished.

'See my beautiful grandchildren. Churchill's bunker. Sherlock Holmes Museum. New umbrella from the umbrella shop. British Museum.'

'What date is your return flight?'

He gave a wolfish, sinister smile. 'Flexible.'

Later, after they had dropped Maxi off at Montessori, she braced herself for a coffee and a chat, but her father yawned once, looked pale, and said it was time to 'rest and recharge'. His hotel was near Liverpool Street station. She put him on the train at London Fields and immediately rang Dan. 'He said his timings are *flexible*.'

'What's that supposed to mean?'

'That he could stay on and on forever? He was so embarrassing at Montessori drop-off. He was reading out the labels on the shelves for the children's shoes. "Olympia, Olive, Land, Leaf…" and then he goes, like he was still reading, "Dirt, Solar Panel, Pussycat, Rubbish Truck." Then he looked into the classroom and said…No, I can't say.'

'Say,' Daniel said, resigned.

'He said, "So there *are* still white children in England." Oh God.' She stared up at the grey sky. 'I won't survive this visit.'

The next day, Friday, was the day Adam didn't do his show, and Montessori pick-up was early, at twelve instead of three-thirty. Adam would take Roger to pick-up. Daniel and Coralie would stay home to prepare lunch. They'd all eat together as soon as Adam and Roger got back with Max.

Florence, at school all day and sad to miss out, had left a drawing of herself behind 'for Grandad'.

'What's this meant to be?' Roger scoffed. 'A bit *remedial*.'

Daniel hadn't arrived by the time Adam and Roger left for pick-up. Coralie feared she'd have to start the lunch prep alone. But at twelve, the bell rang. She opened the door to find a stranger.

Well, it was Daniel, but his ponytail had gone. With his sleek new conservative haircut, he could have been a solicitor or an estate agent.

'It wasn't worth it,' Daniel explained as they embraced. 'I can't cope with Roger's remarks.'

Coralie checked her phone and found a WhatsApp from Adam: *He made the joke about the names again. Rain's mum didn't laugh.*

In the kitchen, Daniel took in her supplies at a glance. 'We'll need some more bread,' he said. 'Because I'm going to use the last of it. Can you tell Adam?'

She watched as, in Dan's hands, the unloved contents of her vegetable box became a delicious gratin and the remains of a sourdough loaf became breadcrumbs for the top. '*Is* he bad, do you think?'

'Roger?' Daniel said. 'Yeah.'

'Self-obsession isn't a crime.'

'Sometimes, I'll be lying in the bath, or sitting at the table with a coffee, and I hear footsteps coming towards me. I know it's only Barbie, the man I love, and who loves me, because I'm in the house we share together, on the other side of the world from Dad. But my heart races, I feel sick—I'm cowering, like Madonna being sniffed by a pitbull. The body doesn't lie. He was bad.'

Was he bad, morally? Or was she, for not being able to love him? Her mother had spent much of their marriage scuttling like a rat to avoid Roger Bower's eagle eye. That was sad. A bit pathetic? Coralie liked to think that she had her father's measure. Little compliment there, little courteous question there! Judicious application of a fascinated listening face; no sudden noises or movements! It wasn't too tricky. If she could do it, handle him—why couldn't Mum? Or Dan?

She remembered a long-ago family trip to Lake Toba, a vast lake in the crater of a volcano. She walked ahead with Dad, as he discoursed at length about the geography of North Sumatra. Trailing far behind them, Mum looked after Dan. Suddenly, Dan (who must have been, what—seven?) collapsed on the ground, wailing with exhaustion and boredom. '*Roger!*' their mother screamed, startling their local guide. 'Here we go,' Dad said. 'Well, you know what they say.'

'What?' Coralie was twelve, on holiday from boarding school, and enjoying being treated (however briefly) like an adult.

'It's hard to soar like an eagle when you're surrounded by turkeys.'

She was an eagle, like him—that seemed to be what he was saying. Wasn't it?

We can do this the easy way, or the hard way. That's what baddies always said in films. What kind of idiot chose the hard way? Mum and Dan, that's who. They couldn't *not* struggle. They couldn't choose the easy way.

Now grown-up Dan got the gratin ready to serve, his cheeks flushed from the heat of the oven. He must have been reading Coralie's mind. 'You were always Team Dad.'

'I wasn't!'

'Well, you weren't on Mum's and my team.'

Even though she'd just been thinking the same thing, hearing him admit they'd had a team, and that she wasn't on it, really stung. 'You had a team, did you? That's nice. I wish I'd had a mother. I would have loved one, actually.'

'You had one,' Dan said. 'You just didn't give a shit about her.'

'Dan!'

'Just a fact.'

'I was there for her small operation, her big operation, the hospital...'

'What about the other thirty years you were both alive at the same time?'

'I suppose there were the eleven years I lived in her various houses as a child? I was left behind after that. Raised by a school instead.'

'You loved your school, you were obsessed by school, you couldn't wait to get back there every holiday, crossing the days off your calendar and ignoring us. You had no idea what life was like for Mum and me, as Dad grew more and more powerful, and we only got more scared. You turned your eyes away. Then you got away for real.'

Coralie's breathing was fast, her vision blurred. 'I don't think I got away. It's followed me around—everywhere!'

Dan looked around at her cosy kitchen. 'You got away.'

'I don't think I did, but I agree I wasn't there. Not in the way you were. And I'm really sorry about it. You *were* there. You were there for Mum. You were a hero with her—an absolute hero.'

'Cor, I wasn't a hero,' Dan said. 'I was a mess. You had no idea—I had a breakdown when I was eighteen. And another one around the time of her big second op. That's why I stayed home, and then why I moved home again. Not to look after her—so she could look after me. So stop, please. Stop being nice to me. I don't actually deserve it.'

What was this feeling inside her? Whatever it was, she hated it. Dan's big eyes and long lashes—so like Max's. She saw his perfect, smooth face, his poreless skin. She wanted to claw and scratch at it. Envy, that's what it was. She was sick with it. Mum had accepted love from Dan and had given him her love back. Why not Coralie?

'Cor,' Dan said. 'What's going on in your mind? I was trying to make you feel better.'

On the kitchen counter, her phone lit up with an alert—she'd missed a call from Adam. She rang back. When the call connected, she could hear Max screaming in the background.

'Max is okay,' Adam said. 'We were on Broadway Market, and I had to take a call. I was gone for *ten minutes*. Roger said he was buying some wine.'

'What happened? Adam!' A car accident. Deliveroo guys on their bikes. 'Is he hurt? Is Max hurt?'

But Adam had hung up.

She could hear the crying from down the street. Roger was pushing the empty buggy. Maxi was sobbing in Adam's arms. Coralie couldn't see what was wrong. His legs were kicking, both his arms were around Adam's neck. There didn't seem to be any blood.

'Oh, shit,' Daniel said.

'See!' Roger gestured at his children. 'Real men have short hair! Even Uncle Danny!'

Coralie started jogging. 'I'm so sorry,' Adam said. 'I'm so sorry.'

318

She took her son into her arms. His beautiful hair was gone. It was shorter than Daniel's. The sides and back had been shaved. He looked like a ketamine dealer, like he should be riding a stolen Lime bike, or wearing a St George's flag around his shoulders with a convicted of journalism shirt.

'For God's sake,' her father said. 'Adam was off doing God knows what. The barber was right there. I was *helping*.'

Maxi was staring at her, wondering how to feel. She pressed him into her chest, gathering the strength she needed to be calm. He'd stopped crying, but was breathing raggedly, periodically racked with sobs. 'That was a bad surprise, wasn't it,' she murmured. 'You didn't know Grandad was going to get your hair cut.'

Maxi whimpered.

'You're very, very beautiful,' Coralie said. His eyes were a startling blue, and his thick lashes curled up like a Rimmel ad. 'I've got you now. I've got you.'

But that's what she always said, that's what she'd made her mission—looking after her children and protecting them from harm. She had failed.

'What the fuck were you doing?' she hissed at Adam inside.

His eyes bulged. 'I was taking a call and buying your bloody bread!'

'Why would you leave Max with him?'

'He's your dad, not Vladimir Putin.'

'You ruined everything,' she sobbed. But he hadn't—*she* had.

When she served the lunch, it was with a smile. If her father knew she was devastated, it would only make everything worse. Better to keep him on side, to soothe, to venerate—as

319

if nothing he did could ever possibly be wrong.

To survive his visit, she had to put the thinking, breathing, feeling part of herself safely away on a high shelf. The problem was, when he finally left, she'd shrunk so much she couldn't get it down again.

21

Weeks after her father had left, and even as spring turned into summer, she found she was still living in fear. Daniel had talked about trembling as footsteps approached while he was in the bath. Now it was Coralie's turn. Sometimes, when the children were in bed, and she was waiting for Adam to get back from the studio, she made him call her from Dalston Junction so she didn't freak out when she heard the front door unlock. When she walked through the streets, strangers seemed to loom and menace her, talking about her, judging her, despising her. She used to take the children to the park after school. Now she was too frightened, of having to talk to other parents, or of her children falling, breaking their legs or even necks. When she closed her eyes, she saw them getting hurt: if not at the park, then on the road; if not on the road, then in a house fire, a terror attack, a flood. Her obsessive concern for them did not translate into solicitude. Every cry or exclamation grated; she experienced every spilled glass of water or smear of yoghurt on the floor as an assault. Being near them was impossible. Being away from them was worse.

All but the most basic parenting tasks suddenly proved beyond her. Taking the children to swimming lessons, in the newest and nicest of Hackney's leisure centres, felt like going to war—the hot chlorine air in the bleachers, the crush to pick up the children, the shouting in the changing rooms, the chemical plumes of spray deodorant and perfume. She began to lose sleep the night before. After a month of insomnia, she cancelled the lessons, but it was too late; her body had made a new rule: she did not sleep on Mondays. Then she didn't sleep if she had an appointment the following day, even something minor like an Ocado slot. Then she didn't sleep at all. She was absolutely fucked.

This does sound like the sort of thing people used to tell you to see your GP about, Lydia wrote, worried.

LOL! Coralie hadn't seen her GP since 2019.

But also (not LOL) she was too scared to call for an appointment.

What do you think about? Lydia asked. *On those nights when you can't get to sleep?*

She thought about the children growing up, and there being no world for them to live in. That she was nigh on forty, and halfway dead, unless she died early like her mother—then she was more like two-thirds dead. That Adam would get hit by a car when he was cycling on London Bridge. That Adam would leave her, because she couldn't laugh, or live a normal life, or get a new job, or even think about having sex. But these fears only took up a few moments each. The rest of the time, she thought nothing.

She was absolutely blank.

As the clock reached one, two, three, four she began to picture the following day, the banging headache she'd have, her bone-deep exhaustion, her savage reactions to noise and stimulus, all hitting her right at the worst possible time: school pick-up, for which she was solely responsible, and the dinner, bath and bedtime routine, which she did alone and unsupported. At 4 a.m., she often cried, carefully sobbing just loud enough to wake up Adam, and because of the crying, or because he wrapped himself around her and crushed her like a python, she was able to get to sleep, and sometimes she could sleep through the children getting up, and claw back two or even four hours, which meant she could exist.

'Do you want me to tell you a story?' One morning, Florence was sitting on the edge of the bed. Her gingham school dress had swamped her at the beginning of Year 1. Now it fitted snugly. Time just kept on passing. It was cruel.

'Okay, Wrennie,' Coralie said, though she'd been asleep, and wished that she still was.

'Once upon a time, there was a mum, the most beautiful mum in the world...'

'Florence!' It was Adam, half shouting through his toothpaste foam. 'Mummy's sleeping! Get your school shoes on!'

After another sleepless night, Maxi came in with a play-silk on his head. 'Ooh,' he moaned. 'I'm a goat.'

'Oh, help, a ghost,' Coralie said. 'There's a ghost in my room!'

'Max!' Adam shouted up from downstairs. Fear filled her at the sound of the shout. Uncontrollable fear.

'You'd better run,' she said. 'Daddy's angry.'

The patter of his footsteps receded. She was alone.

Boris Johnson was in trouble. His MPs were all fed up with him. His health secretary quit his job, and then nine minutes later, his chancellor. 'Rishi Sunak has *resigned*,' she heard on Radio 4 as she dug old rice out of the plughole in the sink. (She didn't listen to Adam's show in the evenings. Hearing his voice but not seeing him confused the kids.) 'Oh, it's all over now!' the commentator exclaimed.

But Johnson simply reshuffled his cabinet and carried on.

When Adam got home, he was giddy with history and drama. 'Everyone's resigning,' he marvelled. 'There won't be anyone left!'

'What about Tory Tom?'

'God, good question, what about him? I'll text.'

After Covid, Tom had been appointed a Parliamentary under-something for—something (she wasn't really sure). It looked good on his Wiki, and apparently came with a pay rise, a small one, which made Marina laugh.

'Ah!' Adam showed Coralie his phone. Tom had responded with a screenshot of the Google Image search results for 'cat holding on to branch with one claw'.

'But is that about Boris, or him?'

'Hard to say.' They couldn't work it out and didn't ask.

Coralie got to sleep at ten-thirty. An hour later, Adam came to bed and woke her up. She didn't sleep again until five.

Was she in crisis? She couldn't tell. It was intolerable, unbear-able. Yet there she was, bearing it. She thought of her life as a train, running between its stations, fixed, unchanging, never deviating from the track. Could she press the emergency stop—shock everyone, inconvenience them, grind the whole thing to a halt? The fact of being alive, the fact of her going on—it made the part of her that couldn't be alive (couldn't go on) a weakling, a fool and a liar. She hovered on the edge, half emergency, half not. If you could press the big red button, you didn't need the help. But if you couldn't...

She typed all this out to Lydia, but couldn't bring herself to share it.

By the next day, so many Tories had resigned Coralie wondered if Boris Johnson would even show up at Prime Minister's Questions. It was brave of him that he did. Labour leader Keir Starmer called the quitters 'sinking ships fleeing the rat'. And 'as for those who are left,' Starmer said, 'they're only in office because no one else is prepared to *debase* themselves any longer—the charge of the lightweight brigade. Have some *self-respect*!' Ouch. Even Coralie felt chastened by the speech, and—apart from being a mental and physical wreck, economically inactive, a failed writer, a shit mother, a shit sister, a shit daugh-ter, and a shitty common-law wife—she hadn't done anything wrong.

That night, exhilarated by events, events, events, Adam stayed late in the News Building. Coralie couldn't sleep because she knew his return would wake her up. By the time he got back at eleven, she was no longer tired. At four-thirty, the Wilton Way seagulls started their usual screaming and flapping. Wednesday 6 July became her first official zero-sleep night. Zero. Nothing! Absolutely no sleep at all.

At five, she gave up, and went downstairs to make the kitchen perfect, tipping loose raisins out of schoolbags, folding up Wrennie's PE kit. She made muffins to use up the apples. She froze the very ripe bananas in chunks for smoothies. She set up drawing paper on the table in case the children wanted art. They came down, warm and cuddly in their summer pyjamas, surprised (in a good way) to see their mother out of bed.

On Radio 4, BBC political reporter Chris Mason was speculating about Boris Johnson's future. 'Mishal,' he told the host, 'as I speak to you, I'm getting a call from Downing Street—so I'm going to take this call and I'll come back on to you in just a second.'

Adam was in the bath, having a shave. (When it was a big day of news, his show also went out live on YouTube, so he needed to look his best.) 'Turn on Radio 4!' she shouted up the stairs.

'Don't let the neighbours hear you!' he called back down. 'She means Times Radio,' he shouted out to no one.

She laughed, delighted. She was so sleepless she'd gone beyond tired and become euphoric. 'Mummy,' Florence seized her moment craftily, 'will *you* take us to school this morning?'

'Yes, Chris,' Mishal Husain said on the radio. 'Let's go

straight back to you. You were just talking to Downing Street?'

'The prime minister has agreed to stand down.'

Coralie was faint, it was quite extraordinary. She leaned back against the counter. A wave of tiredness crashed over her, threatened to pull her under. 'I can't, Flo–Flo,' she said. 'Daddy will take you to school.'

She was a puppet, shaking and waving. Her head was a balloon, floating away. Her vision narrowed, her mouth was dry. She sat in front of the TV, vacant.

'And to you, the British public. I know that there will be many people who are relieved and perhaps quite a few who will also be disappointed. And I want you to know how sad I am to be giving up the best job in the world. But,' Boris said, his voice flat with sudden bitterness, *'them's the breaks.'*

Laundry she could do. Tidying wasn't a problem. She made up her daughter's bed with the summer duvet, and the quilt Sally had made that said florence. She arranged Catty with his long legs crossed, his plush black arms open in a hug. Maxi's special toy was a sheep; she laid him on his side in the cot. The colourful magnets went in one basket, the Duplo in another. Upstairs, she made Zora's bed with sheets she'd brought in from the clothesline. They were warm and smelled of the sun. She couldn't mother the children. The house would do it instead.

That night, Adam was on air as usual until eight. He stayed back in the office for a while, then went on to the *Spectator* summer party. The party—she hadn't factored in the party.

There'd be no point trying to go to sleep before he came back, he'd simply wake her up. In fact, was there any point going to sleep at all, when the morning would simply come, and everything would start all over again? She explained this to Lydia in a text.

I think there is a point, yes, Lydia replied. *To sleeping.*

There is, Coralie conceded. *But I won't be able to.*

Could you ask Adam to come home?

She didn't want Lydia to lose patience with her. She had hogged the role of Friend in Crisis for too long. *I'll try!* she wrote back, with a fake and cheerful exclamation mark.

'When do you think you'll come home?' she texted Adam.

Hi gorgeous, definitely before midnight, he replied. *I love you. CYK.*

Consider yourself kissed. When she was happy, it felt so romantic. When she was broken, it felt like a slap.

Grief is the price we pay for love, that's what the Queen had once said. The price Coralie paid for love was fear and getting lost. Something was wrong with her, it set her apart—she couldn't be *in* love, but she couldn't be out of it either. If she didn't love, she was half a person. But if she did love, she'd never be whole. Her hands shook as she packed her bag. Mother, writer, worker, sister, friend, citizen, daughter, (sort of) wife. If she could be one, perhaps she could manage. Trying to be all, she found that she was none. A high-summer night, still light outside—the seagulls soared and screamed. She loved him so much, more than anything. But when Adam came home, she'd be gone.

22

She woke at nine the next day with a sense of unreality and a very furry mouth. Daniel had given her one of Barbie's sleeping pills. She was downstairs in Amhurst Road, in the guest suite they kept for Barbie's sons. How nullified she felt, how empty. But because no one was around her, needing things from her—how safe. If she could just be herself for a while, be by herself, and *for* herself—she might begin to get back on her feet.

Upstairs, Daniel made her toast with butter and honey. As she held her coffee cup in both hands, she felt as shattered as she had both times after giving birth. But now there was no perfect baby to look after. There was just fucked-up pointless old *her*. It was horrible. Tears slid down her cheeks.

'Go to someone else's house if you want to cry like that,' Daniel gently teased.

'Sorry,' Coralie whispered.

The doorbell chimed. After a few minutes, Daniel brought Adam in.

'Oh,' Adam said. 'Sweetheart.'

'I can't smile.'

'You don't have to.' He wrapped his arms around her from behind. She rested her chin on his forearm as though his hug had snapped her neck.

They all sat at the table. Adam accepted a tea. 'Where's Barbie?'

'Pilates.'

'Well, then,' Adam said. 'What are we going to do about our Coralie?'

'Do you know what you want to do, Cor?' Daniel asked.

Die, she wanted to say. Or be alive again. But not be like this, a dead person going through the motions. A dead mother scaring the kids.

What she wanted was to be alone somewhere safe. But she couldn't be without her children. And she couldn't be *with* her children, not in that ceaseless, unrelenting way. She tried to explain that.

'And what about me?' Adam's face, which had been attentive and tender, became white with sudden terror.

'Remember my flat,' she said. 'When we met.'

'Of course.'

'You stayed there. And I stayed at yours. You didn't make us be together. You let me be on my own. It helped me', she said, 'to fall in love.'

'You're never on your own anymore.' Daniel watched her.

'Are you, Cor?'

She shook her head, tears sliding out again. 'I don't exist.'

'The Graham Road flat,' her brother said. 'One of you can stay there, but who?'

'I will.' Adam raised his hand. 'I'll take the kids, and let Coralie rest at home.'

He couldn't do that. The way she'd set everything up—the house was holding the children when she couldn't. And she couldn't sleep in her own bed. The thought of that bed made her heart race. And she couldn't keep Adam out of his own home. She'd always be sitting to attention, waiting for him to come in, adjusting her face to his face, intuiting his needs and meeting them. The way she had with Richard. Even with Antoinette. The way she had all her life with her dad. *We can do this the easy way, or the hard way.* It hadn't been easy for her.

'I'll stay in the flat,' she said. 'But I need to see the children. But not too much. And I need to not see *you*. I'm so sorry.'

Daniel put the mugs in the dishwasher as Coralie and Adam both cried.

'For how long?' Adam said.

She didn't know.

Daniel walked her to the flat past Marks & Spencer, where she stalled and broke down as she considered all the food. Daniel gathered the basics and hustled her out. 'I'll drop round your meals,' he said. 'Don't worry.'

The two flats in the tall terraced house shared a common hallway. Hers was the second of the internal doors. Behind it was a staircase. Dan gestured for her to go up first. She emerged into a light and airy room, combined living area and kitchen. It took just a few moments to take in the rest, a bathroom and a small bedroom with a double bed. It was plain, attractive and clean.

'This is where Anne and Sally stayed, do you remember? There's no one in the flat downstairs. You've got the whole place to yourself.' Dan put the milk and butter in the fridge. 'There's tea,' he said. 'And sugar.'

'How did you learn all this?'

'Being a dumb old landlord?'

'No, being so good, at…caring.'

He looked out the window. 'I just remember all the times I've felt the same as you.'

He left.

She was alone.

The weather was beautiful, almost shockingly so. She lay on the white bed in the white bedroom and watched as the sun travelled from one side of the linen duvet to the other. Three-thirty; Adam would be picking up Flo from school. How would he manage being on the radio next week without Coralie? Who would have the children? When she tried to think it through, her breathing quickened, and her head started to spin. He would have to solve it. She simply couldn't.

cor, Zora texted at five, in the all-lower-case style she had affected since the beginning of Year 9. *can i ask you a lil q? where's the spinny bit of the stick blender?*

Coralie could see it in the bottom drawer inside the cake tins as if she were standing right in front of it. But she found she couldn't reply.

*'so sorry cor. dad just told me not to disturb you. so sorry about that.
love u. zor.'*

At seven, a message arrived from Adam. One word: *'Ready.'*
She had asked him not to text too much. But one word? It
seemed cold. Was he cold? Was he angry? Did he hate her?
After a second, another one arrived. *'CYK.'* Okay. It was right
this time. It was helpful. She could manage. She walked out of
the flat on Graham Road. Three minutes later, she was at her
own front door on Wilton Way. Down on the corner, Adam
gave her a salute. He walked away, and she went inside. The
children had their pyjamas on. They were ready to be put to
bed. Reading. Cuddling. At eight, she tiptoed downstairs.
Ready, she texted. *CYK.*

An hour with them. An hour she could handle. She did it on
Saturday night. On Sunday, when she did it again, a note was
waiting for her on the bottom step.

> *Dearest Cor,*
> *Anne and Sally will be arriving tomorrow. They'll cover after*
> *school until after radio on Monday to Thursday. They're*
> *happy to text you when the children are ready for bed.*
> *CYK forever,*
> *Adam*

On Monday, at a little past seven, Sally texted. She braced
herself to deal with Anne. Would she be mocking, or (worse)
scathing? *Don't be silly, Coralie.* But as she rounded the corner
near the pub, she saw them waiting in front of the house. As

333

she approached, they waved goodbye. They walked away holding hands. *Thank you,* she texted at eight when she left. And she meant it.

On Friday, Adam was back in charge. He messaged her at seven. She messaged him at eight. When she left, the sun was bright, high and scorching. She looked back down the road. He was standing there, watching. She raised her arm, and he raised his. That was enough.

She remembered when they'd first met, how joyfully they'd opened themselves up and knitted themselves back together, every thread of her fused with every thread of him. What had happened to her? How could a person have everything they ever wanted, and still be empty? How could a person be surrounded, always, by people they loved—and yet still feel alone? In the back garden of the house on Graham Road, a funny thing had happened to a tree. It was, or had been, a birch. Over time, ivy had grown round it, bending the tree within. Now the ivy was as thick as her forearm, and the tree inside was crushed. Could two living beings entwine without one of them having to die?

On Saturday, when Adam texted *Ready,* she let herself into the house, hurried upstairs, and threw herself onto Florence's bed. Her children jumped on her, comb marks in their wet hair, their beautiful faces shining. She read to them and cuddled them. She put them in bed, then back into bed when they got out. She shushed them when they chatted. She sat in the corner until they slept. This was what she'd thought being a mother would be like. Doing one thing at a time, and kindly.

Ready, she texted Adam, and tiptoed down the stairs. As she clicked open the door, she heard the sound of someone rushing from the kitchen. She turned in shock. 'Zora!'

'Oh, that's nice!' Zora was furious. 'She remembers me!'

Adam would be on his way back. 'Zora,' she said again.

'Sorry,' Zora said. 'Did I break the rules? The rules of whatever this is? Sorry for speaking to you, Coralie. Sorry for existing! Sorry for needing you!'

'Oh, Zor.' She could hear Adam's footsteps on the pavement outside. 'I have to go.' And she ran out the door, past Adam, up Wilton Way, hating herself.

She stayed awake half the night, waiting for a breeze to stir the curtains. It would hit forty degrees next week, that was what the papers said. Forty degrees in London? She couldn't believe it was real. At one, she dropped off to sleep. At six, tangled sheets damp with sweat, she woke to find a message on her phone.

write to me as soon as you get this, Zora had texted. *i have something i want us to do.*

Fourteen, and almost as tall as Coralie, Zora had arranged the whole outing, efficiently setting out the plan. But as soon as they met at the station, and before she even said hello, Zora offloaded two big bags into Coralie's arms, just like she'd used to at pick-up. She was still a child, and Coralie was still the adult. It was a relief to be handed the stuff.

By eight, they were marching up through Hampstead Heath,

ground still baked from the day before, grass and wildflowers dry and brown and brittle. 'Are you sure we'll be allowed? Don't you have to book?'

'Not this early in the morning,' Zora said.

'What swimmers did you pack for me?'

'I got the boring black ones, like you said. From your boring drawer of boring black pants.'

'Perfect.'

'Important to be boring at all times,' Zora said.

'Why stand out when you could just...' Coralie shrugged. 'Fade into the background and disappear?'

'No!' Zora's teasing suddenly stopped. 'I know you think you're funny, but you sound really, really sad.'

'It's possible to be both at once, you know. Funny and sad.'

'I don't think you're allowed to make grown-up speeches to me anymore,' Zora said. 'Not after whatever all this is.'

'What do you think it is?'

'Leaving my dad? Moving out? Abandoning us? But not *all* of us. You're still seeing the *good children*. Your real children.'

'Are you a child?'

'No,' Zora said. 'Maybe. I don't know.'

'Whatever you are,' Coralie said. 'You're good. And whatever I am, to you—with you, it's real.'

They walked on, past families straggling across the path, older women in hiking boots with dogs, and sunburnt young people limping home from the night before. 'When you were little,' Coralie said, 'you used to call this Hampstead Heap.'

'I heard Dad crying last night, you know. A grown man, sobbing.'

'Sorry. Sorry you had to hear that.'

'I've heard it before,' Zora said. 'Tom cries all the time.'

Coralie stopped, shocked. 'Really?'

'Not all the time. But they've been fighting *so* much, too. Marina lost her shit in lockdown, and made Tom live in Eastbourne. That's what I heard him crying about—that Eastbourne, and the flat, were so gross.'

'God! Don't tell Anne.'

They both laughed.

After a bit, Coralie waved her arm around at the Heath. 'You know, I've never swum here.'

'What? At the Ladies' Pond?'

'I'm not a cool born-Londoner like you, Zor. I just live my little life in Hackney.'

She'd been aiming for something light, but Zora's cry was desperate. 'Why do you talk like you're basically *dead*?'

'I'm nearly forty,' Coralie said reasonably.

'God, get a *fucking* grip.'

'Zor!'

'Honestly!'

'Okay, since you're the one giving grown-up speeches now, and dealing out reality checks—what's *your* news? What's going on at school?'

'That question's too boring to respond to.'

'Okay!'

WOMEN ONLY

MEN NOT ALLOWED

BEYOND THIS POINT

She'd seen the sign on Instagram so many times.

In the changing rooms, lined in wood like a sauna or cabin, hardy, confident and clearly self-actualised women of all ages were in various stages of undress, chatting, drying, or sharing shampoo in the shower. She handed Zora the tote with her things. Shyly, they diverged into separate cubicles.

When they met out on the deck, she saw something that amused her. Zora was wearing the same style of plain black Speedo that she was. 'What was all that about being boring?'

'It's *practical.*'

'Okay!'

The water was warm, which was spooky. 'Oh, yuck,' Coralie said. 'I just put my foot into a different layer. The water's gone all cold. How can it be different temperatures? Why isn't it all the same? What's on the bottom of this, anyway? And how deep is it?'

'It's nature. Are you scared?'

'Are you *not* scared?'

'Do you think I might be triggered? Because I fell in the lake at Victoria Park?'

'I'm the triggered one; I nearly froze to death after that.'

'I didn't even get to touch the duck. Come on, put your goggles on, swim properly! We'll do a lap.'

'I don't want to put my head under.'

'Fine!'

Coralie swam sedately, keeping her head out of the water. Zora flipped and twisted like a fish. 'You're not supposed to go too close to the edge,' she popped up to say.

'Why?'

'In case you see a dead body. No! You might damage the plants, that's all.'

They struck out into the middle of the pond. Coralie wanted to hold a buoy to rest, but she was scared of the unseen rope trailing against her legs.

'So is this it?' Zora bobbed in front of her. 'Have you and Dad broken up?'

'No—' Coralie started. 'Look at those women.'

Two swimmers had struck out to the deepest part of the pond. They had stopped, and were resting—were they? Or clowning? They started splashing and holding one another.

'They'll get told off,' Zora said.

'Are they kissing? No…Oh, God—they're drowning.'

A whistle blew. A kayak streaked out from nowhere. 'Lady in the red hat!' a woman with a megaphone boomed from the deck. 'Both of you. Stop struggling. Let go. Let go now! You're dragging each other down!'

One of the two heads sank under the surface for a long time.

Screams and cries rang out around the pond. Coralie gasped. 'Fuck!'

'Get apart! Get apart now!' the megaphone woman shouted.

The head popped back up. The rescuer reached the weeds. The two swimmers held the kayak, one on each side. After a while, they began an embarrassed breaststroke to shore.

'That's what we were like,' Coralie said. 'Adam and me. Dragging each other down. I just needed to be alone, so I could rest, and breathe, and save myself.'

'And are you saved?'

'I think maybe I am.'

That night, she did her hour of bedtime as usual. At the end, when the children were asleep, and Zora was up in her room, Coralie slipped out of the house and sent Adam a different message. She was accepting visitors—well, only one visitor—to her flat on Graham Road. Fifteen minutes later there was a tap on the front door. Coralie ran down to open it. His shirt was open one more button than usual. Sweat beaded on his temples and ran in rivulets down his chest. She saw his face again, what he actually looked like—not just how she felt about him. She was nervous, trembling. So was he.

The heat was incredible, she could smell his skin. They kissed, and he rested his chin in her cupped hand. She'd forgotten what he felt like too, that he was a person, warm and alive. He'd been an idea, a shadowy enemy, a ghost reaching out from the past. Now he was Adam again. She remembered that she loved him. 'Do you still love me?' she asked.

'Yes. Do you still love me?'

'Yes.'

They lay on their sides, facing one another, their heads on the same white pillow. 'Do you remember when we first met?' Coralie said. 'In bed for whole afternoons.'

'In your old flat? Under the skylight? I do.'

'Everything was so easy then.' Her eyes filled with tears. She was still crying all the time—when she missed the children, and couldn't wait to see them again; when she thought about the record hot weather, and what the future held; from relief, too—that she'd been to the brink and made it back. There were people around her now. People who cared, and who loved her.

'I'm sorry I let it get so bad,' Adam said. He reached for her hand and held it. '*One more book*, I kept thinking. One more job. And then I'd finally be able to enjoy it.'

'You went on without me,' she said. 'You left me behind. We were so in love. But I moved in with you and everything stopped for me. It took forever to have a baby. It took forever to have another one. It took me forever to start writing. I've been writing the same thing for years. You're wondering when you can stop. I'm wondering if I'll ever start.'

Two matching tears slid down Adam's cheeks and dropped an inch apart on the pillow. 'I don't know how it happened...'

'But it wasn't just you. It was me too.' Because there was something about her, Coralie could see it now. Something that was very like her Mum. Taking on everything like a mule or a packhorse. Plodding along, buckling. Not insisting on things she wanted. Talking herself out of complaining. She'd floated away, mentally. A ghost in her own life. She'd nearly floated away for good. She was crying. Never again. He held her against his chest.

'Remember CYK?'

'CYK? Yes,' Adam said. 'I do.'

'It started off so full of love. But then it was just like ticking a box.'

'It won't be anymore. I promise. I love you the most in the world.'

'I love you.'

'Forever.'

'Forever.'

She sent him home when it got dark. She slept all through the night.

23

2023

The house was in 'an absolute state'. ('The state of it...' an English person would say, really about anything—from a minor breach of queuing etiquette to having five Tory PMs in thirteen years.)

On the top floor, Florence was moving in to Zora's room, and Maxi was moving in to 'Adam's study'. On the floor below, the yellow nursery was now Zora's—painted in Dulux Sugared Lilac so it looked like the set of *Friends*. Controversially, Zora's other request had been for a double bed. That wasn't something Adam wanted to probe. Coralie had agreed, and discreetly changed the planned location of the new built-in wardrobes so the room was a bit more soundproof. Persona non grata between 2020 and 2022, Zora's friend Hannah had recently reappeared on the scene with her head shaved and her septum pierced. Something was going on there, that was for sure, and—when Zora was ready to share—Coralie was keen to hear about it (though not actually to hear *it*—that would be a bit much). Daniel would probably get all the news before her. He and Zora hung out often, and no longer provided readouts of their chats.

Giving up the big front bedroom had not been much of a sacrifice for Zora. As soon as Tory Tom had moved out of Bartholomew Road, Marina had given her the entire top floor as a 'teen retreat'. It would be another 'mature divorce', handled like civilised grown-ups. At Rupert's parents' evening, his teacher had asked how he was coping with a 'broken home'. 'Broken home!' Marina exclaimed. 'She's lucky I didn't make a formal complaint. Anyway, Rup's doing very well out of it, thank you very much.' At Tom's plush bachelor flat near King's Cross, the App Store on Rup's new iPad didn't require a passcode. Every time he bought Minecoins and Robux, Marina received an email—but since it was hooked up to Tom's Visa, she didn't need to mention it. Tom had checked out mentally from his job as Member for Eastbourne and had removed it from his barrister profile. At Westminster, workshops were being held for Tory MPs on how to update their CVs. Labour was predicted to win the next election in a landslide. Coralie would believe that when she saw it!

In Australia, the nation would soon vote on the Indigenous Voice to Parliament, a step on the long road to reconciliation. Coralie's childhood friend Elspeth had emailed her out of the blue: *Happy birthday for next week. I can't believe we're so old—can you? PS Is this your dad? I see he hasn't changed.* She included an iPhone pic of a page from the right-wing *Daily Telegraph*. Four men and one woman had been vox-popped about the Voice. Her father gazed out at her from the passport-sized photograph: lean, ageless, confident, superb. 'I'd advise caution,' read the quote from Roger, 74. 'When you take the boot off someone else's neck, they always put it on yours.'

Coralie had hoped to have the house finished by the time everyone came for Maxi's birthday. Lydia and Nancy, who'd start Reception in two days. Lydia would stay to help, as would Alice. She'd bring Beauty to play with Flo—they were in the same class at school at last. Max would have his Montessori friends: Ottilie, Lyron, Bowie and Mo. But four hours before the party, the hall outside their bedrooms was still piled high with books and toys and mess. She would have to make upstairs off-limits—that was probably a good idea anyway. Last time Lydia had come round, Nancy and Max had disappeared. When they'd returned, giggling, their faces had been covered in lipstick.

Anne and Sally arrived early and inspected the changed-up rooms. 'Beautiful, Coralie.' Sally clasped her elbow. 'You've done a wonderful job.' If she didn't mind, Sally said, she had just one suggestion. Could Zora's painted door move to her new room, and she'd do another one for Florence? Of course— Flo would love it. Sally went off in search of the paints. When Coralie went upstairs to check on progress, she discovered what Flo had asked for: Daddy doing a bellyflop in the pool on holidays; Max picking his nose; herself as a seven-year-old, and Coralie as one too. 'Make us holding hands,' Flo said. 'If she was my age, she'd be my friend.'

'What is she now, then?' Sally asked.

'Silly,' Flo said. 'Just Mum! Oh, and Zora is with us. She's my age too. But I'm in the middle. And the tallest.'

'And the last panel?'

'Zora, Daniel, Barbie, um, Lady Diana Spencer' (Daniel's new black poodle, since sweet old Madonna was RIP). 'And you, and Anne, and my gymnastics teacher, Marley. Oh, and Catty. And Bluey off the TV.'

'I'll see what I can do.'

'Mama,' Max called from the bathroom. 'Come and see my poo.'

His birthday badge with a 4 on it had come undone and the pin was gaping open. Coralie refastened it, wiped his bum, and quickly flushed the toilet.

'Mama!' Max wailed. 'You didn't see my squiggly poo.'

'Was it a funny shape?'

'No, it had noodles in it, that moved.'

Bad news. She sent an SOS to Adam: *Max has worms.*

A howl from the garden told her the message had been received.

'You'll need some mebendazole,' Anne said downstairs. 'I'll get it, my step count today is a disgrace.'

'I'll get it,' Coralie said. 'I have to pick up the cake.'

'I'll come.' Adam poked his head through the French doors. 'You'll probably need a hand.'

This was a transparent ploy to get out of setting up the trestle table and chairs. But Anne just pulled Max onto her lap and waved them both away. They couldn't believe their luck. They snuck out while they could.

'Granny,' Max was saying. 'Can we play BPM?'

'What's BPM?' Coralie whispered at the door.

'It's where they look at the Health bit of her Apple Watch,' Adam said. 'Maxi thinks that it's a game.'

The hollyhocks near the estate bins were waving in the breeze. Above them, the seagulls soared and dipped and screamed. The summer had been a wash-out, but suddenly it was warm. Adam had taken a month off. When he went back to the studio, it would be to host the show at midday. Drop-offs, dinners, bedtimes—he was back. Coralie had started freelancing. Her latest project had ended right before the holidays. Over the summer she had finished a draft of her novel. Lydia was reading it now, and she was reading Lydia's. Every night from eight o'clock they exchanged screenshots of their favourite quotes. *Genius,* the captions said. *Genius, genius, genius!*

In a week, yes, Coralie would be forty. And yes, she was feeling glad about it.

'Worms!' the woman in the pharmacy exclaimed. The other shoppers cocked their ears. 'You'll need the family pack.'

'Oh,' Coralie said. 'I don't think *we* have them.'

Adam bowed his head, dejected. 'Speak for yourself.'

The woman slid two boxes across the counter. 'Liquid for kids, tablets for you. Change your sheets, take the tablet, have a shower, change your clothes. In that order.'

They emerged into the busy Saturday market, red in the face and laughing. 'Oh, look,' Coralie said. 'The flat's for rent.'

They stared up at Coralie's old flat. 'Good old flat,' Adam said. 'I wish we could spend just a day in there, alone. Just the two of us, and our millions of microscopic threadworms.'

346

'Romantic,' Coralie said.

'Very romantic,' Adam said. '*I* think.'

They pulled to side of the market and shared a lingering kiss. 'I don't mind that you have worms,' Coralie said.

'I don't mind you're pretending you don't.'

When they got back, Zora was over, Daniel had arrived with Lady Diana, and Lydia had come with Nancy. Everyone was in the garden, hanging bunting in the bay tree and stuffing the pinata with sweets.

'I hear you have worms,' Lydia said. 'Nothing to be ashamed of.'

'I'm keepin' well out of it,' Daniel made his new poodle say in a Cockney voice.

'I personally *don't*,' Coralie said, 'have worms, actually.' She looked around. 'Where's Adam?'

He came outside looking flushed. 'What's in Daddy's pocket?' Flo asked.

'Gather round,' Adam said. 'And quickly, before the guests arrive.'

Coralie looked around, confused. When she looked back, Adam was down on one knee. Zora's new film camera clicked.

'Oh my God!' Lydia cried.

'Lawd!' the poodle said.

From his back pocket, Adam pulled out one of the worm boxes. 'That was a joke,' he said when everyone laughed. 'But this isn't—Coralie. I've really enjoyed getting to know you.'

'It's been ten years!' Zora said.

'*Ten years?*' Florence was astounded.

'Ten and a half,' Coralie faintly said.

'That's nothing.' Anne put her arm around Sally and pulled her close.

'And I was hoping…' Adam pulled another, smaller box out of his back pocket. 'You might consider making it official.'

'I helped him choose this,' Zora said.

'Ooh,' everyone said when he popped the box open to show the ring.

'Three little stones in the gold. See?' Zora nodded at Flo and Max. 'They're meant to represent us.'

'Thank you,' Coralie mouthed.

'Coralie Bower. Ow.' Adam wobbled. 'My knee's hurting, I'm so old.'

'Silly,' Anne said.

'Will you marry me?'

They knew each other now—properly. The rest of their lives could begin.